I0600301

MIDNIGHT
MULTIPLAYER

A NOVEL

PAUL CHRISTOU

Published in the United States by Shadow Drop Publishing.

Library of Congress copyright registration application pending

ISBN 979-8-9996322-0-3

First Paperback Edition.

DEDICATION

For Lorri, Maria, and Deno
Your support got me to the finish line

CHAPTER 1

THE ASSIGNMENT

G ames can bring people together or tear them apart. A person can play thousands of video games in their lifetime. But it only takes one to change everything.

Half an hour to go. BattleTheatre. *Releasing today.* Charlie thought this as he stared at the "Game Over" royal-blue lettering on his coffee-stained mug resting next to his Kratos *God of War* action figure. The gray handle, shaped like an old-school PlayStation controller, was missing the *X* and *O* buttons that had chipped off when Charlie accidentally banged it on the metal beam of his cubicle last month. It reminded him of the good times playing *Crash Bandicoot*, *Final Fantasy VII*, and *Castlevania: Symphony of the Night*.

Charlie's video game journey began at a young age with *Super Mario Bros*. Then, the floodgates opened with *Donkey Kong Country*, *Super Metroid*, and open-world games like *Red Dead Redemption II*, revealing a fascinating world far removed from the mundane real one. Charlie enjoyed multiplayer first-person shooters like *Destiny 2* and each yearly release of *Call of Duty*, not just for the gameplay, but for the camaraderie of playing with friends. He would never fight in a real war. But he was skilled enough to survive in a simulated one where the rules were simple: press the right combination of buttons, communicate with his team through a headset, and eliminate the enemy. His routine world of work and bills could never compare to the vast open worlds that Charlie immersed himself in.

One of the greatest gaming moments of his life happened when he was nine years old, struggling to defeat the boss Psycho Mantis in the video game *Metal Gear Solid* on the PlayStation. Halfway through the fight, the menacing Psycho Mantis told young Charlie to place his controller on the floor to witness a display of psychokinesis. Charlie leaned forward and set it down on the floor. A few seconds later, his jaw dropped wide open as the controller moved across the hardwood like magic. He leapt off his couch, dove onto the floor, and placed his hand on the controller, waiting for a magic portal to transport him into the game world. The controller vibrated. Numbing his fingertips. It wasn't magic at all. The vibration from the DualShock Analog Controller had caused it to glide across the floor, making him feel like an audience member who figures out a magician's trick right after it's performed. He was blown away by the creative vision of the game designer, Hideo Kojima. *How cool would it be to design a game like this?*

Charlie's cubicle was nestled in the basement of Unlimited Horizons, a run-down Chicago finance company, where he'd worked for the past three years as a junior financial analyst. The carpet was dark gray, thin as a wafer, and hadn't been shampooed in over a decade, while the coffee-colored stains on the ceilings resembled dried-up waste. It was a prison for young wannabes waiting in line to move upstairs so they could kiss the ass of older, executive pretenders who acted smarter than they were. Charlie wanted no part of that. He knew there was more to life than being a servant for the corporate end boss who could never be defeated. He only wanted to get through the day, rush home, and play *Battle Theatre*, a game with the potential to be the biggest multiplayer shooter since *Call of Duty*.

Five o'clock. A group of employees shuffled past Charlie's desk. The click-clack of their Oxfords and high-heeled pumps echoed in the basement louder and faster than they did when they dragged themselves to work in the morning. William, the Head of Security who looked like he spent as much time in the gym as he did on skincare, towered over Charlie in a tight-fitting, blue pinstripe suit with a funky, orange-and-blue Chicago Bears necktie.

"What's up, doofus?"

"Billy Boy. What brings you over to the dungeon?" Charlie said, referring to the lack of windows that made the basement bleaker than a level in *Diablo 3*.

"Any plans for the weekend?" William said.

"My favorite game, *Battle Theatre*, is coming out today on the PS4."

Six months ago, the developer, Warmonger Games, announced a tournament for a hundred players to compete for twenty thousand dollars. Those fortunate enough to register exactly at noon would be among the first to get in. Charlie had clicked the entry button at least a hundred times between 11:59 and noon to earn a spot for his team.

"I'm practicing all weekend to get ready for my tournament tomorrow night," Charlie said, rubbing his hands together.

William tightened his lips and tilted his head. "I'm sure your girlfriend will be thrilled about that."

"I have the perfect excuse. 'Uh, I feel sick. I might be contagious,'" Charlie said, clutching his stomach.

"You're horrible."

"Think about it. The odds of her checking up on me are practically nil."

"I never understood why you love games so much. Such a waste of time."

Ugh. He sounds just like my father.

"Being married is a waste of time," Charlie said, quiet enough so William couldn't hear.

William turned his head to drool over an attractive female coworker walking toward the elevator. "I mean, that's your thing I guess, but you could be making more productive use of your time... like tapping that."

Charlie snapped back, "First place in my game tournament wins twenty thousand dollars, so that could be considered productive."

"You've got no chance against these twelve-year-old gamers. They play all day in their rooms and only leave to eat and take a dump."

"I just wanna play my game to see if I can compete." Charlie had never been good at sports, partially because his father never pushed him. His only path to competitive glory was through video games. And the tournament was a way for him to show that he could accomplish something significant in his life. A chance to be a champion in a virtual world.

"Well, while you're getting smoked by these preteens, I'll be smoking meats this Sunday at a barbecue. I'm the pitmaster. My ribs are the shit," William said.

Charlie, distracted and daydreaming of *Battle Theatre*, said, "Your ribs taste like shit?"

"They *are* the shit," William said. "It's a long drive to my mother-in-law's house. The wife insists I go with her. I dunno. I was planning on watching the Bears game with my boys and some brewskis, but I guess I'll watch the game there. You know, happy wife, happy life and all that bullshit."

"I was planning on having some brewskis and watching the game with my boys too," Charlie said.

"Smart ass. There's no way you're gonna stop playing your little game to watch Da Bears."

"My tournament is on Saturday night, so I might watch the game on Sunday. I'll be playing so much that I'll probably need a break by the time it comes around."

"I can't believe the Bears are nine and four. This is our year, baby. Super Bowl," William said, pointing his two index fingers like six-shooters while walking backward toward the elevators. "The Packers are going down this Sunday."

Charlie yelled, "Have fun with your mother-in-law, Billy Boy," making sure William could hear him.

"Asshole," William said, flipping Charlie the middle finger before moonwalking back into the elevator.

William exited on the tenth floor, heading to his office to gather his things. On the way there, he passed a meticulous-looking office with an incredible view of the Chicago skyline in the distance. The words "Mr. Edward DuPont" were etched into the center of the large glass door. Sitting behind a reddish-brown, mahogany desk polished to a gleaming shine was Mr. DuPont, Senior Vice President of Finance, wearing a double-breasted, virgin-wool Giorgio Armani suit paired with a high-gloss gold tie that screamed "I'm senior management" to anyone in his presence. He saw William wave to him and answered with a half-inch upward nod of his head.

A single photo of his wife, two snapshots of his daughter, and six pictures of his golf buddies adorned DuPont's desk. They were a bit crooked, so he straightened them before raising his coffee cup to reveal a ring stain that blemished the sheen on his desk. He said, "Ugh. Forgot to use the coaster," before shuffling through his bottom drawer to yank out a Clorox wipe. But the stain wasn't going anywhere. "Goddammit!"

He flung the wipe onto his desk, grabbed a laptop and a large file, and stomped into the office kitchen, setting his coffee cup five feet from the sink without any consideration for who'd have to clean it up. His final destination before he left for the day: the basement. In front of the elevator was William, who had already pushed the down button. Both men entered. DuPont pressed the *B* button for the basement. William pressed the *L* button for the lobby.

"Heading home, William?"

"Yeah. Got a barbecue planned this weekend," William said with a half-smile.

Both men stood silent. It was an uncomfortable pause. One that can only exist between a manager and a subordinate.

William tried to be funny to break the awkwardness. "I see you're heading to the dungeon. You going to whip the peasants?"

DuPont never turned his head to look at him. He missed the joke. "I have to talk to Charlie."

William's fake smile disappeared as the elevator reached the lobby. He held the door open and asked, "Did you get a chance to look at my application for the junior financial analyst position?" Even though William was Head of Security, he wanted to carve a path for himself in finance where he could earn more money. He'd sent DuPont three email reminders over the last month but had received no response.

DuPont shot down his chances quicker than a jackrabbit on a date. "I have to say, your lack of formal education is troubling.

You might not have the mental fortitude to be a junior financial analyst. I'd say you have a zero-point-three percent chance of succeeding in finance without a degree. *Statistically speaking.* Stick to security. It's what you're good at."

William stepped out of the elevator, his face blank and expressionless as the doors closed behind him. He bit his upper lip hard, focusing on the pain to distract himself from his failed attempt to advance his career. He knew that DuPont was on his way to destroy Charlie, just as he had destroyed him.

CHAPTER 2

WEEKEND BLUES

D uPont's sinister eyes were fixated on Charlie like a hungry wolf sizing up its prey. Charlie glanced up and wasn't too concerned. After all, it was mid-December. *He must want me to summarize the weekly report. Should take thirty minutes. No big deal.*

"I'm heading out," DuPont said. "Did you get that email I sent you?"

Charlie's cheeks flushed red, and his stomach quivered. "I'll check my inbox right now."

DuPont rolled his eyes upward. "I sent it a few hours ago."

Charlie fumbled with his mouse, clicking furiously for twenty seconds before locating DuPont's message. His index finger twitched, unable to move. He closed his eyes, clenched his teeth, and prayed before clicking again. With each passing word he read, his face scrunched up like someone discovering that a cyber thief had emptied their bank account:

> I need the attached 2018 annual financial report and
> the enclosed loan applications completed by
> Monday. A hard copy of all work is required.
> Thanks.
> Edward DuPont, Senior VP of Finance

Charlie hovered the cursor over the attachment and double-clicked it, transforming the arrow on his computer screen into a spinning hourglass. "I don't know what's wrong with my computer. It's never this slow."

"Wait for it," DuPont said, mounting his chin between his thumb and index finger.

Twenty seconds later, the report erupted onto the screen, listing fifty tasks to complete. Charlie squeezed his eyes shut, hoping that forty-nine tasks would disappear by the time he opened them. He leaned forward to confirm that what he was seeing was real. Searching for an excuse to avoid it, he said, "Um, I can't do this from home. My computer's busted."

DuPont flashed back a devious grin and said, "That's why I have this laptop for you to take home with you. I would never expect you to come into the office on Saturday and Sunday. I'm not a monster."

No, you're a sadistic asshole.

This wasn't the first time DuPont had singled out Charlie. There was a time he had made him stay late on a Wednesday to analyze interest rates. Or when he had him work all day on a Thursday without taking a lunch break to identify economic trends. But he'd never picked on him on a Friday before, and never with an assignment this massive. Charlie thought about asking why this wasn't given to him on Monday, but the fear of standing up to his boss shut down his vocal cords.

"The fiscal year is ending, so this report must be completed by Monday. It's crucial to the success of our company. I'm counting on you, Charlie. You know, I see management potential in you."

That's what all bosses say when they want their employees to do extra work.

Charlie turned on his best happy-go-lucky employee act. "No problem. I've got no plans this weekend."

"Attaboy. Have a great weekend," DuPont said, trotting to the elevator.

As soon as the elevator doors closed, Charlie yelled, "Asshole. Bastard. Prick. Motherfucker."

Charlie imagined DuPont as a boss in *Battletoads, Ninja Gaiden, Dark Souls,* and *Bloodborne* all at once. He pictured his broadsword chopping off DuPont's head, then bathing in his blood, cackling with delight.

How am I supposed to do this? The tournament's my chance to pay Dimitri.

When the NFL season kicked off last September, Charlie had lost the first six games he bet on, plunging him into debt. He'd started betting five hundred dollars per game. Then a thousand. Trying to win his money back. Now he was down four and a half grand. All owed to his bookie, Dimitri, a muscular brute who resembled a bastardized version of Niko Bellic from *Grand Theft Auto IV*, complete with a five o'clock shadow, a thick Russian accent, and a Dracula hairline that pierced the front of his skull, causing his eyebrows to scowl permanently. Dimitri's backers might have had some loose ties to the Russian mob. Or at least Charlie hoped they were loose. Otherwise, he would probably end up with a tight noose around his neck. Charlie imagined a world where sports gambling was legal, so he wouldn't have to deal with the lowest forms of humanity. Maybe someday. If he won, his share of the tournament prize would be five thousand dollars. More than enough to pay off Dimitri.

Charlie thought back to all the good times playing multiplayer games like *Call of Duty, Halo, Gears of War, Rocket League,* and *Overwatch* with his friends. He hated that his friends would be in gaming nirvana, gazing at stunning graphics, while he would be stuck in work assignment hell, staring at a bland computer screen all weekend.

Charlie's desk phone rang. He had no intention of picking it up, but the name on the caller ID was Susan, the girl he'd been dating for a year and a half. Their first year together had been magical. When they weren't texting each other during work hours, they would go on weekday excursions and fun dinner dates. They were both foodies, so finding new restaurants became a passion for them. Spending a weekend making love while camping or attending a local concert was a regular part of life too, since she was a guitarist and loved hearing local bands play in the neighborhood. She shared her dreams with Charlie about making it in the music industry, and he shared his dreams of… well, he had no dreams other than playing games, but he did mention his desire to get a promotion at work from time to time.

When Susan had a bad day at work, Charlie lifted her spirits with his cheerful sense of humor and solidarity against corporate injustice. He'd played video games during that first year but always made time for Susan, watching her practice with her band and attending her gigs. She played multiple rounds of *Mario Kart 8 Deluxe* and *Worms* with him, enjoying the time they spent together on the couch. They loved each other. But over the last six months, it felt as though something was missing.

Charlie answered the phone in a sedated tone. "Hi, babe."

"Hi, honey. You ready for my gig tomorrow?" Susan said.

Her band, the She-Nannigans, was performing tomorrow at the Rusty Spoon, a local venue for independent musical acts. It was a chance for her all-female band to show how they stacked up against three male-dominated bands. Her best friend, Jessica, was the lead singer, while Susan was the lead guitarist. They performed original songs, usually written by the other two band members, Kat and Mimi. But this time, Susan had written a song that she'd be performing in public for the first time. Titled "The Three A's," it was a beautiful ballad that showcased the vocal talent that she'd nurtured by taking over a dozen voice lessons over the past six months. It was her time to shine. And to show Charlie and the world that she could sing.

She kept her lyrics in a wicker basket called the "Dream Bin" that she carried with her wherever the band performed. Inside were mementos and trinkets they had collected over the past six months: pin-back button badges from other indie bands, cloth patches showcasing social justice causes, leaflets from the venues, a few lucky silver dollars gifted to them by family members, guitar picks, sheet music, extra strings for their guitars, and even some encouraging printed-out emails from fans. It was a treasure chest of sentimentality. Their lucky charm. Always with them on stage and even during practice. Susan hoped the bin would make her dreams come true someday. The upcoming gig was her chance to show what she could do as a singer and songwriter, since scouts were scheduled to attend the performance. It was an important night—not to be missed.

Charlie was silent. His tongue was tangled and numb. At least he didn't have to lie to her about being sick. The truth was easier to explain, even though it would be difficult.

"Charlie? Are you there?"

He whispered, "I'm here." After a long pause, he raised his voice and said, "Babe, I'm fucked."

"What's wrong?"

Charlie rested his forehead on his desk and said, "My boss gave me a financial report that's due on Monday."

Susan waited for Charlie to say more, but he stayed silent. "It's only one report. How bad could it be?"

"It has, like, fifty parts to it. It's an end of the fiscal year report. It requires a ton of research before I can even begin to write it, not to mention all the loan applications the bastard gave me."

"How long will that take you?"

"All weekend with minimal sleep. I don't think I'll have time to watch you perform. I'm so sorry."

Susan stomped her feet around her apartment. "Goddammit, Charlie. This gig is important to me. I'm singing for the first time. I've been practicing for months."

"How is this my fault?"

"I never said it was your fault. I'm just pissed that your boss would do this."

"I tried to come up with an excuse that my home computer was busted, but the son of a bitch had a laptop in his hand and said, 'Here you go, Charlie. Ha, ha, ha.'"

"Well, you can do your work and still make it to the gig. It doesn't start until ten tomorrow."

"I can't afford to waste four hours. It takes an hour to get there, an hour to get back, plus an hour for dinner beforehand. I'll get fired if I don't finish it on time."

There was a pause before she pleaded, "I've worked so hard on this."

"I don't want to miss it, but my boss has got me by the balls," Charlie said. "Sorry."

Silence.

"I love you," Charlie said.

More silence.

Susan responded with "I'll talk to you later."

The line disconnected, and Charlie let out a long sigh. She didn't argue. She just hung up. Never said "I love you" back. He couldn't remember the last time she'd conceded an argument that fast, and it was clear that she was upset with him.

I feel bad, but if she loves me, she'll understand.

CHAPTER 3

FRIDAY FOLLY

harlie jammed his overstuffed manila folder, USB flash drive, and DuPont's low-end laptop into his backpack. The mustiness, lack of natural light, and despair of weekend work made the basement walls close in, tightening his throat and making his head spin. He wobbled to the elevator and banged his head against the doors like a zombie in *Left 4 Dead*. He imagined DuPont's tiny head on the lobby button before kicking it like Kratos' Spartan kick in *God of War*. As soon as the elevator doors parted on the lobby floor, a slender, dark-skinned woman appeared near the front desk. Her eyes were locked on Charlie. She looked like she meant business. It was Jasmine, one of Charlie's coworkers, who had occasionally worked with him on past projects. He did his best to walk past her, but she grabbed his arm and pulled him close.

"Charlie, we need to talk."

He'd never had a woman be so assertive with him, and for a moment, he thought she was flirting. But the look in her eyes was not one of passion. It was one of concern. His stomach churned as he stared deep into her eyes.

"Let's take a seat," Jasmine said, gently tugging Charlie's arm toward the couch in the lobby.

"What's going on?"

"I know DuPont gave you that weekend assignment. You wanna know how I know?"

Charlie rested his cheek on his fist. "I'm afraid to ask."

"He put me in charge to make sure you stay on track. I'm responsible for checking in on you over the weekend. He asked me to wait here in the lobby to grab you before you leave for the day."

"What the hell is going on? You're not even my boss."

Jasmine turned her head away from Charlie, stared blankly into the distance, and whispered, "I think he's getting back at me."

"Getting back at you for what?"

"It's nothing. I shouldn't have said anything."

"You can't say something like that and then not explain it."

"Listen, Charlie. You were gonna get this assignment anyway. I had no bearing on that. That's the truth. I was talking about myself and why he made me responsible for keeping you on track. It's personal. I'd rather not discuss it."

"It might make you feel better to get it off your chest."

"It's personal. Please let's just leave it at that."

"This fucking sucks. So, you're DuPont's minion calling me every hour to make sure I'm working?"

"It's not like that," Jasmine said. "I can help you get the work done. I'm familiar with most of those reports, so I can answer any questions you might have. Please answer your phone and texts so I know how things are coming along."

"Fine. I have to go home and work. Some more. God, that sounds so pathetic," Charlie said. "Just don't tell me to have a good weekend or I might lose my shit."

"I'm sorry, Charlie. I'll talk to you tomorrow."

Charlie sprang up from the couch and glanced back at Jasmine as he walked out the front door. She was hunched forward with her head down.

What does DuPont have on her?

Charlie's head, heavy and muddled, drooped as he dragged his feet across the parking lot. He lifted his head for a moment, only to have it flop down again after a sharp slap to the back of his skull. Dom, the Italian forty-three-year-old maintenance manager of Unlimited Horizons, was laughing. He was the kind of guy who would throw someone against the wall if they looked at him funny. Despite their sixteen-year age difference, he and Charlie could chat for hours about video games. Dom had an encyclopedic database of games in his brain, ranging from *Combat* for the Atari 2600 to *Red Dead Redemption II* for the PlayStation 4. He'd also introduced Charlie to hidden gems like *Illusion of Gaia* and *Future Cop: LAPD*.

Charlie had collected games before meeting Dom, but he only got serious about it after their long discussions at work. They both loved horror games like *Silent Hill 2* and *Dead Space*, but Dom's favorite was the *Resident Evil* series. He ranted about how newer games needed to take a page out of its perfect blend of puzzles and scary, action-based gameplay. He believed that no other game had ever scared him more than the dogs jumping through the windows in *Resident Evil*, although the chainsaw-wielding maniac with the burlap sack over his head in *Resident Evil 4* was a close second. Like Charlie, he'd started playing video games at an early age, and he was the only one who knew more about the subject.

Dom had witnessed Charlie's discussion in the lobby and said, "You tryin' to bang Jasmine or what?"

Charlie rubbed the back of his head and said, "No. It's work related."

As they approached Charlie's car, Dom punched him on the arm and said, "Ready to get online and fuck shit up this weekend?"

Charlie, feeling deflated, lowered his head and said, "Sure."

"What da fuck? You sound like your dog just died."

Charlie said, "You know my dog, Daisy, died when I was a kid."

"Shit. I forgot. Sorry, man. But seriously, what's happening with you?"

"DuPont fucked me today. He gave me this massive financial report due on Monday."

"Typical DuPont. What an asshole. He couldn't give it to you at the beginning of the week?"

"There's no way I'm gonna have time to play this weekend. I gotta get this report done."

Dom sat on the hood of Charlie's beige Honda Accord, crossed his arms, and said, "You ain't doin' shit," inflecting every single word to drive his point home.

"I don't have a choice. I'll lose my job."

Dom stood up, clutched Charlie's left arm, and gently slapped him on the cheek three times like a Mafia boss. "You've been waiting, no, *we've* been waiting, four years for this game. Twenty thousand dollars, man. The tournament's worth twenty g's. Tim and Johnny cleared their schedule this weekend to practice, even though high-ass Johnny doesn't have much of a schedule. I'm even telling my wife to fuck off so I can play. What could be better than that?"

Charlie rubbed his cheek. "I'm in deep shit."

"You at least gonna buy the game?"

"I preordered it from GameStop. I'll probably pick it up on the way home."

Dom said, "Just buy it digitally."

"Not a chance."

Charlie loved collecting games as well as playing them. He was smart enough not to trade them away for a measly amount of trade-in credit at GameStop. The center of his apartment was adorned with custom-built shelves dedicated to his collection. He had games from just about every era. Each had its own special moment that he never forgot: holding the thick double jewel case of *Final Fantasy VII* when he was six years old; slamming *The Legend of Zelda: Ocarina of Time* cartridge into his Nintendo 64 with unbridled excitement after getting it for Christmas; falling in love with the Subaru WRX in *Gran Turismo 2* before buying the car in real life eleven years later. Memories of joy. Seared into his brain for eternity. Many of his games had become rare over time, and his entire collection was now worth at least seven or eight thousand dollars.

Nothing could make him part with them.

Dom walked back to the office building, turned around, and yelled, "See you online, jagbag," referencing a Chicago slang term fusing the words "jagoff" and "douchebag."

Charlie opened his car door and yelled back, "No, you won't."

"Yes, I will," Dom said. "Don't kid yourself, man. If this game were a drug, you'd be injecting it into your veins like a junkie. Just go with it, baby."

Charlie gripped the steering wheel, his thoughts twisting like a soft pretzel. *I hate my boss. Susan's pissed. I need to win this tournament to pay off Dimitri.* During his drive home, he couldn't stop thinking of the day his dog died. It had been almost sixteen years now, and he tried to block it from his memory so many times, but something would always remind him.

Fucking Dom.

CHAPTER 4

GAMBLING AND RAMBLING

C hicago. Home of Italian beef, Polish sausage, deep-dish pizza (although most Chicagoans prefer thin crust), and Old Style beer—four pleasures that somehow never caught on anywhere else. A great sports city that produced Michael Jordan's Bulls dynasty and Mike Ditka of the Chicago Bears. Da Coach would definitely be elected mayor if he ever chose to run. Famous for Oprah Winfrey, the Bean sculpture in Millennium Park, Second City, and Al Capone's mob.

Except now it was the Russian Mafia that had taken over gambling in the city. Charlie met his muscle-packed bookie at O'Malley's pool hall three years ago. It was the prime place for hustlers and bookies to prey on local suckers who liked to gamble. A cocktail of drugs from cocaine to ecstasy could be acquired within five minutes or less. Charlie had started off betting twenty-five dollars a game, but that soon increased to a hundred. If he'd bet on basketball, like his father did, he would be financially ruined, since basketball had sixty-six more games than football each season.

Down a few hundred some weeks, up a few hundred other weeks, it was a manageable financial risk. Until recently. Charlie had lost a thousand dollars to Dimitri last season, which was why he'd gambled so heavily at the start of this one to try and win his money back. Soon, he was betting with money he didn't have. Dimitri had let it slide for a few weeks since Charlie was a regular customer.

But Charlie had kept digging his hole deeper.

Dimitri was cruising past Wrigley Field, home of the Chicago Cubs, in his jet-black Ford Mustang, polished to a high-gloss sheen. He was on his way to collect a debt from another hapless gambler when he called Charlie. "Six weeks. Time's up. Tell me you head to ATM to get my four and a half grand."

Charlie, driving in his dull, not-washed-for-over-three-months Accord, said, "I need a little more time."

"What part of 'Time's up' you not understand? You're overdue. Boss made it clear. Pay up today or we find other ways to get money."

"Come on, Dimitri. How long have you known me? This is the first time I've been in a hole like this. What are you going to do? Break my legs like it's the seventies?"

"No. We break precious little video game thumbs of yours."

Charlie caressed his left thumb before rubbing his right one. They were, after all, his most prized possessions. "Just give me till Monday. I've got something in the works."

Dimitri parked his car in front of the other gambler's house and walked to the trunk. "Books out of balance because of you. We wait long enough."

"I only need three more days. Just tell your boss that I'm sorry."

Dimitri grabbed a baseball bat from the trunk and tapped it on his palm three times. "You're the one who's gonna be sorry." The line disconnected.

Charlie rubbed the back of his neck, his mind racing like a stampede of horses. Worry was in the passenger seat and wouldn't leave the car. He thought about calling Dimitri back, but money was the only language he understood. *I'm not buying the whole "balancing the books" thing. I just need to win.* The odds of winning the *BattleTheatre* tournament were twenty-five to one. A hundred players were set to compete in twenty-five teams of four. His team just needed to be better than the other twenty-four teams. Easy.

Charlie's veins bulged out of his temples as he gripped the steering wheel. A headache was coming on. He needed to talk to his best friend, Johnny, a cannabis aficionado who'd started smoking at the age of eleven. When other kids were reading *Highlights for Children*, Johnny was reading *High Times* magazine. If marijuana was kung fu, Johnny was a ninth-degree black belt grandmaster. He believed that aliens gave us weed to help us love each other, but we found a way to mess it all up by making it illegal. His most prized possession was a glorious bong with magnificent gold etching all around it, given to him on his sixteenth birthday by his uncle, a talented glassblower. It had sparked his obsession with creating the perfect bong, and he spent a lot of his time making his own with the lessons he'd learned.

Johnny, sitting on his once-white couch, now stained tan from all the weed smoke, placed his pineapple bong on the table in front of him. He twirled his Bic lighter in his hand and said, "Brah, I was wondering when you were gonna call me. I'm about to get online with the boys."

Charlie gazed at the Christmas lights on the buildings as he drove past. Chicago was cold and cloudy during the winter. Hell, it was cloudy during most of the spring and fall, too. But there was something magical about Christmas in the city, with its snowy white canvas providing the perfect backdrop for the kaleidoscope of shimmering lights. Right now, though, Charlie's gambling debt dulled all the bright colors along the road.

"I just got off the phone with Dimitri."

"I told you not to bet against our hometown heroes," Johnny said, referring to Charlie's losses from betting against the Bears earlier in the season.

"He sounds serious this time. He said I'm going to be sorry if I don't pay him. I'm worried."

The bubbling sound of Johnny taking a hit echoed over the phone.

"Worried? About Dimitri? Brah, he'll get his money when we win the tournament tomorrow night. And even if we don't, everything will be fine. He likes to act tough, but he ain't gonna do shit."

"Yeah, about the tournament," Charlie said. "My boss fucked me over. He gave me this stupid work assignment that's due on Monday. It's like thirty hours of work, maybe more."

The bong continued to gargle. *Plop, bloop, plop, bloop.*

"Dude, your interpretation of problems needs some serious adjusting. I thought you were gonna tell me that your PS4 Pro died."

Charlie swerved around a slow-moving minivan. "If I don't finish this assignment, he's gonna fire me."

There was a moment of silence before the crack and fizz of a can of soda hissed from the phone.

Charlie said, "There's more."

Johnny took a swig of Mountain Dew Code Red, the stoner's drink of choice. "Are you gonna mention an actual problem this time?"

Charlie turned the corner and said, "I forgot about Susan's gig this weekend. It's happening a couple of hours before the tournament."

"I have an easy solution to both your problems," Johnny said. "It involves the word 'fuck' multiple times."

"I think I know where you're heading with this."

Johnny walked over to his pantry and grabbed a bag of Cool Ranch Doritos, the stoner's snack of choice, and said, "Fuck Dimitri, fuck your boss, and, I'm sorry, fuck Susan. What kind of boss gives someone thirty hours of work over the weekend? And what kind of girl gets mad about her boyfriend playing in a video game tournament worth twenty thousand dollars?"

"She told me about her gig a couple of months ago. I said I'd be there since the *Battle Theatre* tournament was supposed to be on November thirtieth, but then it got delayed by two weeks. It's like my brain never registered the change. She gets nervous when I'm not in the crowd and she's scared she's gonna mess up her song."

"Brah, I hear what you're saying, but you can't miss this tournament. If you don't play, *Battle Theatre* is gonna assign a rando to us. I'm not playing with some fucking rando," Johnny said.

Of course, when Charlie had gained entry into the *Battle Theatre* tournament, he had named himself and his three regular teammates in the four-person team. But the rules of the game stated that if any team member could not play, a random person would be selected from a waiting list to fill the vacant slot.

Charlie stopped at a red light and placed his palms on his face. "Fuck me. I don't know what to do."

"I know you love Susan, but can't you, like, promise her a spa weekend or something? Girls love that shit."

Charlie was getting a call. He looked down to see the name "Joe" on his phone. "Shit. It's Joe. He only calls if there's an emergency. I gotta go."

Johnny pleaded, "Brah..." before the line went dead.

Charlie had called his father "Dad" for the first eleven years of his life, but his view of him had changed at the age of twelve. He no longer called him "Dad." He called him "Joe" to signify that he was a distant acquaintance who just happened to be his father.

"How's it going?" Joe said.

"Fine."

"I was hoping you could do me a favor and help me move a cabinet from the living room to the garage. I found someone on Craigslist who wants to buy it."

"Why can't you move it?"

Joe placed his hand on the furniture and said, "You know I can't lift anything heavy. It'll only take five minutes."

"Yeah, five minutes, but I have to drive an additional twenty minutes to get to you."

"When do I ever ask you to do stuff for me? Huh? Hardly ever. I'm asking you for a favor."

It was true. Charlie's father, a recently retired construction foreman who looked like an obese Bob the Builder, rarely asked him for anything. He was better at curling a can of beer while watching and betting on the Bulls than doing anything physical. Charlie wanted to say no, but he knew that Joe would either hurt himself or suffer a heart attack attempting to move the cabinet by himself, and he didn't want his injury or death on his conscience.

He blew a loud sigh out of his cheeks and said, "Fine. I'm on my way."

The rush-hour traffic on the powdery, snow-covered streets of Chicago made Charlie wonder if the twenty-minute drive would turn into an hour. He glanced at the bright-green digital clock on the dashboard: 5:35 p.m. *I still need to pick up* BattleTheatre *from GameStop.*

This wasn't the first time the allure of buying a game had overpowered Charlie's good sense. If it wasn't a new game, it'd be one on sale. Every week, he scoured the PlayStation, Xbox, and Nintendo Switch online stores for discounted games. FOMO ravaged his brain. *If I don't buy it now, it may never go on sale again.* Thousands of games purchased over the years. Many of them never played. Physical games still in the shrink wrap. Digital games unplayed on his hard drive. Ten lifetimes wouldn't be enough to play his full collection. It was no surprise that he was willing to go out of his way to buy a game that he wouldn't even be able to play until after the weekend.

CHAPTER 5

SHOVEL YOUR SNOW, JOE

Three inches of wet snow blanketed Joe's driveway. Charlie parked his car on the slush-filled street and trudged through it, his footsteps crunching like a soft drumbeat. The walkway hadn't seen a shovel either. *This son of a bitch is going to ask me to shovel, too.* Charlie reached the doorway and brushed the snow off his ankles. He scowled at his father's smiling face in the doorway.

"Charlie. Come inside, my boy."

"Really? You couldn't shovel your driveway?"

"It's too cold to shovel. I'll just wait for it to melt."

Charlie's eyes, colder than the frigid air outside, locked onto Joe's face. "Let's get this over with." He continued to wipe the snow off his shoes and looked up to see his sister, Emma. She was wearing a black T-shirt that looked like a long-sleeved shirt because of all her tattoos. Not an inch of bare skin in sight. Her fierce independence on display.

Growing up, Emma had learned the joy of playing video games from Charlie and looked up to him. Especially around the mid-2000s when she started playing on PC. *Half-Life 2* made her fall in love with PC gaming. Years later, *Counter-Strike: Global Offensive* made her a lifelong fan of multiplayer shooters. She was highly ranked as one of the top players in competitive *Fortnite*,

PUBG, *Overwatch*, and *Destiny 2*, even though her PC struggled to handle the demanding graphics. She'd started saving, hoping to buy a new graphics card so she could play *Apex Legends*, which was still a month away, studying it almost as closely as Charlie studied *Battle Theatre*. She'd recently started playing her favorite shooters on both the PlayStation 4 Pro and Xbox One X in preparation for the release of *Battle Theatre*, which was exclusive to consoles for now. She wanted to talk to Charlie about it, but she could tell he was in one of his moods.

They used to play games together all the time when they were younger, but that stopped around fifteen years ago, when he gravitated toward consoles. She'd asked to play on his team, the Chi-Town Crew, a few times, but the last thing he needed was his little sister embarrassing him in front of his friends. Like most older siblings, he could never imagine that she might be cool enough to hang out with them, especially given the significant age gap. Consequently, he never appreciated just how good she was. Multiple crews were desperate to recruit her, but all of them were online acquaintances she'd never met in person.

Charlie said, "Why are you here?"

Emma grabbed the side of the entertainment center and said, "Dad didn't want to call you, but I told him there was no way I could move it. Sorry."

"Never send a girl to do a man's job."

"You're gonna need my help when you see how heavy this sucker is," Emma said. "You excited for *Battle Theatre*? I'll be online tonight. We should play a match together."

Charlie was silent, his ears disregarding her last sentence. He directed his attention to the entertainment center. It looked bigger than he remembered.

"What? Afraid to play against me? You'll need some good competition if you're gonna compete tomorrow."

Charlie ran his palm against the side of the cabinet, not answering her again.

"God, I wish I was playing in the tournament. You're so lucky," Emma said, bowing her head down. She had tried but failed to earn a spot.

Joe waddled into the kitchen and yelled, "How about some hot chocolate? You always love hot chocolate on cold days like this."

"I haven't had hot chocolate in years. Can we please get this over with? I have work to do this weekend," Charlie said.

"Work? On the weekend?"

"It doesn't matter."

Joe started fidgeting with the couch cushions, unsure of what to say next. Finally, he said, "I found a guy on Craigslist who's coming tomorrow. Gonna give me a hundred dollars for it."

Without a word, Charlie grabbed a corner of the entertainment center and began to tilt it toward him, but stopped when he felt its heft. He knelt down and opened one of the fully packed drawers. "What the fuck?" he yelled. "What's all this in here? You expect us to lift it with all this junk inside? Are you giving away all this shit, too?"

"Oh my God. I forgot there was stuff inside," Joe said.

Charlie, in a frantic rage, grabbed everything from the drawers like he was looting a chest in *Borderlands*, tossing everything over his shoulder. The flip-up covers from VHS tapes of *Romancing the Stone*, *Rocky 3*, and *Big Trouble in Little China* slammed on the floor, breaking the hinges that held them in place. The ears of cute porcelain bunny knick-knacks broke off, while the jewel cases of Pink Floyd's *The Wall* and The Eagles' *Greatest Hits* cracked open, causing the disks to roll on the floor like tiny frisbees.

Joe gazed at the woman's face on the cover of Styx's *The Grand Illusion* as it landed at his feet, then back at Charlie. In a high-pitched tone, clearly inspired by his son's demeanor, he started singing a verse from the album track "Fooling Yourself (The Angry Young Man)."

Emma covered her mouth to hide her smile, then stepped back to avoid being hit by any more of Joe's old media relics. While his attempt to lighten the mood may have worked with Emma, it only increased Charlie's anger.

"You asked me to move this thing, and you didn't even bother to empty it. You knew I was coming and didn't shovel your walkway. My boss is breathing down my neck to get this impossible task done. Dimitri keeps asking for his money. Susan's pissed at me. A game I have been waiting four years for releases today, and all I want to do is play it and forget about all this bullshit in my life!"

Joe took a sip of his whiskey on the rocks. "Son, what's wrong?"

"I just fucking told you what's wrong!"

"Can we sit down at the kitchen table and talk about it? I'll make some tea if you don't want hot chocolate."

"Oh, spare me. Let's just move this thing so I can get the fuck out of here," Charlie said, his eyes glossy.

Joe downed the rest of his whiskey and said, "You need to relax."

"I just want to go home. Emma, grab your end and let's move this thing."

Emma tilted the side of the entertainment center toward herself, while Charlie crouched down to grasp the bottom shelf. His muscles quivered. The weight of the cabinet caused his face to turn blood red. After ten minutes of grunting and shouting, they finally maneuvered it into the garage.

Joe said, "Thanks, Charlie. I'm sorry."

Charlie stormed out of the garage, took three steps, and slipped on a patch of ice hidden underneath the snow. His heels flew into the air, making him weightless for a fraction of a second, before he fell flat on his back with his arms and legs spread wide like a snow angel. A sharp pain coursed through his spine.

"Oh my God, Charlie!" Joe yelled. "Are you okay?"

Charlie staggered to his knees, then his feet, and said, "I'm fine."

He took off his jacket and twirled it like a matador's cape to shake off the snow. He could hear his father's muffled voice, but he didn't care to decipher it as he got into his car and drove away. He never engaged in long conversations with his father or spent any meaningful time with him. They'd been close during Charlie's younger years, from five to eleven, but then something had changed. A pot filled with anger and resentment toward his father raged inside him. It had started boiling when he was twelve and continued to overflow to this day. Joe only called Charlie in emergencies. Charlie never called Joe. They never needed much from each other.

Emma watched Charlie's car spin its wheels on the ice before speeding away. She turned to her father and said, "Do you know how much he owes his bookie?"

"He never tells me anything."

"It's over four thousand dollars. He told me a few weeks back."

"His problems are his own. They have nothing to do with me."

Emma grabbed her jacket and said, "You really should start shoveling your snow and salting your driveway."

CHAPTER 6

DAISY AND THE DRUNK

October 2002. Eleven-year-old Charlie immersed himself in the virtual worlds of *Kingdom Hearts*, *Final Fantasy X*, and *Super Mario Sunshine*. Completing missions and defeating enemies was a lot more fun than riding his bike around the same six-block radius for the hundredth time. He even convinced his mom to buy him *Grand Theft Auto: Vice City*, telling her it was a racing game. Charlie lived on the northwest side of Chicago, twenty minutes west of Wrigley Field. His father, Joe, spent most of his free time sprawled back in his recliner with a glass of whiskey resting on his massive gut, losing most of the bets he placed on basketball games on TV. His mother, Mary, was a part-time administrative assistant whose slim figure and heavy makeup suggested a former prom queen. His sister, Emma, was five years old and loved watching Charlie play video games for hours on end, especially the ones with colorful graphics and cartoon characters. Her favorites were *Crash Bandicoot*, *Spyro the Dragon*, and *Jax and Daxter: The Precursor Legacy*. Charlie sometimes let her play a level or two. Her tiny hands were barely big enough to grasp the controller, yet she always sat up straight with eyes of wonder.

One evening, Charlie asked to be excused from the dinner table to play Hideo Kojima's latest masterpiece, *Metal Gear Solid 2*, in his room upstairs. He was down to his last five dollars of allowance after renting it for the third time from Blockbuster Video. He loved the original *Metal Gear Solid* for the PlayStation, but was even more excited about the sequel, which had the power of the PlayStation 2 behind it.

Joe polished off his plate and downed his fifth whiskey on the rocks, while Mary drank a glass of water. Unlike Joe, Mary practiced portion control and rarely drank alcohol. She left a few fatty chunks of steak along with some potatoes on her plate. Daisy, their playful Shih Tzu, sat with wide eyes, waiting for food to drop from the table.

Twenty minutes later, Charlie's mom called for him to come downstairs so they could go shopping. He paused his game and shut off the television, but left his PlayStation 2 on so he could continue later without losing his progress. Mary strapped Emma into her booster seat in the back of the car and buckled up Charlie next to her. They were off to the mall to buy Charlie some sneakers. Since Joe had bet a hundred dollars on the Bulls game, he stayed behind to watch his money slowly dwindle away.

Joe scraped some of the leftover food from Mary's plate into the garbage bin when he spotted Daisy sitting next to it. She was waiting for a morsel to be tossed her way. He grabbed a lump of gristle and threw it to her. His buzz was kicking in. He plopped himself onto his recliner to watch the game and tried to stay awake, but the soft chair, paired with five glasses of whiskey, made his eyes droop. The movement of the basketball on the screen was like a hypnotist's pocket watch—back and forth, back and forth. Two minutes of lucidity was all Joe could manage before he succumbed and fell into a deep sleep. Daisy dashed throughout the house in a state of panic, but couldn't bark. The fatty piece of steak was lodged deep in her throat.

The mall didn't have the shoes Charlie wanted, so he settled for Nike sneakers. He wasn't about to tell his mom that he wanted New Balance. That would mean going to another store and wasting precious time that could be spent beating *Metal Gear Solid 2*. Mary bought a black leather purse and a couple of blouses, while Emma got one of those magic sandbox sets with blue sand that molds into animal shapes.

When they arrived home, Joe was asleep in his chair, snoring like a jackhammer. Emma called out for Daisy, but there was no answer. Odd. Daisy always came running when called. Mary asked Charlie to look for the dog upstairs, since he was eager to return to his game. He sprinted up the stairs and checked his mom and dad's room, Emma's room, the bathroom, and the guest room, but found nothing. As soon as he opened his bedroom door, his legs trembled like twin flames blowing in the wind. It was the first dead thing he had ever seen in his life. *If only I had a Phoenix Down revival potion from* Final Fantasy VII, *I could bring her back to life.*

Looking back, the only thing Charlie could clearly remember after that moment was his mother punching his father in the chest, screaming over and over, "How could you let our baby die?

It was the end of his childhood.

CHAPTER 7

GAMING RIFT

F riday, 6:25 p.m. Susan slouched on the faded brown leather couch inside Starbucks, waiting for Jessica to arrive. She glanced out the window at an older woman selling roses. It reminded her of how Charlie gave her a single rose on her birthday and Valentine's Day. A full bouquet of flowers would have been nice.

Susan clenched her teeth and thought of Charlie's lame excuse of having to work. *How could he not spare a few hours to watch me sing?* If only she lived with him, she could see firsthand if he was really working. About a year ago, they used to sleep at each other's apartments all the time. He would play games whenever she stayed at his place. But he always set them aside when they had plans. Games were a hobby back then, not an obsession.

Susan envisioned moving into a larger apartment with Charlie at some point, but she couldn't get out of her eighteen-month lease. Both their places were way too small for them to live together, especially with her vast collection of shoes, which rivaled Charlie's enormous collection of games. She wanted to move in with him for many reasons: his capacity to bring her back to center whenever she spiraled out of control; his ability to make her laugh with ease; his support for her music, which boosted her confidence. His kindness. She shivered when she played poorly, barely noticeable to an outside observer, but it screamed "Help!" to Charlie. He'd walk behind her, wrap her in his arms, and say, "Breathe in. Then out. You're okay. Clear your mind. Start over." If that didn't work, he would say silly things like "Zu, Zu, Zu, Zu, Zu, Zu, Susan is Gru, Gru, Gru, Gru, Gru, Gru, Groovin'." To anyone passing by, his antics weren't particularly amusing. But to Susan, they were enough to make her laugh out loud and calm her nerves so she could play again.

Over the past six months, things had started to change. He'd get lost in his games. Continue playing when she was around. She could tell he was reluctant to move in with her because of the limited gaming time he would have. Maybe it was for the best, because the more time she spent watching him play, the more it reminded her of his growing obsession.

Charlie had become an expert at making excuses to avoid his obligations. When *Assassin's Creed Odyssey* was released a couple of months ago, he'd come up with all kinds of reasons not to go to the park or visit her parents' house so he could play it. He'd missed plenty of milestone events because of games, and today was the release of *Battle Theatre*, the King of All Games. She was aware of it because it was all Charlie had talked about for the past month.

It was clear to Susan that gaming had created a chasm between them. It wasn't that she disliked video games, but she hated how they affected their relationship. Charlie was kind and affectionate when games weren't involved, but distant when they were. Like the time they were late for her cousin's birthday party because he got stuck on the final boss in *Dark Souls 3*, or when they missed a movie Susan wanted to see because he was determined to finish a *Destiny 2* match with his friends.

Sometimes, Charlie would even leave the bedroom immediately after making love to her. He'd shuffle into the next

room, and she'd hear the beep of his PlayStation 4 turning on.
Like a robot powering up. Ready to follow its prime directive.
She couldn't help but think that the entire time they made love,
he was fantasizing about playing video games.

Why doesn't he just fuck his PlayStation?

Last month, their relationship had started to sour. Especially after
a particular lovemaking session at Charlie's apartment. Susan
had opened the fridge to grab the only food Charlie always had
plenty of: cold cuts and white bread. Probably because a sandwich
could be made quickly without taking time away from gaming.

"I'm making ham and cheese. You want one?" she asked,
curious to see if he would get up off the couch.

"I'm not hungry."

Why am I even with him?

Most things in Charlie's pantry weren't fresh, including
the ham, which was two days past the expiration date but still
somewhat edible due to all the nitrates. The American cheese was
fine, but that stuff lasts even longer than butter. She sat at the
kitchen table and took a bite of her sandwich, chomping through
the stale bread. She paused a YouTube video on her phone and
asked, "How's your game?"

"Good," Charlie said. "You good?"

Despair washed over her. "I don't know. Am I good?"

Charlie could have easily put down his controller and sat
with her, bored while watching her eat, but where was the fun
in that? Besides, he was in the middle of a boss fight that he'd
spent the last ten minutes trying to win. He continued jamming
on the buttons before asking, "What's going on?"

Susan stood up like a wooden plank, blocking his view of the television. Daggers shot out of her eyes. "Let's see, Charlie. We just made love, and you went straight to your PlayStation."

"Here we go again," Charlie said, getting ready for a fifteen-round heavyweight fight.

"I said I was making a sandwich. You could've eaten with me."

"I said I wasn't hungry."

Susan let out a loud sigh as she walked back to the kitchen table. "It doesn't matter. You could've sat with me at the kitchen table instead of playing your game."

Charlie paused the game and walked into the kitchen, towering over her. "Why do you hate games so much?"

She set her sandwich down and said, "I don't hate video games. I just think they're more important to you than I am."

"That's not true. If I was watching TV, you wouldn't have said jack shit to me. You're mad because it's a video game."

"If you would've watched a show, I would've watched it with you."

"You don't even like the shows I want to watch."

"We could've decided on one *together*."

Charlie paced around the kitchen. "How many times have I asked you to play a game with me? I have games that we can play together, but you never want to."

"You only like games where you kill things. That doesn't appeal to me."

Charlie placed his hands on top of his head. "Oh my God. I asked you to play *Overcooked*, that game where we work together in a kitchen, but you didn't want to play. I also asked you to play *Pac-Man Championship Edition* and *Puyo Puyo Tetris*."

Susan took the bread off the top of her sandwich and slapped the exposed ham onto the plate. *Thwap!* "We're getting nowhere. I'm going home. You clearly don't want to spend time with me."

"Fine. I'll stop playing."

"It's not that. I want you to *want* to stop playing."

"That makes no sense. Why would I want to stop playing?"

"Exactly."

Susan knew that there would always be another boss, level, or world to conquer. That was priority number one on Charlie's list. Sometimes, it felt like she wasn't on it at all. She put on her jacket and said, "I'm leaving. That sandwich sucks, by the way. Buy some fresh bread and meat."

The sun had set when Jessica, Susan's best friend since high school and the lead singer of her band, arrived at Starbucks. A rebellious party animal who could down any drink in a few minutes, Jessica was also kind and caring. Although she had the strongest voice of the four band members, she was always encouraging Susan to write songs and sing. She expected to see the usual Smiling Susan, a nickname she'd given her years earlier, but instead found her friend with her head down.

"What's wrong, baby?" Jessica asked.

"Charlie's not coming to our gig tomorrow."

"Why the hell not?"

"His boss gave him this big project that's due on Monday."

Jessica flung off her coat. "Wait. Wait. Wait. You're telling me he can't spare a few hours to see you sing at our gig? Bullshit!"

"He said it would take all weekend and that he would barely have enough time for sleep."

"He probably wants to play video games," Jessica said as she walked up to the counter to order a cappuccino.

Susan took another sip of her latte as she pondered Jessica's words. When she returned, Susan asked, "Do you think he's lying so he can play his game?"

"If he is, then it's obvious he's prioritizing games over you," Jessica said.

"Thank you. I'm not crazy to think that, right?"

"Not at all. Why don't you ask that guy who works with him?"

"Dom? I can't do that. Charlie will hear about it and think I don't trust him."

"It already sounds like you don't trust him. At some point, you gotta decide whether you do or not. He loves video games, but honestly, I don't see him lying about something like this. He knows how important the gig is to you."

"He might not be lying," Susan said. "But maybe he's exaggerating the amount of work he has to do. Whatever. You know what? We're gonna rock tomorrow night. His loss."

Jessica placed her hand on Susan's shoulder and said, "You know what helps me get over a guy's bullshit?"

"No. No. No."

"Yes, yes, yes. We're going to the club and getting drunk as shit tonight."

CHAPTER 8

PHYSICAL MEDIA

C harlie winced at the sharp sting at the base of his spine. He'd probably injured his tailbone during the slip on Joe's driveway, but the thought of holding *Battle Theatre* in his hands was enough to ease his pain. He wanted to display the physical copy prominently on his shelf, next to the hundreds of other games. As soon as he arrived at GameStop, he planted each foot like Frankenstein's monster, slow and deliberate, listening for the crunch of the cold, hard snow before taking another step. *I'm only buying the game. I can wait until Monday to play it.* After making his purchase, he was browsing the store, looking for something on sale to add to his collection, when Tim, the youngest member of his gaming crew, called.

Tim looked like Urkel, but talked like a dime store version of 50 Cent. He was a whip-smart engineering student who acted as if he came from the streets, yet still lived with his mother. He'd played online with Charlie for the past three years but never met him in person. Outside of gaming, he had no other friends. The click-clack of his controller grew louder as he said, "Guess what *I'm* doing."

Charlie said, "Masturbating?"

"Oh, yeah. Ugh. Ugh. Give it to me, baby. You so tight. Imma bust a nut," Tim said, barely making it to 20 cents on his 50 Cent scale. "I'm jerking off to the dope experience of *Call of Booty.* Oh wait, wrong game. *Battle Theatre.*"

"It's that good?"

"It's on point, playa."

"You heard what happened?" Charlie said, knowing that Dom had probably spilled the beans.

"Yeah, Tony Soprano with muscles told me while we were playing a half-hour ago. Come on. Play a few matches with us, then you can go back to jacking off your boss for the weekend."

Charlie grabbed a copy of *Octopath Traveler* off the shelf, unconsciously fondling it between his fingers. "I really shouldn't."

Tim scored a headshot online before bobbing his head to the side. "Why not?"

"Because if I start, I won't want to stop."

"Kind of like those late-night *Rocket League* matches we used to have."

"Good times. No jobs. No girlfriends," Charlie said, recalling the time before he met Susan.

"I still don't have a girlfriend. Or a job. All I have is *Battle Theatre* and my boys."

"Yeah, well, I do have a job, and a girlfriend, but no *Battle Theatre.*"

"You didn't buy the game?"

"I'm holding it in my hand, but I can't play it until Monday. I don't think I'll be able to play in the tournament."

Tim munched on his Doritos and mumbled, "Oh, you playin' this weekend. Guaranteed."

Charlie trudged back through the snow, holding his copy of *Battle Theatre* in one hand and his phone in the other, trying not to slip again. "You don't know what it's like to have this kind of work pressure, Tim."

"I go to school. That's kind of a job. Look, I get it man. But a cokehead don't buy an eight-ball and have it sit on his desk all weekend without taking a few bumps. Know what I'm sayin'?"

Charlie recalled Dom's earlier comment about the game being like a drug. *What's with these guys comparing games to hard drugs?* His mild headache was now heading into migraine territory. He got in his car and said, "I gotta go. I'll talk to you on Monday."

"You trippin'. I'll be talking to you in a couple of hours online."

"Don't count on it."

CHAPTER 9

WORK OR PLAY

C harlie balanced the laptop, copy of *Battle Theatre*, and three manila folders stuffed with work documents while fumbling with his keys. As soon as he entered his apartment, he flung the laptop and folders onto his couch like a disgruntled fast-food worker tosses trash in a dumpster after a long night of serving ungrateful customers. He gently set the copy of *Battle Theatre* on the coffee table and tapped the case twice with his fingertips, mesmerized by the lettering. Bold. Deep hunter green. Set against a desert backdrop of sand. Crumbled buildings. Bright-orange explosions.

The cover screamed, "Play me! You know you want to."

His living space existed in another universe, far removed from the harmony of feng shui. The centerpiece of the apartment was a sixty-five-inch OLED 4K high-definition Samsung television, smack dab in the middle of the room. The PlayStation 4 Pro had its own shelf, just like the other consoles in his entertainment center. RGB lighting matched the colors the consoles were known for: royal blue for the PlayStation 4 Pro, bright green for the Xbox One X, and candy red for the Nintendo Switch. The entire wall behind the television was lined with a dozen polished walnut shelves, each proudly displaying his games in alphabetical order like a library bookshelf. A hundred or more portable system games, from the Game Boy to the PlayStation Vita, were organized on the bottom shelves, since those games were much smaller. Two rotating glass towers, one on each side of the TV, displayed the game-related merchandise he'd collected over the years, including unopened copies of PlayStation 2 games and a replica of Link's Tri-Force shield. Daylight was no match for the blackout curtains installed on the two windows. Illumination was the enemy. Reflections would not be tolerated. Some of Charlie's most prized games were *Little Samson*, *Chrono Trigger*, *Suikoden II*, *Super Mario 64*, *Pokemon: HeartGold*, and a rare lenticular cover copy of *Xenosaga 3*.

He stared at the laptop and three manila folders. His vivid imagination drifted to the point of hallucination. His work materials began to evaporate into the ether. The *Battle Theatre* case melted into a neon-blue puddle on the coffee table. A massive syringe stood upright in the center of the pool. The plunger drew back as the chamber filled with game liquid. He imagined grabbing the needle and thrusting it into his left forearm, watching the blue liquid disappear into his veins. *If I can't play the game, I might as well inject myself with its essence.* That's what happens when the one thing you desire the most is right in front of you. And you can't do a damn thing about it.

Charlie imagined a third date with a beautiful woman. The dinner—great. Conversation—amazing. Values—aligned. This could be his soulmate. Back at the apartment, she comments on his impressive game collection while gazing at him with her seductive eyes. She peels off her clothes to reveal black lingerie, complete with a lace garter belt holding up translucent stockings that look as if they've been painted on her body. She is perfect. She lies on the bed, naked. *Take me.* Then, like an aberration, DuPont, the ultimate cock block, appears in front of the goddess.

Charlie, you know I see real potential in you. If you do well, this could lead to a big promotion. The woman vanishes. DuPont laughs like a maniac. And Charlie finds himself back at his desk, the rancid stench of his body odor lingering from working nonstop for the past three days.

Charlie shuffled to his desk in the corner of the room, far away from his gaming setup. He turned on his laptop and stared at the email, afraid to open it. Clicking on it meant he had to start working. He gazed at his copy of *BattleTheatre*, resting on the coffee table like a delicate flower. *I just want to play you.* A dark cloud loomed over him as he opened the email attachment. The ring of his cell phone snapped him out of his trance. It was Dom.

"Hey, *paisan.* What're you, lost? Why aren't you online?"

"I'm getting ready to work," Charlie said. "After I just finished working all day."

Dom said, "Why're you wastin' your time with dat crap? The boys are waitin' for you to play *BattleTheatre*."

Charlie heard Dom's wife and kids yelling in the background. He couldn't make out what they were saying, but it was always noisy whenever Charlie called him or played with him online. Dom's wife, Marie, yelled so often that he became better at dodging verbal bullets than virtual ones.

"How's the game?" Charlie asked.

"Like getting a blow job from a supermodel while eating your favorite slice of pizza," Dom said.

"Do you even remember what a blow job feels like, old man?"

"That's what my birthday's for."

Charlie's stomach churned at the thought.

Dom asked, "How much work did this *stronzo* give you?"

Charlie opened the email attachment and scrolled through all the single-sentence assignments that would take multiple pages to complete. "I'll have to work nonstop with minimal breaks and almost no sleep to get this done on time."

"You know what? So fucking what? You can work and play. It's *Battle Theatre, leccaculo.*"

Charlie was familiar with these Italian swear words by now, as Dom tended to use them whenever he was passionate about something. *Stronzo* meant asshole, and *leccaculo* meant kiss-ass.

"I'm afraid if I start one match, I won't be able to stop. One match will turn into ten, then twenty, then God knows how many," Charlie said.

"That's a good thing. We need to practice if we're gonna win this thing. Fuck 'em. Call in sick Monday. And Tuesday."

"That's not gonna work. Apparently, this is a really important report. If it doesn't get done, it'll affect the company."

"*Ingenuo*, you believe that bullshit?" Dom said. "C'mon, brother. He's blowing smoke up your ass."

"Doesn't matter. If I don't get this done, I'm gonna get canned."

Out of the blue, Dom yelled, "Shut the fuck up. I'm on the phone."

Marie's voice shifted from a distant buzz to a deafening foghorn. "Who da fuck do you think you are, talking to me like dat?"

"I'm trying to listen to my friend Charlie, and you're yapping over there."

Some questionable shuffling noises followed a ten-second pause.

Dom returned to the call. "You know how long *Battle Theatre* has been in development for?"

"Is everything okay?" Charlie said.

"What?"

"With Marie?"

"She'll be all right," Dom said as he walked outside. "I'll apologize to her later. What were we talking about?"

"*Battle Theatre* being in development for four years."

"Oh, yeah. Look. If you want to suck your boss's dick this weekend, by all means, pucker up buttercup, but don't let him ruin our weekend. Marie wanted to go hiking at Starved Rock. I said, 'Hell, no. This weekend is for me and da boys.'"

Dom's words cut Charlie deep. He was one of the boys. Hell, he was the main boy. Except now he wasn't. *Battle Theatre* was supposed to be *his* game. The rest of them hadn't followed its development over the past four years. Reading every article, watching every video, and entering them in the tournament. Charlie was the reason they had a spot. And now he was going to miss it because of DuPont's merciless assignment. He rested his head on his desk and glared at the laptop. "I gotta go."

"See you tonight," Dom said. "On the battlefield."

CHAPTER 10

INTOXICATION ALIENATION

Jessica's house had a basement bar with more spirits than a haunted house. Her plan: get drunk with Susan, call an Uber, and head to the club. She was on her fourth Moscow Mule when the doorbell rang. She leapt from the couch, swung open the door, and hugged Susan with the might of a boa constrictor.

Susan said, "I see you started without me."

"It's only my third drink. Or was it my fourth?" Jessica said. "Who cares? Come inside, baby. Let me fix you a drink."

Jessica knew vodka cranberry was Susan's favorite drink, so she mixed one and handed it over with blinding speed. Susan raised the glass to her lips and downed it in seven seconds flat. Jessica immediately mixed another. "That's my girl. You've got some serious catching up to do."

Susan ran her index finger along the rim of the glass and fell back onto the couch, spilling some of her drink. Her chin sank into her chest.

Jessica grabbed a towel and tossed it on the spill. "Honey, don't let him ruin our night. I want a happy drunk tonight, not a sad one."

A single tear fell from Susan's left eye. Her lips began to quiver. "Why do I keep letting him make me feel this way?"

Jessica sat beside her and hugged her tight. "He's an idiot for not seeing what I see. You are, like, the fucking best. I can't believe he chose a fucking video game over you."

"Maybe he's telling the truth."

Jessica sat up straight, grabbed Susan by the shoulders, and said, "He's lying. I bet he's playing his game. Men suck. Accept it."

"I don't know. Maybe I was too harsh with him. We got into a pretty bad argument."

Jessica took a large swig. "Fuck him. Now chug that drink."

Susan let out a soft chuckle, took a sip, and said, "Why do we need to get wasted?"

"Because getting blitzed is fun, and it means I don't have to think about all the asshole guys in this world. I think I'm gonna start, like, asking girls out," Jessica said.

"Maybe we're picking the wrong guys."

Jessica sighed. "My mom's always saying there's a perfect guy out there for me, but I haven't met him. It's like a lie that mothers tell their daughters so they can have grandchildren. It really is a messed-up dynamic."

She continued to slam down Moscow Mules while Susan took slow sips of her vodka cranberry. They talked about Charlie, their upcoming gig, playing guitar, immature men, and Jessica's possible newfound sexual orientation. They were bonding, and it was exactly what Susan needed. Eventually, Jessica's phone alarm went off, prompting her to say, "Time to call the Uber."

"I don't feel like going out tonight."

"Why? So you can cry all night over him?"

"How could he not sacrifice a couple of hours to hear me sing?" Susan said.

Jessica placed a hand on her shoulder. "You don't need him, you know. You're a strong, beautiful soul."

"I don't know what I need right now. Maybe I should just go home."

Jessica sprang up and said, "No. Stay. I'll make some popcorn and we can watch a movie."

"Sorry. I know you wanted to go out tonight."

Jessica said, "Who cares about some stupid club?"

About half an hour into the movie, the Moscow Mules knocked Jessica unconscious. Susan stared at her eternally single friend. She wanted things to work out with Charlie, but her thoughts spiraled into an endless abyss of doubt. *Why does he have to be so obsessed with games? Was I too hard on him?* She thought she'd invested in a partner who could share her dreams. A man she might marry someday. But maybe she was watering a dead plant instead of nourishing an elegant garden of flowers. She felt her soul withering.

She covered Jessica with a fleece blanket and shifted her gaze to her lyric sheet, which was lying on the lid of the band's Dream Bin next to the couch. At least her music was still alive. She turned to the still-sleeping Jessica and said, "Love is hopeless, isn't it?" Then she grabbed the spare key and let herself out, locking the door behind her.

By nine-thirty, Susan was lying in her bed. Staring at the ceiling. Wondering if she should call Charlie. Thinking that he was either working or playing online. She twirled her phone in her hand for another minute before finally calling him.

He answered with a ragged "Hello?"

"You don't sound too good."

"I'm stressed out from all this work."

"I know you have a lot going on, but I'm hoping you'll reconsider and come to my gig?"

Charlie began clicking on the laptop keys. Part of him felt the need to keep working, but another part wanted to make sure Susan could hear him typing. "Didn't we already have this conversation? There's no way."

"Are you lying to me?"

Charlie said, "Wait a minute. You think I'm lying about work? That I'm playing a game?" He wanted to please her, but he was facing an unreasonable time crunch to finish this assignment. He simply couldn't spare four hours for her gig.

"I don't know what to think, but we can't keep going on like this."

Charlie slammed the laptop shut and said, "Like what? Why are you blaming me for this?"

"I dunno. I feel like you're using this assignment as an excuse not to be with me. You know how much this gig means to me, but you don't seem to care."

Charlie flung his pen across the desk. "Fine. I'll forget the assignment and come to the gig."

"No, I don't want you to come. You're just gonna be miserable the whole time," Susan said. There was a long pause before she added, "You're not worth it."

There it is. The sentence no man ever wants to hear. She should have just called me a loser. At least that's more direct. Charlie was trying to be responsible and get his work done, yet he was now worthless in Susan's eyes. He wanted to yell at her. Not just yell. Full nuclear meltdown. But he held himself back. All he could muster was "I gotta go. I don't have time for this."

"You know, Jessica was right. You don't have time for me. You never have. That's the problem. But you always have plenty of time to play video games."

Charlie rubbed his temples as he shook his head. "Who told you I was playing games right now? Jessica?"

"Yes, and she has a point. You prioritize games over me. You love games more than me."

Why can't she just accept the fact that I like to play video games?

"You play games when I come to your apartment, and you bring your Nintendo Switch whenever you come to mine."

"Yeah, but I don't always play it."

"It's not about playing it. It's the fact that you feel the need to bring it in the first place. You'd rather stay home, play your games, and smoke weed with Johnny."

"I don't smoke weed all the time. Besides, you drink a lot with Jessica. How is that any better?"

"Charlie, I don't want to fight, but I need more."

"I gotta get this done or I'll get fired. I didn't ask for this shit. I'm in a tough position. Why can't you see that?"

"Have fun with your game," Susan said before hanging up.

Charlie placed his hands on his face and shook his head. She didn't believe him. He thought about FaceTiming her so she could see all the files on his desk and the email from hell. But he knew it wouldn't make any difference.

Charlie and Susan's last six months of dating were a stark contrast from the first year. He made excuses to avoid doing things together, either mysteriously falling ill or being in the middle of a crucial multiplayer match he couldn't quit. He only wanted to watch his movie choices, labeling hers "the same rom-com over and over again." While the relationship seemed fine to him, it was fading in her eyes. He was kind and made her laugh, but he avoided doing fun things with her and could be incredibly thoughtless at times. He got what he needed from her: sex, someone to take care of him, and almost unlimited gaming time. For him, the more time they spent apart, the happier he was and the stronger the relationship felt. When they were together, he took advantage of when she was busy to get in more gaming. On the phone with her friends: game. Making dinner at his apartment: game. Preparing a meal at her place: bust out the Switch. Helping her make dinner was as rare as an unopened copy of *Stadium Events* for the Nintendo. Why cook when you could game?

On nights when he stayed over at her place, Charlie would lie on the couch with her. But if he didn't like the movie, he would put on his noise-canceling Bose headphones and play on his Switch. And he'd continue to play once the movie had ended. He figured Susan probably wanted to watch another movie, so it would be fine to play for a couple more hours. She complained about it at first, but over time, she just let it happen and ignored it. She received sex, a little companionship, and not much else.

Susan's anxiety shot into overdrive. She couldn't escape the terror of singing for three and a half minutes on stage tomorrow. *I'm gonna suck.* Charlie's face in the crowd would have calmed her, but she knew he wasn't going to be there. Tomorrow was supposed to be a joyous night—a milestone in her music career. Her first time singing one of her own songs on stage. She continued to stare at the ceiling and imagined Charlie playing his game while laughing with his friends. *How could I have let this go on for so long?*

A tidal wave of doubts swirled in her mind. Her hints about his excessive gaming should have led to long, deep conversations about how his selfish behavior was tearing apart their relationship. She gazed at her turquoise electric guitar in the corner of the room with the same admiration that Charlie probably felt when looking at his game collection. She got out of bed, walked to the closet, and pulled out her amplifier. Then she plugged in her guitar, and turned the volume knob to maximum, causing a high-pitched squeal. As she played "Sweet Child O' Mine," her mind gradually drifted away from Charlie. Halfway through the song, she started singing. She didn't care if she woke her neighbors or if the police were called. Every note she played felt like a decayed piece of armor falling away from her body. She shut her eyes and imagined dancing on the strings, free from Charlie. The damage was done.

Games had ruined their relationship. Again.

CHAPTER 11

PIZZA PAL

C harlie worked on the financial report without eating anything except for the crumbled remnants of a bag of potato chips. The phone call with Susan had disrupted his focus, and he felt like he'd spent the past three hours doing only an hour of work. He opened the fridge, which contained a half-carton of milk, half a loaf of bread, some moldy salami, and a grapefruit. Francisco's Bar & Pizzeria, a local pizza joint half a block away from his apartment, was open until 1:00 a.m. He felt like he was about to pass out, so he grabbed everything he needed to continue working and headed there.

As far as Charlie was concerned, it served the best pizza in the world. He ate there at least once a week. Francisco was a middle-aged Italian man with salt-and-pepper hair who was more fit than anyone who worked at a pizza place had any right to be, especially since he was always behind the counter. And he was a true artist when it came to crafting a tavern-style pizza. A crispy, cracker-like crust was topped with hand-crushed San Marzano tomatoes, whole-milk mozzarella, and a generous helping of basil and oregano. Only a handful of places in Chicago could rival Francisco's.

Charlie trudged inside, dragging his backpack along the floor before bumping into Francisco's Christmas tree with his shoulder, causing a plastic ornament to fall to the ground. He bent down slower than an arthritic old man to pick it up and place it back on the tree, inches away from another trinket, disrupting Francisco's perfect tree. He was a regular enough customer that Francisco instantly sensed something was wrong.

"Charlie? You okay? You never come in this late."

Charlie reached into his backpack, pulled out one of the manila folders and the laptop, and set them on a table in one of the booths. His eyes were wells of tears. "My boss gave me this bullshit assignment to do." He took a deep breath, sat down, and tucked both hands inside his shirt.

"You all right, kid?"

"I can't take it anymore," Charlie sighed. "I don't know what to do. It's just too much. It can't be done."

Francisco walked over and picked up the thick folder. "Let me see that." He began leafing through the reports while Charlie turned his laptop toward him to reveal the dreaded email.

"And that's just a taste of my nightmare," Charlie said.

Francisco put on his reading glasses. "This sure looks like a lot of work. When is this due?"

"Monday. I'm toast."

"Hang on a second."

Francisco scampered back to the kitchen, picked up the cordless phone, and called his brother Vince, who answered after five rings. "Did I wake you? Good. I need you to look at an email one of my customers is about to send over. Hold on." Francisco held the phone against his apron and yelled to Charlie, "My brother is in finance. You mind sending him your assignment?"

Since Charlie was probably going to be fired anyway, he didn't care about the legal ramifications of sending a confidential document to a stranger, so he replied, "Why not?"

Francisco recited his brother's email address and Charlie started typing.

"Vince, he's sending it over now." There was a long pause before Francisco spoke again. "No, I'm not bringing you a pizza. What? Just look at the fucking email, okay? Now, listen. *Listen.* Are you listening? We need to know how long it would take you to do the work." Francisco paused for a second and sighed before continuing. "No, I'm not asking you to *do* the work. I'm asking how long it would take you to do it." Another pause. "You can't just do me a favor without getting something in return, eh? Fine. I'll bring you a pizza tomorrow. Call me back in ten minutes." With that, Francisco hung up the phone. "You got a brother, Charlie?"

"I have a younger sister."

"This guy. Successful in finance, and he acts like he's too good for me. I've been feeding his ungrateful family for over twenty years," Francisco said.

"Thanks for doing this," Charlie said, taking a sip from the Coke Zero Francisco had placed on the table.

Ten minutes later, Francisco read out a text from Vince. "'The assignment is impossible to complete in three days. It would take at least a week of work, maybe more. Fifty to sixty hours billable.'"

Charlie's head dropped into his right palm as he shook his head. His soul was crushed like the San Marzano tomatoes on Francisco's pizza.

"Look at this guy. He sounds like a robot with this 'billable' shit," Francisco said.

Charlie's voice cracked as he said, "I feel sick."

"I know my brother makes a lot more than I do, but I wouldn't trade places with him. I can tell he hates his job. No passion. No creativity."

"Pizza's creative?" Charlie said, trying not to cry.

"Let me ask you something. Why do you come here every week and eat my pizza?"

Charlie straightened up and said with conviction, "Because it's the best pizza in Chicago."

"How do you think it became the best?"

"I don't know. Good ingredients?"

"Time. Ingenuity. Passion. I make pizza different from other places. I studied the craft and experimented for six months before I even opened this place. I trained with some of the best chefs in the world and used what I learned to create the perfect pizza through trial and error. There's no better feeling than building something you can call your own."

"I didn't mean to imply your pizza's not creative. Sorry."

"Don't be sorry, kid. You're figuring it out, just like the rest of us. The question you should ask yourself is: 'Can I learn something new and put it out in the world?'"

"Thanks, Francisco."

"Mushroom and pepperoni with garlic?"

"You know it."

Charlie inhaled his heavenly pizza, burning the roof of his mouth. It tasted better than ever. The crust—crispier. The sauce—spicier. The cheese—gooier. A pizza made with love, by a sympathetic soul, at the end of a bleak night was the cozy blanket Charlie needed. After savoring the final slice, he returned to his apartment, sat at his desk, and opened his laptop. He stared at the immense amount of work in front of him for over thirty minutes.

Francisco's brother was right. This is impossible.

It was two o'clock in the morning. He could barely keep his eyes open. Time for bed.

CHAPTER 12

DEPLORABLE DUPONT

Around the same time Charlie finished his last slice at Francisco's, DuPont's plane landed in Naples, Florida. One of his golf buddies, Todd, was a private jet pilot who whisked his friends away to exotic destinations during the winter. This weekend, he'd offered to fly DuPont and two other pals to a lush green haven of a resort. A far cry from the snowy concrete jungle of Chicago.

After a few hours' sleep, DuPont strolled into the golf course lobby at 9:00 a.m., wearing a Burberry polo shirt, Celine soft lambskin jeans, and Berluti leather golf shoes. His clubs were Callaway Big Berthas nestled in a premium-leather Heritage Brown bag. While some people saved their money for a comfortable retirement or family vacations, he saved his for personal belongings that reflected his insecurities. He had no foresight or concern to save money for his family's financial future.

He slid up to the nearby bar and ordered a Bloody Mary, the alcoholic breakfast drink of champions. Todd arrived a few minutes later and ordered the same thing.

"You ready to lose, Eddie?" Todd said. The only ones who called DuPont "Eddie" were his golf buddies.

DuPont said, "Not today. Feeling especially good this weekend."

"Let me guess? You finally bagged that hot little number. What's her name again?"

DuPont took a sip of his drink. "A gentleman never fucks and tells."

Both men cackled.

"I *can* tell you who I'm fucking with, though. Scrawny guy named Charlie. Gave him this huge work assignment on Friday and told him it was due on Monday."

"Why didn't you just give it to him earlier in the week?"

DuPont pulled the celery stalk out of his glass and bit down hard on it, producing a loud crackling crunch. "I could have, but you know, I like to see them sweat."

"Man, that's—"

DuPont interrupted, "Oh, and William, a glorified rent-a-cop posing as Head of Security, actually had the balls to hand in an application for a junior financial analyst position. With no education. He's not even qualified to be an intern."

"You need serious help. Maybe I should teach you some humility and beat your ass on the golf course."

"Humility is for losers. You gotta swing your dick around to keep these losers in line." DuPont extracted the toothpick with three olives speared on it from his drink, raised his eyebrows, and waved the tiny, bulbous phallus. "Sometimes they gotta be slapped in the face with my kielbasa."

DuPont's home life was lacking, to put it mildly. His wife probably would have left him years ago, but the money was too good. A sleek Lexus, Ralph Lauren clothes, and Fendi purses at least made her misery more bearable. She'd made the mistake of disrespecting him one time. His response—he pushed his index finger into the middle of her chest, causing all 115 pounds of her to fall backward onto the bed. She lay stunned as he said, "Imagine what I can do with the rest of my hand." After that day, she never disrespected him again. But she got her own little form of revenge by complaining of a migraine whenever he wanted sex. He also had a daughter who moved away to California at nineteen years of age, likely due to the psychological abuse she had suffered at home.

DuPont's wealth, power, and status in the social hierarchy made him feel good, but it wasn't enough. He took pleasure in seeing others suffer and adding them to his list of defeated subordinates. He'd done it to William, Jasmine, and plenty of others over the past fifteen years. Dominance was his drug. And he hadn't had a fix in weeks, so Charlie was the next victim. The impossible assignment was a way of keeping him in check. *Domination cannot thrive in a comfortable environment.*

Todd said, "You're not beating me today. Prepare to go down."

The corners of DuPont's mouth curved up slower than molasses. "I'll bet you a thousand bucks I win."

Todd stood silent for thirty seconds.

It was time for DuPont to go in for the kill. "Let's make it two thousand."

Todd rubbed his forehead, squirmed in his chair, and said, "Too rich for my blood, Eddie."

DuPont stretched his arms in the air, pleased by Todd's reaction. He raised his drink and tipped his visor toward his golf buddy, his eyes cold and insidious. Todd clinked his glass against DuPont's, downed the rest of his drink, and slunk over to the golf shop to buy some tees.

DuPont smirked. He had prevailed over his opponent before even taking his first swing on the golf course.

CHAPTER 13

TEQUILA

Last year, DuPont invited a male employee of Indian descent to attend the company's annual diversity conference in Atlanta. The year before that, he brought along an Asian man. This year, it had to be a woman, an African American, or, ideally, an African American woman. By checking both boxes, Jasmine enabled DuPont to satisfy the company's illusory quota.

On the final day of the conference two months ago, he invited her to join him for a drink on the hotel's rooftop bar, adding that he would flag her as "not a team player" in his report to the CEO if she refused. When she arrived, two shots of light-blue tequila and two limes were sitting on the bar in front of him. She ordered a glass of white wine while he ordered a Jack and Coke.

Two minutes later, he said, "Come on. Have a shot with me."

"Uh, hard liquor isn't really my thing. I'm all right with just my wine."

"Come on. Live a little. This is top-shelf tequila. Not the cheap stuff you're probably used to."

Jasmine rolled her eyes when he wasn't looking, clearly offended by his comment. "I'm good. Thanks."

DuPont raised one of the shot glasses and said, "This is a toast to you. It's my way of saying that I appreciate all your help. You can't just turn down a toast like that."

One shot. That's all I'm having. I'll be damned if he gets me drunk.

"Here's to Jasmine, the greatest assistant financial manager in the world."

Jasmine downed the other shot and noticed it tasted incredibly bitter. To her, all tequila tasted strong, so she usually couldn't tell the difference between a bitter one and a smooth one. She sucked on the lime to try to mask the harsh taste in her mouth.

DuPont yelled, "Bartender! Two more shots over here."

Jasmine knew he was trying to get her drunk, and she wasn't going to fall for it. "We already had our toast. I'm good."

"Come on, darling. We work hard, so we play hard."

The bartender poured two shots of tequila and placed them on the bar. DuPont said, "Come on. You can handle one more itty-bitty shot."

"I don't need another. I'm already buzzed," Jasmine said, her eyes blinking rapidly.

"I'm a gentleman, so I won't pressure you to drink more than you can handle," DuPont said before downing both shots.

After twenty minutes, Jasmine said, "It's getting late and we have an early flight. I'm gonna call it a night."

"No problem," DuPont said. "Oh, before you go. We need to go over the prospectus. I left it in my room. Let's head up there together. It'll only take a few minutes."

"Why can't we just go over it in the morning?"

"The email has to be sent tonight because our client is in Japan. It's already three o'clock in the afternoon over there, and they need it before five."

Jasmine's mind raced. A million red flags flapped in her head. The Senior Vice President of Finance was inviting her to his hotel room to review a document that conveniently needed to be checked right away because of a client in Japan. She remembered a lesson her mother had taught her: *Never go into a man's hotel room, especially when you've been drinking.*

"I'm sorry, but I'm uncomfortable going into your hotel room."

"Tell you what, why don't you come up and wait in the hallway while I look for the prospectus?" DuPont said.

Jasmine paused for a second before replying, "I guess that would be fine."

As they rode the elevator to DuPont's room, Jasmine's buzz intensified, causing her lips to tremble. *Why didn't I just tell him to meet me in the lobby?*

When they arrived on the fifth floor, DuPont marched down the hallway, swiped his keycard, and strutted into his room. Jasmine stood steadfast outside.

After fumbling around for five minutes, DuPont poked his head out and said, "You sure you don't want to come in? It might be a while before I find this thing."

Drowsiness started to set in. Jasmine remembered thinking about something important a few moments ago. Something about a lobby. The thought eluded her. Confusion. She slurred her words as she said, "I'll… just… wait… here." She didn't feel drunk. It was more like the moment before drifting off to sleep after taking a sedative or driving for six hours without a break.

"Fine," DuPont said before closing the door on her.

All Jasmine wanted to do was lie down in the hallway and take a nap.

Three minutes later, DuPont's shuffling stopped. Jasmine peeked at the tiny, bright light emanating from the peephole, which briefly turned dark. It happened again. And again. *The son of a bitch is watching me. Waiting for me to pass out.*

Then it dawned on her. *He must have drugged me.* It was the only thing that made sense. The waving red flags wrapped tightly around her like a nylon blanket, impossible to escape from. The decision was clear: stay here and pass out or run back to her room.

Jasmine dashed toward the elevator. Her legs were burning. Her arms went numb. As soon as the elevator doors opened, she heard DuPont yelling something down the hallway. She thought, *If he grabs me, I'll scream.* She stumbled inside the elevator and pressed the button for the third floor. She struggled to stand up straight. The elevator doors closed. The sudden descent made the urge to pass out even stronger. Fortunately, her room was only a few feet from the elevator. Any further, and she would have collapsed in the hallway. She swiped her keycard, turned the security lock to the left, and collapsed face down onto her bed.

Never again. I am never putting myself in that situation ever again.

CHAPTER 14

INTO THE STRATOSPHERE

S aturday, 11:00 am. Charlie's usual dreams of hopping on a kaleidoscope of colored platforms as Super Mario or swinging his chain blades as Kratos in *God of War* were replaced with one where his head was stuck in the metal jaws of a vise, with DuPont turning the handle until they dug into his skull. The earsplitting crunch of bone woke him up, leaving him with a pounding headache and a sore jaw from grinding his teeth. He glanced at the laptop and paper files spread all over his desk of doom, his irritability erupting like a raging volcano. He stomped over to the desk, grabbed the laptop, and held it against his chest like a Frisbee. *Son of a bitch. That son of a bitch.* The urge to fling the laptop into the drywall was tempting, but a text from Jasmine asking him about his progress snapped him out of his rage. He wanted to text her back and let her know that the task was impossible, but couldn't bring himself to do it.

There was a knock on the door.

Who the hell's that? What other monstrous mountain of shit can happen now?

As soon as Charlie swung open his front door, the woodsy aroma of weed flooded inside. The sun shone behind Johnny, making him look like a lion in the savanna, with his long blond hair flowing in the breeze like golden wheat.

"'Sup, brah?"

"Hey, Johnny," Charlie said, stepping aside to let him pass.

Johnny strutted in, ran his hand through his hair, and said, "I've got some really good cannabis for you. Super fresh."

"This is the worst weekend of my life," Charlie said.

Johnny just smiled and started singing lyrics from "My Console" by the techno band Eiffel 65, making it clear he expected they would be playing all day long.

"I'm really not in the mood."

Johnny continued singing, inflecting each letter. "P-L-A-Y-S-T-A-T-I-O-N."

"It's too early for this shit."

Johnny said, "It's eleven o'clock, man." As he walked around Charlie's apartment, he glanced at the collection of in-box copies of rare games spanning every console generation.

Tail Concerto, *Clock Tower*, *Persona 2*, *Tactics Ogre*, and *Galerians* for the PlayStation.

Rule of Rose, *Haunting Ground*, *Silent Hill 2*, and *God Hand* for the PlayStation 2.

Contra Force, *The Legend of Zelda*, and *Snow Brothers* for the Nintendo.

EarthBound, *Mega Man X3*, and *Super Turrican 2* for the Super Nintendo.

Paper Mario, *Conker's Bad Fur Day*, and *Ogre Battle 64* for the Nintendo 64.

Aero the Acrobat 2, *Ristar*, and *Vectorman* for the Genesis.

Johnny selected *Haunting Ground* from one of the shelves and said, "I should dig out my PS2 and borrow this sometime."

"Yeah, I don't think so. The last thing I need is for that game to disappear. Do you know how rare it is?"

"What? You don't trust me?"

"I do, but losing even one of my games would send me into a panic attack."

Johnny flopped onto the couch and said, "I got a chance to look at the level editor in *BattleTheatre* last night. It looks sick."

Charlie shrugged before joining Johnny on the couch. "I wouldn't know."

"I'm surprised you're not more excited. Remember how you used to create all those levels and mods for *Half-Life* on your PC when you were a kid? You were always showing off those levels you designed."

"I dabbled."

"*Dabbled?* Dude, you were fucking obsessed with it for over a year. Don't you remember? You were pretty good at it."

"I'd rather not remember those days," Charlie said, recalling that his parents divorced shortly after.

Charlie hadn't just created mods. He'd used his PC to hack games, developing a primitive AI system that adjusted a game's difficulty based on player performance. All those lines of code. All those hours. It was hard to remember the exact reason why he gave it up. Was it because *playing* games was so much easier than *making* them? Why was there so much math involved? He was terrible at math. Did it stop being fun?

Why did I feel so bad when I was coding?

The more he thought about it, the more painful the surge of humiliation coursed through his body.

Around the same time, when Charlie was twelve, his father confiscated his PC for an entire month because his math grades were slipping. He would sneak into his parents' room to make and play games on the banned PC whenever his father wasn't home. But one day he got caught. Joe punished him by deleting all his game files, including the mods he was working on. Deleting those files right in front of Charlie made it even worse. He begged his father to stop, but it was no use. All that work—vanished. Charlie had never cried as much as he did that day. The more he tried to talk to his father about how serious he was about game design, the worse he felt. His father's words thundered in his brain: "Games are a waste of time. How are you going to make a video game with terrible math grades? This is not normal."

Johnny glanced around the room until he spotted *Battle Theatre*, still in its shrink wrap, on the coffee table next to the TV. He reached over, grabbed the game, and held it inches from Charlie's face. "What the fuck is this?"

"Don't start."

"I know the shit I smoke is good, but I didn't know it could make me hallucinate. All right. What the hell is going on?"

"I told you. My fucking boss gave me a ton of work to do this weekend. I'll have no time to play if I want to get this assignment done."

"Brah. We've been waiting four years for this game. We need to practice."

Dom and Tim had already played half a dozen hours of *Battle Theatre* in preparation for the tournament, with Johnny joining them for about two hours. It would've been longer if he hadn't burned himself out playing way too much *PUBG* the night before. At the start of the game, Tim had instructed Johnny not to bother Charlie because of the work assignment.

"Ugh," Charlie said. "Why aren't you playing with Tim and Dom right now?"

"I saw you weren't online again. I'm not playing any more matches without Sir Bud."

Johnny had given Charlie the nickname several years earlier because of an encounter with a marijuana bud the size of a grapefruit. The bigger the bud, the stronger the high. Or at least that's what Charlie believed in his late teens. He paid a local dealer more for a massive bud that looked like a strange artifact from an alien planet. The orange and red hairs interwoven into it were more intricate than a human brain's dendrites. He resisted the urge to smoke it for two days because he wanted all his friends to see the freakish specimen. Ever since, Johnny had called him Sir Bud whenever they got high together.

"I went to Francisco's last night," Charlie said. "He called his brother, who said it would take at least a week to finish the assignment. If I don't show my boss that I made an attempt, I'll get fired for sure. I don't know what to do."

Johnny sprawled on the floor, closed his eyes, and placed his fingers and thumbs together like a meditating Dalai Lama. "The choice is easy. You've been trying to fuck this hot girl for four years. She finally spreads her legs, and you say, 'I need to blow my boss.' Brah. Don't blow your boss. Fuck the girl."

The burden of DuPont's impossibly heavy weight started to melt off Charlie's shoulders. Like a phoenix flapping its regenerated wings, he finally understood his flight path. The task he'd been given was not only impossible but incredibly unfair.

Why should I make myself miserable only to fall short?

Charlie stood up, thrust his shoulders back, and said, "You know what? You're right. I'm gonna fuck the girl."

Johnny wagged a finger and said, "I knew Sir Bud was still in there somewhere." He plucked a gallon-sized Ziploc bag of weed from his jacket pocket, opened it, and held it to Charlie's nose. Charlie took a deep whiff, savoring the fragrant bouquet of fresh apples, lemons, and pine. Then he gave Johnny *the look*. Of finally giving in. Of accepting everything at face value and just going with it.

Johnny immediately understood and said, "Welcome to Wonderland."

Charlie smiled, realizing it was the first time he'd done so all weekend.

Johnny opened his backpack and pulled out one of the dozen bongs he'd made over the years. It was shaped like a pineapple, leafy green with yellow stripes running vertically down the sides. Hand-painted by Johnny himself. He only brought it out on special occasions.

Charlie smiled again. "The famous pineapple bong."

Johnny held it high in the air, like Rafiki held Simba in *The Lion King*. "Imagine you're on a tropical island. It's just you, the sun, and this glorious pineapple bong in your hands." He trotted to the kitchen sink and filled it with water, then reached inside the refrigerator for a handful of ice cubes. He placed them in the ice catcher to cool the smoke for smoother hits. Finally, he lit the extra-wide bowl with his trusty Bic lighter and declared, "Let the games begin."

Johnny took no more than a baby hit because he wanted Charlie's to have the maximum impact. There was no turning back now. Like a peace pipe offering, Charlie accepted the bong and inhaled as if he were taking his last breath. He held the smoke in his lungs for a few seconds, then exhaled a cloud that was as thick and dense as a cumulonimbus. Haze filled the entire apartment. After a few minutes of passing the bong back and forth like Michael Jordan and Scottie Pippen, Charlie was not just feeling good. He was feeling joyous. Untethered elation coupled with anticipation. He was about to experience a game he had dreamed of for four years. The crinkle of Johnny removing the shrink wrap off the game case sounded louder than usual. The weed was kicking into high gear.

Charlie ran his fingers around the circumference of the game disk. It was as smooth as the glass of Johnny's bong. He inserted it into his PlayStation 4 Pro and waited for the game to load. A few seconds later, a message popped up on the console: "An update is required. Please update the game before starting. Update size: 84 GB."

Johnny said, "Eighty-four gigabytes! Fucking updates. It's gonna take at least an hour for it to download. Remember when you could just pop in a cartridge and the game would start right away?"

"Yup, good ol' early Nintendo days. I'm so hungry, I could eat a burger the size of a Nintendo 64," Charlie said.

"That reminds me of this chick a few years back. Remember skinny Jenny?"

"I don't even know where I am right now," Charlie said, his high intensifying.

"Lightweight," Johnny said. "Anyway, she was anorexic all her life. Her mom took her to all these doctors. She saw all these therapists. Nobody could help her. She took a few hits of my sticky icky bud and scarfed down a double cheeseburger with fries in minutes." There was a long pause before he added, "And she polished off a large vanilla milkshake!"

Charlie replied, "Incredible."

"She threw up all over my car and me. But you know what? I wasn't even pissed. I changed her life," Johnny said, clearly proud of himself.

Charlie raised his eyebrows. "You cured her anorexia?"

"Absolutely," Johnny said. "I mean, she's a two-hundred-and-fifty-pound pothead now, but she's as happy as ever."

"You're an idiot. All this talk is making me even more hungry. I think it's burger time," Charlie said, rubbing his belly.

"*BurgerTime.* Great fucking game. Remember we used to play it every day at that shitty arcade?"

"Yup, that and *Galaga* were the best," Charlie said. "Let's walk over to Windy City Dogs and get us a double cheese and a char dog, baby."

"Can't game on an empty stomach. It should be ready to play by the time we get back."

A few seconds later, Charlie's cell phone rang. "Shit. It's Jasmine. Should I answer it?"

"Hell, no. Let that shit go to voicemail."

"Dammit," Charlie said. "I told her I would pick up if she called. I have to take it." He swiped the screen and said, "Hey, Jasmine. How's it going?"

"I was about to ask you the same thing," Jasmine said.

"Well, you know, it's going. I'm just working away. Day by day. In my own special way."

Jasmine paced around her apartment. "You sound strange. Is everything okay?"

Charlie's eyelids drooped while his head bobbed from side to side. "Everything's great. But I'm hungry, and when I'm hungry, I eat."

After a five-second pause, Jasmine said, "Okay."

"Okay," Charlie replied.

"Do you want to call me after lunch so we can go over the report?"

"I mean, I don't *want* to call you. I *will* call you. But I'm not sure I *need* to call you," Charlie said.

"You sound drunk."

Charlie lifted his head, lowered the cell phone to his right thigh, and started laughing.

Jasmine yelled, "Charlie!"

He brought the cell phone back up to his ear and said, "Listen, Jazzy. I'm going out to eat with my buddy Johnny. I'll call you later."

Jasmine bit her bottom lip and paced even faster. "Okay. Please call me right after you're done eating."

Charlie responded with a deep-voiced "Yes *ma'am!*" then hung up.

Jasmine's worry escalated from a light breeze to a category-five tornado. Her mind spun and twirled in all directions as she took three deep breaths in a futile attempt to calm down and convince herself that Charlie wasn't drunk. A lot was riding on this report. If Charlie didn't finish it, both of them would likely be fired. This time, there would be no escape from DuPont's crosshairs, targeting them for termination.

CHAPTER 15

GRAND LARCENY

C harlie and Johnny were sufficiently high to embark on their culinary adventure. Charlie grabbed his keys and wallet, but forgot to lock the front door when they left. He was usually careful when it came to locking up his apartment, but the weed broke down his inhibitions. The char dog and double cheddar burger were on his mind, and not much else.

They waded through the powdery white snow to the shoveled sidewalk on their way to Windy City Dogs, which was three blocks away. Both of them were unaware of the two scruffy-looking men who were staring at them from inside a rusted light-blue Chevy Impala. The car had been parked in front of Charlie's apartment all morning. The occupants worked for Dimitri and were planning to collect Charlie's gambling debt by any means necessary, even if that meant rummaging through his apartment for something valuable. Dimitri had told them that Charlie lived alone, so they knew the house would now be empty.

Steve, the more sympathetic of the duo, asked, "Who's the guy with Charlie?"

Mike, the irritable half of the crime team, put on his tight-fitting gloves and said, "Doesn't matter. We go inside in two minutes."

"This doesn't seem right. Robbing him like this."

"This numb nut owes over four grand," Mike said. "He's a deadbeat and way overdue. He deserves what's comin' to him. Probably doesn't have a penny to his name, but maybe he's got something valuable we can pawn."

"Why am I here?" Steve asked. "I have no idea how to break into an apartment."

Mike stepped out of the vehicle, opened the trunk, and grabbed a large black duffel bag containing a toolkit and a crowbar. He walked over to the open passenger-side window and tossed the bag into Steve's lap. "You're lucky that I do."

Steve put on his gloves and asked, "What if he's got a dog in there?"

"You know, for a smart motherfucker, you sure are dumb. That's what knocking on his door is for. I've never met a dog that doesn't bark when someone knocks on the door," Mike said. "Let's go, pussy. The clock's ticking."

"Do *not* call me that," Steve replied. "It's disrespectful. I'm out here risking my ass too, you know."

Mike, a full foot taller than Steve, with tattooed arms as thick as two-liter Mountain Dew bottles, snapped back, "Poor little snowflake. I promise we'll go to Starbucks afterward to get you a pink drink."

Steve squinted at Mike and said, "Let's just get this over with," as he exited the car and slung the bag's strap over his shoulders.

On the way to the front door, Mike's head darted around, scanning the street for nosy neighbors. He rang Charlie's doorbell, waited thirty seconds, then knocked three times with his closed fist. No barking dog.

Mike rolled up his sleeves and said, "Hand me the bag."

Steve passed it over and said, "Jesus. It's cold out here. What if you can't unlock it?"

Mike reached into the bag and pulled out the crowbar. "I got this, just in case." Then he placed the torsion wrench at the bottom of the keyhole and set to work with a rake pick, but something didn't feel right. He switched to a half-diamond pick, but still couldn't locate any pins to open the lock.

Sensing Mike's frustration, Steve reached over his crouched body, twisted the doorknob, and laughed when it opened.

Mike glared at him and said, "Good job, Stevie."

As soon as they entered the apartment, a pungent, skunky odor invaded their nostrils. The light haze of Johnny's super-fresh marijuana smoke still lingered in the air. The open bag of weed was resting against the bong on the coffee table.

"Jesus Christ. These guys must be real potheads," Mike said as he grabbed the ounce of weed and took a whiff. "We could probably get two hundred bucks for this bag alone… but I think I'll keep it for myself."

Steve peered around Mike's hulking body and stared at Charlie's gaming setup. It was worthy of a museum exhibit. "PS4 Pro, Nintendo Switch, Xbox One X. Some older consoles, too. I haven't seen a Nintendo 64 in ages. And he has so many games."

Mike grabbed the duffel bag off Steve's shoulders, unzipped it, and dropped it on the floor. "Not for long. Fill 'er up. I'm gonna check the other rooms."

Steve couldn't stop smiling as he marveled at Charlie's impressive collection of portable consoles on the bottom shelf. There was a Game Boy, Game Boy Advance, Nintendo DS and 3DS, PSP, PS Vita, even a Game Boy Micro, with a screen the size of a postage stamp. Not one of them had a scratch. Out of the corner of his eye, he saw *Battle Theatre* updating on the TV screen. Steve was an avid gamer himself, so he was fully aware of the hype surrounding it. He wondered if he should eject the disk and slide it into his pocket without telling Mike.

In Charlie's bedroom, Mike found a gold chain and pendant—a gift from Susan. He rummaged through the chest of drawers, but found only clothes. He flipped over the mattress to check for hidden cash, but there was nothing there either. He walked back into the living area to find Steve frozen, seemingly in a trance, still gazing at the shelves of games. The duffel bag remained empty.

Mike smacked him on the back of the head with enough force to make him lose his balance. "You out of your fuckin' mind? You sure you didn't smoke some of that weed?"

Steve rubbed his skull and took two steps back. "This game collection is incredible. One of them is worth at least three hundred dollars."

Mike snatched Steve's phone from his hand and saw the asking price for a pristine copy of *Haunting Ground*. "We're in a rush here, and you're shopping on eBay? No pink drink for you, sugar tits."

"I told you to stop disrespecting me."

Steve clenched his right hand into a fist and took a swing at Mike, who sensed the telegraphed punch from a mile away and easily dodged the futile attempt at retaliation. Then he grabbed Steve's right arm like a twig and spun him around, placing him in a chokehold.

"Let's get this straight, little man," Mike said. "You do what I tell you to do. I can easily make you pass out and leave you here for the cops." He tightened his grip on Steve's throat.

Steve gasped, struggling to inhale the last few molecules of oxygen that were left in his constricted airway. "I'm sor… I'm sorry."

"Goddamn right you're sorry," Mike said as he released the chokehold and hurled Steve to the floor. "Now, fill up that bag before I fuck you up again, which for me would be easier than putting on my underwear."

Steve, embarrassed and emasculated, sprang to his feet and started stuffing the bag with games and consoles. Then, while Mike checked the street from the window, he quickly ejected the *Battle Theatre* disk from the PlayStation 4 Pro and slipped it into his jacket pocket, making sure he zipped it up so it wouldn't fall out. He also pocketed the Nintendo 3DS and Game Boy Micro for good measure. Only then did he call over to Mike. "What about the TV?"

"Leave it. All it takes is one person to see us leaving this apartment with a TV, and they'll call the cops."

"What about the laptop? The bong?"

"Nah," Mike said. "It's a shitty laptop and I'm not using something these stoners have slobbered over." He grabbed a sheet of paper and a pen, scribbled a message for Charlie, and placed it in the center of the work desk. Finally, he pocketed Johnny's bag of weed and said, "Time to deliver this stuff to Dimitri. Then I'm gonna smoke some of their shit to celebrate a job well done."

Steve was afraid he might aggravate Mike further, so he never asked what the message said.

CHAPTER 16

WINDY CITY DREAMS

The bitter wind slapped Charlie and Johnny in the face as they walked. Charlie took his hands out of his pockets and rubbed them vigorously to try to warm them up. A thick layer of snow blanketed the cars and the shoulders of people walking in the streets. Snowflakes as large as confetti at a ticker-tape parade started to fall as a group of little kids bundled up like marshmallows tossed snowballs at their parents' knees. The line of bungalows, decorated with green Christmas wreaths, red ribbons, and white snow, looked straight out of a Christmas card.

But Charlie didn't notice. His head was down, fixated on the icy path to make sure he didn't slip like he had at his father's house. He was so focused on the ground that he nearly walked into oncoming traffic, but Johnny grabbed the back of his jacket and pulled him back just in time. "Just because you're not driving doesn't mean you can't get killed on these streets. Pay attention, brah."

Charlie, realizing he'd almost been splattered, said, "You saved my ass, bro. Thanks."

"Friends don't let friends walk high by themselves."

As they stumbled into Windy City Dogs, a light haze of savory smoke lingered in the air from the charcoal grill that was jam-packed with dogs and burgers. It was the best place to eat when the munchies kicked in. They both ordered a double cheddar burger, a char dog, and a large cheddar fry. The cheddar fry was a sight to behold—a mountain of fries topped with a dollop of cheese the size of a grapefruit. Likewise, the double burger overflowed with so much melted cheddar that it spilled over the sides. The char dog was the perfect shade of red, with golden grilled onions piled high.

Johnny said, "Check this out," and pulled out his phone to show Charlie a picture of his Dragonstone bong. Charlie stared at it for over two minutes. Not eating. Mesmerized by the intricacy of the design. He zoomed in on different areas of the picture at least a dozen times. The dragon had a full set of razor-sharp teeth and was covered with bumps that resembled real scales. It was similar to one of the dragons from *Game of Thrones*, yet subtly different. Almost good-natured. Its face was fierce but friendly, like Falkor's in *The NeverEnding Story*.

Charlie tossed a handful of fries in his mouth and mumbled, "How come I've never seen this before?"

"It's a prototype. Something I've been messing around with for the past few months."

"This is the most beautiful piece of glass I've ever seen. If we win this tournament, you should start selling your bongs online. Five grand would go a long way toward launching a business."

Johnny swatted the air with his palm and said, "Nah. I just do it for fun. I can't imagine being a businessman."

Charlie chomped on his last fry. "All your bong designs are incredible, but this Dragonstone… This is something special. Have you ever reached out to anyone about it? You could make real money."

"You really think so."

"You should look into it."

"Sure," Johnny said, his voice lacking enthusiasm.

"I'm serious, man. Promise me."

Johnny went from slouching to sitting up as straight as a tightly rolled joint. "Fuck it. I mean, you said 'fuck it' when I convinced you to play in the tournament, so what the hell? Why not? I'll look into it. Thanks, man."

"For what?"

Johnny twirled a fry in his hand and said, "For believing in me."

"That's what best friends do. It's like an unwritten law or some shit," Charlie said.

Johnny smiled, took a deep breath, and looked up at the ceiling. "I guess it is. You ready to go to war?"

"Brother, I've been waiting four years for this."

CHAPTER 17

CHARLIE'S WORST NIGHTMARE

On the walk home, a peaceful ocean of serenity washed over Charlie. No longer concerned about what he should do. It was time to do what he wanted before everything got in the way. Time to play. For as long as he liked. Until his thumbs were numb. The sheer joy of playing *Battle Theatre* for the first time was minutes away. The tournament—only hours away. He found himself skating over the icy sidewalk, head held high, admiring all the dazzling Christmas lights in the storefronts.

But when they arrived back at the apartment, Charlie noticed that the front door was slightly ajar. His stomach twisted like it had during his first roller-coaster ride when he was a kid. He considered calling the police before entering the apartment, but logic took a backseat to dread that his prized possessions might have been stolen. He flung open the door. In a microsecond, his eyes darted to the gaming area. He placed a hand on his forehead and yelled, "Fuck! Fuck! Fuck!"

The pulsating RGB lighting, switching from dim to bright, illuminated the empty spaces where his consoles and games used to be. The television was still there, but that somehow made him feel even worse. *What good is a TV without games?*

His mouth dropped open. He paced back and forth, stomping his feet. His hands flailed in the air like a day trader witnessing a stock market crash. "I... I... I don't... I don't know what... What should I do, Johnny? My games. All my games. All my consoles. Even the portable ones. I think I'm gonna... I don't feel too good." He put his hands over his mouth and collapsed to his knees. He felt like vomiting.

Johnny, unsure of what to say, blurted out the first thing that came to mind. "Well, at least they left your TV."

"This isn't a fucking joke, man," Charlie cried. He stood up, but the queasiness in his stomach surged to his head. The apartment started to spin. He stumbled over to his work desk and saw the crude note written in bold pen strokes: "Thanks, Charlie. Next time, pay up, loser."

Charlie's forehead creased, his nose scrunched up, and his lips tightened. "Oh, no. No. No. No. I was gonna pay. After the tournament."

Johnny folded his arms and let out a deep breath. "Assuming we win."

"I fucked up."

"What do you owe? A grand?"

Charlie collapsed on his couch, thrust his face into his hands, and mumbled through the spaces between his fingers, "Forty-five hundred dollars."

"Jesus, brah. Why didn't you tell me you were in a hole that deep?"

"Because I should have won on the last Bears game. I bet big on the Rams. But their fucking quarterback threw four interceptions. That wasn't supposed to happen. I thought it was a sure thing. I should have won most of my money back."

Johnny said, "What do we always say?"

Both he and Charlie called out in perfect unison, "Never bet on a Bears game."

Charlie's mind was racing, but it made no sense to call the police. Exposing Dimitri and the Russian mob would only create more problems.

He had never considered himself a habitual gambler. *It's not a gambling problem if I win.* And he'd won plenty of times in the past, with the winnings usually put toward buying another rare game. But this year his luck had faded faster than his relationship with Susan, with every bet becoming an unwelcome reminder of his father.

From the time Charlie was five years old until his parents' divorce, his father yelled at the TV during some basketball games and laughed during others. Charlie had thought he was just a multiple-team fan, but Joe was a gambling addict who chased the highs while trying to avoid the lows. Losing was nothing more than collateral damage on the way to glory.

Charlie scanned the room again and wailed, "All my shit. Gone." That included his prized copy of *Final Fantasy VII*. His mind drifted back to when he was six years old. His father had driven to five different stores to buy the game on release day. All of them sold out. The next day, when young Charlie arrived home from school, he found a copy right next to his PlayStation. He hugged his father as tightly as any child could. Those were the days when his father was his hero.

Charlie's feet, heavy as cinder blocks, prevented him from moving. The *Battle Theatre* tournament was over before it had even begun. He never even bothered to check his bedroom to see if the gold chain and pendant were missing. All he could focus on was his once golden shrine, which was now an empty vessel. Decades of joy. Vanished. He turned toward his work desk and stared at the blinking red light on DuPont's laptop. He pictured it as the bastard's eye winking—a mocking reminder that Charlie had no chance of winning against him.

Johnny called Dom and begged him to come to the apartment as soon as possible.

He arrived fifteen minutes later. "How did this happen?" Dom said.

"It has to be my bookie, Dimitri," Charlie muttered. "He must have robbed me because of the money I owe him. We were only gone for an hour. My dumbass must have left my door unlocked."

Dom, exhibiting his street-smart powers of deduction, said, "He must have been casing the apartment. Don't beat yourself up about not locking your door. He would've broken in anyway."

"Well, I certainly made it easy for him."

"How much do you owe?"

"Forty-five hundred."

"*Fanculo.* We've been waiting four years for *Battle Theatre* and this *merda* happens." Dom stood still for a couple of seconds, then said, "You know what? Fuck this. I'll be back in an hour." He turned around and exited the front door.

Charlie yelled after him, "Where are you going? Please don't go after Dimitri."

But no words were going to stop Dom. He was determined to right the wrong. Charlie and Johnny watched from the window as his car sped away and disappeared at the end of the block. Charlie feared that Dom would be melted gelato if he tried to get the games and consoles back with violence. Messing with Dimitri would be a slap in the face to the whole Russian mob. The only thing worse than stealing from them was disrespecting them.

Charlie tried to call Dom on his cell phone, but it went straight to voicemail, so he sent a text instead: "I know you're pissed, but please don't go after Dimitri." He plopped onto his couch and leaned his head back. Johnny sat next to him and tilted his head back as well, not knowing what to say.

The *BattleTheatre* Midnight Multiplayer Match was meant to be the culmination of Charlie's two decades of gaming, but his reckless gambling had reduced it to a distant dream. His PS4 Pro was gone. He was already deep in debt, unable to afford a new one. He was bound to lose his job.

And possibly Susan, too.

Sure, she wasn't into video games. But she supported him in so many other ways. Planning vacations to Wisconsin Dells and Lake Geneva. Letting him try out new recipes she found online. Hugging him when he needed it. Kissing him when he wanted it. Loving him when he was close to falling off the edge of depression over his job. Listening. Helping. Caring.

If only he were brave enough to call her and tell her about the mess he was in.

CHAPTER 18

GEARING UP TO GO DOWN

T im, the brains behind Charlie's gaming crew, had spent most of his time playing *Battle Theatre* since its release. Clocking in far more hours than anyone else in their group. The innovative new shield system and realistic damage to the environment were next level. No other shooter could match the chaos of rocket launchers blasting plaster off collapsing buildings like Lego bricks, and bullet holes denting metal and shattering glass. It was a glorious symphony of destruction and a technical marvel. And it ran at a buttery-smooth sixty frames per second.

Games like *Sniper Elite 4* and *Sniper: Ghost Warrior 3* focused exclusively on precise marksmanship. Small adjustments for wind speed and elevation determined the trajectory of each bullet, while its path was tracked in slow motion by a camera positioned directly behind it. There was no better feeling than nailing the perfect shot while watching the bullet travel over a hundred yards to shatter an enemy's skull. *Battle Theatre* juggled many different elements, so it was impressive that its sniper gameplay was on par with those games. Tim was studying to be an engineer, and his mathematical mind could easily plan strategies based on geometry and physics to gain an advantage on the battlefield. He was in his element.

Emma's PC wasn't powerful enough to handle the latest games. Since she couldn't afford a new graphics card, she was playing

Battle Theatre on console for the time being. She was on her fourth match with Tim when a phone call from Johnny interrupted them.

Tim muted his headset, held his phone up to his free ear, and addressed Johnny with "Ready to get schooled, playa?"

Johnny blurted out, "Charlie got robbed."

"What? Hold up a second."

Tim unmuted his headset so he could reconnect with Emma. "Did you know Charlie was robbed?"

Emma said, "No. What? What the hell?"

"I have Johnny on the phone. I need to quit this game. We'll talk later."

"Is he okay?" Emma asked.

There was no answer. Tim had already disconnected from their group chat. He tossed his headset aside and asked Johnny, "What happened?"

"I was over at his house. We went out to lunch, and when we got back, all his shit was gone. The PS4 Pro, Xbox One X, Switch, and his entire game collection. Gone. His TV is still there, though. I don't get that."

"Muthafucka. Should I call him?"

"Just leave him alone for now."

"Man. Did he call the cops?"

"He thinks it was his bookie," Johnny said. "He owes him four and a half grand. Reporting it to the cops would be a death sentence."

"Damn. They took *all* his shit?"

"His shelves are as barren as your sex life."

Tim slammed his controller on his thigh. "Why you gotta go there?"

During a multiplayer match six months ago, the crew had discussed all the women they'd dated. Everyone shared their horror stories about ex-girlfriends, except for Tim, who admitted he'd never had one. He was single, lived with his parents, and sometimes asked Charlie what it was like to have a girlfriend. All he wanted was a woman who accepted him for who he was. He'd considered joining a dating website, but who would want to date someone like him? Women wanted a strong man who could sweep them off their feet. Tim couldn't do that. He'd been unable to walk since being hit by a drunk driver when he was twelve. He'd asked four different girls to his high school prom and was rejected every time. That was seven years ago, and he'd never asked out another girl—his fear of rejection held him down like a world-class wrestler.

Charlie told him to keep asking girls out because the law of averages meant that someone would eventually say yes. Although they'd never met in person, Charlie thought that Tim looked handsome enough when they FaceTimed, so he couldn't understand why he was so terrified to try again. Tim told everyone that he didn't have time for girls because he was busy with school, but that was a lie. He desperately wanted a girlfriend but was convinced that no girl would ever be interested in him. Well, maybe a gamer girl, but finding one of them was like finding a unicorn.

Johnny's thoughtless remark only reminded Tim of his hopeless situation. His mind drifted to a dark place. He slouched back in his chair and said, "I gotta go."

"Come on, man. You know I didn't mean—"

Tim hung up the phone and glared at the *Battle Theatre* title screen on his TV screen for what felt like an eternity, his despair invading like an unwanted relative during the holidays. Johnny was only doing what most guys did with their friends. Busting balls. But all it took was that one little comment to send a furious rage coursing through Tim's veins and push him well beyond the boiling point. He gripped his controller and hurled it to the floor, which sent the trigger buttons gliding through the air like tiny flying saucers. There was no need to worry, though. Tim had two more controllers sitting in his drawer, waiting to be connected to his PlayStation 4 Pro.

Charlie started biting the skin off his hangnails. Starting with his index finger. Moving on to his middle finger. Then his thumb. He chewed off enough skin to make each one bleed. He started sucking his thumb like a newborn child trying to soothe himself after a long bout of crying. The habit he'd conquered months ago had returned, and his fingers were paying the price.

At that moment, his phone pinged with a message from Emma, which started a new thread:

> EMMA: I'm so sorry you got robbed. That's awful. Are you okay?
> CHARLIE: All my shit is gone, but I'm not hurt. Who told you?
> EMMA: Tim. We were playing *Battle Theatre*.
> CHARLIE: Why are you playing with my friends?
> EMMA: Tim wanted to practice. Am I not allowed to game with them?
> CHARLIE: Do me a favor. Go back to playing *Fortnite* with your friends. You're not on our team.
> EMMA: I know you're upset, but you don't have to take it out on me.

Charlie decided not to reply to the final message because he was afraid of writing something he couldn't take back. He was often mean to her, but didn't know why. Charlie was getting pretty good at making women mad at him.

Two hours passed. Dom still hadn't replied to Charlie's text, so he sent him another and called him. Once again, no response. Charlie wished he had a two-way communicator like Solid Snake in *Metal Gear Solid*, with Dom acting like Colonel Roy Campbell, always answering the call.

Dom had learned to fight dirty in countless street fights. And he outweighed Dimitri by at least a hundred pounds. Charlie pictured him grabbing Dimitri by the shirt collar, slapping him around a bit, and demanding the return of the stolen goods. An act like that would cause the Russian mob to either kill or seriously injure him. And Charlie would be next on their hit list. He squeezed his eyes shut as his headache throbbed like a thunderclap. He eventually dozed off into a light sleep, but then a loud thud jolted him awake. *Another robber? Who cares?* All that was precious had already been stolen. He closed his eyes again, hoping to fall back asleep.

"Charlie? You home? It's Dom."

Charlie's eyebrows raised high enough to meet his hairline. He darted toward the door and swung it open, ready to yell at Dom for beating up Dimitri. Those feelings vanished faster than Solid Snake hiding in a cardboard box. Dom was standing in the doorway, holding a brand-new PlayStation 4 Pro and a copy of *Battle Theatre*. Charlie's mouth gaped open in confusion and disbelief.

"I thought you were going to kick Dimitri's ass."

"I'm a forty-three-year-old father of two. You think I want the mob after me?"

Charlie wiped the beads of sweat off his forehead and said, "Why didn't you answer my calls and texts?"

Dom shrugged. "I wanted to surprise you. Ready to practice? We got a lot of catching up to do."

Charlie ran his fingers through his hair. "I can't afford to pay you back."

Dom laughed and said, "It's a gift, dumbass."

"Marie's going to kill you. Isn't she a tight-ass when it comes to money?"

"Yeah. She is. When it doesn't involve her spending it," Dom said. "She'll bitch at me for throwing away expired coffee, but when *Hamilton* first opened on Broadway, she spent a thousand dollars to fly to New York and another thousand on the ticket. For three hours of entertainment! I'm spending less than a quarter of that for this once-in-a-lifetime experience. This is your *Hamilton*, my boy."

"I don't know, man. I've heard your wife on the phone. She can be scary. I wouldn't want that wrath crashing down on me."

Dom set down the PlayStation 4 Pro in the corner and said, "Not worried about it. I'll just tell her I'm helping a friend."

"I'll pay you back someday. I don't know how, but I will. I won't forget this, Dom."

"You ain't gotta pay me shit. This is my gift to you. I won't let that scumbag Dimitri ruin our magical weekend. Pull up your bootstraps, soldier. I'll see you online."

Charlie hugged Dom with all his might and said, "Love you, brother."

Nothing was going to stop Charlie now. Not a robbery. Not a weekend work assignment. Not anything. Until…

The doorbell rang.

Is Dom back? Johnny? An Amazon package? Dimitri with a heartfelt apology?

What Charlie didn't expect was Susan, carrying a large bag of Chinese takeout.

CHAPTER 19

CHINESE FOOD

C harlie loved it when Susan comforted him with warm surprises. She was considerate and affectionate—two qualities he'd once possessed. He found her intelligence incredibly attractive and adored the stimulating conversations they often had. She had taught him that love existed in the world and that it was a beautiful thing. Even though he had a game to play, he was happy to see her. Eager to explain his dilemma. Maybe she would have some sympathy for him.

Susan hugged him, set the Chinese food down in the kitchen, and said, "I felt bad about our last conversation." She turned her head to see the empty shelves and bare entertainment center. For a moment, she thought he might have gotten rid of all his games and was finally ready to grow up. Then she came to her senses. "What happened?"

Charlie crossed his arms and pressed his lips tighter than a trash compactor. "I was robbed."

Susan put her hands on his shoulders and said, "Oh my God. Are you okay? Why didn't you call me?"

Charlie bowed his head and said, "It happened a couple of hours ago. I was gonna call you soon."

The stench of marijuana lingered on his clothes. "Why do you smell like weed?"

"Johnny stopped by."

Susan scratched the back of her head, wondering how he had enough time to smoke weed, but not to attend her gig. She wanted to say something but decided to let it go, thinking that he probably needed it to calm his anxiety over the massive work assignment. "How did they get in?"

Charlie said, "I left the door unlocked."

Susan couldn't hold in her laughter. "Wow! I can't believe it. You're always so anal about that." She might not have shared Charlie's passion for gaming, but she understood his obsession with locking his door. They'd both grown up on the tough streets of Chicago, where crime, especially theft, was commonplace. "Jesus Christ. How high were you?"

"High enough to abandon all my security protocols."

"Did you call the police?"

Charlie didn't want to lie to her by saying he'd called the police. But if he told her he was robbed because of a gambling debt, then she would break up with him for sure. Maybe there was a third option? Delay the lie. "I'll do it later," he said.

Susan tore open the bag of Chinese food, grabbed some forks from Charlie's kitchen drawer, and divided the Kung Pao chicken and rice between two plates. She ate at a normal pace while he devoured his food, savoring the spicy flavor, but desperate to get back to *BattleTheatre*. After six bites, Susan glanced over at the corner of the living room and spotted the PlayStation 4 Pro box. "Why is there a PlayStation over there? And why didn't the burglars take it? What's going on, Charlie? Please don't lie to me."

For a moment, Charlie thought he had food poisoning as the room began to spin. He'd managed to keep the truth about why he was robbed to himself, but there was no hiding a brand-new

PlayStation 4 Pro and a copy of *BattleTheatre*. "Dom bought me one after he heard I was robbed."

Susan's head dropped as she sighed. "So you can play your game tonight?"

Charlie sighed back. "Yes. My friends want to play. There's a chance to win twenty thousand dollars, Susan."

"Did your boss really give you a weekend assignment?"

Charlie stomped over to his desk and opened the laptop so fast it was a miracle the hinges didn't break. He clicked on the fifty-part email attachment and pulled out all the loan applications from one of the manila folders, then brought them over for Susan to see. "In case you don't believe me."

Susan skimmed through the document and some of the applications. "I still don't understand why you didn't at least try to do this. Your job's at stake."

Charlie walked back to the kitchen table and started playing with his food. "I planned on giving it a shot. But you know Francisco from the pizza place? He told me it couldn't possibly be finished on time."

Susan sat opposite him at the kitchen table and squinted before saying, "What the hell does he know about it?"

"His brother's some sort of financial whiz."

Susan slammed her fork on the table, causing grains of rice to launch into the air. "And you believed him?"

Charlie's mind wandered into a world where Susan was the perfect gamer girlfriend. Sitting next to him during a match and feeding him Cheetos so his hands wouldn't get orange dust on the controller. Holding the straw of his favorite drink, Mountain Dew Code Red, up to his lips so he could take gentle sips while sniping his targets. Cheering him on with every successful kill. Rubbing his neck and shoulders after a tense battle.

It was a short-lived fantasy that barely took root before Susan said, "So, you decided to blow off your work assignment, get high, and play your silly little game with your friends. You could have done at least some of it, so your boss could see that you put in some effort. I can't believe you just gave up."

"It's done, Susan. I'm not gonna kill myself just to get a fraction of the assignment done and still get fired. Maybe I'll tell him I got sick or was hit by a car? I'd rather spend my time playing *BattleTheatre* and competing for the grand prize. I've been waiting four years for this."

Susan couldn't hold back the question that was swirling in her mind. "But it doesn't start till midnight. So, you'll be able to come to my gig, won't you?"

Charlie turned away. "About that…"

"Are you serious? You know how much this means to me. I get nervous when you're not around. I should be done by eleven, which will give you more than enough time to get back home for your tournament."

"I need to practice," Charlie said. "If I go in cold after watching you sing, I'll have no chance to win. My boys are counting on me. It's a four-man team. It doesn't work with only three. I can't let them down."

Susan crossed her arms and asked, "Why aren't you part of *my* team?"

"It's one night. I've been waiting so long for this game. Why can't you just let this one go?"

"It's not about 'this one.' It's about us," Susan said, "How many times have we been late or missed things because you were playing online? I can't believe you're choosing a game over me again."

"I understand the gig is important to you, but this tournament is important to me."

"You really think you can win?"

Charlie raised his hands in the air and said, "I just want the chance to find out."

Susan stood up, dashed to the front door, turned around, and shouted, "Have fun playing with your friends while I sing my heart out. Maybe I'll meet a cute guy at the gig. Who knows what'll happen?" Then she stormed out of the apartment.

Charlie flinched as the door slammed.

Am I really going to lose her over a video game?

CHAPTER 20

PRE-GAME

E ight hours to midnight. Charlie set up the new PlayStation 4 Pro and placed the *BattleTheatre* disk into the console. The update screen popped up again. Charlie clenched his fists. *Goddammit. Last time this happened, I was robbed.* If the game had loaded immediately, like an old-school Nintendo cartridge, he never would have left the apartment. He would've skipped lunch with Johnny and ordered food delivery. This was one of the trials and tribulations of the modern gamer—waiting for updates before engaging in digital pleasure. The *BattleTheatre* update had four minutes to go. Four minutes versus four years of waiting for the game.

The update finished downloading. But the excitement of pressing *Start* on the controller faded immediately as his mind returned to the argument with Susan. For the first time, he found himself questioning his decision to play in the tournament. It was a bad sign. If his heart wasn't in it, his chances of winning were slim to none. *Why couldn't I just go to the gig? It's not like I'm going to win the grand prize.* He was well aware that most of his competitors would be die-hard multiplayer gamers who excelled at *Call of Duty, PUBG, Titanfall 2, Tom Clancy's Rainbow Six, Battlefield V,* and countless others.

He needed to call Dom—the only member of his crew with a functioning relationship. He sent him a group chat invite before navigating the user-friendly menus of *Battle Theatre*. Thankfully, they weren't cluttered with the usual pay-to-win loot boxes. Instead, there was just a small tab link in the corner of the screen for in-game cosmetics, a far cry from the constant bombardment of monetization that plagued the vast majority of multiplayer games. The menus themselves were crisp and clean, focused on gear, weapons, and the new ten-second shield that was set to revolutionize multiplayer gaming. No more "one shot and you're dead" scenarios. Ten body shots, or five head shots, would be needed to eliminate a player.

Even the tournament tab was discreet. Almost everyone who bought a copy of the game already knew about the Midnight Multiplayer Match from the heavy promotion on IGN, Game Informer, GameSpot, and other popular sites, so there was no need to advertise it on the menu. Savvy gamers were well aware that the registration process had taken place months ago. Those who weren't lucky enough to earn a spot would have to play in their own private matches.

The console chimed to indicate that someone had just joined the group chat.

"Man, it's so good to see you back online," Dom said.

"Seriously, thanks again," Charlie said.

"You ready to get some practice in?"

"Sure," Charlie said, sounding like a mouse gasping for its last breath.

"Come on, bro. You should be happy. What's wrong?"

"Susan's pissed. She's singing tonight. Told me about it months ago, but I got the dates mixed up."

Dom sat up straight from his slouched position on the couch and said, "If bad luck has a middle name, it's you."

"The world hates me."

"Video games—destroying relationships since 1985," Dom said, referring to the year when the Nintendo Entertainment System catapulted gaming into most of the nation's living rooms.

"I told her I had nothing going on this weekend when she told me about her gig two months ago," Charlie said. "Then the tournament got delayed by two weeks, and I forgot that it landed on the same day as her gig."

"You know what I need when the wife pisses me off? I'll give you a hint. It's digital. It's always turned on and ready to go. And it never asks me to take out the trash," Dom said.

Charlie slumped forward. "That's not going to work for me this time. I don't even feel like playing right now. Things ended badly."

"*Svegliati!*" Dom yelled.

The reaction reminded Charlie of a long-running, campy Chicago TV show, which made him say, "Svengoolie?"

"Snap out of it. Don't make me regret buying you that PS4 Pro. What's done is done. Playing with your boys is the exact medicine you need," Dom said.

"I messed up. I know I owe four and a half grand, but it's not worth losing my girlfriend over it."

Neither of them said anything for fifteen seconds. For Dom, each second was like one year of his fifteen-year marriage, as he tried to access memories and open up about his own relationship challenges for the first time.

"Did I ever tell you that Marie asked me for a divorce?"

"Shit, man," Charlie said. "I'm sorry. You're splitting up?"

"No, we love each other."

"I'm confused."

"She asked me for a divorce last year. Three times, in fact. Three times within a year."

"Now I'm even more confused."

"I refused to give up on us. I fought for her. Thought about all the good times. Our trips to Italy with the kids. All the incredible meals she's cooked for me. My huge belly is proof of that. I looked at how she's raised our two boys. Without her, they'd probably be fucked up because of my temper."

"You convinced her to change her mind?" Charlie asked, raising his eyebrows. "All three times?"

"Yup. We went to counseling. Which I fucking hate, by the way. But it's not about who's right or wrong. For me, it was about listening without always trying to butt in. Giving instead of taking," Dom said. "If you love Susan, you'll fight for her."

"So, I should go to her gig?"

Dom batted his right hand in the air like he was swatting a fly. "Hell, no! We got a game to win."

Charlie buried his face in the couch. "So, everything you've just told me was bullshit?"

"Look. Women need time to cool off. Treat her to an expensive dinner. Talk it over. Tell her you're willing to change. I'm sure she'll give you another chance," Dom said. "Now get your head in the game, and let's win this fucking twenty thousand dollars. I need to buy some new software for my channel."

Dom was referring to his bare-bones, failing YouTube channel, which consisted of his ugly mug talking about gaming. No fancy graphics with snappy, colorful words and phrases popping up on the screen. No exciting gameplay. It was dull. Amateurish. He wanted to invest in expensive software to make it look more professional, with high-end CGI and bursts of color to attract viewers. Marie usually never allowed him to spend such a large sum of money on himself, as opposed to her and the kids, but she could hardly refuse if he won it in the tournament.

Seven hours to midnight. Charlie sent a chat invite to the rest of the crew. They needed to practice. Sixty thousand people were currently playing *Battle Theatre* online, but only a hundred would be competing in the Midnight Multiplayer Match. And ninety-six of them had probably been practicing relentlessly since the game's online launch on Thursday at midnight. Allowing for five hours of sleep a night, they probably already put in thirty-one hours of practice. In comparison, Tim put in just over a dozen hours, Dom and Johnny each had five or six, and Charlie himself had a big fat zero.

As Charlie waited for the others to join the chat, the intuitive menus on the screen reminded him of those he'd designed when he was twelve years old. Simple, yet elegant. If he had been better at math, he might have been able to design a game himself. He shook his head and forced a laugh. Who was he kidding? Making games was too hard. Playing them was a lot more fun.

"How the hell are you online?" Tim asked. "I thought all your stuff was stolen."

Charlie replied, "Dom bought me a PS4 Pro and a copy of *Battle Theatre*."

"Go, Dom! I've been playing all day," Tim said. "The competition is tough. Lotta good players out there. And most of them ain't even in the tournament. We need you."

"I knew you'd get pwned without me," Charlie said. "How many matches have you played so far?"

"No idea. I lost count. Maybe thirty? I'm in one right now. I just sent you an invite to spectate."

The spectator mode in *Battle Theatre* had a bird's-eye tactical view of the action for players who were either eliminated or just wanted to watch a match. The camera could be zoomed in or out, as well as rotated 360 degrees.

Dom said, "Just quit that pathetic match so we can all play together."

"I'll be done soon," Tim replied. "Imma take these fools down." A minute later, he screamed, "Fuck! I'm hit." His health points were down to ten. One more bullet meant death.

Johnny yelled, "Look out, Tim."

"Where? Where?"

"Behind you!" Dom screamed.

But it was too late. A bullet found Tim. His health meter hit zero. With his dead avatar slumped over a V-shaped tree, an enemy positioned himself behind and began thrusting back and forth. Of course, the rest of the Chi-Town Crew had a perfect view of his defilement in spectator mode.

Tim shrieked, "Goddammit! Look at this muthafucka,"

"You're finally getting laid, just not in the way you imagined," Johnny said.

"Fuck you!" Tim yelled.

"Looks like only one of us is getting fucked," Johnny said with a chuckle.

The match finally ended when the sadistic enemy player pulled out his sidearm and shot Tim point-blank in the back of the head.

"Jesus. This is like some sick underground porno snuff film," Charlie said. The screen went blank for a moment before the in-game lobby appeared. "This is not how I expected to be introduced to *Battle Theatre*. I feel, I don't know... *violated*."

Five seconds of silence followed before Dom said, "War is hell."

Charlie opened a new game lobby, and they all waited for an available match.

Breaking the silence, Tim said, "Dom told me that you and Susan got into a fight."

"Tim, why the fuck would you mention that now?" Johnny said. "We're about to play and you're fucking with his head."

"I can't offer support to my friend?"

"I have a lot of groveling to do when this is all over," Charlie said.

"Was it about the games?" Tim said.

"Of course it was about the games, numb nuts," Johnny said.

Charlie tried to shift their attention back to the match. "Everyone needs to select different weapon types so we're balanced. I'm the commander, so I'll issue the orders on the battlefield. Is everyone okay with that?"

As if they shared the same brain, the other three hollered in unison, "Sir! Yes, sir!"

"Remember," Dom said, "we're playing for five grand each. But more important than that, we're playing to get Charlie's game collection back from Dimitri. So, focus and discipline, okay?"

"Enough jibber-jabber. Let's go," Johnny said.

CHAPTER 21

PRACTICE MAKES IMPERFECT

attleTheatre, like *Fortnite* and *PUBG*, is a battle-royale game in which a hundred players fight to survive until the end of the match. The problem with most multiplayer games is that one well-placed shot to the head or a couple of bullets to the chest means game over. *BattleTheatre*'s solution? Point-driven bullet damage to specific body parts and an innovative ten-second shield system. A headshot costs a player twenty health points, or HP. Being near an explosion knocks off fifteen. And a torso shot subtracts ten. More importantly, though, after each bullet strike, a ten-second shield protects a player so they can find cover or run away to avoid further harm. Once the ten seconds have expired, they're vulnerable again. This forgiving game mechanic eliminates one of the major problems of other multiplayer games, as it gives novice players a fighting chance against more experienced opponents.

Each match takes place inside an ever-shrinking death circle. The objective is simple: stay inside the circle. Flirting with the outer edge results in a slow death from purple lightning strikes. Every few minutes, the circle shrinks by a few hundred miles, forcing players to move toward the center or risk elimination. Medkits are rare and only restore health to living players. There is no respawning. If a player's health points drop to zero, it's game over.

The Chi-Town Crew's first practice match was seconds away. All the bullshit. All the drama. None of it mattered now. The only thing that mattered was *BattleTheatre* and winning the prize money so Charlie could reclaim his game collection.

Charlie's gamertag was CyberLancer15, a juvenile-sounding name he'd created at the age of fifteen and was too lazy to change. He selected the Dragunov semiautomatic sniper rifle as his starting weapon because of its accurate, long-range capability and rapid reloads. He paired it with frag grenades known for their large-range explosive capabilities. Johnny's gamertag was DonkeyBong57, in honor of the world's favorite gorilla. He chose the M4 fully automatic assault rifle, which was excellent for mid-range combat, with flashbang grenades. Dom played as Dominate28, and opted for the VLK Rogue shotgun because he excelled at close-quarters combat, along with smoke grenades. Finally, Tim was NightHawk34. He chose a PP-29 submachine gun and claymore mines. Between them, they were a well-balanced team with a good selection of close, mid, and long-range weapons.

The countdown to the first practice game, set in a condensed version of North America, appeared on screen:

Three.

Two.

One.

Deploy.

The cargo plane, large enough to hold a hundred players, appeared, flying high above the battlefield. Charlie believed that most of the players would parachute out over the central 75 percent of the map. The plan was for his crew to jump out early so they would encounter fewer opponents, reducing the risk of a potentially lethal firefight. Unfortunately, this strategy was about to fail faster than a D student in an AP calculus class.

"Focus and discipline, everyone," Charlie reminded the rest of the crew before leaping out of the plane, just five seconds after it had appeared from the west. Then he added, "Jump now!" Tim and Dom responded immediately, but Johnny didn't leave the plane for another fifteen seconds.

"How do I jump out?" he shouted.

"*R1*," Tim said, referring to the controller's right shoulder button.

"Who the hell designs a game where *R1* is used to jump out of a plane?" Johnny cried. "It should be *X*. I'm hitting *R1* but nothing's happening."

"Jesus Christ. You're probably hitting *R2*," Charlie said.

"Fuck," Johnny said. "I'm always getting those two mixed up."

The fluffy white parachutes resembled puff pastries waiting to be devoured by the insatiable appetites of a hundred hungry soldiers craving warfare. Charlie and Tim touched down on the rainy northwest side of the map, near Seattle. Dom landed somewhere in dusty Idaho, while Johnny glided just south of Miami to catch some rays.

Charlie called out, "Remember your ABCs. Always be crouching."

But the team didn't have time to crouch as a barrage of bullets swarmed them like locusts during mating season. Dom chucked a grenade that filled the air with thick white smoke, providing just enough cover for him to retreat from the carnage. Johnny stepped on so many landmines that he might as well have been playing *Goat Simulator*. At least the ragdoll physics of the game were accurate. Despite clocking over a dozen hours in *BattleTheatre*, Tim was like a lost preschooler circling a playground and screaming for his mommy. Everyone was losing health points fast.

Charlie spotted a truck with crusty rust patches all over its frame. He shouted, "Tim. On my six. Now!" before sliding underneath it faster than a hyperactive kid on a Slip 'N' Slide.

Tim fumbled with his controller and took a bullet to the cranium, losing twenty points in a millisecond.

Charlie peeked at the minimap in the lower-right corner of the screen. The small green blip that was Johnny was now a tiny flashing boat heading toward Texas. "Johnny, how'd you find a boat?" Charlie said.

"There are tons of them in Florida, if you haven't noticed. I'm heading your way. Wait. What the… Oh no!"

"What?" Charlie said.

"Why can't I—? Why is there land underneath Texas?"

Tim said, "Welcome to Mexico, dumbass."

"Why is Mexico here? This is supposed to be a map of the United States."

"You know Mexico is connected to the United States?" Tim said, flexing his geography muscle.

"Get to shore and find a vehicle," Charlie said, seconds before a grenade exploded nearby, sending shards of rust flying off the truck. He glanced at the minimap again and saw that Dom's blip was now motionless near Spokane, Washington. "Why'd you stop, Dom?"

"I see a supply crate. There might be a medkit inside."

Bullets ricocheted off the truck, causing sparks to fly through the air. "Forget the medkit. We need help. We're pinned down behind this truck."

But it was futile. Over the next five minutes, Charlie was shot three times in the head, while Tim fell victim to his own grenade.

The best way to eliminate an enemy with a grenade was to pull the pin and hold it for two seconds before tossing it toward the enemy so it would explode upon landing. Despite his intelligence, Tim forgot how to count. He pulled the pin on his grenade and held it for four seconds, at which point it exploded, killing him instantly. The horror of war can turn even the brightest genius into a bonehead.

Johnny and Dom had already perished in a hail of bullets. Sure, the new shield mechanic protected them for ten seconds after each hit, but then another bullet would invariably find them. *Battle Theatre* wasn't Disneyland. It was a violent and inhospitable place.

Charlie said, "We suck."

"It's our first game together," Dom said. "Relax."

"First, we all need to jump out of the plane at the same time," Charlie said. "Second, keep the unit tight. No wandering off. We stick together. Third, never parachute into an open field. Fourth—"

Dom cut him off. "We're still learning, Charlie. Don't worry. We'll get to where we need to be."

After a ten-second pause, Charlie, Tim, and Dom all heard a bubbling sound followed by a loud exhalation. Then Johnny asked, "Is Dom short for Domino? Like Domino's pizza?"

"It's Dominic. You know that," Dom said. "Are you high?"

"I'm talking about Domino's pizza. I saw a YouTube video where they used to have, like, a thirty-minute-or-less delivery guarantee until a bunch of delivery drivers got into accidents," Johnny said. "Can I call you Mr. Domino?"

Charlie remembered an obscure 1998 PlayStation game and blurted out, "No one can stop Mr. Domino!"

"Oh my God. I was wondering how I came up with Mr. Domino. I remember watching you play that game when we were kids," Johnny said.

"Stop smoking fucking weed," Dom said. "You sound out of it. *Bastardo strafatto.*"

More bubbling, another prolonged exhalation, then Johnny's strained voice came over the headsets. "Last hit. I promise."

"So much for focus and discipline," Tim said.

BattleTheatre launched with five maps, representing North America, South America, Africa, Asia, and Europe. Australia and Antarctica would be added later as downloadable content. The maps were condensed versions of the continents, allowing travel from one end to the other in about eight minutes. For their next game, Charlie selected South America.

This time, he and his crew were in sync as they all jumped out of the plane at the same time. The wind carried them toward the northern tip of the lush Amazon rainforest. Charlie bit his lip while gazing at dozens of parachutes floating through the sky like a paper lantern festival. The dense green canopy hid the horrors that awaited them beneath. The only unrealistic part of the game was that parachutes ignored foliage on the way down. Almost as if it wasn't even there. But that was probably for the best, since dozens of players stuck in trees would have been easy targets for those on the ground.

The rain sliced through the fog like long glass needles as Charlie and his team landed on the muddy terrain. They could barely see ten feet in front of them, and the thick undergrowth made movement difficult. Tim, Dom, and Charlie sloshed through the sludge toward Johnny, who had drifted a hundred yards from them during the descent. Then a single bullet struck Charlie in the head, instantly deducting twenty points. "Dammit! We're not alone," he said. "I just took a bullet."

Dom, like Ezio in *Assassin's Creed 2*, snuck behind an enemy and shot him in the back with his shotgun. The stricken player retreated into the jungle, heading back to his team. Dom chased after him, yelling, "I've got the son of a bitch on the run." Charlie and Tim followed until a barrage of bullets danced in the air, striking all of them. The sounds over their headsets, which were usually used for clear, calm communication, were "*Oomph, waaaa, whyyyy, noooo, ha ha, boooo!*" The last noise couldn't be explained. Maybe Dom was trying to scare someone.

Johnny said, "I see a guard tower. I'm gonna climb it to see if I can get a bead on them." He ascended the wooden tower about as fast as a morbidly obese Spider-Man and pulled out his assault rifle. He could only see blended colors of gray and green, similar to a Monet painting. Then a rocket struck the tower, sending Johnny flying into the air along with hundreds of splinters.

Charlie shot four players in the back before taking on more gunfire. Dom took down three. Tim hit two. Johnny continued to play the *Goat Simulator* version of *Battle Theatre* by repeatedly stepping on landmines. All their HP was dwindling. Fast.

An enemy started sprinting toward Johnny. Charlie needed to warn him, or he was toast. "Johnny! Go left. Left!"

"I am going left."

"He's right up on you!"

"Where?"

"Turn around," Charlie said. "God, you're playing like a pussy."

Before Johnny could turn his avatar around, an entire clip of bullets pummeled his back. Panicking, he tossed his grenades like rice at a wedding. The series of explosions alerted another four-person team to their location. Dom blasted his shotgun into the fog, hoping to land a lucky hit. But the new enemy crew, along with the original terrorizing attackers, dispatched Charlie's team with incredible precision and efficiency. Since they were already low on health, they all died within three minutes.

Charlie said, "Johnny, why the fuck didn't you listen to me?"

"Take it easy, Charlie," Dom said forcefully.

"No. I'm not gonna take it easy!" Charlie yelled. "He cost us the match with all his commotion. He's hurting us more than helping us."

A message popped up on the screen: "DonkeyBong57 has left the match."

"And now he's offline," Tim said. "Do you think it was his internet connection or your verbal abuse?"

"Give him a break," Dom said.

"Who the fuck is gonna give *me* a break?" Charlie said. "Instead of spending time with my girlfriend, trying to patch things up, I'm fucking around with all of you. I knew this was a waste of time. We aren't winning shit." He couldn't believe he used those words—*a waste of time*. The guilt and self-doubt were creeping back.

"Like I said, just take her to a nice dinner after the tournament. You'll have to grovel and apologize, but she'll listen," Dom said.

"I don't know. It's just—"

"Charlie, we need you," Dom interrupted. "If we're going to win this thing, there can't be any animosity between us. Go apologize to Johnny."

"Fuck that."

"If you want me to play, then you need to apologize," Dom said. "There cannot be any bad blood on this team. We're going up against some of the best players in the world. It doesn't matter that *BattleTheatre* has only been out for two days. A lot of these guys have no jobs and play *PUBG* and *Fortnite* all day long."

"You're right, man," Charlie conceded. "It's just everything's getting to me. I'll apologize."

"You're our commander, Charlie. Find a way to communicate with us so we stay alive," Dom said. "Lemme call Johnny. I'll try to get him to rejoin. One sec."

Johnny immediately answered his phone when he saw Dom's name on the screen. If Charlie had called, he probably would have let it go to voicemail. "Hey."

"Charlie wants to apologize for what he said. Please come back online."

"Why is he treating me like shit?"

"You know how important winning the tournament is to him. It's no big deal if we lose. But if he loses, his game collection is gone forever. He's having problems with Susan too, and he's just taking it out on you. Swallow your pride. We need you. We have to be a team. There's a lot of money at stake here."

"Is he really gonna apologize?"

"He better. Or I'm gonna drive over to his house and slap him silly."

As soon as Johnny came back online and reentered the group chat, Charlie said, "Sorry I yelled at you, bro. I'm just overwhelmed with everything."

"Thanks for apologizing," Johnny said. "I feel bad that this happened to you. You're my best friend, man. We shouldn't be fighting. And I'll try not to be such a pussy."

"You're not a pussy," Charlie said. "I'm an asshole."

Dom added, "Tim, I guess that makes you the taint."

They laughed like only best friends could. The magic ingredient in the bowl of their friendship was closeness. Along with a dash of forgiveness.

They played for five hours, right up until 11:30 p.m. It was pandemonium. Bullets flew by, limbs were blown off, buildings collapsed, cars exploded, and feelings were hurt. In the third game, Johnny threw a grenade that dinged off a metal beam, causing it to bounce back and explode right in front of Charlie. In the fourth, Dom accidentally fired his rocket launcher at the ground, blowing up the whole crew. In the fifth, Tim and Johnny wandered into an open field looking for a medkit and lost seventy-five points within a minute. More games ended in defeat than victories.

Charlie knew he had to do a better job of leading if his team was to have any chance in the tournament. He took charge in the seventh game: Tim was told to check their six at least once every thirty seconds; Johnny's task was to search for snipers lying on the ground and take them out; and Dom was responsible for scouting around corners for surprises, especially inside buildings. Charlie's head was always on a swivel, scanning for enemies in the distance. His instructions were tailored to specific situations, but still focused on his teammates' strengths. Communication was key if they were going to survive.

CHAPTER 22

A PERFORMANCE TO FORGET

Forty minutes to midnight. The Rusty Spoon, a spot where bohemians occupied the same space as six-figure executives, was known for showcasing emerging, raw talent in the Chicagoland area. With its unpolished, untreated wooden beams, exposed ventilation ducts, and a grimy floor that hadn't seen a mop since the early 2000s, it was a perfect venue for musicians and their fans. The tunnel leading to the main stage was plastered with stickers of local bands, musical instruments, peace signs, rainbows, and at least six different renditions of a marijuana leaf. The skunky smell and hazy cloud of weed filled the air, masking the body odor of sweaty hipsters.

The She-Nannigans were scheduled to perform at ten o'clock, but their start time was pushed back to after eleven because of last-minute changes by the club's owner. It probably had something to do with the two talent scouts who were there. They sat near the front of the stage, trying to be discreet by wearing grunge clothing from the nineties, but the notepads on their table were a dead giveaway. Hushed whispers spread through the room. Talent scouts only visited the Rusty Spoon every few months, so when they showed up, it was a big deal.

Three plush couches, reserved for band members, were nestled in a back room where the performers could drink, smoke weed, or gossip while waiting for their slots. Susan sat on one of the couches, staring at Jessica, who was drinking a Corona Light and chatting with another band across the room. She wondered if that band was any good. Her mind kept drifting. If only she could focus on Charlie's face and listen to his tranquil voice to calm her nerves. His support blanket of affection was missing in the freezing-cold storm of her anxiety-riddled mind. It felt like a dozen tiny spiders were crawling inside her throat, making her cough every five seconds.

Jessica wandered over and sat beside her on the couch. "Do you, like, have a cold or something?"

Susan said, "I cough when I'm nervous."

Jessica rummaged through the Dream Bin and said, "I think there's some cough drops in here somewhere."

"I don't need a cough drop. I need a Xanax."

Jessica nodded toward the other band and said, "Should I ask one of those guys? I'm sure they'll have one."

"Why would I take a pill from someone I don't know?"

"The owner of this place has their information. They'd get in trouble if they gave us fentanyl or Molly or something," Jessica said. There was a long pause. "You know what, forget I said anything."

"I'm sorry," Susan said. "I'm just upset that Charlie's not here. He always makes me laugh when I'm nervous. It helps to calm me down."

"He has his charms, I guess. Unlike my ex… God, he was so dull. No passion. No sense of humor," Jessica said. "I swear I'm gonna do it. I'm gonna start dating women."

Susan's thoughts drifted away from her disdain for gaming and crash-landed in the warm, cozy, and hilarious antics of Charlie for a brief moment. If he were here, he'd make some silly comment about Jessica's not-so-secret desire to become a lesbian. Or he'd make fun of one of the other performers, probably the guy with a tattoo of a single curlicue on his forehead, who looked like he was trying to be John Travolta from *Grease*, but didn't have time to style his hair.

Charlie's heart was always pure. He supported Susan's dreams by going to her band's practices and offering helpful feedback. He helped her pick out a Fender when the mono jack in her old guitar failed. He even slipped little love notes or a single rose into the Dream Bin when she wasn't looking. He was a peaceful oasis in her chaotic desert.

An older man with a long gray beard and a Rusty Spoon T-shirt at least two sizes too small set down a sheet of paper next to the array of doughnuts and snacks on the main table and announced, "Here's the running order. The band on the top of this list is on in five minutes."

Susan sprang up from the couch and ran to the table. No one else in the room seemed to care. The She-Nannigans were second on the list.

The first band on the lineup took the stage and began their set. To Susan, they sounded like one of the teachers from a *Peanuts* cartoon. Muddled. Like her mind. They were on their last song when Susan started clearing her throat again. Jessica held up a cough drop she'd found in the Dream Bin. "My God. Just take one of these."

The cough drop was as effective as a single raindrop in a five-alarm fire. Her coughing continued.

Kat, the band's drummer, said, "Maybe you shouldn't sing tonight?"

Susan took a long drink of water, then snatched what remained of Kat's apple martini from her hand and downed it in one gulp. "I'm not going to miss my chance to sing in front of those talent scouts because of this stupid coughing fit. I'll be fine. I just need a shot of whiskey. Maybe the alcohol will numb the itchiness in my throat."

Jessica perked up and said, "I got you," before pushing through the crowd and heading toward the bar.

On stage, the She-Nannigans were crushing it, with the crowd lapping up all the energy from their first three songs. Now, it was Susan's turn to sing. She cleared her throat one more time and approached the microphone. Her queasy stomach rumbled like the Grand Rapids, while her throat burned like a Los Angeles wildfire. A bead of sweat fell from her forehead, hitting the mic. She stared at the Dream Bin on the floor near the front of the stage in the hope of seeing a rose from Charlie. But she knew it only contained the usual hodgepodge of trinkets. She looked up and scanned the crowd. Hoping to catch a glimpse of Charlie's cheerful grin. Instead, she saw a three-hundred-pound stoner with an unkempt goatee wearing a Phish shirt.

Her guitar trembled in her hands as her lips moved closer to the mic. She squeaked out the introduction like a wounded mouse. "This next song is called 'The Three A's.'"

The song began with a heavy bassline from Mimi and a fast drumbeat from Kat, followed by a frail guitar riff from Susan, who sang:

> Attention, you never gave it to me.
> Admiration, is what I seek.
> Affection, do you know what it means?
> I wanted them all, but I came up empty.

She strummed the chords out of key in a choppy melody that left the rest of the band struggling to keep up. Her voice was equally erratic—one verse was crystal clear, while the next was rough and muddled. She coughed twice in the first thirty seconds, and three more times during the chorus. Drenched in sweat, she wondered if the Phish-loving stoner was gawking at her nipples. She forgot the words to the third verse after her guitar pick hit the wrong note.

I'm done. I'm cooked. I quit.

The crowd stared in confusion as Susan stopped singing. One by one, the rest of the band stopped playing. Silence filled the room. Susan crumpled up her lyrics sheet and tossed it like trash into the Dream Bin. She coughed three more times before rushing off the stage in tears.

She was finished with music. How could she ever recover from that embarrassment? She pictured the two talent scouts writing on their notepads: "Band played well, but they should stick to their main singer, because the new one is clearly not ready for prime time."

She had ruined not only her own but the band's one big shot at success.

CHAPTER 23

MIDNIGHT MADNESS

Midnight was twenty minutes away. The non-stop, five-and-a-half-hour practice session had caused Charlie's pupils to dilate, blurring his vision. He was worried about burning out before burning the midnight oil, so he told the team to take a break before the tournament started.

"My stomach's in knots," he said. "How's everyone else feeling?"

"I'm pretty queasy myself," Tim said. "Man, twenty grand is a lot of money."

Dom said, "The real question is, are we good enough?"

"Probably not," Johnny said.

Charlie sighed. "Focus and discipline, guys. We can do this. We're a team. We watch each other's backs. And stay in cover as much as possible. ABC. Always be crouching. Avoid large open areas, and always scan before making a move."

"And for fuck's sake," Dom added, "stay away from windows when you're in a building. These guys can easily take you out from over a hundred yards away."

Tim closed his eyes and said, "Less than twenty minutes to go. Should we meditate or something?"

Johnny packed his bong with more weed. "Forget meditating. I'm *medicating*."

Charlie said, "Please tell me you're not stoned out of your mind right now?"

"What? I'm nervous. Cannabis relaxes me. I play better when I'm stoned."

"We're fucked," Dom said.

"Relax, guys. I'm not stoned. I'm in my usual slightly buzzed state of mind, which is where I excel."

"I might need some of that weed to relax. My nerves are killing me," Charlie said, his hands cold and clammy. "And I need to rest my eyes."

Eight minutes to midnight. Charlie wasn't meditating. He was thinking of Susan. Here he was, about to enter the most important match of his life, and all he could think about was her. He recalled all the beautiful moments they'd shared—feeling her soft lips during their first kiss, caressing her hair while they made love, the sweet smell of her perfume. He prayed she would forgive him.

Midnight. The team logged into the Midnight Multiplayer Match and waited for it to begin. *This is it. It all comes down to this. Focus, Charlie. Focus.*

Four minutes later, a message popped up on the screen:

BattleTheatre's Midnight Multiplayer Match is experiencing server issues due to matchmaking problems. Please stand by. Do not exit the match.

Johnny took a massive hit from his bong and exhaled a thick plume of pure white smoke. "Wouldn't it be funny if the Midnight Match didn't work?"

"*Funny?*" Charlie said. "This shit better work. My girlfriend might break up with me over this."

"You'd think the developers would have made sure they could pull this off before attempting a tournament. And it's not like there are a lot of players. It's only a hundred people. This makes no sense," Dom said.

"I bet their anti-cheat protocol is causing the delay," Tim said.

Since twenty thousand dollars were on the line, *Battle Theatre* had implemented a sophisticated anti-cheat system specifically for the Midnight Multiplayer Match. Any player caught using a hacked console to gain an unfair advantage would be immediately disqualified. The developers even recruited overseers to monitor each individual player to ensure they weren't cheating with aimbots or using physics hacks like the ability to jump fifty feet in the air.

Charlie crossed his arms and continued to stare at the message on the screen. *What if it gets canceled? Was all this for nothing?*

Five minutes later, another message popped up:

> We apologize for the delay. Since this match involves significant prize money, we are verifying the legitimacy of all participants through an authentication system and implementing an anti-cheat protocol. This process is taking longer than anticipated. Please stay logged in as we work to resolve this issue as quickly as possible. Thank you for your patience.

Charlie jumped up off the couch and placed both palms on the side of his head. "Why? Why is this happening?"

"Chill, bro," Tim said. "The match hasn't even started and you already buggin'. Why don't you meditate with me? That goes for the rest of you, too. Close your eyes and breathe in and out slowly."

Dom said, "Fuck it. I'll try it."

Charlie closed his eyes and tried to calm himself, but his heart was pounding against his chest like a SWAT team using a battering ram on a door in *Rainbow Six Siege*.

After a minute of silent meditation, everyone heard the familiar sound of a bubbling bong in their headsets.

Charlie was the first to react. "Jesus Christ, Johnny. Again?"

Johnny fumbled with his controller. "Shit. I forgot to mute my mic."

"We need you sharp, man."

"Who knows how long we'll have to wait for this match to start? Sorry, but I need my low-level buzz."

Dom said, "If we lose this match because of you, you'll need a surgeon to remove my Timberland boot from your ass."

Thirty minutes past midnight. The only onscreen action was a bouncing animated message that continued to inform the players of the delay in the Midnight Multiplayer Match. Anticipation and excitement had morphed into disbelief and boredom for the Chi-Town Crew. No one was talking to each other: Tim was meditating; Johnny's mic kept muting; and Charlie had resumed his habit of biting his cuticles.

A few minutes later, all three of them were startled by a strange sound on their headsets.

Cahhh. Haghhh. Cahhh.

"Oh my God," Charlie yelled. "Is that Dom? I think he's snoring. Dom, wake up!"

No answer.

Tim shouted, "Dom!"

Still no answer.

"Dom. Dom. *Dom!*" Johnny screamed. "Wake up. Wake up. *Wake... up!*"

Nothing.

Dom's head had tilted back against his recliner at just the right angle for his headset to slip off his ears and rest around his neck. He couldn't hear anyone. But the rest of the team could hear him along with his labored breathing through his mic, which was an inch away from his mouth.

Tim cried out, "Is the old fuck having a stroke?"

"Maybe he's fucking with us. Come on, you ol' dirty bastard. Say something," Johnny said.

Charlie's hands trembled as he grabbed his cell phone and scrolled through his contacts for Dom's number. He called four times in a row, but there was no answer. Dom had set his phone to silent six hours ago so no one would disturb him during the practice matches.

Charlie put his headset back on and addressed Johnny and Tim. "He's not answering his phone."

"What do we do?" Tim said.

"I'm texting everyone his address. Let's see who's closest," Charlie said, fully aware that it was almost certainly him.

A minute later, Tim said, "I'm an hour away."

"Twenty-three minutes for me," Johnny said, "but I'm pretty high, and I have a personal rule never to drive stoned because—"

"Shut it," Charlie said. "I'm nine minutes away. Fuck! Fuck! Fuck!"

"You gotta go get him. We're fucked without his old sleep-apnea ass," Johnny said. There was a twenty-second silence over the group chat before he added, "Don't think, Charlie. Drive!"

"Okay. Okay. Fuck it. I'm going. Call me if anything changes with the match."

"We will," Tim said. "Drive safe."

Charlie tossed his headset on the couch, grabbed his car keys, and remembered to lock the front door before rushing to his car. His Accord peeled out as if it had received a starting boost in a *Mario Kart* race. There were no power-ups to make it go faster, but at least there was minimal traffic since it was the middle of the night. Charlie couldn't believe the risk he was taking to wake up Dom. Then again, he would have lost his place in the tournament if it hadn't been for Dom's generosity in buying him a PlayStation 4 Pro and a copy of the game.

It was 12:42 a.m. when Charlie slammed on the brakes in front of Dom's house. He sprinted up the driveway, clenched his fist, and banged on the front door while ringing the doorbell at least a dozen times.

All the commotion woke up Dom's wife, who turned her head to see that Dom wasn't in the bed beside her. She assumed he was on the couch playing in the tournament and couldn't hear anything because of his headset. *If this is a prowler, he'd better drop that game and protect his family.* She grabbed Dom's baseball bat from the closet and lifted it to her right shoulder, ready to swing at anything that got in her way. Tiptoeing down the stairs, she saw Dom fast asleep on his recliner. His headset was around his neck, not on his ears. She placed the bat in his lap, grabbed his shirt with both hands, and shook him four times before he woke up. Then she screamed, "There's someone at the door, banging like crazy. Take the bat and check it out."

Dom's eyes slowly focused on the same standby screen he'd seen before falling asleep. Instead of worrying about a prowler, he thought, *Thank God the match hasn't started yet.* The banging and doorbell ringing stopped. Dom tightened his grip on the bat, rose from his recliner, and approached the front door. Ready to strike.

Outside, Charlie had his phone to his ear.

"I hate to be the bearer of bad news," Tim said, "but the match is starting in three minutes. Where are you?"

"In front of Dom's house. He's not answering his door," Charlie cried. "I can't believe this bullshit. Are you sure it's starting this time?"

"Yup, there's a countdown clock and everything. Two fifty-three, two fifty-two…"

"That's it. I'm fucked. My God. My God. My God."

Charlie pounded on Dom's door again with fists faster than the drum solo on Rush's "Tom Sawyer." Dom peered out of his side window to see Charlie banging away. He tossed the bat aside, unlocked the door, and said, "Oh my God. I'm so sorry."

Charlie, now hunched over and breathing heavily from all the exertion, stood up straight, pulled his arm back, and slapped Dom square in the face. He was probably the only one who could do that to Dom without getting pulverized. "The match is starting in two minutes. Get back online. Help our team. I'm heading back home."

He then made the terrible decision to run down Dom's icy driveway. His ass slammed hard on the pavement as he slid all the way down to his car like Nathan Drake in an *Uncharted 2* action scene. He jumped into the driver's seat. The searing pain from his already bruised tailbone was unbearable. He smashed his foot on the accelerator, causing the tires to spin five or six times before they finally gripped on the slush-covered asphalt. Only then did the Accord disappear into the chilly night.

Marie peeked over Dom's shoulder. "God, I hope he doesn't kill someone."

Dom rubbed his bright-red cheek. "If he does, it'll all be my fault."

"I can't believe he slapped you," Marie said, covering her face to hide her amusement. "And that you fell asleep before the match started. You really *are* getting old. Maybe it's time to end these late-night gaming sessions."

Dom scrunched up his face as he bit his tongue. Hard. He took a deep breath and sighed, but didn't say a word. This was no time for temper tantrums. He dashed over to his PlayStation 4 Pro and put on his headset.

"Well," Marie said, "since I'm up, I might as well watch you play this life-changing match you keep talking about."

Dom pressed his chin against both fists, furious that he might have cost the team the match. "Baby, I love you, but go back to fucking sleep. The match is about to start. I don't need your ass hovering over me."

"What if I make you a cup of coffee before I go to bed?"

Dom turned to her and said, "That would be wonderful, babe. I'm sorry. I'm mad at myself, not you."

Marie put her hand on his shoulder and said, "I forgive you. I know I don't always support your gaming, but... I really hope you win."

"Thanks, honey. That means more to me than you know. You'd better make that coffee extra strong. I got a lot of motherfuckers to kill tonight."

CHAPTER 24

THE BATTLE BEGINS

Charlie's foot stayed firm on the accelerator. *Six minutes from home.* He glanced at the dashboard clock: 12:48 a.m. His cell phone rang.

"We're on the North America map," Dom said. "I got good news and bad news."

Charlie's knuckles turned white as he clutched the steering wheel. "I'm locked out, right? It's over for me."

"The match started a couple of minutes ago. You got kicked out of the plane and your chute failed to open."

"Am I dead?"

"That's the good news. You landed in the safe zone and you're alive," Dom said. "The bad news is that you've got only twenty-five HP left."

"The game must have automatically ejected me when I reached the edge of the map," Charlie said. "But why didn't my parachute open? No wonder I lost seventy-five HP."

Charlie was well aware that any player who fell from a height of more than a hundred feet, equivalent to a ten-story building, lost three-quarters of their health points and became disabled until healed with a medkit. What he hadn't realized was that a player's parachute deployed only when there was some activity on their controller.

Dom said, "There's worse news."

"What?"

"You're in Philadelphia and we're in Salt Lake City."

"Why didn't you jump out near me?" Charlie said, confused.

"Fucking Johnny. The plane was heading from left to right across the screen, and he thought you'd die once it reached the edge of the map, so he convinced us all to jump out near Salt Lake City. The idea was to use the mountains for cover."

"I'm gonna need a medkit. Did anybody find one yet?"

"No," Dom said. "But I'll protect your ass until we do. We're coming for you, Charlie."

The safe zone was a large circle covering the entire United States, which was scheduled to shrink by a set amount every ten minutes. The area outside was toxic, causing players to lose ten health points every ten seconds. Even with shield activation, a player with full health could be eliminated in three minutes. If no one killed Charlie while his controller was unattended, then the deadly outer edge of the play zone certainly would. Although the ten-second shield was active for any player who was shot, armor was disabled for the duration of the Midnight Multiplayer Match. And while medkits could heal players, they could not revive them.

While Charlie navigated the icy side streets of Chicago, the rest of his crew sprinted across the apocalyptic landscape in search of a vehicle that would give them a chance of reaching him in time. Nobody said a word for a full minute.

Finally, Dom leaned forward in his recliner, tightened his grip on his controller, and said, "We need to find a car and a medkit. Keep running toward Charlie's position on the map. Johnny, I need you to focus. You're responsible for checking our six when we're in open areas, so get used to looking behind you every few seconds. Tim, check the left side. I'll check the right. And for fuck's sake, stick together. This is a rescue mission. Now, run. Run like the motherfucking wind."

In a stroke of luck, Charlie had landed on the roof of an abandoned building that resembled a Jenga tower with large sections missing. The fragments that remained were charred black from what looked like multiple rocket launcher hits. The windows were broken, with only shards of glass remaining in the frames. The entire structure looked like it could topple at any moment. The only good news was that there were no enemies around. At least for now.

In *Battle Theatre*, the drive from Seattle to Miami usually takes eight minutes. The crew found a car and drove from Salt Lake City to Philadelphia in four minutes. It was an impressive feat, especially as their car took a few hits along the way. They saw the dark purple skies and lightning bolts of the death zone just beyond the outskirts of the devastated city, no more than a couple of football fields away. The safe zone of the circle was set to shrink in exactly four minutes, as indicated on the map timer.

Tim found Charlie's green number-three icon inside a large rectangular shape on the map. "He's inside that building."

Johnny parked the car and shouted, "Charlie, are you there? Charlie?"

No response.

Overgrown vines hugged the side of the decayed building, which looked straight out of *The Last of Us*. Old sheets of newspaper and masonry littered the ground floor.

After the team entered, Dom said, "We have about three minutes before the circle starts closing in. We need to do a sweep. Floor by floor. Tim, Johnny, one of you will have to stay on the ground floor to warn us if anyone approaches."

Tim said, "I'll do it."

"Head on a swivel, Tim."

"Yes, sir."

"Johnny, let's go."

"Right behind you," Johnny said.

It was 12:54 a.m. when Charlie skidded to a halt on a patch of black ice in front of his driveway. His whole body was shaking, so he had to grab his key with both hands to insert it in the keyhole. *Please don't be dead. Please don't be dead.* He bolted straight to the TV, which displayed a bird's-eye view of the map, with his green number-three icon right in the center. At least he was still alive. He grabbed his controller and exited the map view to see his avatar lying on the roof of a tall building.

After putting on his headset, he yelled, "Guys, I'm back! I'm on the roof of some building."

Dom said, "Me and Johnny are running up the stairs now."

The staircase to the roof was in ruins. The handrails were rusty and curled like spaghetti, blocking some sections. Many of the steps were damaged, while others were missing. Instead of a straight ascent, Dom and Johnny had to keep hopping over lumps of rubble and twisted metal.

"Watch my six," Dom said as he leapt up the staircase.

Johnny walked backward right behind him, scanning for enemies.

Then, there it was: a medkit, balanced on a metal beam three feet above and ten feet away from their current position. If Dom missed the next jump, he'd plummet all the way to the ground. But it was a risk he had to take. He ordered Johnny to stop moving before preparing to leap onto the beam. He wiped the sweat off his left thumb and clicked in the left joystick to start the sprint animation as he flung the joystick up to run. As soon as he pressed the *X* button, his avatar jumped and clutched the edge of the beam, legs dangling loose. He pressed up on his joystick to pull himself up, grabbed the medkit, then made the much easier jump back down to the staircase.

Charlie looked around the roof. It resembled a junkyard, with old bicycles, washing machines, rubber tires, and dozens of barrels scattered throughout the area. *Why do all shooter games have so many barrels in them?* Their presence was like an unspoken rule in video game architecture. Charlie was just glad that none of them were red, because anyone who plays video games knows that a red barrel is an explosive barrel. His avatar was disabled from the fall, so his only option was to crawl toward a stack of tires and hide. He was a few feet away from cover when an enemy player opened the rooftop door. The gunman, named Demented87, quickly aimed his assault rifle and shot Charlie in the torso from thirty feet away. Minus ten health points. Fifteen remaining.

"There's an enemy on the roof!" Charlie yelled. "He shot me. He's walking toward me. I'm crawling behind some tires. You'll see them as soon as you exit the stairs. About thirty feet straight ahead. Hurry!"

Dom and Johnny were on the third floor, running and bunny-hopping upward like Master Chief in *Halo*. The broken and twisted staircase made their progress slow and difficult.

Demented87 was now just twenty feet away. He could see Charlie's legs protruding from the mound of tires. As he drew closer, he noticed the fifteen points displayed over Charlie's avatar and the shield protection counting down. One twenty-point headshot and it would all be over. He aimed his handgun and waited for Charlie's shield to disappear. Waiting to deliver the final blow. Execution style.

Charlie squeezed his controller and stared at his helpless avatar. The match was over before it had even begun. *I waited four years so that I could die like a dog. I pissed off my girlfriend. And I'll never get my games back from Dimitri. This is the end.*

The shield counted down: three... two... one. Demented87 aimed at Charlie's head and fired.

In a perfect world, Dom and Johnny would have burst through the rooftop door and killed Demented87 seconds before he shot Charlie. But the reality was that they didn't arrive in time. What did arrive in time was a fluke. Or a glitch. Wait, not a glitch, but a twitch. Not the interactive live-streaming service for gamers, but a sudden involuntary movement of Charlie's left thumb on the controller's joystick a millisecond after his ten-second shield had counted down to zero, which caused his avatar's head to jerk out of the line of fire. Demented87 immediately lined up for another headshot, but Charlie had just enough time to start spinning his avatar like a mid-eighties breakdancer. Frustrated, Demented87 sprayed him with bullets from his assault rifle, but none of them struck him in the head. Charlie's torso may have been Swiss cheese, but he lost only ten health points. *Five HP left. Ten-second shield activated again. I'm still alive.* It was only then that he noticed Demented87 had only ten HP himself.

At that moment, Johnny kicked open the rooftop door and ran directly toward Demented87, firing about as accurately as a non-gamer picking up the controller for the first time. Demented87 crouched behind a barrel and shot back. Johnny absorbed more bullets than an enemy in *Borderlands 2*, losing ten points, but his shield protected him for the next ten seconds, so he kept running. Demented87 didn't notice Dom sprinting directly behind Johnny until it was too late. As soon as they reached the barrel, Dom dove sideways like Max Payne, which gave him the perfect angle for a shotgun blast right into the enemy's chest.

"Take that, motherfucker!" Dom shouted as he made his way to Charlie. Then he used the syringe from the team's only medkit to bring him back to full health. "I got you, buddy."

"Holy shit. You won't believe what just happened," Charlie said. "I was down to fifteen HP, he aimed at my head, and—"

"Tell us about it later," Dom said. "We gotta get the hell out of here. The edge of the circle is closing in. And it'll take forever to get down them stairs."

Tim, still on the ground floor, looked up at the roof and said, "Why don't you just jump?"

Most multiplayer games feature reusable parachutes that players can utilize at any time, but the designers of *Battle Theatre* had removed that option. Instead, each player was able to use their parachute only once—when first jumping out of the plane. Charlie knew this and had planned to tell the rest of the team at the start of the match, but the start was anything but normal. "The fall from the building is over ten stories," he said. "We can't jump off. We'll all lose seventy-five HP."

The deadly edge of the circle was less than a minute away.

Dom yelled, "Stop blowing each other and start running down them stairs. Now!"

Fortunately, they all had extensive experience with platformers, so they were able to navigate the various hazards faster than the little pixelated guy from *Downwell*. As soon as they exited the building, Charlie spotted Tim's avatar and said, "Oh. Hi, Tim."

"Why I gotta miss all the fun shit?" Tim asked.

Dom stared at Tim. Then scanned the empty wasteland. "Where da fuck did our car go?"

"Someone stole it," Tim said.

Dom yelled, "And you let them?"

"I was hiding. You told me to stand watch. I didn't want to draw attention," Tim shrieked.

Charlie said, "Stop arguing. We need to find another car."

Charlie pulled out his rangefinder binoculars and scanned the battlefield in search of another vehicle, but it was difficult to see anything through the swirling dust devils dancing in the air. The top of his viewfinder displayed a cylindrical compass, while the bottom showed the distance to objects in meters. He could just about make out a dark shape.

"I think that's a jeep to the west. Eight hundred meters. Everyone, follow me," Charlie said as he rushed ahead.

The edge of the circle was now less than a hundred yards away. They headed west, but each of them lost ten HP as the toxic area coming in from the east enveloped them. Their shields activated, giving them just enough time to reach the jeep without losing any more health. Charlie hopped into the driver's seat and drove at full speed toward the safety of the inner circle.

Their mission for survival had only just begun.

CHAPTER 25

THE THEATRE OF BATTLE

The arid terrain of *Battle Theatre* was full of players waiting for a vehicle to pass by so they could destroy it with an RPG. But the team had no choice—they had to get out of there. The jeep barreled due west, leaving a large plume of dust trailing in its wake. They had no clear destination. All Charlie could think about was how he had escaped death thanks to his band of brothers. Sure, Dom's narcoleptic tendencies had nearly cost them the match. But none of that mattered now. He was alive, with ninety HP, and grateful that he still had a chance to win. The team had risked sacrificing themselves to save him even though the odds were against them. That was more than enough to motivate him to become the leader they needed.

Tim asked, "Where we going?"

Before anyone could reply, several bullets ricocheted off the jeep's fender.

Ting! Ting! Ting!

It was unclear where the shots were coming from, but they continued to hit. Charlie's screen counter indicated that forty-one players were still alive. Avoiding other teams of four was essential for survival, as being tracked by an entire squad meant trouble.

After a minute of zigzag driving, they finally escaped the hot zone of gunfire. Two more minutes of straight driving landed them outside Dayton, Ohio. It was quiet. A perfect chance to look for supplies. The team hopped out of the jeep, searched a few houses, and found ammo but no medkits. The edge of the circle was only four minutes away.

Charlie said, "We're wasting too much time here. We need to head to the center of the circle."

As they trotted across an open field, a bullet whizzed past Charlie's ear. An enemy player was firing at them from behind the jeep.

"What do we do?" Johnny yelled.

"Slither around and head toward that tall patch of grass," Charlie replied.

The team had used the zigzag movement of a snake in previous multiplayer games as it made it difficult for snipers to zero in on them, especially when they were firing from a distance. Soon, they all looked like they were in the closing credits of an episode of *Benny Hill*, sprinting from side to side like banshees. The sniper continued to fire shots that whizzed through the tall grass toward them, but none of them hit.

"This guy must think we're noobs, running around like this," Tim said.

Johnny yelled, "Fuck this. This slithering shit is slowing us down. I'm running straight at him."

"Me too," Tim agreed.

They ran side by side in a dead-straight line, making it easy for the sniper to land two well-placed headshots. As a result, they each lost twenty points before diving into the grass. The sniper could still see the top half of Johnny's head, so he lined up another shot, but at that moment, he was hit himself. A random shot from another sniper. Some unknown savior must have decided to take him out.

Dom said, "Guys, we're no longer taking fire."

Tim asked, "Are we clear?"

"I heard a single gunshot from those houses behind us," Dom said. "I think someone killed the son of a bitch."

The team slowly rose to their feet and looked around. Nothing.

"Why ain't they shooting at us?" Tim said.

"Dunno," Dom replied, "but I have a feeling they're looking at us right now through a scope."

Tim sprinted toward the jeep and found the blood-splattered sniper lying on the ground beside it. He looted the body, collecting some extra ammo and a drone, which could be an invaluable tool on the battlefield. After placing the prized object in his inventory, he turned around to see Dom frozen in place. "What the hell you doing standing there like that? Let's go."

Dom was staring at the line of houses, his feet stuck like they were embedded in quick-drying concrete. Then he raised both hands. Almost daring the player to shoot him. *I know you're watching me.* But the shot never came. The next sound he heard was the spinning of tires as Charlie drove over to him, with Johnny in the backseat and Tim riding shotgun.

Johnny yelled, "What the fuck is wrong with you, brah? Get in."

Dom muttered, "I'm sure we'll meet again, *uomo del mistero,*" before jumping into the jeep.

After three minutes of driving, they were approaching St. Louis, Missouri.

"Are we just gonna drive around all day?" Dom asked.

"I'm heading into town," Charlie replied. "We have to find another medkit."

He eased off the gas and let the jeep coast toward the annihilated city center. Angry weeds infested the streets. Dark green foliage clung to most buildings. A once bustling area filled with car dealerships, luxury hotels, and coffee shops was now a wasteland decimated by war. The middle of the Gateway Arch was missing, leaving two curved metal beams facing each other. Probably destroyed by players who had nothing better to do than waste their rockets on a national landmark. Half the neon signs were broken, missing their faceplates and exposing hundreds of half-broken light bulbs. Others hung down vertically, about to fall. Piles of rubble littered the streets.

Tim called out, "Two guys near that brown-and-blue building straight ahead."

Charlie pulled over near a tall concrete barrier, used his rangefinder binoculars to scan the dozen oddly shaped buildings arranged in a perfect grid pattern ahead of them, then zoomed in on the two enemies. According to the rangefinder, they were ninety-three meters away. "I see them," he said. "Everyone out. We're taking them down."

"Why we fuckin' with them? Why can't we hide?" Tim said.

Dom chuckled. "This is *Battle Theatre*, not hide and go seek. I agree. Let's take 'em out."

"Agreed," Johnny said.

"Tim. While we're moving, scan the open area behind us for any stragglers," Charlie said.

"Fuck that. I'm not doing that boring shit again."

"Fine," Charlie replied. "Johnny, you scan for enemies while I go after these guys with Dom and Tim. I'll check the windows and balconies for any snipers. Get ready to sweep the area. Military alphabet for all the buildings we pass. Alpha One, Bravo Two, and so on. We're southwest. The building in front of us is Alpha One. Got it?"

The team always used the same technique when sweeping a town in a multiplayer match, starting from the closest corner building. Picture a chessboard, or a game of Battleship. The buildings on the outer horizontal perimeter were Alpha, Bravo, Charlie, Delta, and so on. The vertically stacked buildings were numbered One, Two, Three, Four, and so forth. So, if an enemy was spotted two buildings north of a Bravo building, a player would call out Bravo Two. It wasn't the best tactical system, but it had worked well before, so Charlie felt it was worth trying again.

The team inched their way along the outer edge of the grid. Heading east, they moved toward the middle corridor, where Tim had spotted the enemies near the brown-and-blue building. Now acting as a scout, he shuffled a few steps ahead and peeked between the Delta and Echo buildings before springing back into cover. "Delta Three. Enemies on ground level. I think they saw me."

"They might have a full team," Charlie said. "We either go down that corridor or walk past it."

"I say we walk past it," Tim said.

Johnny scoffed, "Stop being a wuss, Tim."

"Leave him alone," Charlie said. "If you're so tough, why don't you head down there and scout instead?"

Johnny shrieked, "By myself?"

Charlie said, "Guess what you sound like."

"Fuck you," Johnny said. "Fine. I'll do it."

Johnny crouched low between the Delta and Echo buildings, moving slower than a grandma in the walking simulator *What Remains of Edith Finch*. The dried vegetation at his feet made it difficult to spot any enemies lying on the ground. He drew his assault rifle, ready to fire, but the coast was clear.

Charlie instructed Tim and Dom to walk along the city's edge. Then he looked behind him to see the open field transforming into an enormous cloud of swirling beige dust. Worried that a group of enemies might be using it for cover, he slithered ahead of the rest of the team. "There's a dust storm coming. We have to go into the city."

Charlie, Tim, and Dom crouched between Echo and Foxtrot, while Johnny was picking daisies at Delta Four. Charlie spotted an enemy on Echo Two's balcony, but before he could say anything, a single bullet struck Dom in the head. Twenty points instantly disappeared from his HP bar, but his shield activated, giving him just enough time to dash toward a pile of dusty cinder blocks. Seconds later, Charlie and Tim dove to the ground near a dilapidated shack.

"Motherfucker shot me in the head," Dom said.

"I see a guy," Johnny said. "Ground level at Delta Four."

Three seconds later, a bullet struck Charlie. Pink mist sprayed out from the back of his skull, splattering blood onto the shack behind him. Doubt seeped deeper into his brain than any bullet could. *Why the fuck didn't I hit the deck when Johnny called out the enemy?* His lack of focus had cost him twenty health points, but it felt more like a hundred. The confidence he'd built up over the last four years had disappeared in a flash. In his mind, the match was already lost. He didn't feel like a leader. They would all be dead soon.

"I got shot in the head too," Charlie said as his protective shield counted down. *Five... four... three.* He used his sniper scope to zoom in on the enemy at Delta Four, hoping to take him out, but he was nowhere to be seen. Charlie was the victim of a snipe-and-run.

Dom crawled behind a pile of twisted metal and rubble and shouted, "*Paisan*, what da hell you doing? Get down."

But Charlie's avatar remained glued to the spot as his shield vanished. His attention had shifted to a couple of dark blips near Echo and Foxtrot Five. He zoomed in with his binoculars and saw the two dots morph into a full, four-person team. Hungry for blood and closing in fast. *One hundred and thirty meters. One hundred and twenty meters.* A barrage of bullets speared toward him, forcing him to retreat behind a rusty truck with missing doors. Meanwhile, Dom and Tim returned fire.

Johnny rushed back to them and asked, "What the hell is happening?"

Charlie used his sniper scope to zoom in and opened fire. He scored a head shot and a body shot, but the enemy players weren't slowing down. They were within a hundred meters now. Determined to kill. "Team of four approaching." More bullets danced in the dust storm. One struck Dom's dome again, costing him another twenty points. The shooting stopped for a few seconds, which gave Tim enough time to stand up and unload his machine gun in the direction of the enemies, but he took a shot to the chest. After five seconds of silence, a grenade rolled toward them and exploded right next to Dom. Another fifteen points were deducted. He was down to his last thirty-five.

"Johnny, get your ass over here," Charlie said.

"Where am I going?"

"Charlie Four. Flank them from the side. They're between Echo and Foxtrot Four."

Johnny started to sprint toward Charlie Four, but then paused for a second. It was enough time for an enemy to nail him with a bullet to the shoulder. The activation of his shield allowed him to shoot three of the four-person team kamikaze-style. But as soon as his shield counter dropped to two, he ran away faster than Han Solo doing an about-face after chasing down stormtroopers in *Star Wars*.

The enemies' snipe-and-run tactic had lured the boys into town and set them up for an ambush. Dom and Johnny reunited at Delta Two, only to get pummeled with heavy fire that struck Dom in the head yet again. In just a few minutes, he had lost fifty-five health points. He had only fifteen left.

"I'm hit!" he yelled.

He and Johnny scurried like little lost soldiers in the real-time strategy game *Company of Heroes*. Aimless. Terrified. The cascade of bullets flying in every direction meant that there had to be two separate teams hellbent on their annihilation. Almost as if they were coordinating with each other to take out the Chi-Town Crew.

"It's an ambush!" Charlie yelled. "It's gotta be two teams. Retreat! Everyone, back to the jeep at Alpha One. Now!"

Tim asked, "Why don't we hide in one of these buildings instead?"

Charlie glanced at his map. The closing circle was about three minutes away. "We can't. We'll be trapped with two teams waiting for us. And if they don't get us, the death zone will. We have to run."

"You guys go," Dom said. "I'm gonna waste as many of these motherfuckers as I can."

"This isn't some movie where you sacrifice yourself to help us escape. We live and die as a team," Charlie replied.

"I only have fifteen HP left. We don't have any medkits. And I won't make it to the jeep if I make a run for it. These guys are pros. If I take another shot to the head or a grenade explodes near me, I'm dead."

Charlie hesitated. His throat tightened. The back of his neck ached. He couldn't just leave Dom behind. His coworker. His mentor. His friend. "I can't do it, Dom. I couldn't live with myself knowing that I left you behind."

"I'm doing this," Dom said. "So, either we all die here, or you and the boys live."

Charlie's eyes filled with tears at the thought of abandoning Dom. It would be yet another example of his selfishness. Just like his refusal to attend Susan's gig. Or the way he'd declared himself the crew's commander months before the game was even released, confident that he would be the best *Battle Theatre* player and lead his team to an easy victory.

"I need a rocket launcher. Does anyone have one?" Dom asked.

"I do," Johnny said.

"Give it to me."

"How do I do that?"

"Jesus Christ. See the bottom-left corner of your screen, where your gun icon is?"

"Yeah."

"There should be an icon of the rocket launcher under it."

"I see a pistol and… Oh, shit, is that a rocket launcher?"

In a monotone voice, Tim said, "We're dead."

But Dom remained calm. "Select your rocket launcher."

"I'm trying, but it keeps jumping to the pistol."

"Press the triangle button twice, quickly."

"Oh, there it is. Who the fuck designs a game where you have to press a button twice to select a weapon?" Johnny said.

Gunfire bounced off the buildings.

Dom said, "Now, drop it in front of me."

Johnny fumbled with his controller for four seconds. "How do I do that again?"

Dom finally lost patience and yelled, "Charlie, will you tell him before I beat his ass?"

"That's no way to treat a friend," Johnny answered. "I'm just—"

Charlie barked, "Hold down on the *D* pad and press the *R1* button at the same time."

"These controls keep getting better and better," Johnny said, before finally dropping the rocket launcher at Dom's feet.

Dom picked up the weapon and primed it. "I'll be right behind you… shoving this rocket launcher straight up their ass. This is my moment, brothers. I love you guys."

"Love ya, brah," Johnny said, as he bolted toward the jeep with Tim.

For a second, Charlie just stood there, but then Dom shoved his avatar aside and sprinted north toward the attacking enemies like a menacing mech in *Titanfall*. He fired his rocket launcher at the two buildings directly in front of him, creating a bright orange glow of explosions that could be seen right across the battlefield. Shards of glass and chunks of masonry burst into the sky. No building was safe from his destructive frenzy as he continued to fire while chucking smoke grenades, creating a thick cloud around himself. An enemy grenade exploded nearby, but it was far enough away that he didn't lose any HP. A bullet struck his leg, but it didn't diminish his appetite for destruction. He still had five health points left, and he'd be damned if he wasn't going to make the most of them.

Charlie glanced at his minimap and ran southwest toward Tim and Johnny's green blips. Johnny was so far ahead that he escaped without a scratch, but Charlie took a bullet in the back during the chaos. It was a miracle he didn't lose more HP, considering two teams were fixated on his demise. The silhouette of the jeep at Alpha One emerged after the smoke from Dom's onslaught started to clear. A nearby sniper fired, hitting the jeep's hood, but Charlie continued to run at full speed and dove into the back seat. Johnny floored the accelerator, and the jeep dashed away from the city. Into the open wasteland.

Dom wanted to go out like Leon in *The Professional*. Lying on the floor. Mortally wounded. With the enemy standing over him. Looking him in the eye before pulling the pin on his grenade and saying, "This is for Charlie." Instead, his body was riddled with more bullets than Tony Montana at the end of *Scarface*.

Although he didn't get his epic finale, Dom's parade of destruction saved the rest of the team. He lay on the floor, smiling, as he watched the jeep icon speeding across the map, fleeing from both the death zone and the town of terror. Mission accomplished.

He died so his friends could live. And that was enough for him.

CHAPTER 26

THE BRIDGE ON THE RIVER CHARLIE

Sunday, 1:15 a.m. Jasmine was cursing at her phone. She couldn't sleep. She had called Charlie six times and sent him eight messages. She couldn't even watch TV to relax. All she could do was glare at her phone, waiting for Charlie to respond. Her job was on the line. She looked at her long list of sent text messages again:

> Charlie, you were supposed to get back to me about the assignment.
> Why aren't you answering your texts?
> Charlie, please reply.
> If you don't answer, I'll have no choice other than to tell DuPont that you're almost done with the assignment. My ass is on the line too, you know.
> Oh, what does it matter?
> Fuck him and fuck you.
> If by some miracle you read this message, call me. We need to talk. I'm not even mad anymore. You're probably not the right person to talk to about this, but for some crazy reason my gut tells me you might be. I must be losing my mind.
> Please! I need to talk to you.

Jasmine closed her eyes and thought about how her fate had become intrinsically tied to Charlie's. They were either moving up or crashing down together. She pictured him working so hard that he had no time to check his messages. Burning the midnight oil. Perhaps he'd call her in the morning and tell her that most of the work was already finished. *That must be it, right?* But she knew she was fooling herself. The completion of the assignment could save her job, but what then? Continue working for a boss who drugged her and tried to get her alone in a hotel room? For what? A crappy paycheck every two weeks. Her desire to tell Charlie about DuPont's evil intentions was growing stronger. The assignment would have to take a back seat for now.

Three members of the team may have escaped with their lives, but their health was dwindling. Charlie and Tim had sixty HP each, while Johnny was down to fifty. Their jeep was moving at a steady clip toward the southwest corner of the map when Dom, who could still chat with the rest of the crew despite his elimination, said, "No more going into towns. It's too risky."

Charlie replied, "You definitely earned your share of the prize money if we win."

"I don't know," Johnny said. "I mean, technically, he *has* been eliminated from the tournament."

Dom snapped back, "Don't make me come down there and whip your skinny ass."

Charlie cut in, "We need a plan. Only eighteen players left, and the edge of the circle is close."

"At least we're in the top twenty percent," Tim said.

Three minutes later, the Chi-Town Crew crossed the Colorado border. Plenty of houses lined the side of the road, but seeking cover in one of them would be a death trap if an enemy team used the death circle's edge to lure them out for an ambush. There had to be a safer place to hide.

They arrived at a rusty metal bridge suspended over a crystal-blue river near Colorado Springs. Burned-out cars with shattered windows were stacked on top of each other, while others were resting on their sides.

Charlie said, "Maybe we should hide under the—"

Then…

Boom!

A well-directed shot from a grenade launcher exploded under their jeep, flipping it into the air like a slow-motion explosion in *Grand Theft Auto V*. All three of them immediately lost fifteen health points. Charlie's first-person view spun around half a dozen times, making him dizzy, before the bridge reappeared in his vision. A word salad of gibberish came through his headset. The only word he understood was "bridge," but he wasn't sure whether Tim and Johnny were warning him there were enemies on it or telling him to run toward it. Another grenade exploded. Thankfully, Charlie still had two seconds left on his shield, so there was no further damage. The smoke and shrapnel from the blast formed a dense white cloud, but he was able to make out the dark image of Johnny running toward the bridge at full speed.

"Three enemies on the west side of the bridge. Why can't I find a fucking medkit anywhere?" Johnny said.

They reached the safer east side of the bridge in just under ten seconds and took cover behind a dusty blue pickup that was resting on its side. Half a dozen smoldering cars lay between them and the enemy team. The toxic edge of the circle was less than five minutes away. A firefight was about to begin. And only one team was going to make it out alive.

Charlie blinked rapidly as a hail of bullets dinged off the pickup's chassis. The enemies had perfect cover: a junkyard stack of four overturned cars with a clear line of sight through a small opening between the vehicles that enabled them to fire endless rounds without getting hit. Charlie and his team had no such luxury. The only way to return fire was to peek around the sides of the truck. Tim stuck his head out to fire a shot, but a bullet pierced his brain after two seconds, causing him to lose twenty-five points. The closest car was thirty feet away, near the center of the bridge.

Charlie lay prone on his belly, shuffled around the edge of the pickup, and quickly zoomed in with his sniper scope. "Dammit! They have great cover. We're pinned down."

Even though Tim hated the task of covering their rear, something told him to turn around during the chaos on the bridge. "Three coming up behind us. About a hundred yards away."

They were trapped. Enemies on both sides of them. Not to mention, the toxic edge of the circle was less than a minute away. Charlie thought of Indiana Jones on a rope bridge in *The Temple of Doom*. In the movie, Indy wraps his arm and leg around one of the ropes to hold himself in place, then cuts the rest with his machete, causing most of his enemies to fall to their deaths. This bridge was made of steel, so that strategy was useless.

Tim cried out, "Oh, man. We're fucked."

Charlie fired at the enemies behind them, hitting one in the chest. The well-placed shot must have pissed them off, because an RPG sailed right over the pickup seconds later. All three members of the enemy team continued on their warpath toward the Chi-Town Crew.

"The play zone is shrinking," Johnny said.

Tim yelled, "They've got RPGs. Oh, man. Oh, man, Oh, man. Charlie, what do we do?"

A five-second pause.

"Charlie?"

There was no way they would survive if they moved either forward or backward. Too many bullets. Too many grenades. The only way out was... *down*.

"We have to jump off the bridge," Charlie said.

Johnny yelled, "We what?"

"*Jump!*"

Charlie's avatar bunny-hopped off the bridge quicker than a preteen playing *Fortnite*, falling fifty feet and splashing into the river. Without thinking, Tim and Johnny leapt off after him. They bobbed in the water, going from pinned soldiers to sitting ducks. Enemies above to the left. Enemies above to the right. Jumping had been an act of desperation, an attempt to live just a few seconds longer. All three avatars were helpless. Ready to die. Even if there had been no enemies, there was no way they could outswim the toxic zone, which was closing in fast. Charlie closed his eyes and waited for death's bitter kiss to arrive.

It was a good thing Johnny's eyes were open, because the next sound Charlie heard was him yelling, "*Holy shit!*"

Like a mirage, a shiny red speedboat appeared beside them in the water. Its foghorn blared out a three-note melody, which proved to Charlie that this wasn't a dream. Hovering above it was the gamertag RedBird21 with a remarkable HP of ninety. There was no attack coming from the little craft. It was clear that this player, like an elegant dove, had come in peace.

"I can't believe it," Johnny said. "I think this RedBird guy wants to help us. Everyone, hop in the boat."

Charlie's avatar continued to tread water for a few seconds while he weighed his options. But he knew there was only one.

Johnny yelled, "Charlie, come on."

With bullets skimming across the river like smooth stones next to his head, Charlie started smashing the X button on his controller to swim faster toward the boat. As soon as he hopped in, he joined Tim and Johnny in pointing their guns at RedBird21. The three of them waited for the inevitable firefight. But it never came.

Overjoyed, Johnny shouted, "RedBird!"

Then Tim and Charlie joined in, all three of them chanting, "RedBird!" in unison as the speedboat glided across the water.

Seconds later, Charlie accepted a chat request from RedBird21 and linked everyone in a new chat room. He half-expected their savior to sound like a whiny teenager. Instead, a soothing female voice said, "All right, boys. Stay crouched in the boat while I get us out of this mess."

The voice sounded eerily familiar, but Charlie's adrenaline was so high that he thought nothing of it.

The speedboat was heading north, leaping higher on the waves than a six-year-old kid in a bouncy house. Enemy players fired countless rounds, but it was hard for them to score any direct hits. Just one bullet struck RedBird21 in the back, costing her ten points.

Charlie looked at the purple, lightning-filled circle's edge that was coming up behind them. It was moving at blinding speed. "Can't this boat go any faster?"

RedBird21 replied, "It's already at full throttle."

"We're all gonna lose ten HP if the circle reaches us," Tim said.

The death zone started to cast a shadow on the rear half of the boat as it continued to speed along the river. The boys crawled to the front, stacking on top of each other, which caused RedBird21 to shout, "Spread out. You're messing up the balance of the boat."

In a flash of total recall, Charlie recognized the voice. *Oh my God. It can't be.* "Emma?" he said.

"You got it, punk ass," his sister replied, her voice booming with confidence.

"Wait, what? How'd you get in this match?"

"I was near the top of the waitlist. Someone dropped out, so I was assigned to their team."

"Why didn't you tell me you were on the waitlist?"

"I didn't think I'd get in," Emma said. "Anyway, the team was really crappy, so I broke away from them and wandered around on my own for a while until I saw your gamertags in the distance. I've been following you around ever since."

Dom piped up. "You were the one who killed that *bastardo* near Dayton, weren't you?"

"It was kinda fun watching you guys run around like noobs," Emma replied.

"Why didn't you text me when you joined the match?" Charlie asked.

"I dunno. I guess I wanted to prove to you that I could compete and that I was just as good as all these testosterone-filled bros."

"There must be a few other girls in the tournament," Tim said.

Emma said, "Seven that I know of, but they're all dead. I checked their gamertags before the match."

Emma's randomly assigned team had barely communicated with each other and took unnecessary risks, so her decision to go off on her own had been a smart one. Using her wits to hide, she'd rarely shot at anyone. On top of that, most players wouldn't have thought to change their clothes in the middle of a match to camouflage themselves, but she did. She wore a tan outfit in the desert and a green one in the forested areas.

She had driven her speedboat for ten minutes before coming across Charlie's gamertag on a distant bridge. After parking beneath it, she sat there and awaited the outcome of the firefight. She had thought about sending Charlie a chat request or calling his cell phone to tell him she was under the bridge, but she wanted to win too. It was a lot of money. All she had to do was wait for everyone else to kill each other.

Then Charlie jumped into the river. Right in front of her boat.

He was her brother. She had to save him.

The bastard.

The lightning edge of the circle overtook the boat and raced fifty feet ahead of them. All of their HP instantly dropped by ten points. Even worse, the boat wasn't going fast enough to break past the circle's edge. They all lost another ten points as soon as their shield protection expired.

Tim, who was already down to his last five health points, screamed, "No! I can't die like this."

"Wait for it," Emma said.

The shrinking of the play zone stopped, exactly as it was supposed to after a certain time. Emma made a sharp left into a side channel of the river, drifting the boat like a car in *Mario Kart 8 Deluxe*. Everyone's shields continued to tick down. *Four…*

three... two... Then the boat broke through the border of the death zone and into safety.

The team remained quiet for five seconds before Johnny said, "I could smoke a thousand bowls and still not get the high I'm feeling right now."

Charlie glanced at the onscreen counter. Only five players remaining. *The team on the bridge and the crew behind us must have killed each other. Or the death zone got them.* That meant only one enemy was still out there. The odds were in their favor. Four against one.

But he knew that a single person could change the outcome of a war. And that person was out there. Somewhere.

CHAPTER 27

SNIPERSNAKE

S hards of blustering rain drummed on Charlie's helmet in a steady rhythm as the pale gray sky darkened. Emma's boat glided across the water, bobbing up and down with each passing wave. The peaceful lull of the boat ride was the first time Charlie had felt calm since the match began. He closed his eyes for a moment. When he opened them, he saw a patch of land a few hundred yards ahead.

The boat reached the shore. Everyone hopped out and trudged through the mud past the stone embankment. The play zone, once a sprawling representation of the entire United States, was now a quarter of the size of a small Midwestern town. Roughly two square miles. They were right in the middle. Safe for ten more minutes before the circle would close again.

Charlie turned his avatar toward his sister and said, "Emma, I don't know what to say. You saved our—"

Whoosh!

A bullet hissed past Charlie's ear and pierced Emma's skull, subtracting twenty points. Another bullet, clearly meant for Johnny's head, grazed his right shoulder blade. His health ticked down to five HP.

Charlie turned to his left and spotted a mammoth-sized tractor. It was their only salvation. "Sniper! Go left. Head to that tractor."

The entire team slid behind its two massive wheels as the lone sniper continued to fire, chipping off rust and paint faster than a summer wind blows away the delicate bristles of a dandelion. A bullet pierced one of the tires, causing it to lose pressure.

Tim slithered through the soft mud between the two wheels, then scanned the area with his binoculars. He zoomed in on every building to the east and west. Searching for the bright glint of a sniper scope. Nothing. "Where the hell is this guy?"

Since Dom wasn't playing anymore, he clicked on the enemy's gamertag, SniperSnake47, which showed over five thousand hours spent on the *Sniper Elite* and *Sniper: Ghost Warrior* series. And another ten thousand hours on all the yearly releases of *Call of Duty* and *Battlefield*. Dom muttered, "Jesus. This guy's played more multiplayer matches than you, Tim. He's a pro."

"Great, we're up against Agent 47," Tim sighed. It seemed they were doomed to die at the hands of the famous bald video game hitman.

Johnny chimed in. "The edge of the circle is closing soon. I'm gonna get him to reveal his position. He's probably in one of these two buildings in front of us."

"Please don't do what I think you're going to do," Charlie said. "Don't pull a Dom. You only have five HP. Going out there would be suicide."

"It's a sound strategy," Tim said.

Johnny sighed again. "Brah, we all know I'm the weakest player. The only reason I'm on this team is because I'm your best friend. I can't even shoot straight. But at least I can zigzag. It's our only option."

Charlie wanted to tell Johnny that he would sacrifice himself instead, but the words never came out. He couldn't even admit to himself that his main concern was self-preservation. All he could do was go into commander mode and yell, "You heard him, everyone. Get ready. As soon as Johnny runs, keep your eyes peeled for the sniper's muzzle flash. Johnny, you ready?"

"It's been an honor fighting with all of you," Johnny said.

First Dom. Now Johnny. Why are they sacrificing themselves for me?

From their vantage point under the tractor, Charlie, Emma, and Tim all had a clear view of the smaller of the two buildings in front of them. Most of its windows were opaque, covered in dust and ash. Others were half-broken.

Johnny asked, "On three?"

"On three," Charlie confirmed. "One. Two. Three!"

Johnny galloped like a wild bronco, flailing his hands in the air and heading northeast from the tractor. Charlie, fascinated by Johnny's erratic dancing, failed to follow his own advice and kept switching his attention from the building to Johnny and back again. After ten uncoordinated steps, Johnny was shot in the chest and eliminated from the tournament.

Charlie bit his knuckle hard as he watched Johnny fall back from the bullet that killed him, mortified that he'd lost focus at the critical moment. How would he explain that to Tim and Emma?

"Please tell me you got his location," Johnny said.

"Sorry, man," Tim said. "I got nothing."

"Nothing here either," Emma said.

Silence.

Johnny, now reduced to the role of a spectator, asked, "Charlie? Did you see a muzzle flash?"

Charlie didn't want to lie to his team, so he said, "I was looking at the windows, but then I got distracted by your goofy-ass run. Sorry, bro. I missed it."

Dom barked, "What da fuck, Charlie?"

Charlie stared at the small building. Then at Johnny's corpse. Then at the taller building in the distance. "Hold on. I have a theory."

It was all a question of ragdoll physics, which has been a key element of gaming for years. *Hitman: Codename 47* and *Max Payne 2* were early examples of showing players' bodies and limbs flailing in the air after they were shot or blown up. This revolution in realism was enhanced by the Havok physics engine in *Half-Life 2*, which many games still use today. *Battle Theatre* took the technology a step further by showing each dead player falling directly away from the source of the bullet that killed them, just as they would in real life.

"When Johnny was shot, he fell straight back," Charlie continued. "If he was shot from the west, he would've fallen to the right. If he was shot from the east, he would've fallen to the left. The sniper has to be dead ahead of us."

"He's definitely not in the small building," Emma said. "I was looking at it the whole time. There was no muzzle flash."

"So, he must be in the high-rise behind it," Charlie replied.

Tim laughed. "Son of a bitch. If he's up there, he's got the perfect angle to wipe us all out as soon as we break cover."

Charlie closed his eyes. Half a dozen scenarios ran through his mind. They could probably make it to the wooden shack that was fifty yards away. *Wood is terrible for cover.* They could throw a smoke grenade, run to the small building, then climb up to the roof in the hope of getting a bead on the sniper. *But the small building's at least a hundred yards away. And the smoke grenade cloud lasts only ten seconds.* He imagined strapping on a jet pack, flying right up to the sniper, and shooting him at point-blank range. *But there are no jet packs in this game.* There had to be another way. *What if we could fly?* Then it hit him. *Oh my God! Of course.*

"Tim, you still have that drone you found earlier, right?"

"Hell, yeah. I know not to waste that."

"I need you to fly it up to that high-rise and keep it positioned above the roof."

Tim was confused. The drone could track an enemy's movements and relay them to an operator. But in this case, it was useless because snipers rarely moved. If it was shot down or destroyed, it was gone forever. Why risk such a valuable piece of equipment? Then, it dawned on him. "You want me to look for the reflection off his scope, don't you?"

"Bingo!"

"I don't know, Charlie. He'll probably spot the drone and shoot it down."

Emma said, "We could toss a smoke grenade."

"That won't work," Charlie replied.

"Why not?"

"Because he'll be on high alert as soon as he sees the smoke. He'll be looking for anything unusual away from the smoke," Charlie said. "We need to distract him. I'll make a run for it. If we're lucky, he'll be too busy tracking me with his scope to notice the drone."

Dom had done it. Johnny had done it. Now it was Charlie's turn to sacrifice himself for the good of the team. It was a step in the right direction. He was finally thinking of others.

"I'll run far enough so he can't see the drone in his peripheral vision," he continued. "Remember, Tim, you have to fly that drone straight up. Like a rocket. What do you think, three seconds after I start running?"

Tim agreed. "One second for him to see you. Another to zoom in with his scope. And another to fire. Sounds about right."

"Here goes nothing," Charlie said. He took a deep breath and sprinted away from the tractor.

As predicted, SniperSnake47 peered down his scope and fired a well-aimed bullet, striking Charlie in the ribs.

A microsecond later, Tim pressed the X button and pushed the left stick on his controller, launching the drone into the air faster than an intercontinental ballistic missile. He gripped the controller to steady his shaking hands and guided the drone forward, then into a hover, twenty feet above the high-rise roof. He pressed the triangle button, activating first-person mode, which gave him a breathtaking view of battle-worn America beyond the building. Scorched black. The charred ruins of collapsed buildings littered the landscape. Peaceful now, but sad. Like every war-ravaged area. After a few seconds of wonder, Tim turned his attention back to the high-rise. "Drone's in position. You should see the view from up here."

Charlie's ten-second shield gave him just enough time to scurry back to safety under the tractor. "Emma, you have a rocket launcher?"

Emma pressed her triangle button twice to select the rocket launcher from her inventory. "I've been itching to use this thing. What do you want me to do?"

"Run and fire some rockets at the top floors of the high-rise. Your shield should give you enough time to take a few shots."

Puzzled, Emma asked, "Why do we keep acting like bait for this guy?"

"I'm hoping it'll scare him enough to move so we can get his location."

Emma took a deep breath. "What if I fuck it up?"

"Did you fuck it up when you saved our asses with the boat?" Charlie said. "You're part of our team. And I don't just mean today. I mean from now on. Does anyone have a problem with that?"

"Sir, no sir," Johnny said.

Dom and Tim both yelled, "Sir, no sir."

"You heard it, Private. You ready to save our asses again?"

"I'm not calling you 'sir,' but, yes, I'm ready," Emma said. "Hey, Charlie…"

"Yeah?"

"Thanks."

Tears flooded her eyes. All those years. Desperate to play games with her big brother. Only to be rejected by him every time. He was the reason she wanted to become a professional esports player. She'd played even more multiplayer games than Charlie over the last few years. But she kept it to herself. Afraid of telling him how good she was at *Fortnite* and *PUBG*. Afraid to tell him she needed a safe space too, away from all the chaos of their family falling apart. Playing *Battle Theatre* with him filled what had been a chasm in their relationship. She was part of his crew… forever. And it felt good.

Emma bent her avatar's right knee like a world-class sprinter, waiting for the starting gun. She zigzagged away from the tractor, then slid to avoid the first whistling bullet. She fired a rocket that struck right in the center of the high-rise's top floor. It was a graceful ballet of destruction. It took six seconds for her avatar to load another rocket, so she kept dashing and dodging while maintaining her aim. No easy feat. A downed telephone pole lay fifty feet away. Not the best cover. She took a closer look and spotted a concrete slab resting on top of it. Three more steps and… *Thwack!* A bullet penetrated her chest, causing her to fall backward. She lay flat on her back, gazing at the clouds in the bright, blue sky for a second before uncoiling like a spring and dashing under the slab. The sniper fired three more shots, grazing the concrete each time. Shards of masonry flew into the air like confetti.

Charlie shouted, "Tim, did you see any reflections off his scope?"

"Sorry. Nothing."

"Emma?"

"I'm trying to dodge bullets like John Wick. You think I've got time to look for reflections!"

Charlie's lips parted, ready to offer advice, but before he could utter a single word, she said, "Deploying smoke."

Attagirl.

The smoke grenade obstructed the sniper's view, granting Emma a few seconds. She waited until the dark silhouette of the high-rise reappeared through the haze, then fired her rocket launcher again, this time striking the second floor from the top. After another annoying six-second reload, she fired a third shot, hitting the top floor again. Her fourth rocket shattered all the windows in an explosion of clear glass and orange flames. Then the sniper fired a bullet right between her eyes. The impact caused her to flip onto her back. She stared up at the sky again. Pleased she hadn't let her brother down. She'd demolished most of the building's upper floors. More than that, she proved to herself, and the gaming world, that a girl can excel at video games. She was a better player than Charlie. But she was also a player with only ten health points left.

"Did I get the bastard?"

"He moved! Oh my God!" Tim cried. "He moved to another window. You spooked him, Emma. I have his exact position. He's on the top floor. Eighth window from the right. Near the middle. He has twenty HP left. You must have injured him."

Emma crept back under the concrete slab and said, "Okay, Charlie. What's next?"

"I don't know."

"What do you mean, you don't know? I'm a sitting duck here."

"My plan was to reveal his position, but now I'm not sure how to kill him."

Emma shrieked, "Don't look at me. I'm all out of rockets."

Charlie was supposed to have all the answers, but he faced a dead end. He couldn't leave the shelter of the tractor without getting shot. Emma had no more rockets. Tim's drone was unarmed. They were stuck. Running out of time.

There's no way out.

But sometimes all you need is a fresh perspective.

CHAPTER 28

WHO SAID MATH WAS USELESS?

Most people don't use geometry in their daily lives. But then again, most people aren't Tim. He remembered a *BattleTheatre* preview article from last month's *Game Informer*. He and Charlie had discussed it at length. According to the article, a drone could see team members as heat signatures. In turn, team members could spot their drone by entering the game's Active Drone Detection mode. Players who hadn't read the article probably wouldn't be aware of these features, especially as drones were extremely rare on the battlefield.

Tim cried, "Why didn't I think of it before?"

"Think of what?" Charlie asked.

Tim traded his fake street-smart persona for a more credible book-smart one. "I can calculate the angle of elevation using the drone."

"Huh?" Charlie said.

"I'm going to fly the drone into one of those broken windows on the top floor," Tim said. "Next, I'll fly through the hallway until I find his room. Then I'll hover right behind him. That'll give you his exact position so we can calculate the best angle to take him out. You'll essentially be aiming directly at my drone that will be right behind him."

"Of course," Charlie replied. "I'll be able to see its position by switching to Active Drone Detection mode. Tim, that's brilliant."

"Jesus Christ," Johnny said. "My brain hurts. I need another bong hit."

Charlie said, "Tim, you're assuming he won't see or hear the drone. He may have planted a motion sensor behind him."

Tim huffed. "You have a better idea?"

"I'm all out of ideas, buddy. Let's just hope he's run out of motion sensors."

Although Dom couldn't participate anymore, he was still paying close attention to the match. "Five minutes before the edge of the circle starts closing."

Tim's left thumb trembled. He grasped it with his right thumb and index finger to try to stop it shaking. Then he set down the controller and wiped his sweaty palms on his shirt. He grabbed the controller again and switched to first-person mode. The drone inched forward. The broken window was large enough for the drone to fly straight through, but there were shards of glass around the splintered frame. Clipping even one of them might alert the sniper. But Tim's hands were steady now, and he expertly guided the drone through the gap like a surgeon using robotic controls for laparoscopic surgery.

"I'm in," he confirmed. "Just looking for the door to the hallway. Looking. Looking. Damn. It's shut. I can't access the hallway. Need to fly back out. Find a different room. Hopefully one that doesn't have a closed door."

"This is gonna give me a heart attack," Charlie said.

Tim's drone exited the window as gracefully as it had flown in. He guided it to the left and through another broken window, but the result was the same: another closed door. The drone whizzed outside again.

Charlie brought up the map to check on the progress of the death circle. "Tim, whatever you're doing, please hurry."

"Every room has a closed door. I see one more cracked window. It's going to be a tight squeeze, but I think I can do it."

The drone hovered in front of the final broken window that wasn't within the sniper's field of vision. Tim eased it forward, lightly tapping it on the remaining intact glass, but the opening was too small.

"I can't do it, guys. The drone won't fit."

"Just back it up and smash through the window," Johnny suggested.

Tim sighed. "That's a dumb idea. The sniper will hear it."

"Not necessarily," Charlie said. "We might be able to mask the sound. What if I throw my two grenades and count down before they explode? You'll just have to smash through the window at the exact moment of the explosions."

"And what if the drone is destroyed as I'm doing that?" Tim asked.

Charlie said, "How fragile does the glass look?"

Tim zoomed in on the spider web of cracks that ran from the tiny opening to the edges. "I guess we'll find out." He moved the drone back ten yards and prepared to go full speed ahead.

"I can't believe our hopes and dreams rest on the durability of that drone," Charlie said.

"And the probability of you not getting shot in the head," Tim said, fully aware that Charlie would have to break cover to toss the grenades. Not to mention that Charlie only had fifteen HP left.

"I guess we don't have a choice. Get ready to fly in when I yell 'now' on the countdown, since it'll take you about a second to reach the window."

"Sounds good."

Charlie made sure nothing but his arm was exposed as he threw the two grenades. A bullet caught him just above the elbow, but that didn't stop him from yelling, "Three... two... one... now!"

Boom! Boom!

The drone crashed through the window, causing hundreds of tiny glass shards to cascade into the room. Tim pressed his right palm to his heart and let out a huge sigh of relief. "The drone is undamaged. And the door is open. Praise the Lord Jesus!"

He piloted the drone through the open door, then turned left down the hallway. According to his calculations, the sniper was just three rooms away. Within seconds, Tim had a clear view of the enemy, crouched down and looking out the window. He had neglected to close the door.

The lump in Tim's throat grew. "He's right in front of me. Holy shit!"

Charlie said, "Tim, take a deep breath. Just go slow and position the drone right behind his head."

Emma whispered, "Don't get too close."

"Moving the drone," Tim confirmed. "Getting closer. God, I hope he doesn't turn around. Okay, I'm right behind him. What now?"

Charlie ran his left hand through his hair before placing his thumb on the right stick of the controller—the one responsible for aiming. He'd spent countless hours playing every game in the *Sniper Elite* and *Sniper: Ghost Warrior* series, calculating range, wind direction and velocity, target elevation, and bullet drop. He'd also played enough of the sniper class in the *Call of Duty* and *Destiny* series to know the intricacies of handling a sniper rifle. But this would be the toughest shot he'd ever had to make.

"Stay in position," he said. "I'm gonna shoot through the window of the small building to hit our target."

"That's your plan?" Johnny said. "No way that will work."

"Stop being so negative, Johnny," Emma said.

Charlie rubbed his chin. "There's no other option. I've got to take the shot from here." He peeked out from under the tractor and aimed his rifle at one of the lower windows of the smaller building. Then he toggled on Active Drone Detection, which displayed green wireframe shapes of the buildings ahead. Everything now looked like the vector graphics from the Atari classic *Battlezone*, which Charlie had played at an old-school arcade. The bright red outline of the drone stood out vividly among the hundreds of green lines. But this was much more difficult than just aiming at the red shape and pulling the trigger. The bullet needed to clear both the front and rear windows of the smaller building, then travel another hundred yards to reach the enemy who was perched in the high-rise behind it. And he would be shooting at an upward angle, so the effect of gravity would be reduced, meaning less bullet drop. Calculating the bullet drop for a non-level shot was notoriously difficult. "Tim, which window am I aiming at?" he asked.

"Standby," Tim said as he switched back to his avatar's view. For a brief moment, he was back with Charlie behind the tractor, able to see the windows as Charlie saw them. Then he toggled back and forth between the drone's view and his avatar's view to try to get the exact location. He did all this within ten seconds, then switched back to the drone's view. He couldn't risk leaving it unattended longer than he had to. "Okay, I think I've got it." He activated the drone's thermal imaging mode, which allowed him to see through the buildings and spot three small, multicolored blobs: Emma, Charlie, and himself. "I can see all three of us from the drone. Make sure you stay in the middle, Charlie. Don't move."

Charlie said, "I'm not going anywhere."

Dom called out. "Two minutes until the circle starts closing in."

The thermal view also showed the exact distance between the drone and the three avatars. Tim zoomed in on Charlie's position with 4X magnification and said, "Stay in that exact position. I'm trying to figure out the distance and height of where you should aim." His brain started to crunch geometrical calculations faster than a supercomputer. "Okay, the distance is one hundred eighty-three meters. You need to shoot at the second-story window. It's one window to the left of where you're currently aiming. If it goes through there, it'll reach the drone."

"My left or your left," Charlie said.

"Yours," Tim said. "I'm not an idiot." Then he added, "Aim ten inches above the bottom of the window. And don't forget to add another four inches to account for the bullet drop."

Charlie aimed fourteen inches above the bottom edge of the window frame. Then he switched back to Active Drone Detection and saw that he was aiming slightly higher than the drone's red outline. It was the angle he wanted to account for the bullet drop. He held his breath. And fired. The bullet pierced through the front window but then stopped dead in its tracks as it struck the concrete wall at the back of the building.

"Did I get him?"

"The bullet didn't go through the rear window," Tim said.

Emma asked. "How do you know?"

"Because I would've seen it shatter."

Charlie sighed. "It must be those extra four inches to account for bullet drop."

"Try it without them," Tim suggested.

Charlie aimed again. This time, ten inches above the bottom edge of the window. After he fired, the bullet sailed through both windows of the small building but hit the masonry above the sniper's window. Luckily, SniperSnake47 never saw or heard it hit the concrete.

Tim pulled out his phone and googled "bullet drop upward angle." As he waited for the results to load, he said, "The back window broke on the small building. But you aimed too high. Wait. What? 'The pull of gravity on bullet drop is reduced if ...' Wait a second, Charlie."

Silence for five seconds.

Dom chimed in, "Whatever math computation you're doing, hurry. The circle's closing in. It's about a minute away."

"Quiet. This shit's not easy," Tim said. "Okay. Charlie, I did a Google search. Since you're shooting at a steep upward angle, the bullet drop is minimal. Probably no more than an inch or two. Try four inches above the bottom of the window."

"Got it."

Charlie lined up his shot precisely four inches above the bottom edge of the window frame. He took another deep breath and held it in. This time, the bullet went through both windows of the small building as well as the sniper's open window, flying mere inches over his head and the drone.

Tim saw the enemy flinch through the drone's camera and yelled, "Shoot just above the bottom of the window. Now!"

The sniper turned to face the drone and lunged at it like a jaguar attacking its prey. Charlie took aim and fired. His bullet grazed the bottom edge of the window frame, sending tiny splinters of wood flying, but it continued on its path through all three windows.

Tim whispered, "The drone. My God. The drone."

"I shot the fucking drone instead of him, didn't I?" Charlie said, squeezing his eyes shut.

"I… I… I can't…" Tim stammered.

Johnny yelled, "Spit it out!"

Tim, still in the drone's first-person view, said, "Red."

Dom yelled, "*Red?* What da fuck does that mean?"

"All I see is red," Tim said. "From all the blood. You got the son of a bitch."

"We got you, you *figlio di puttana*!"

"Tim, you're a genius," Charlie said.

"It's just simple physics and geometry."

"Simple to you," Dom said. "Complicated as fuck to *idioti* like the rest of us."

Both Charlie and Tim had five health points left. Emma had ten. The outer edge of the death circle was now thirty seconds away. One touch from it would mean instant death for all of them. There was nowhere left to run.

"We're the last three players left," Emma said. "What happens if we all get killed by the death zone at the same time? I'm technically not on your team. Does that mean nobody wins?"

"I hadn't thought of that," Charlie said. "I guess… either you kill us… or we kill you. I can't believe we've ended up in this position."

Emma didn't hesitate. "Kill me."

Charlie rubbed his forehead and stretched his neck from side to side. "No."

"You have to. Not just for you, but for your whole team. If I win, I get five thousand dollars, but fifteen thousand will go to some randos I don't even know. I'd rather see the money go to you and your friends. Come on. It's just a quick shot to the head."

"I can't. I can't do it."

"You've got to."

This was it. The moment he'd been waiting for. All he had to do was shoot his sister. The one who'd saved them all. He paused for a moment and said, "We couldn't have done it without you."

"I know," Emma said.

Charlie gripped his controller. *I shouldn't be like this.* He aimed at Emma's head. *This isn't fair.* Then he fired.

A message popped up on the screen of every *Battle Theatre* player around the world:

CONGRATULATIONS! CHI-TOWN CREW WINS THE MIDNIGHT MULTIPLAYER MATCH AND $20,000 IN PRIZE MONEY

"We're gonna be famous," Johnny said.

Dom, talking like a mobster after a jewelry heist, said, "I can't believe you shot your own sister in the head. But *congratulazioni*! I'm still expecting my cut, by the way."

"Yeah, yeah. Don't worry. You'll get your money, Dom Corleone," Charlie said. "Let's give it up for Tim, our amazing drone pilot."

The entire team clapped their hands as Emma yelled, "Woo hoo!"

Johnny said, "Charlie's getting his game collection back."

"Everyone played great. Thanks," Charlie said.

Tim was still clapping. "Give it up for Charlie, our fearless commander."

Charlie asked, "What do we do now?"

Johnny took a big hit from his bong and exhaled into the mic. "We gotta celebrate. This bong has all your names on it."

"I need to sleep," Tim replied. "For a very long time."

"I promised the wife I'd go to church this morning if she left me alone to play *Battle Theatre*," Dom added. "Sorry."

With that, they both disconnected.

"Emma?" Johnny said.

"Maybe another time."

"Charlie?"

"I don't know, Johnny. It's really late."

"Don't leave me hangin', brah."

"We'll celebrate after a well-earned night's rest. I promise."

"Fine. I'm gonna hold you to that."

Charlie logged out.

A few minutes later, he received an email notification from the *Battle Theatre* developers with instructions on how to claim the prize money. He wanted to call Susan and share the good news, but something made him pause. He closed his eyes and leaned back on his couch.

I should be happier than this. I won the tournament, for Pete's sake. She'll forgive me once she hears that I won. Maybe I'll buy her something nice.

His thumb hovered over Susan's name on his phone for nearly a minute. All he had to do was tap the screen, but he couldn't bring himself to do it. The pain in his thumb from the long gaming session seemed trivial compared to the pain of having to justify his actions to her.

CHAPTER 29

THE LATE-NIGHT STREAMER

Sunday, 2:30 a.m. Dom rubbed the back of his neck, his droopy eyes struggling to stay open as he searched YouTube for *Battle Theatre Midnight Multiplayer Match*. At the start of the match, he had pressed the *share* button on his controller so he could record their gameplay and conversation. He'd wanted to preserve the memory of their match, never expecting to win. But now that they had, he sensed an opportunity.

After scrolling through a few preview videos, he found the official match video from the developers, seen from the winning team's perspective. *His* team. He watched the first few minutes, then fast-forwarded to the middle. *It's not here.* He clenched his fists, raised his arms in a V-shaped victory pose, and yelled, "It's not fucking here."

The developers had uploaded a video of the match. Every blade of grass and piece of flying debris was displayed in stunning 4K high-resolution. Orange flames burned, white smoke billowed, and blood-red bodies flung into the air. Dolby Digital 5.1 surround sound rang out a symphony of bullets striking stone, metal, and flesh, accompanied by the room-shaking boom of explosions. But the most crucial element was missing—their in-game chat. The developers didn't have access to it for privacy reasons. But Dom did. And it was gold to him. *The world will want to hear how we won.*

In the past, Dom had uploaded only two obscure videos to his YouTube channel: *Top Ten RPGs of the 90s* and *The Fascinating History of the Game Boy*. Together, they'd generated no more than a thousand views, completely lost in the vast landscape of online video game content and Twitch streams. Dom wasn't about to miss his chance to go viral. He had to post it on YouTube before anyone's first cup of morning coffee, even if it meant getting yelled at by Marie for not waking up in time for church in the morning.

He struggled for a while, unable to post the video because his YouTube and PlayStation accounts wouldn't play nice. His gentle sighs turned into loud grunts, making him sound like a crazed wolf hunting its prey. He bellowed loud enough to wake up Marie, who waddled down the stairs to see lines of text on the TV, unsure of what he was doing.

"You woke me up with all your noise. Just because you lost, doesn't mean you have to be so loud."

"I didn't lose."

Marie rubbed her eyes and said, "Wait. You won? How much?"

"Five thousand dollars."

Marie stomped up and down like she'd just hit the jackpot at the Grand Victoria casino. "We won five thousand dollars… and you're yelling?"

Dom, thinking that Marie was already planning how to spend his newfound money, said, "*We* didn't win anything. *I'm* the one who won,"

"Then what the fuck are you yelling for?"

"I'm trying to post the match on YouTube and it's giving me fucking problems."

"Why are you wasting time with that at this hour? Come to bed."

Dom shouted, "Why do you waste your time shopping at the fucking mall?"

"Do *not* yell at me, Dominic. We talked about your temper."

Dom's temper went nuclear whenever he worked on something unfamiliar. A few Christmases ago, he couldn't assemble a bike that Marie bought for their son. Frustrated, he threw his wrench at the Christmas tree, but it missed all the branches and crashed through the plate-glass window behind it. It was thrown with such force that it ended up in the middle of the street. It was a Christmas miracle that nobody got hurt.

"I'm sorry. You know how I get when I can't figure shit out."

"Yes, I do. You need to control your temper instead of throwing shit through windows," Marie said.

"Well, if I don't figure *this* shit out, the PlayStation is going through the window."

"Oh, please. You love that thing more than your children," Marie said. "Why are you trying to post a video in the middle of the night anyway?"

Dom clenched his teeth and held his breath while grumbling out the side of his mouth. "It needs to be posted tonight because people will be searching for our match in the morning."

"Wait. People watch videos of other people playing video games?"

"Yes, darling."

"I don't get it," Marie said, shaking her head. "That's like going to Thanksgiving dinner and not eating anything. Just sitting there and watching your family eat."

Dom wasn't surprised by her reaction. Most people didn't understand gaming culture. In many ways, he struggled to understand it himself. But video game content on YouTube and streaming platforms like Twitch brought gamers together. Content creators like Ninja and PewDiePie were major celebrities among gamers who came for the gameplay but stayed for the commentary. One minute they would laugh at funny comments, the next they'd bite their fingernails while watching a boss fight. Dom hoped that posting his video would be a springboard for his channel, so he could become a popular content creator himself someday.

"People like watching gaming videos for the commentary. They might wanna hear our in-game chat during the match."

Marie tapped Dom on the shoulder twice. "Well, just remember you're coming to church with me and the kids in less than five hours. And you better not be grumpy. Good night."

Dom raised his eyebrows and said in a high-pitched voice, "Good night, my love."

Thirty minutes later, his tenth Google search gave him his answer. After uploading the video to his desolate YouTube channel, *Dominating Games*, he flopped back into his BarcaLounger and let out a booming sigh. He had won two battles tonight: the tournament and getting his version of the match online. His relatives always looked down on him because he was a maintenance manager, and most people at work ignored him unless something needed to be fixed. Who could have imagined that a maintenance manager would have a dream?

Back in 2006, when Marie got pregnant, he had to find a decent-paying job to support his new family. He worked multiple odd jobs, including one as an exterminator, which he hated. Nothing was more degrading to him than having to drive around in a Toyota Yaris with mouse ears. A year later, he started his career with a small company as a maintenance apprentice, before eventually advancing to supervisor. It was enough to pay the bills. After bouncing around other companies, he landed at Unlimited Horizons, where he met Charlie. It was fulfilling to meet someone who shared his passion for video games.

Plenty of young streamers made money playing games online. Dom never believed his forty-three-year-old ass could compete with them, but he had a treasure trove of video game knowledge in his head. There had to be people other than Charlie who wanted to hear about it. Maybe he'd make a little bit of money off this video. A couple of thousand subscribers and around fifty thousand views would be enough to get him started.

CHAPTER 30

THE AFTERMATH OF WAR

S unday morning. The bright-orange glowing rays of the sun crept through a tiny crack in Charlie's blackout blinds, poking at his eyelids. As soon as he woke up, Susan was the first thing to enter his mind. He thought about all the ways to get her to forgive him. A verbal apology over hot dogs and fries wouldn't be enough. He figured most women love endless mimosas, so taking her to a fancy brunch place might be a good place to start. He half-heartedly raised a fist in the air, trying to remind himself that he was a champion. Out of thousands of multiplayer matches he'd played, from *GoldenEye 007* to *Call of Duty: Black Ops 4*, none had ever come close to delivering the euphoria of winning last night's Midnight Multiplayer Match.

Dom's, Emma's, and Johnny's sacrifices swirled in his head like blades in a blender trying to puree a large piece of frozen pineapple, but producing only tiny amounts of pulp. They had given up their chance to experience glory at the end of the match. And for what? So he could use his winnings to pay off Dimitri and get his games back. *It's all about me.* For a brief moment, he thought about calling the cops to bust Dimitri during the exchange. But doing that would either be hazardous to his health or land him in jail for admitting to the police that he had gambled illegally.

He flung open the blinds, and a thick ray of white light slapped him in the face. He turned his head away to check his phone for messages, but the sun's reflection on the screen burned his retinas again. Like a glaring warning. He blinked half a dozen times before his eyesight returned to normal. Then he scrolled past eleven messages to find the only one from Susan:

> Congratulations on winning your game. I'm happy for you.

Charlie figured she must have searched for the *Battle Theatre* results online. He expected a phone call or at least a longer text. This felt… cold. Susan would have to forgive him after he won five thousand dollars, wouldn't she? Winning the tournament was financial justification for missing her gig as well as a golden ticket to pay off his gambling debt to get his games back.

He clicked on Jasmine's name. Eight messages popped up. He held his breath while reading her increasingly frantic cries of desperation. He let out a sigh, then opened a single text from DuPont:

> Hi Charlie. Jasmine assured me that the assignment is near completion. This pleases me greatly. I knew you had it in you, buddy. Great job. See you on Monday.

Charlie couldn't care less about DoucheBag's message, but Jasmine's worried him. He'd set his phone to silent before embarking on his *Battle Theatre* journey so nothing would disturb his Zen-like state. But now he found her last two messages troubling:

You're probably not the right person to talk to about this, but for some crazy reason my gut tells me you might be. I must be losing my mind.

Please! I need to talk to you.

Charlie had ignored her cries for help. He clasped his hands behind his back and paced back and forth. Preparing. For the wrath of not only Susan but also another woman. He picked up his phone again and noticed that he'd received a voicemail from his father. *Who leaves voicemail messages anymore?* He decided to call his father first since it would be the shortest conversation. Short, but never sweet.

"Hello," Joe said.

"Hey."

"Emma just gave me the news. Congratulations. She told me how she was there waiting with the boat to help your team. It's so cool that you and your sister were playing with each other. I can't believe your team won."

Charlie rolled his eyes and said, "That we did."

Joe took a sip of whiskey. "Good job."

Charlie thrust his phone away from his ear, scowling at it. He cocked his hand back, ready to fling the phone across the kitchen table. For as long as he could remember, his father had always made him feel ashamed of playing video games. And now he was congratulating him? For what? For all the design notes and mod levels he'd created for *Counter-Strike*, *Star Wars: Knights of the Old Republic*, and *Half-Life* fifteen years ago? Or for the D he'd received in pre-algebra, which had led to his PC being confiscated for an entire month? His father's words had been etched into his subconscious: "If you're not smart enough to handle pre-algebra, how will you handle regular algebra in high school next year?

And you want to make video games? You know you need to be good at math, especially calculus and trigonometry, to do that. You'll never stop playing enough to actually make them." But that's the thing about the subconscious—it locks away painful words in a sealed vault until insecurity floats them to the surface with no idea how they got there.

Charlie set down his phone and put it on speaker. If he could have punched his father through the screen, he would have.

"Well? Say something," Joe said.

Charlie paused for a few seconds, then said, "I gotta go. Talk to you later."

"Wait. Wait. Wait. What's wrong?"

"Nothing."

"You should be happy."

Charlie shook his head. "I am."

"You don't sound like it."

"Look. We don't need to talk. You called to congratulate me. Thanks a lot, but I gotta go." Charlie hovered his finger over the red button on his phone, ready to disconnect the call.

"Please don't hang up."

"What?" Charlie said.

"Err… I dunno."

"If you don't have anything else to say, then we—"

"Should celebrate," Joe said, raising his whiskey glass in the air.

Charlie said, "The last thing I wanna do is celebrate with you."

"Well, then, celebrate with your teammates."

"What are you getting at?"

"We'll throw a party."

Charlie pouted like a child. "Why?"

"It's a great accomplishment. You deserve to have fun with your friends. Let me do this for you."

Charlie despised this lame attempt to bond with him. He knew that Joe wanted to celebrate the prize money, not the skill it took to win it. Winning cash was a language Joe understood, despite the hundreds of basketball games he'd lost on. Charlie's gut told him that his father would never have offered to throw a party if there was no prize money involved.

He didn't value the same macho traits that Joe cherished. To his mind, parents who acted tough were often the weakest. Too afraid to face their own emotions or support their children's passions. Worried about what others would think if their son wasn't on the varsity basketball team or, even better, played linebacker in high school. Sacking quarterbacks and bagging cheerleaders was more respected than designing an entire digital world. By contrast, the only macho hero in Charlie's life was his onscreen avatar. Brave, valiant, and fearless. Games were his comfort zone and provided the stability he never got from his father. When he stayed at his father's house on weekends, he would just lock himself in his room and play all day. His father only checked on him when it was time to eat. They barely spoke to each other. The only joyful memory from his parents' divorce was receiving a Game Boy Advance SP that Christmas. Games were predictable, consistent, and safe. Joe was volatile, broken, and insecure.

Nevertheless, Charlie had to admit that a party would be the perfect way to thank his team. He might even get to meet Tim in person. Three years was a long time to wait, especially given the amount of time they spent together online. Then there was Emma. Charlie went online and bought her the jeans she'd told him she couldn't afford. But she deserved so much more. After all, she had helped his team win twenty thousand dollars.

A huge celebration with friends and family would also allow him to show Susan the fruits of his labor and that missing her gig had been a wise decision. Maybe he could buy her a nice gift with whatever was left over after he'd paid off Dimitri? Then Johnny could get her so high at the party that she'd forget how angry she was at him. Oh, and an apology. He couldn't forget about that.

"Fine. We'll have a party," Charlie told his father. "We should have it at Francisco's. I want to give him some business since he helped me realize that this dumb work assignment is impossible."

"I'll call him and let you know what he says."

"Just make sure you mention my name. He'll take good care of us," Charlie said.

He hung up without thanking Joe. He wasn't about to give him the satisfaction. It was only a party. A single step on a long, winding road to a possible relationship with his father. One he wasn't even sure he wanted. Or needed.

CHAPTER 31

JASMINE AND THE JAGBAG

Time to call Jasmine. Charlie cracked his neck from side to side like an extra in a martial arts movie preparing to get pummeled. She was going to go ballistic when she found out he had ignored his work to play in a video game tournament, especially since she'd offered to help him with the assignment back on Friday. He would just tell her that Francisco's financially savvy brother had said the assignment couldn't be finished on time. Getting high with Johnny yesterday had been a "fuck you" to DuPont, not Jasmine, but he was sure she'd think differently because of all the text messages he had ignored.

It wasn't like he was going to do a mad dash and try to finish the assignment today anyway. He would simply tell her the truth and try to convince her that they should both stand up to DuPont about the assignment. Two against one would be much better than facing him alone.

Charlie dialed Jasmine's number, half-hoping it would go to voicemail.

She answered on the first ring. "Charlie, my God, I thought you were dead or something."

"Sorry for not calling you back. I was…" Charlie paused and squeezed his eyes shut, bracing for a deafening reaction.

Four seconds of silence.

"Hello?" Jasmine asked. "Charlie, are you there?"

His next words were "playing in a video game tournament," but he said them so fast that it sounded like he was saying "playing in a vinegar determinant." He held his phone away from his ear to protect his hearing from the inevitable onslaught.

"What was that?" Jasmine asked.

Charlie swallowed hard and paced around his apartment. "There was this little tournament. Actually, a really big video game tournament last night. My friends and I have been looking forward to it for years. We needed to practice."

Jasmine's heart fluttered. "Let me get this straight. You blew off your assignment for a... video game?"

Charlie curled his lip and spoke out the side of his mouth. "Is that bad?"

"No, it's not bad. It's a monumental fucking disaster!" Jasmine yelled. "I told you my ass was on the line. I can't believe you did this to me."

"Did I mention that my team won twenty thousand dollars?"

"Wait. You won twenty grand?"

"My team of four did. So, we get five thousand each. Actually, it was more like a team of five, since my sister Emma showed up and saved us all." For the first time, Charlie considered splitting the prize money five ways. Then again, he'd have to get Tim, Johnny, and Dom to agree to that. *I can't do that to my friends.*

"Well, you still have the rest of today to work on the assignment. You just need to hunker down and see how far you can get."

Charlie whispered, "Jasmine, I like you. You're always so nice to me at work. I like our chats and the funny videos we share during lunch. You bought me Starbucks last week, which I really appreciate. So, it hurts me to say this..." He channeled Johnny's attitude, raised his voice, and said, "But fuck the assignment. And fuck DuPont. He almost robbed me of not only all the joy I felt after winning but also of five thousand dollars. And for what? A stupid assignment that's probably not even time sensitive. I've never heard of him giving a weekend assignment to anyone else."

Jasmine huffed. "How can you know that? Maybe it happens all the time?"

"Nope. He singled me out. Probably because he knew I wouldn't say no, since I'm still at the bottom of the totem pole. Even after working there for three years. Do you know I've never said no to him? Ever. Well, it's time to say no now. He took it too far with this impossible assignment. What I wanna know is why he singled you out as well?"

Jasmine's cheeks puffed up like two balloons before she let out a breath of discomfort. "I don't have the answer to that."

Charlie said, "Your text message said I might be the right person to talk to. About what exactly?" There were ten full seconds of silence before he asked, "Why didn't he just give *you* the assignment? You're obviously more qualified to complete it than I am. Why is he tying your fate with mine?"

Jasmine sobbed like a dying car engine. "Because he's jealous of us."

"But there is no *us*. Please tell me what's going on."

"He sees us joking around," Jasmine said. "Do you remember when I had my arm around your shoulders while you showed me that video of the guy slipping on ice a few weeks ago?"

Charlie wanted to play it cool and say he didn't know what she was talking about, but of course he did. If there's one thing a man never forgets, it's when a woman other than his wife or girlfriend puts her arm around him. In any way, shape, or form. At the time, the gesture sent a chill down his spine. But deep down, he knew they were no more than work friends. Especially as it had never happened again.

"I kind of remember," he said. "But what the hell does that have to do with DuPont? Are you, like, dating him?"

"Oh, God. No," Jasmine said, disgusted. "It's just…" She paused again. "I could get in a lot of trouble for telling you this."

"I'm probably getting fired on Monday," Charlie said, "so anything you say won't come back to bite you. And even if that doesn't happen, I would never betray your trust. Your secret is safe with me."

Jasmine grabbed her shirt collar and pulled it up over her face. "DuPont's pressuring me to sleep with him."

A fifty-six-year-old executive trying to sleep with his twenty-nine-year-old coworker made Charlie sick to his stomach. "What did he do?"

"He always invites me to go to this local neighborhood bar after work for happy hour."

"Have you ever gone?"

"No. But then he punishes me with tons of extra work, like putting me in charge of you this weekend. He said it was a test of my leadership abilities or some such bullshit," Jasmine said. "He was insanely jealous when he saw me with my arm around you that day. Asked me why I would want to hang out with such a loser."

Charlie slumped back onto his couch and muttered, "That bastard."

"There's more," Jasmine said.

"Oh my God. What?"

Jasmine hadn't told anyone about the Atlanta conference. It was just too painful. But now she gathered her courage and said, "He tried to get me alone in his room. I'm pretty sure he expected me to sleep with him."

"Jesus. Can't you go to Janet from HR about this?"

"I can't. He's best friends with Janet. She'll just sweep it under the rug."

Charlie said, "But it's sexual harassment."

Jasmine rested her chin on her clenched fist. "Who are they gonna believe? A white male vice president making half a million a year, or a young black woman who's barely cracking sixty thousand. If he finds out I reported him to Janet, everything will get a lot worse for me."

"Man. Now I'm really glad I didn't bust my ass for that son of a bitch. I wish there was a way we could get back at him."

Jasmine laid her cheek against the soft gel of her mouse pad. "He'll probably fire you, but he won't fire me. He'll just make my life a living hell. I swear he gets off on it. It's like he's waiting for me to break, so he can get what he wants."

"Why don't you quit?"

Jasmine had thought about quitting every day for the past three months. Every morning, it was the same. The dread of going to work made her stomach queasy and her head throb. "I can't afford to. I need this job. I also think he would do everything in his power to prevent me from getting another job by getting Janet to tell anyone who called for references that I was 'not eligible for rehire,' which is like a death sentence."

"I had no idea he was such good friends with her," Charlie said. "Fucking HR. So much for it being an independent department." He paused for a couple of seconds. "I know you need the money, but I still think you should quit. You can't let the asshole have this unrelenting grip on your life."

DuPont's control and manipulation ensnared Jasmine like a fly in a spider's web. Any attempt to escape only made her more stuck. She wanted to tell Charlie that DuPont had drugged her in Atlanta, but suspected he would go straight to the police if she did. She wasn't ready for that, so she said, "Let me think about it. I gotta go. I'm sorry I dragged you into my mess."

"This is not your fault," Charlie insisted. "I wish I could do something to help, but finishing this assignment is the last thing that will solve your problem with him. He'll just find another way to make your life miserable."

Charlie thought that free pizza and Italian beef might be just what she needed to get her mind off her troubles. "One more thing…"

"What's that?"

"I'm thinking of hosting a party tonight to celebrate my *Battle Theatre* victory. You should come along."

"Oh, I don't know," she said. "I won't know anyone there."

"Dom, the maintenance manager from work, will be there."

"I barely know him."

There was a long pause before Charlie added, "Tell you what, bring a friend. Maybe I can set up my online buddy, Tim. He's looking to meet a nice girl."

"Let me guess… Tim's black."

"How'd you know?"

"And you figured all my friends are black, too."

"Tim's a great guy," Charlie said. "I don't think he's ever dated a girl. This could be my way of thanking him for helping us win the tournament. Sorry if I offended you."

"It's fine. I just find it funny." Jasmine chuckled. "This always happens with you white boys. Trying to hook up your one black friend with a friend of the only other black person you know."

"I have plenty of black friends," Charlie said.

"Really?"

"Well, no. Not really. But isn't that what all of us white boys say when confronted with how many black friends we have?"

Jasmine laughed again. "At least you're honest."

"What do you say? Free food. Free booze. Free weed, courtesy of my buddy Johnny."

"Where's the party?"

"Francisco's Bar and Pizzeria. My father's talking to the owner right now to see if he can accommodate us. I'll let you know the details once he's confirmed everything."

"I might stop by with my friend if I have the time."

"Fair enough. Hope to see you both there."

CHAPTER 32

MAKING PLANS

C harlie meandered around his apartment like a malfunctioning robot, trying to think of where to take Susan. Then, it hit him: LeFleur's. The fanciest, and most expensive, brunch place in town. Forgiveness always comes at a price. And in Charlie's case, it would be sixty dollars a plate. Ninety with infinite mimosas. But it had to be done. Thanks to a last-minute cancellation, he secured a reservation for noon.

Charlie had played more than three thousand video games and pressed the buttons on his controller millions of times. But the hardest button to press was Susan's name on his phone. Once he did, there would be no turning back. She was going to be mad, but maybe the allure of dining at LeFleur's could diffuse her anger.

Should I call Dom, Tim, or Johnny instead? Or a couples therapist...

Charlie's thumb trembled as it hovered over her name. He was more nervous than he'd been when lining up the winning shot in *Battle Theatre*. Maybe it would all be fine. Maybe their relationship could be fixed with nothing more than a full belly of fancy food and mimosas. A gesture of love could be the metaphorical dessert.

The real war was about to begin.

"Hello?"

Charlie said, "Hi," followed by a lame, "How are you?"

"I'm okay."

Charlie waited for Susan to continue talking, but silence followed for a grueling four seconds. Finally, he said, "Thanks for the congratulations text earlier."

Susan held the silence for another four seconds before saying, "You're welcome." She was playing the two-word response game with him. The sign of a woman scorned.

"I'm sorry I missed your gig. I know it was important to you. Can you forgive me?"

"Thank you for apologizing, but an apology isn't going to fix what's wrong with our relationship."

"Okay. Then tell me what I need to do."

Susan sighed. "You're not emotionally available, and I don't know if you ever will be. We do things together, but I can tell you're just waiting for me to leave so you can go back to playing your games. I'm just a placeholder for your obsession."

"That's not true. I love spending time with you. How can you say I'm not emotionally available? And why haven't you mentioned any of this before?"

Susan shook her head. "I shouldn't have to, Charlie. I can *feel* that you hate spending time with me. It's in your body language and how you get squirmy whenever we go shopping. It's like you can't wait to get back to your apartment to play your games."

"At least ninety percent of men get squirmy when they go shopping with their girlfriends. Guys hate shopping."

"Not all guys."

Charlie made a feeble attempt to lighten the mood. "I guess gay guys love shopping."

"That's not funny," Susan said. "I'm sorry, but I need someone who puts me first. Why would I want to be in a relationship with someone who puts me last?"

"I don't put you last. Can we please continue this conversation in person? I've made a reservation for us at a great brunch place downtown. I'd like to see you."

Susan pressed her hands to her temples. "What's the point?"

"Please," Charlie said. "Let me make it up to you."

Susan didn't say anything for ten seconds.

Charlie's heart dropped into his stomach. "Please say—"

"Fine. Where is this place?"

"In the Loop," Charlie said, referring to Chicago's bustling downtown area. "It's called LeFleur's. Meet you there at noon?"

"Sure."

"I love you," Charlie said.

Susan replied with "I'll see you soon."

Charlie rested his face on his closed fist as he stared at his phone. *She didn't say "I love you."* The conversation was just a preview for the main event. Charlie was Marvis Frazier facing Mike Tyson. Most people don't even know who Marvis Frazier is because Iron Mike knocked him out in twenty-five seconds flat. And this afternoon, it would be Charlie Frazier vs. Susan Tyson at LeFleur's for the Relationship Championship of the World.

But first, he had to call Tim and invite him to the party. Convincing him to show up would be tougher than winning a late-game battle in *Tactics Ogre*, but it would be worth it if it forced him out of his cocoon and into the arms of a woman.

Four rings later, Tim answered. "Hello."

"Timmy, baby. How you feelin'?"

"Still trying to process what happened last night. When I woke up, it took me a full minute to realize it wasn't a dream."

"My father is throwing a party tonight to celebrate our victory. Please tell me you'll come."

Tim fidgeted in his chair, his throat tightening. "Yeah, I don't think so."

"Why not?"

Tim hesitated before saying, "Parties aren't my thing."

"Maybe this will convince you," Charlie said. "I'm pretty sure one of my coworkers is bringing one of her girlfriends to meet you. I think the two of you might hit it off."

Tim's voice, bitter with sarcasm, said, "Oh, right. She'll fall in love with me, no problem."

"Of course she will. You're a catch."

Tim's head spun, making him dizzy with contempt. "Why you trying to set me up? I didn't ask for that."

"You kinda did with all our online chats about your perfect date scenario."

Tim, annoyed and irritated, said, "That was months ago."

"Love never dies," Charlie said. "Don't worry. I'll make it easy and introduce you."

"Do you even know anything about this girl?"

"No. But Jasmine is kinda cute, so I'm sure her friends are too."

Tim adjusted his glasses on the bridge of his nose with his index finger. "That's a common fallacy. I'm still not coming."

"Why not? What's the worst that could happen?"

"Listen, Charlie. I know you mean well, but you've never met her. And, even more concerning, you've never met *me*. I could be a five-hundred-pound guy."

"Your face looks skinny."

Tim pushed himself away from his desk so hard that his wheelchair didn't stop rolling until it collided with one of his tower displays. One of his *Halo* action figures toppled over, knocking the tiny gun out of its hand. "That's not the point. People get matched up over similar interests. No one goes on blind dates anymore. This isn't the nineties."

"Look. You never know. She might be the girl of your dreams. Maybe one day you'll get married in *World of Warcraft*," Charlie said. They'd both watched real-life weddings in that game, complete with a priest, guild members, and a rocking DJ spinning dance music at the reception.

"I appreciate the invitation, but I'm not going. And that's final," Tim said. He placed his phone on speaker and flung it onto his desk.

"Dude, what the hell? Are you really five hundred pounds? If not, then you have no excuse. Unless you're, like, deformed or something…"

Tim hunched over and wheeled himself back to the desk. "Don't be an asshole."

"I'm sorry, but I really want you to come. The only way to learn about women is by putting yourself in social situations, not avoiding them."

Tim crossed his arms and said, "I'll pass."

"Ugh. If you don't want to talk to her, then fine. Don't talk to her. But this is a chance to meet the rest of the crew. If you're not there, I'll be upset, and so will Dom and Johnny. It won't be the same without you. Please come."

Tim gripped the armrests of his wheelchair, bowed his head, pressed his lips together, and mumbled, "Fine. I'll think about it."

"Dress sharp."

"I'm crazy to even consider this. Goodbye." He tapped the red button on his phone and spun his chair around to see his mother, Vonda, standing in the doorway. *Of course, the one time I forgot to close my door.*

"Hi, sweetie. Who was that on the phone?"

Tim groaned. "Charlie."

Vonda had heard Tim shout out Charlie's name so often during their late-night online matches that she felt like she knew him. "Was he calling about last night's match?"

"Yeah."

"Did he say anything else?"

Tim punched his thigh hard enough to leave a bruise. "You were eavesdropping, weren't you?"

Vonda placed her hands on her hips and said, "Yes, I was. Is he trying to set you up with a girl?"

"Can't I have some privacy?" Tim yelled. "Why are you sneaking into my room and listening to my conversations?"

"Baby. You left your door half open."

"He's throwing a party tonight to celebrate our victory. He's invited his coworker, who's bringing her friend to meet me."

"Well, that's very nice of him," Vonda said.

"Mom, it'll be a disaster."

"This one might be different."

"No, Mom. She won't. She'll be just like the rest of them. Nobody wants anything to do with me," Tim said, his head drooping.

Vonda rested her hand on his shoulder. "That's not true, honey. You're such a sweet boy. Any girl would thank her lucky stars to find someone like you."

Tim flinched away from his mother and slapped his other thigh. "Girls aren't looking for a sweet boy. They're looking for a strong, confident man. Which I'm clearly not. Who the hell is gonna want me like this?"

Vonda lifted Tim's chin with her open hand. "Don't be sad, honey. Be happy that your friend is giving you a chance to meet someone. Don't run away from your fear."

Tim looked at his mother with eyes as slippery as freshly polished glass. "I can't run anywhere. That's the problem. You know I'm gonna be judged. God, the look on this girl's face when she sees me…"

"She's going to see a beautiful, caring soul. You'd be surprised how many girls would love to have someone like you in their lives."

Tim wasn't buying what his mother was selling. Acting like he was some flawless, compassionate jewel who could melt women's hearts and make their panties fly off. He had no game. He was a geek with a disability. Isolated from the world. Taking online classes and working part-time from home as a customer service rep made it tough to form real connections with anyone. Vonda did her best as a mother. Tried to make her son feel special and unique. But that doesn't get the girl.

"At the very least, you'll finally meet Charlie and your other teammates," Vonda added.

Tim's head dropped back to his chest. "That's what I'm afraid of."

Vonda knelt in front of her son, grabbed the chair's armrests, and pulled him closer to her. "They'll love you no matter what. *They* love games. *You* love games. Maybe you can love people, too. Go and have fun. And don't worry about what a girl you've never met might think of you."

Tim looked into his mother's big brown eyes. She wasn't turning away without an answer. "I can't believe I'm considering this."

"That's my brave boy," Vonda said.

"I'm not a boy anymore."

"Well, then, prove it and take a chance."

Tim stared out the window. It was time to go out into the real world and risk losing everything—his pride, his friends, his dignity. He let out a sigh and said, "Can you find my dress shirt and black tie?"

Vonda smiled and said, "Gladly."

CHAPTER 33

VIRAL DENIAL

C harlie spent more time than usual in the shower. Thinking. About what he was going to say to Susan to convince her that their relationship was fine despite his gaming habit. After all, he did nice things for her from time to time. On her birthday, he gave her a necklace along with a thoughtful note and a single rose, expressing how special she was to him. He also gave her a single rose on Valentine's Day and Sweetest Day, even though the latter was just a card manufacturers' marketing ploy for money. He wanted their brunch to be a positive experience and was prepared to focus on all the good times they'd shared so he could emerge victorious from the Charlie vs. Susan championship bout.

After he dried himself, he checked his phone and saw that Dom had left a voicemail just as his father had earlier. *What is it with old people and voicemail?* Charlie tapped the screen and heard, "I posted the video of our match on YouTube last night. Call me."

Charlie was confused. The official video was already posted on the *BattleTheatre* website. Why would Dom post it again?

When Dom picked up, Charlie said, "Got your message."

"How you feeling, champ?"

"Pretty good. I'm meeting Susan in about an hour for brunch."

"Did you put on a lot of ChapStick for all the ass kissing you're gonna be doing."

"Very funny," Charlie said. "So, why'd you post the video? The *Battle Theatre* devs already did that."

Dom uttered the only French he knew. "*Au contraire, mon cheri.* The official *Battle Theatre* video doesn't include our voice chat. Mine does. I was expecting a couple of thousand views. Guess how many I have?"

"I don't know. Ten thousand?"

"I have over ten thousand *comments*. And half a million views. Half a fucking million!"

Charlie responded with a high-pitched "Get the fuck out of here."

"I just sent you the link. Most of the comments are positive. People love it. Except this one asshole who said we suck and got extremely lucky."

"Probably SniperSnake47," Charlie said. "I didn't even think about recording our chat during the match."

"Winning the tournament was incredible. But *this*? This is like a dream come true. I've always wanted one of my videos to go viral, but I never thought any of them would become this popular."

"You should post some of those retro games you're always raving about. Strike while the iron's hot. I mean, what's stopping you?"

"I don't know," Dom said. "My job, my kids, a nagging wife…"

"You know a lot about gaming. And you've got charisma. You could be really good at this."

"You think so?"

"I know so," Charlie said. "I have a feeling you'll get a lot more views by the end of the day. I'm really happy for you. I'm sorry, but I gotta get off the phone. I have to get ready for my brunch date with Susan."

"Want some advice?"

"More ChapStick?"

"Well, yeah. That goes without saying. But also…" Dom's tone changed. "A woman wants to feel special. Make her feel like she's the most important person in the world."

Charlie paused, then said, "Don't worry. I have a plan to do just that."

"See, you didn't need my advice after all."

"One more thing. My father is planning a party for us tonight at Francisco's."

"Awesome. Count me in."

"I gotta go. We'll talk later."

Charlie knew he had to look his best. Convincing Susan to forgive him was going to be a tough task. Nothing could be left to chance. He wore a gray wool blazer, black dress slacks, and a hunter-green shirt paired with a red tie. Might as well look festive for the holiday season. He sprayed himself and the blazer with Cool Water cologne, then looked at himself in the mirror. He resembled a seasonal employee at Macy's. He glanced at his phone: 11:00 a.m. He called the restaurant and they confirmed that the surprise for Susan was all set.

Charlie thought back to all the single roses he'd given her on special occasions. She had loved the first one, but her excitement faded with each given rose. He clearly needed a new strategy. So, this time, he planned to present her with…

Well, let's just say it was more than one rose.

CHAPTER 34

THE BRUNCH CRUNCH

High noon. As soon as Charlie walked into LeFleur's, he gazed at the dozen Greek columns, each one as thick as a sequoia and decorated with bright green and red flowers. Intricate branches hung down from the ceiling, adorned with hundreds, if not thousands, of sparkling Christmas lights. A stack of chopped wood, neatly arranged in a wire frame, stood ten feet tall. White, red, and green candles were lit along the top of the glossy marble retaining walls that led from the foyer to the main dining area. Charlie felt proud of himself for choosing such an elegant establishment.

He went to the men's room to fix his hair. Seconds after he walked out, he saw her. Standing in front of the maître d's desk. More beautiful than ever. A stunning ivory dress with delicate white lace hugged her shapely figure. Her shimmering gold necklace and emerald charm sparkled under the bright overhead lights. Charlie's throat felt dry and coarse, his stomach uneasy. His legs almost buckled as he walked toward her.

"You look incredible. Wow!"

"Thanks. You look nice too. I'm surprised you got dressed up," Susan said.

"I mean, they have a dress code here, so I figured I'd better follow the rules this one time," Charlie said, hoping to get a laugh that never came.

The maître d' escorted them to their table near the center of the restaurant. This was fine dining at its best, at least for Charlie, whose usual diet consisted of burgers, pizza, and Italian beef.

They looked at each other for fifteen seconds without saying a word.

Charlie started the conversation in the worst possible way. "So, how was your gig last night?"

She squinted and said, "A disaster. Thanks for asking."

"It couldn't have been that bad." Another bad response.

"My voice cracked. Then I forgot the words. In front of everyone. Who's going to sign a band with a singer who can't sing?"

"I'm so sorry," Charlie said.

Susan caressed her fine china plate. "I needed you there, and you let me down."

If Charlie hadn't already felt like shit, he did now.

"I wanted to be there. I really did, but—"

"Your game was more important. I get it," she said, sounding like a wounded bird.

"If it was just a normal night of gaming with the boys, I would've canceled. But this was a once-in-a-lifetime tournament. Gaming companies never do this. It was worth it. We won twenty thousand dollars."

"So, the fact that you won some money means I should forgive you? What if you'd lost? Would it have been worth it then?"

Charlie didn't know how to respond. Fortunately, the waiter came to take their order. Charlie ordered the brunch special for two, which included cream-cheese-stuffed blueberry French toast, a spinach and truffle omelet, candy-coated bacon, and a selection of fine pastries. As the waiter walked away, Charlie was tempted to answer Susan with a resounding "Yes!" Instead, he told her what she wanted to hear. "I guess not."

"At least we agree on something," Susan said.

They sat in silence for more than a minute. Charlie knew he couldn't justify his participation in the tournament or his absence from the gig. At least not to Susan. So, he just continued down the path of telling her what she wanted to hear. "I messed up. I'm sorry."

Susan rubbed her thick, silky napkin and said, "I'm sorry too. Sorry that you love your games more than you love me. You don't need me, Charlie."

"That is so not true. Look, maybe I've been a bit selfish this weekend. But I thought you were fine with the way things were, because you've never said anything about hating my games."

Susan banged her fist on the table softly enough so only Charlie could hear. "Oh my God. I have said something. More than once. You just never hear me. Also, let's be clear, I don't hate your games. I hate the amount of energy and time you devote to them. You do the bare minimum in our relationship."

Charlie leaned forward and said, "In what way? Give me an example."

"You canceled that double date I arranged with my friend from work last month."

"Yeah, because I was trying to beat a world record for a speedrun. And I came pretty damn close."

Susan shook her head. "What else? Lemme see. You didn't get me a gift last Sweetest Day."

"I gave you a rose and a card."

"Once again, the bare minimum for me to throw in my Dream Bin," Susan said.

Charlie had told the restaurant owner he would raise his hand as a signal for the waiters to bring Susan's surprise to the table. Now seemed the perfect time. *Let's see her call this the bare minimum.* He raised his right hand high and said, "I'm actually glad you said that."

One of the waiters approached the table with a dozen bright red roses intertwined with tiny white baby's breath and placed them in Susan's arms. Then another arrived with twelve more roses. Then another. And another. By the time the sixth waiter had dropped off his bouquet, Susan had seventy-two roses in her lap. Charlie pulled out his cell phone to take a picture, but before he had a chance, she pitched all the flowers aside like a worker at Seattle's Pike Place Fish Market. The waiters exchanged confused glances, but then just smiled as they walked away.

Susan's cold-steel scowl was enough to pierce Charlie's heart as she said, "Why did you do that?"

"You keep saying I only do the bare minimum. I'm trying to show that you deserve more than that. I thought you'd be happy."

Susan sat quietly for about thirty seconds. Then her eyes started to fill with tears. "You're not making this easy for me."

Charlie sank into his chair, slid his hands over his knees, and puffed out his cheeks. What should have been a joyful moment was turning into a horrific nightmare. His insides twisted like garlic knots at Francisco's. *Is she breaking up with me?*

Susan turned her head away from Charlie and said, "I shouldn't have reacted like that, but this was very unexpected. Your idea of this brunch is very different from mine."

Charlie whispered, "What the fuck," under his breath. He lowered his head like he'd just been pummeled ten times by Sister Friede in *Dark Souls 3*. He was fighting a battle he knew he couldn't win. No piece of armor or ability stat boost could protect him from what was coming. All the gaming know-how in the world was powerless to stop it. "I was hoping you'd see the roses and realize that you're not the bare minimum to me. I love you, Susan. I thought you knew that."

"I know you love me. And you're the kindest person I know. But your games will always be in the way. When you play them, you barely even notice that I'm there. I just don't think you know what you want out of a relationship."

"I want *you*," Charlie said. "I love *you*."

"Let me say this in a way that you'll understand," Susan said. "You think everything should just fall into place like *Tetris* blocks, with no effort on your part. Instead of growing, it feels like we're dying. And you're probably going to lose your job on Monday. All because of a video game."

Charlie entirely missed the point and asked, "So, you're breaking up with me because I'm about to get fired?"

"I don't care if you get fired. And I don't care if you quit. I needed you last night, but you weren't there for me. You won your game, but you quit on me."

Charlie raised both hands in the air. "What do you want from me? It feels like you're being a bit needy. You want me to stop playing games, work my dead-end job, and become some boring guy like that Mr. Wonderful doll who kisses his girlfriend's ass."

When the string on the doll's back gets pulled, it makes comments like:

"You're going shopping by yourself? How about if I tag along and carry your bags?" or "The ball game really isn't that important. I'd rather spend time with you."

"I just want a partner," Susan said. "I don't think you're capable of being that anymore. And what kills me is that you never used to be like this. You get lost in your games and don't care about anyone else. I mean, when was the last time you even called your parents? Don't you think they're sad that you never call them?"

"I had no idea you felt this way," Charlie said. "Sometimes I need to be beaten over the head before I get it. As for my parents... I mean, my mom calls me sometimes, but my father only calls when there's an emergency. So, why should I call him?"

"Maybe that's why you're the way you are," Susan said.

One of the waiters returned and set their food on the table. A venerable feast for two. Charlie pressed his clenched fist into his right cheek. His eyes stayed fixed on the French toast. They both remained silent for a full minute.

Susan spoke first. "I know you're a good person, but you're not invested in me or our relationship. You were always my priority, but I wasn't yours."

"So, what happens now?" Charlie said.

"I think you know the answer to that."

"Are you sure about this? I can cut down on my gaming."

"You'll just end up resenting me. I couldn't live with that," Susan said. "It's better that we just go our separate ways."

Charlie continued to stare at the French toast as he thought about all the asshole guys in the world who cheat on women. All the guys who stay out late. Drinking. Belittling their girlfriends. Charlie didn't do any of that. Yet, here he was—getting dumped.

He didn't touch his food. If he had, he probably would have thrown up.

Susan didn't eat anything either. She sprang from her chair and said, "I'm sorry you spent so much on this. Maybe it would have been enough for another girl. But it's not enough for me. I hope you find someone. Or, if you decide to be alone, then I guess that's fine too."

And with that, she was gone. Out of Charlie's life forever.

CHAPTER 35

THE LIGHT IN THE DARKNESS

C harlie returned to his lifeless apartment. The drawn blackout shades reflected his bleak mood. No artwork on the walls. No photos of him and Susan. No plants on the windowsill. He might as well have been living in a dungeon. At least that would have some character, with its stone walls, Gothic windows, and Victorian metal bars. His apartment was a stark contrast to the bright, colorful, open game world that he loved to escape to. The only place where he was truly free.

He thought about playing a few more matches of *Battle Theatre*, or maybe some *Hollow Knight*, but it didn't feel right to start gaming now. The idea didn't make him feel safe and comfortable. Instead, it was a reminder of what he'd sacrificed for the "love of the game." He didn't have enough love left over to give Susan the attention she deserved. The Midnight Multiplayer Match had simply been a manifestation of the underlying problem in their relationship. *Just one more level and we'll go out to dinner. I'm in the middle of an important match.* There was a place for playing games, but they could never be a replacement for someone who loved him. He could have saved their relationship if he'd found a healthy way to incorporate them, but he let them become an obsession. He wept. It was supposed to be the best day of his life. A day that began with an improbable *Battle Theatre* victory, followed by a grand celebration with Susan and all his friends.

When did I get so empty inside?

Charlie opened his email to see interview requests from IGN and Kotaku, but he had about as much enthusiasm for that as he did for DuPont's work assignment. He never called them back. He didn't care about fame. He didn't even care about games right now. All he could think about was holding Susan in his arms, telling her how sorry he was, and swearing that he would take on the most dangerous quest and risk his life against the end-game boss just to be with her for a few moments longer. It would have made a great ending to a video game. But in this real-life game, the princess was not only in another castle. She tossed Mario aside and ran off with Bowser because he had more ambition.

Charlie's phone vibrated. The caller ID read "Joe." He'd be damned if he ever listed him as "Dad" on his contacts list.

Before his father reached the second syllable of "Hello," Charlie said, "Cancel the party."

"What do you mean?"

"I don't want it."

"Yeah, but I already—"

"Just cancel the fucking party. Bye."

Charlie flung his phone into the cushions on his couch.

After ninety minutes of hating himself and wanting to smash every plate and glass in his apartment, Emma snapped him out of his trance with a phone call. "What's this about you canceling the party?"

Charlie closed his eyes. "I don't feel like talking. I gotta go."

Emma raised her voice and said, "I thought we were pals."

Charlie raised his voice even louder. "I said I don't feel like talking."

"You know what? You never feel like talking with me. Even online. How many times have I invited you to play *Fortnite*?"

"I've told you before, I don't like *Fortnite*."

"Yeah, but I do, Charlie. *I* do," Emma said before hanging up on him.

Charlie tossed his phone aside again and shouted, "God! What is wrong with these women?"

He cracked open a can of Dr Pepper, took a monster swig, and called Johnny. He needed to talk to one of his brothers.

Johnny, a secret Prince fan who owned at least one blouse with fluffy fringes at the wrist, answered with "How's our little soldier? Ready to party like it's 1999?"

"I see Dom told you about it."

"Dom told the whole fucking world about it. I lost track of how many people are coming to Francisco's. Dom is probably buying glow sticks and hiring DJ Khaled."

"Jesus fucking Christ," Charlie said, followed by a long pause. "Well, he should save his money. The party's canceled."

"Brah! What the fuck?"

"Susan broke up with me."

Johnny ran his fingers through his blond mane and said, "That's no reason to cancel a party, man."

"I took her to LeFleur's. I apologized to her. I even had the waiters bring six dozen roses to the table. It wasn't enough. Maybe I should have brought out twelve dozen roses and a hundred sparklers."

"She still broke up with you after you did all that?" Johnny said. "I don't think I ever bought a girl a single flower."

"I feel like shit. I just want to sleep. For, like, ten hours."

"Fuck that. I'm coming over."

Charlie said, "I don't think that's a good—"

But the call had already disconnected.

Charlie dropped his phone on the hardwood floor. A loud thunk echoed around his normally silent apartment. He didn't bother to check if the phone was damaged. Instead, he fell back onto his couch, took a deep breath through his nostrils, then exhaled a heavy burst of air out of his mouth. *He's not changing my mind about this party.* His eyes drooped shut. He was asleep within seconds. A brief reprieve from the sorrow.

Johnny had spent the last six months perfecting a bong prototype named the Fiery Phoenix. It was shaped like the mythical bird, with hand-painted, flared wings in a dazzling array of red, yellow, and orange. Intricate metallic silver swirls were etched into the massive black talons, which served as a stable base. A large chamber ran through the center, designed to direct white smoke to the wings when the bowl was lit. As soon as the drop pipe was lifted, the smoke flowed out of the wings and into the user's lungs. It was Johnny's masterpiece.

He opened his closet door and carefully lifted out the box that contained the precious, bubble-wrapped bong. Then he noticed another box in the top-right corner, partially buried under clothes he hadn't worn in years. *What the hell is that?* He set down the Fiery Phoenix box, grabbed a stepladder, and retrieved the mystery box. After blowing off the dust, he flung open the lid to reveal an intriguing relic: his father's old Sony Camcorder, model DCR-HC20e. A high-end video recording device, at least when it was released in 1998, long before smartphones could record video. He kept it solely because of its supposed ability to see through people's clothes thanks to its special IR filter. But there was no way of knowing if this was really the ultimate Peeping Tom gadget or just an urban legend, since the camcorder could no longer record. Probably due to his father overusing it in the late nineties.

Johnny last used it to tape an interview with Charlie when they were twelve years old. A memory that had been long forgotten until now. Luckily, the charging cable was still in the box. *God, I hope this thing still plays.* He carried the camcorder and the Fiery Phoenix bong to the trunk of his car and set off for Charlie's apartment. He needed to show him something… and it wasn't X-ray videos of girls.

CHAPTER 36

WHAT'S A CAMCORDER?

Johnny was a few minutes from Charlie's apartment when he called Dom, who sounded like he was half asleep.

"What do you want?" Dom mumbled.

Johnny said, "Wake the fuck up, Cheech. I need you,"

Dom's face was buried in his pillow. "Why am I Cheech?"

"Duh. 'Cause I'm obviously Chong," Johnny said. "I need you at Charlie's. Now."

Dom rolled onto his side, hugged his body pillow, and closed his eyes. "I had to get up early for church. I just went back to bed. I need sleep."

"He *needs* us," Johnny said. "His girlfriend broke up with him, and now he wants to cancel the party."

Dom rubbed his eyes. "What can I do?"

"I need you to help me cheer him up. I'm bringing the Fiery Phoenix bong."

Dom opened his eyes wide and raised his voice like someone who'd just beat a late level in *Ninja Gaiden*. "Really?"

"Oh, now you're interested?"

Dom, who liked to partake on special occasions, said, "Free weed's hard to turn down."

"Just follow my lead when you get there."

Dom swung his legs over the side of the bed. "The hell does that mean?"

"Once we get there, just play along with whatever I do."

"You better not do some dumb shit."

Johnny pulled up to Charlie's apartment. "Yeah. Whatever. Just get over here."

He grabbed the two boxes from the trunk and shuffled across the icy sidewalk, dragging his feet so he wouldn't drop either of his fragile, prized possessions. He knocked five times on the door before it opened. He noticed that Charlie's eyes were even redder than his own. Not from weed, but from all the crying he had done earlier.

"Dude. Why'd you take so long to open the door?"

"I fell asleep."

"Why is everyone sleeping? We should be getting ready to party!"

Within seconds of walking in, Johnny lifted up the blackout shades. An intense beam of sunlight pierced through the darkness and onto Charlie's face, causing him to squint. Johnny plugged the camcorder into an outlet. The tiny red light illuminated, indicating it was charging.

Johnny took a long look at Charlie and said, "*Dead by Daylight*," recalling the multiplayer survival horror game they played a couple of years ago.

Charlie groaned and flopped face down on the couch. "I wish you'd kill me like you used to in that game."

"Man, I lost count of the number of times I snuffed you out. What's one more?" Johnny said. He leaned in to get a better look at Charlie's face. "You all right, man?"

Charlie flipped over, put his hands behind his head, and stared at the ceiling. "I never cheated on her. I never got drunk, or hit her, or even smoked that much weed. She broke up with me because I didn't go to one gig."

Johnny sat on the couch and slapped his palms against his thighs. "I don't see it."

"What don't you see?"

"I don't see why she would break up with you over that. I have a hunch why she *really* broke up with you."

"Yeah, it's painfully obvious. She broke up with me because of video games."

"Brah, a lot of gamers have girlfriends."

"I guess I played them too much or something. The gig was the last straw for her. It was a test, and I failed."

Johnny got up and carefully started unwrapping his bong from the bubble wrap. "Is she aware that we won twenty thousand dollars?"

"She knows. It didn't matter." Charlie finally dragged his eyes away from the ceiling and looked over at Johnny. "Put that thing away and go home. I wanna go back to sleep." He flipped over and lay face down again.

Johnny packed the Fiery Phoenix with weed and walked over to the sink to fill it with water, then raided the refrigerator for ice. "But I brought you a present."

Charlie raised his head to look at the bong and asked, "Which one is it?"

"This is the Fiery Phoenix, man. And you're about to ride its wings of radiance."

"I honestly don't want to get high right now," Charlie replied.

Johnny ignored him and packed in even more weed. The extra-wide bowl overflowed a full half-inch above the rim. "Watch this." He took a monster hit to produce thick white smoke that filled the chamber before spreading to the wings. Next, he removed the drop pipe, causing all the smoke to vanish into his lungs. He held it for a few seconds, then exhaled a ridiculously large white cloud. "The Phoenix has landed," he gasped. "Ride on the wings, baby."

Charlie took a much smaller hit, just to get Johnny off his back. He was afraid that any more would make his depression worse.

"Come on, brah. You didn't even turn the wings white. Why are you hitting it like a bitch?"

Charlie took another draw. This time, a really big one. What did he have to lose? Maybe it would help him forget. But after another large hit, he said, "All right. Time to go."

"You aren't even gonna comment on my bong?"

Charlie leaned back on the couch and said, "It's cool."

Seconds later, the doorbell rang. Johnny sprang up off the couch to answer it. "Look who it is! The Italian Seth Rogen," he said, poking fun at Dom's pudgy stature and fondness for weed.

Dom said, "If I'm the Italian Seth Rogen, you're the white Snoop Dogg."

Johnny mimicked wiping a tear from his cheek and said, "That is the nicest thing anyone has ever said to me."

Dom walked over to Charlie, who was still on the couch, and asked, "What happened?"

"She broke up with me. I thought she was okay with me playing games. But I guess I missed too many special occasions. I wish she would've told me how she felt."

"She never complained about your games before?" Dom said.

"She got upset when I played my Nintendo Switch in the hotel room at Lake Geneva last month. She told me to put it away and said it was supposed to be a romantic weekend," Charlie said. "I mean, I stopped playing as soon as she asked me to. She never yelled at me or even raised her voice. Maybe if she had, I would've realized how much it bothered her. Sometimes, I need to be hit over the head for things to register."

Dom asked, "Did she complain about the Switch right away?"

"No, not until Sunday morning."

"So, you were playing on Friday and Saturday?"

"Yeah, I guess I was. But not all the time."

Dom raised his right hand and swung it down like he was chopping wood. "I'm telling you. When a woman plans a weekend getaway, the video games need to stay far away."

"Or when she's singing at a gig," Charlie said. "Maybe I should stop playing games and just grow up."

"Fuck that," Johnny said. "If you stop playing, you won't grow up. You'll grow old."

Charlie closed his eyes as if he were about to fall asleep, wishing he could slip into the great abyss of oblivion.

Johnny knew what he had to do. It was time to fuck with Dom. He placed his hand on Dom's shoulder and shoved him hard enough to make him lose his balance. "Dude! What the fuck? You didn't bring anything. I told you to bring Italian beef, you *guido* bastard. You forgot, didn't you?"

"You never told me to bring Italian beef," Dom replied. "And don't call me no fuckin' *guido*."

Johnny sighed. "I said, 'Dom, bring Charlie a beef. Dipped. With giardiniera peppers, the way he likes it.'"

Dom paused for a moment as he finally realized what was happening. A faint smile appeared on his face as he pushed Johnny back. "You said no such thing."

Johnny pushed Dom again. "I did."

Dom slapped Johnny's chest with both palms and said, "You didn't."

Johnny grabbed Dom by the shirt and wrestled him onto the couch next to Charlie. If this had been a real fight, Johnny would have been shredded into thin strips of Italian beef. Instead, Dom writhed around, pretending to be helpless, while Johnny got him in a headlock and continued to berate him.

"I told you not to smoke weed before you ordered the beef. I knew you'd forget. And now look what you've done. You've upset Charlie, and you've agitated me."

Charlie leapt off the couch, stunned by what was happening. He was wide awake now.

Dom wriggled free from the headlock, stood up, and pointed his index finger inches from Johnny's face. "*I* didn't forget. *You* forgot."

"Did I?" Johnny said. "Maybe you're right. Oh my God, I did."

Dom straightened his shirt, waved his hand upward, and calmly said, "Fuhgeddaboudit."

Charlie cracked a smile, then laughed. Hard. Maybe it was the weed. Or maybe it was watching these two forgetful idiots wrestling on his couch. But, for a moment, he forgot why he was sad.

Johnny laughed with him and said, "Yes! That's what I like to see."

Dom fixed his thinning hair and said, "I'm glad you find this so amusing. Did you really believe this scrawny little bastard could kick my ass?"

Wrestling with Dom had been just the first part of Johnny's plan to force Charlie out of his funk. Now it was time for step two, which involved a camcorder from the nineties. Who said old technology was useless?

Johnny walked over to where the camcorder was charging. Its battery had reached 20 percent. More than enough power to lift Charlie's spirits. He unplugged it from the outlet and connected it to the TV.

"What the hell is this?" Charlie asked.

"Probably some old-school porn," Dom said.

Johnny pressed *Play*. The screen turned blue, displaying the date, March 17, 2003, in the bottom-right corner. There was a brief flicker, then twelve-year-old Charlie appeared. He was sitting at his Pentium III computer. Creating mods for the PC game *Half-Life* and showing off designs for a platform game in the style of *Super Mario*. If this were the only thing on the video, it would have been a nice dose of nostalgia and nothing more. But there was something else. Something that had lain dormant for the past fifteen years. And it was about to be revealed through Johnny's interview with Charlie. The image scrambled every five seconds or so, probably due to the age of the tape. But the sound was mostly clear, apart from a few inaudible words:

> JOHNNY: Here we ____ with Charlie making ____ latest masterpiece. Tell us, what ____ working on?
> CHARLIE: It's my own real-time strategy game, called *Charlie's War*. I made ____ AI system ____ adjusts ____ difficulty ____ statistics.
> JOHNNY: And what does that mean?
> CHARLIE: It ____ the worse you play, the easier the game gets. The better ____ play, the harder the game gets.
> JOHNNY: Hmm, interesting. How ____ create ____
> CHARLIE: I just wrote ____ artificial intelligence program ____ adjusts ____ player.
> JOHNNY: But why bother? Aren't games perfect ____ way are?

Charlie's next response on the video was completely intact. No audio issues. No scrambled image. Almost high-definition, as if divine intervention had taken place. The camera zoomed in on his face, capturing every detail of his expression:

> CHARLIE: Games are pretty perfect, but I just wanted to make them better. I'm tired of playing games that are too hard to beat. It's really sad that a lot of players will never see the endings to some games because of how hard they are. I have a really cool ending for my game that I want everyone to see, so I designed it to reduce the difficulty when it gets too hard. Every player will be able to beat it if they keep trying. I just want my players to be happy... want my players to be happy... want my players to be happy... want my players to be happy...

The video kept replaying the final phrase. Over and over. Speaking to Charlie from the past. Reminding him of who he once was. A boy with a gentle smile and a gleam in his eye, eager to express himself. The video skipped another ten times before Johnny stood up and pressed *Stop*.

Then it happened. The moment. Describing what the moment feels like is difficult, especially if you've never experienced it. It's like a spark. But where does it come from? Is it spiritual? Does it come from an ethereal place in the cosmos? Or just from being in the right place at the right time with the right people? Either way, most people ignore it. Too busy to notice its significance. Distracted by their boring jobs. Their fractured relationships. Their hobbies. Yes, even their video games. But this time, the spark was an explosion. The heat was far too intense for Charlie to ignore.

His eyes pooled with tears. "Why didn't I remember this?"

"I'd forgotten about it too," Johnny said. "But as soon as I saw that camcorder, the memories came flooding back. That's why I wanted you to see the video. It reminded me of what you went through after your parents got divorced. I begged you to keep making game levels, but you said it was a waste of time."

There was that phrase again—*a waste of time*.

"I still can't believe they got divorced," Charlie said. "All because my dog died from choking on that piece of meat my father fed her. They yelled at each other for months."

Johnny shook his head. "Brah, you needed therapy. Your parents probably thought you were fine because you're so easygoing. But they fucked you up. Stopped you from doing what you were born to do."

Charlie's subconscious bubbled to the surface, revealing all the times his father had made him feel ashamed for playing and designing video games. "I don't know. Making games? It's too hard."

"Tell that to Team Meat," Dom said, "the two guys who made *Super Meat Boy*. It sold a million copies. Or Jonathan Blow, the guy who designed *Braid*. That made over four million dollars. And he did it all by himself."

"Team Meat. Jonathan Blow. Are you sure you're not—" Johnny said, before Dom cut him off.

"Finish that sentence and see what happens."

"Gay?" Johnny said.

Dom clenched his fists and lunged at Johnny, but stopped a few feet short. He lightly slapped Johnny's face and turned toward Charlie. "It won't be easy. It'll take a lot of work. But you're probably gonna lose your job tomorrow anyway, so you might as well go for it."

"Mr. Testosterone is right," Johnny agreed. "Most people live their whole lives not knowing what they're capable of. How do you think I learned to make my majestic bongs? I watched a ton of YouTube videos and spent hundreds of hours shaping glass with my uncle. Think of it as a quest in *Skyrim*, or a level in *Celeste*."

"I dunno. What if I fail?" Charlie said.

"Brah, you've failed a million times in a million different games. But you always keep playing. You know how many times I've shattered glass on a bong or made it so hot it turned into a jumbled mess? But I keep at it. Some people make music, or write books, or make movies. I make crazy-ass bongs. You can make games."

"Yeah, and they'll all be unsuccessful," Charlie said.

"That doesn't matter," Johnny said. "You get to live the life you're supposed to live and do what you're supposed to do. How's that not success?"

Dom threw a verbal jab back at Johnny. "Mr. Pothead is right. Most people don't go after what they want. Then they wake up one day and wonder where twenty years of their life have gone."

Charlie knew Dom was talking about himself.

"Just promise me you won't make a hard-ass game like *Battletoads*. I never got to see the end of that one," Dom said.

"He could design a game like *Battletoads* that gets easier after multiple playthroughs," Johnny suggested. "He already knows how."

Johnny was right. It was all there on the video. But the knowledge Charlie needed was buried deeper than Atari had buried a million unsold cartridges of *E.T. the Extra-Terrestrial* in the desert of New Mexico.

Charlie turned on his TV as soon as Johnny and Dom left the apartment. Not to play video games, but to watch YouTube videos on how to program them. Instead of sitting through *The Top 100 PlayStation 4 Games of All Time* or tips on how to complete a difficult game level, he searched for developers' videos on how to code with Unity. Although not simple by any means, Unity was one of the easier game engines to learn. And Charlie knew that it could be used to create a retro platform game in just a few months. One video became two. Two became four. Four turned into twenty. It was incredible how quickly Charlie's brain absorbed all the information, almost like slipping into a soft, comfortable sweatshirt.

During the two hours Charlie spent watching coding videos, he smiled and was… entertained. It was a feeling he thought he could never experience outside of gaming. It was just coding. But it was fun. *How is this happening?* He clutched his phone and called his father.

Joe answered in a glum tone. "Hi, Charlie."

"Cheer up. Today's gonna be a great day."

Joe, stunned, asked, "Have you been smoking weed again?"

"I did earlier, but I'm straight as an arrow now. The party's back on. Please call Francisco and see if we can still have the place tonight."

Joe chuckled. "Oh, Charlie. This is kinda last minute. What if he says no?"

"Tell him that I'm finally making my own pizza. He'll understand."

Charlie hung up and was about to disconnect the camcorder from the TV, but something made him pause. *Is there something else on this video?* He'd already gotten what he needed from it, so there was no point in watching hours of himself sitting at a desk, designing game levels. But curiosity dug its nails in deep. He fast-forwarded a few seconds to clear the skipping section and pressed *Play*. It was a decision that would change his life. For better or for worse.

The screen filled with another close-up of young Charlie—beaming, with a huge smile on his face. Creating a mod for a game. Happy. In his element. Then he turned his head away from the camera to ask his offscreen father to check out a level he'd created for *Warcraft III: Reign of Chaos*.

Twenty seconds later, his father appeared and nudged Charlie's shoulder with the palm of his hand. It was gentle enough not to be construed as physical abuse. But it was emotional abuse. And sometimes that pain runs deeper. Onscreen, his father said: "Charlie, how many fucking hours you gonna waste on that shit? You know you've got to be good at math to make games, and your grades show me otherwise. Stop trying to be the next great game designer and do your homework. Or, better yet, why don't you go outside like a normal kid?"

The camera remained tight on young Charlie's face as his smile transformed into a frown. Something that should never stain a twelve-year-old's face. It was impossible to miss the tears.

Charlie watched in silence as the younger, better version of himself continued to fade away, like an old Polaroid of happier times. The personification of a dream suffocated right before his eyes. He bit his upper lip as he recalled the shame his father had made him feel. The memory had always been there. In his mind. But now he actually *saw* it. With his own two eyes. A random-access memory was thrust to the surface like a voltage spike. A memory corrupted. By his father. It was time to do something about it.

CHAPTER 37

BREAKING THROUGH

Joe called Charlie to tell him he had managed to rebook the party room. "We're all set for seven," he said. "Francisco was reluctant at first, but when I mentioned you were making your own pizza, he said, 'Say no more.' I still don't get what that means. Can you meet me there so we can organize everything?"

"Do you need me there for that?" Charlie asked, unable to suppress the extra layer of bitterness he now felt toward his father.

"Yes, we need to coordinate with Francisco."

"Fine. I'll be there in fifteen minutes."

"Great. See you then."

When Charlie arrived at Francisco's Bar and Pizzeria, only a handful of people were drinking at the bar, while a single family was eating pizza in the restaurant. It was a far cry from the dozens of customers who had been there earlier to celebrate the Bears' victory against the Packers.

Francisco waved to Charlie and said, "Your dad's waiting for you in the back room."

"Thanks again for letting us have the party here."

"How can I say no to one of my favorite customers? Plus, I wanna hear what kind of pizza you're going to make."

"Video game development."

"Of course. Glad the door opened up for you. All you gotta do is walk through."

Charlie smiled, clasped Francisco's hand in his own, and pulled him in for a side hug. He headed to the back room, which had enough capacity for about forty people. Joe, drinking whiskey on the rocks, was fixated on the wall-mounted TV, which was showing highlights of the Bears game. He turned around as soon as he heard Charlie's footsteps.

"We need to discuss who's coming to the party. Your mom will probably invite her brothers and sisters, along with some of your cousins. I've already invited my brother and his two boys."

Charlie found it telling that his father called his nephews "boys," instead of referring to them as Charlie's cousins. Joe barely saw his brother and was lucky to talk to him twice a year, if that. Charlie didn't even know the names of the "boys." They might as well have been strangers.

"Why the hell did you invite them?" he asked. "We never see them."

"Your uncle reached out to me a few months ago. What's the big deal if they come?"

"I don't want your brother and his weird-ass kids at my party."

"This is a chance for me to get together with my brother, and for you to see the boys."

Charlie yelled, "I hardly know them."

Joe took a large swig of whiskey and sat in silence for fifteen seconds. "What's wrong with you? Why are you being so mean?"

Charlie's usual strategy with his father was to let him speak and then move on with his life. But this time was different. Of all the people to call him mean. The needle on his aggravation meter swung from medium to high.

"Do you even know why I want this party?"

"Because you won a tournament."

Joe's condescending tone drew more aggro than a tank in *Overwatch* or *World of Warcraft*. Charlie's DPS character was ready to unleash hell and take him out.

"This is so typical you," Charlie said. "But I could never quite put my finger on it until Johnny showed me an old video on his camcorder."

"What video?"

"A video of me. When I was twelve. Talking about creating my own video game. It was like a part of my memory that I'd erased. The video brought it back." Charlie paused for a moment. When he spoke again, his voice cracked. "I was really happy making games."

"I remember you used to spend a lot of time in your room on that computer," Joe said. "I never understood your obsession. Always in front of a screen. Never going outside. You can't get a tan from a computer screen."

Charlie's aggravation meter was now at maximum. Needle to the right and shaking. "I spent a lot of time on my computer making something magical. Then it died," Charlie said. "It died because of you."

"What the hell did *I* do?"

"I saw the smile on my face when I was making games," Charlie said. "Then you yelled at me to 'turn that shit off.' Told me it was a waste of time. You said I wasn't normal and that I could never become a game developer because I wasn't good at math. You made me feel... I don't know... *ashamed*. For making video games."

Joe rubbed the top of his bald head. "I was going through a divorce. I wasn't in my right mind."

"I went through it too. I was just a kid," Charlie said. "I needed you, and you dismissed me. Why do you think I played so many games? They gave me the attention you never did."

"Why didn't you ever tell me that you felt this way?"

"It wasn't my job to tell you," Charlie said. "You're the parent. You should have figured out something was wrong. I would always play games in that tiny room whenever I stayed at your apartment after the divorce."

"I just thought you loved playing games."

Charlie had no tears left for his father. "I did. But I loved you too, and you didn't care."

"I did care. I *do* care. I love you, son. Please believe me. The divorce tore me apart."

"I know it wasn't fair that Mom divorced you after Daisy died. But you could have done some things that other fathers did, like play video games with me or toss a ball around."

"I tossed a ball with you."

"Yeah, like, three times."

"Most of those fathers you hold in such high regard used to beat their sons," Joe said. "Did I ever lay a finger on you?"

"Well, thanks for doing the bare minimum and not physically abusing me," Charlie replied, subconsciously echoing Susan's comment from four hours ago.

"All you remember are the bad times," Joe said. "What about all the times I took you to the park to play on the swing set, or when we went on vacation to Disney World? You act like I'm the worst father in the world, but when was the last time you called me other than when you needed something? You gotta meet me halfway here. You never let me get close to you."

"I never got close to you because you made me feel like I was a burden. Getting close to me was too much work for you. Oh, and by the way, Susan broke up with me. Probably because I could never get close to her, either."

Joe looked down at the floor and shook the ice cubes in his whiskey glass. "Why didn't you say anything earlier?"

"What could you possibly say that would make me feel better? I'm also gonna lose my job tomorrow, because I blew off a weekend work assignment to play in the tournament. What do you have to say about that?" Charlie didn't give his father a chance to answer. "I don't even know why I'm telling you all this. You don't give a shit about my life, you never have, so just go back to feeling sorry for yourself and blame everything on the divorce."

Charlie turned away and stared at the room they were supposed to be setting up. "You know what? Forget about this stupid party. I'm done." He pushed himself away from the counter and left without another word.

Joe cupped his palms around his forehead and gently thumped his head three times on the table. Then he felt Francisco's hand on his shoulder.

"Kids. Moody little bastards, aren't they? So, are we canceling the party again?"

"You might wanna pour me another drink. I gotta do something I really don't wanna do," Joe said.

"Oh, yeah? What's that?"

Joe let out an enormous sigh and said, "Call his mother."

CHAPTER 38

THE REVEAL

Joe had tried to cut down on whiskey more times than he could remember, but he could never give up the euphoria of drinking with his friends. Or the numbing effect of drinking alone. It relieved the depression from working all day as a construction foreman. But it came at a heavy price. His ex-wife endured many years of his alcoholism before finally asking for a divorce. And he gave it to her. It was perhaps the only thing he gave her that made her truly happy. They had rarely spoken since, but this was a call he had to make... for Charlie.

"Hi, Mary."

Mary put her phone on speaker. She was in the middle of putting away groceries. "Which one of them needs something now?"

"Not this time," Joe replied. "Charlie and I got into a fight over a party we're trying to plan tonight."

"What party?"

"A victory party for winning his video game tournament last night."

Mary placed a few cans of beans in the cupboard and slammed the door. "Jesus Christ, that kid. You'd think he'd call his mother and tell her about it."

Francisco set another whiskey on the rocks in front of Joe, who took a huge swig before continuing his conversation with

Mary. "He saw an old video of himself making video games when he was twelve, and it set him off. Apparently, he showed me his game creations back then, and I told him it was a waste of time. Then he mentioned how Daisy's death led to the divorce and—"

Mary interrupted to make sure Joe had kept the long-standing family secret. "You didn't tell him the real reason, did you?"

Joe spun the large square ice cube in his glass a few times. "That's the thing. I feel like he needs to know. But I can't just blurt out, 'Actually, son, your mom divorced me because of my drinking.'"

"We agreed it was easier for him to think the divorce was over Daisy's death. You didn't want him to grow up resenting you for being a drunk."

"He may not resent me because of that, but he definitely resents me," Joe said, gulping down the rest of his drink. "He wants to cancel the party. Can you talk to him? Maybe tell him the truth?"

Mary placed a bag of tangerines in a bowl but kept one in her hand. She squeezed it so hard that some juice started to drip onto the countertop. "This is a conversation you should be having with him."

Joe let out a hiccup, which happened whenever he drank whiskey too fast. "I will. But first, I need to get him to the party. How do I do that if he won't talk to me?"

Mary remembered his hiccuping from years before and yelled, "Jesus, Joe. Are you drinking right now?"

"I'm at Francisco's, planning the party. What do you care?"

"I don't," Mary said, flinging her hands in the air. "Fine. I'll tell him you ignored me, missed most of his school plays and soccer games, and dismissed him because you're in love with the bottom of a bottle."

"Just don't make me out to be an asshole."

"Sure. I'll just make you out to be a *drunk* asshole," Mary said before hanging up.

For the first time in her life, she wasn't looking forward to calling Charlie. Even though he rarely called her, she would check in with him at least once a week.

The call began in the usual way. "Hi, Charlie. How are you? I miss you."

Charlie answered, "I'm okay."

Then Mary said something she couldn't recall saying over the last fifteen years. "I just spoke with your father." She paused. "He's upset that you don't want to have your party."

Charlie moved the phone away from his ear for three seconds to calm himself down before asking, "Did he tell you why *I'm* upset?"

"Something about a video of you designing games when you were twelve?" Mary said.

"It was upsetting, Mom."

"We had a lot of marital problems during that time."

"I don't understand," Charlie said. "You guys were fine before Daisy died."

Mary was silent for ten seconds. "We haven't been entirely honest with you."

Charlie rolled his eyes and shook his head. "Do I wanna hear this?"

Mary tilted her head back and sighed. "We didn't get divorced over Daisy. We got divorced because your father was an alcoholic."

Charlie's brain went into instant denial. He thought about how alcoholics can't keep jobs, stumble around, and slur their words whenever they talk. His father didn't do any of that. Then again, he did always seem to have a drink either in his hand or within reach. It just seemed normal, like drinking a soda.

Charlie said, "He likes to have a few drinks, but he's not an alcoholic."

"No, Charlie. He's a *full-blown* alcoholic," Mary said. "I wanted to be the good, supportive wife because I knew how hard he worked. He had a tough life growing up. I don't think his father ever loved him. I lied to myself. Told myself that's how men are supposed to be. But he loved the bottle more than me. More than you. More than Emma. I'm so sorry I kept this from you."

Charlie sank into his couch. "That coward couldn't even tell me himself. He had to get *you* to do it."

"He knew you'd refuse to talk to him. For some reason, he's acting like the world is gonna end if this party doesn't happen," Mary said. "He wanted me to prepare you for it, so you wouldn't flip out."

"Let me get this straight," Charlie said, his voice rising. "You divorced him without getting him help? You gave up on him. Just like Susan gave up on me."

Mary jumped up from her chair. "What happened with Susan?"

"She broke up with me."

"Oh my God. Why?"

Charlie sank deep into his couch. "Video games. What else?"

"I knew this would happen," Mary said. "You're more like your father than you realize."

Charlie hopped up from the couch faster than a white rabbit emerging from a magician's top hat. "Wait. Are you comparing my gaming to Joe's drinking? They're hardly the same thing."

Charlie was thrust into a position he'd found himself in plenty of times: defending his hobby. Protecting his right to play games. It's not like they could damage your liver. They were digital, and much better than binge-watching TV or endlessly scrolling on a phone.

But then he started to wonder. Games had always dangled in front of him like a carrot that could never be reached, no matter how many he played. The urge to gamble and chase that high must have come from somewhere.

Am I really like him?

"Did you want to play games more than spend time with Susan?"

Charlie stormed into the kitchen. "No... I don't know... Maybe... Sometimes... God, why are women so needy?"

"You should've been grateful that she wanted to spend time with you," Mary said. "She was just looking for the same thing from you."

"I swear, men are like *Pong* and women are like *Civilization Six*."

"I know *Pong*, but what's *Civilization Six*?" Mary asked.

"Something beyond the capacity of human comprehension."

Charlie's mind reflected on all the times he chose to play games rather than go out with Susan. Like when he faked an illness to get out of a double date on the day *God of War* was released for the PS4. *I mean, it's Kratos!* Or when he was so close to beating *Shadow of the Tomb Raider* that he invented a migraine. Or when they were late for a concert by Paramore, a band Susan idolized, because he was in the middle of a long strike mission with Tim in *Destiny 2*. These were just three examples among dozens of others.

The Midnight Multiplayer Match was the breaking point for Susan. It didn't matter that Charlie had a chance to win the grand prize. Their relationship was hanging by a thread. And her gig was a desperate, outstretched hand, reaching out to pull him up before he plunged into the abyss of hopelessness.

"She'll never take me back," Charlie continued. "She never wants to see me again."

"It's up to you to decide if you want to try and get her back," Mary said. "But I'm telling you, it's not too late for you to repair your relationship with your father. He's trying to show you that he loves you."

"It'll be even harder for me to get close to him now that I know he used to be a raging alcoholic," Charlie said. "He was probably drunk when Daisy died."

Mary didn't answer.

"Oh my God, he *was*, wasn't he?" Charlie cried. "Jesus fuck! He was too drunk to notice our poor dog choking on a piece of meat."

"Yes, he was drunk," Mary said calmly. "He kept calling me afterward, saying how sorry he was. But I couldn't get past the fact that he could have saved her if he'd been sober. Did you know that he cried more when Daisy died than when his father died? Three days straight. I think that dog gave him the attention his father never did."

Charlie grabbed the back of one of the kitchen chairs and flung it across the floor. "Unbelievable."

"Your grandpa was a tough man, but I never thought that your father would follow in his footsteps," Mary said. "I know he didn't *want* to be like that. He needs this party more than you know. And he needs *you*. Don't make it so hard for him to show his love for you."

Charlie was still mad at his father. Just like he always had been ever since the day Daisy died. Now he knew why. He wanted to tell him to fuck off forever. Eating a whole pizza by himself and playing *BattleTheatre* seemed like the best way to spend the rest of the night.

He plopped down on the couch, powered up his PlayStation 4 Pro, and stared at the title screen on his TV. He grabbed the controller. Ready to play. But he couldn't press *Start*. Like a tiny husk of popcorn stuck in his teeth, something was bothering him. His mother's words. Asking him to give his father another chance. He clasped his hands over his head, pulled his elbows in, puffed out his cheeks, and blew hard enough to extinguish a birthday candle from three feet away. He shut down the console, tossed the controller onto the couch cushion, and texted Joe: "Go ahead with the party."

The party was happening. No more cancellations.

CHAPTER 39

BECOMING

Charlie sent a group text to his crew to let them know the party was back on. *If only I could invite Susan.* He wanted to share his joyous victory with her, but it was clearly over between them. He had to accept it. At least he could play matchmaker for Tim by calling Jasmine to see if she was bringing her girlfriend. They also needed to discuss what they were going to do about that jagbag DuPont. The party would be a good chance to do that in a relaxed and familiar setting.

Jasmine was driving to her brother's place, as she did every Sunday, when Charlie called. She put her phone on speaker and said, "Hi, Charlie."

"The party is set for seven o'clock at Francisco's. Did you talk to your girlfriend about Tim? Can she make it?"

Jasmine turned onto Milwaukee Avenue and said, "I feel a little weird about setting her up like this."

"She'll really like Tim once she talks to him. He's a gentle soul."

"Well… maybe we could stop by for a little while."

Charlie jumped up and down, then clenched his fist and punched the air three times in a row. "Great. We can talk about how to deal with the assignment at the party."

"I'm pulling up to my brother's house," Jasmine said. "I'll see you later."

Charlie had about an hour and a half before the party started. More than enough time to watch another YouTube video on game design. He typed "Unity game development" in the search bar, which brought up a bunch of videos. He double-clicked on a forty-five-minute tutorial.

Around twenty minutes in, Charlie's fascination turned to confusion because of the complicated jargon, so he paused the video to make sure he wasn't watching an advanced lesson. The title was *Unity 101*.

Charlie's bewildered education was interrupted by the doorbell. He stood up and opened the door to find his father standing there with a shit-eating grin on his face.

"Why are you here?" Charlie asked. "Did something go wrong with the party?"

"No. It's all set. I wanted to see you. See where your head's at with Susan and all."

Charlie turned away from his father. "I don't wanna talk about it."

"It might make you feel better."

"I don't even think this party is gonna make me feel better."

"Well, maybe *this* will," Joe said as he handed Charlie a shoe box.

Charlie's mouth dropped open. *It can't be.* He opened the lid and looked down in disbelief as he leafed through the sheets of paper. The box contained precise, handwritten details of the mods he'd created for *Half-Life*, *Quake II*, and *Counter-Strike*. A small notebook inside detailed an AI system that adjusted the difficulty of *StarCraft* based on player performance, along with notes on cel shading, animations, and polygons. It was a treasure chest of technical jargon that, to Charlie, was infinitely better than discovering twenty rare NES games. It was almost like reconnecting with an old friend and picking up right where he left off.

"Where did you…? How do you even have these?" he asked, holding up a couple of precious pages.

"They were in the attic," Joe said.

In the midst of his parents' divorce, Charlie's father had punished him for failing at math by confiscating all his notes. His math scores improved, but his passion for creation declined. So much so that he never asked for his notes back.

"I thought you threw these away?"

"I figured you might ask for them someday. I'm so sorry that you never did."

Charlie spread the notes across the kitchen table like he was organizing spell scrolls in *Skyrim* before embarking on a quest. "These could be useful if I decide to start making games."

Joe took a seat at the table and said, "Like a video game side quest?"

Charlie blinked and looked up from the papers. "I'm surprised you know what a side quest is."

"I've been reading up on video games. Your notes are quite impressive, by the way. I took the time to read a few of them. You might have a gift for this."

"Yeah. A gift that disappeared because of you and your drinking."

Joe bowed his head. *I guess Mary told him.* Then he said, "I'm not proud of it."

"Were you really drunk when Daisy choked on that piece of meat?"

Joe struggled to respond. After rubbing the back of his neck for ten seconds, he finally said, "Yes, I was drunk. Passed out on the couch. Drinking cost me my marriage… And Daisy's life.

Believe me, as much as you hate me, I hate myself even more. I'll always love you, even if you don't love me back or forgive me."

Charlie bit his knuckle, wondering what to say next.

"The hardest part was when I would come to you with a problem, you would say, 'Just deal with it.' Like you were trying to toughen me up," Charlie said. "You never asked me how I felt about *anything*. I don't have the same hypermasculine traits that you have. I know Grandpa was a hard-ass, but you didn't have to act like him when you were dealing with me."

"I'm not going to use my father as an excuse," Joe said. "He was an angry man. His favorite move was to grab my wrists and squeeze them so hard that I would lose the circulation in my hands. Then he would pull me toward him, so my face was inches from his. He yelled so loud and for so long that my ears rang for hours afterward. Over the tiniest thing, like not cleaning my room the way he wanted, or when I broke a shitty three-dollar toy. He acted like I'd broken his thousand-dollar stereo system. I can still smell the alcohol on his breath whenever he yelled at me. To this day, my wrists sometimes hurt for no reason. I always told myself I would never physically abuse you or Emma, and I never did."

"You never hit us, but I watched you shove me in that video," Charlie said.

"I don't even remember doing that. I was in a haze most of the time. I must have thought a little shove was okay because at least I wasn't hitting you. But you're right. It's still bad."

Joe began to weep as years of sorrow bubbled to the surface.

Charlie covered his mouth with his hand and murmured, "Don't cry. It's okay."

"It's not okay. I want to throw this party to show you how much I love you," Joe said. "But you deserve so much more. I want to hear about your dream of making games. I'll listen this time. I want to know. I *need* to know. I promise I won't shit all over it like I did in the past."

"When Johnny showed me that video, I realized how happy I could be making games," Charlie said. "But programming is so hard. I can't even understand a simple Unity tutorial. I don't think I'm smart enough for game development."

Joe stood up, grabbed the kitchen chair he'd been sitting on, slid it closer to Charlie, and sat back down. Then he gently squeezed Charlie's shoulder—a far cry from the shove he'd given him in the video. "Look at me, son."

Charlie turned his head. His father's face was redder than a maraschino cherry in a Martini. Joe's eyes darted back and forth as he prepared to tell Charlie something he had never told anyone, not even his ex-wife or his closest friends. It was time to make up for the shame and insecurity he'd caused so long ago.

"Did you know that I always wanted to be a teacher?"

Charlie sat up, puzzled. "A teacher of what? Bartending?"

Joe placed his hands on his knees, looked down, and said, "High school."

Charlie shoved his father's shoulder just as his own had been all those years ago. Not out of spite, but to wake his father from his delusion. "You need to go to college for that."

"Yeah, I know. But I never did."

"Why not?"

"Because I gave up," Joe said, wiping a single tear from his eye. "It still haunts me to this day. I picked the perfect college. The internet didn't exist back then, so I had to submit a paper application. My father saw me filling it out in my room. He told me it was a waste of time because I wasn't smart enough for college."

Joe grabbed the sides of his chair, stood up slightly, and slammed the chair's legs onto the hardwood floor. He rolled his eyes upward and said, "God, I can't believe I did the same thing to you that he did to me." Two teardrops rolled down his cheeks. "'Get a trade,' he said. 'Work with your hands. Build something. Be useful, instead of a flake like all those prissy college students.' Then he left me in my room to be alone with my thoughts. I kept saying to myself, 'Fuck him. I won't let him discourage me.' But I looked at all the coursework, and I got scared. Scared that I really wasn't smart enough and that it would be too hard for me. I sat on the floor in my room with my back against the wall. I wanted to stand up, walk over to my desk, and finish that application, but I couldn't do it. Instead, I just kept sitting on the floor, saying over and over again, 'You can't do this, Joe. It's too hard, Joe.' I've been sitting like that ever since. You *are* smart enough, Charlie. Don't be like me. Stand up."

Tiny streams of tears ran down Charlie's face. His father finally believed in him. And for the first time, he felt love from this broken man.

No man should ever fall to his knees unless it's for love. And Joe did. He knelt in front of Charlie and wrapped his arms around him. "Please don't quit, son."

Charlie rose from his chair. Instead of squeezing his father's wrists to pull him up, he held them like wounded birds, gently helping him to his feet. Then he said a word he hadn't spoken since the divorce. "Stand up, Dad."

Joe got to his feet and lifted his head until his eyes were level with Charlie's.

"I can't imagine how tough it's been for you," Charlie said. "Grandpa was such an asshole."

Joe gently held Charlie's wrists and pulled him in for a hug before whispering, "I don't dream of being a teacher anymore. I dream of helping my son become the best fucking game developer on the planet."

Charlie's determination to do just that rose faster than a voltmeter needle swinging from zero to maximum during a power surge. All he had needed was for his father to believe in him.

He was going to go to school. He was going to learn. He was going to live.

CHAPTER 40

THE PARTY

The celebration was minutes away. A few Bears fans were drinking at Francisco's, still rejoicing from the victory against the Packers and discussing the possibility of a first Super Bowl win since 1985.

Despite all the commotion, Francisco had set up the private room for Charlie's party in grand fashion. With a lot of help from Joe. The room was decked with oversized plush chairs, black silk tablecloths, and white carnation centerpieces. Cloth napkins were neatly folded, with plastic silverware on top that resembled real gold. The glossy white plastic plates looked like fine china, much fancier than one would expect in a bar and grill. A shiny, gold-colored plastic trophy sat right in the center of the serving table. A small plaque underneath it read: "Chi-Town Crew—2018 BattleTheatre Champions." An extra-long serving table with large stainless-steel trays was set up for food. And plenty of food would be coming. The standard overhead fluorescent lights had been turned off. The only illumination came from a combination of white spotlights shining on the menu and blue spotlights shining on the walls, creating a soft glow that resembled a trendy nightclub. Two large speakers were playing classic rock. Not too loud. A large spotlight shone on a banner that read: "Congratulations to the BattleTheatre team on an amazing victory!"

When Charlie arrived, he shook Francisco's hand and said, "Wow! I've never seen the room looking like this. You've got some style."

Francisco smiled. "My parties are usually a lot simpler than this. Your dad's the one with the style. He came up with everything, including the crazy lighting. Congratulations, by the way."

"Thanks, Francisco. I see you have Italian beef on the menu. Nice."

"Of course. The only thing as good as my pizza is my beef," Francisco said. "What are you wasting your time with me for? Go talk to your dad and sister. They're right over there." He nodded to the far corner, where Joe was bending down to adjust some lights. Emma stood next to him, waiting to see if he needed more help.

Charlie tapped Emma on the shoulder, causing her to turn around. "Hi. I wanted to apologize."

"For what?"

"For not playing *Fortnite* with you all these years. And for shooting you in the head at the end of the match. I still feel bad about it. This party's just as much for you as it is for me and the guys."

"I don't feel like it's for me," Emma said. "Everyone's here for you."

"That's because everyone knows I love video games. You're a video game savant. You shouldn't try to hide it."

Joe stood up and let out a loud, old-man groan. "Hey, there's the champ."

"Everything looks good."

Joe reached in and hugged Charlie for a few seconds longer than he ever had before. "You like it? You don't think I overdid it?"

"The trophy's a bit much, but everything else is great."

"What a day, huh? The Bears beat the Packers, and you won the grand prize."

Charlie shifted his gaze to the door to see Dom and Marie arriving. "Dom just got here. I'm gonna say hi. We'll talk later."

"Don't mind me. You're here to have fun with your friends."

Dom was wearing a dark gray suit and a sleek black tie. He had his hands clasped behind his back, examining the food like a curious health inspector who secretly wanted to chow it all down. Marie was in a pink dress with a fading blue fringe. Charlie wondered if she'd made Dom wear the same outfit he'd worn to church that morning.

"We did it," Dom cried, enveloping Charlie in a rib-crushing bear hug before he had a chance to escape.

"Yes, we did," gasped Charlie. "Thanks for coming."

"Hello, Charlie," Marie said.

"Hi, Marie. Ready for a fun night?"

Dom released Charlie for a second, but then instantly grabbed his arm and gently slapped the side of his face. "As long as you got booze, she'll have fun."

"You're such an asshole," Marie said. "You act like I'm an alcoholic or something."

"Noooo," Dom protested, stretching out the word for a good three seconds. "Plenty of people use whiskey as mouthwash and then swallow it afterward."

Marie waved a hand in Dom's face as if she were dismissing him. "This fuckin' guy. Always bustin' my balls." She turned to squint at Charlie before saying, "I don't drink that much, Charlie. Only in social situations."

Dom nodded and flashed a devious grin. "Yeah, she never drinks alone. Only when she's with someone... which is all the time."

"I'm talking to Francisco," Marie said. "I can't listen to this *idiota* any longer."

As she turned her back and walked away, Dom whispered to Charlie, "I always know how to get rid of her."

"You're bad," Charlie said.

"You wanna know the secret to a long marriage?" Dom said. "Always keep your woman on her toes. That means bustin' their chops every once in a while. Did you see the views on my video yet?"

"I got so much shit going on right now that I haven't had a chance."

"We're up to a million, with four hundred thousand likes," Dom said. "We're, like, famous."

"So, six hundred thousand people didn't smash that *Like* button?"

Dom laughed and said, "'Smash that *Like* button'... You're a funny guy."

"You can make money with that many views. You should make more videos. Maybe some retro content."

"I do love to talk retro games. Nothing beats them."

"I mean, you introduced me to sprites when all I knew were polygons."

"Sprites will never die. Fuck your millions of tiny triangles," Dom said.

Charlie laughed. "Seriously. You should do it."

"I'm not creative enough to make good content."

Charlie remembered the long conversations they had about *Portal 2*, *The Legend of Zelda: Breath of the Wild*, and plenty of other games. "You always help me solve puzzles when I can't find a good walkthrough on YouTube. I'd call that creative," he said. "And you love game history. You could put your own spin on that."

Dom rubbed his chin. "It would be cool to make a mini-documentary about the video game crash of 1983."

"I'd watch that," Charlie said.

"Atari released all those crappy games and nobody bought them. They went from selling three billion a year to less than a hundred million," Dom said. "Then Nintendo came along two years later and saved gaming with the NES. That's when games started to get really good. Then *Tecmo Super Bowl* came out and—"

Like the dog from *Duck Hunt*, Johnny appeared out of nowhere to interrupt their conversation. "Is this fucker talking about *Tecmo Super Bowl* again? Jesus Christ, give it a rest, man. We've heard this, like, a million times."

Dom said, "Fuck off, Johnny. You don't know shit."

"I know retro games are shit. Why would I play that garbage when I have *Madden*, *Battle Theatre*, and *Red Dead Redemption 2*?"

"Because you wouldn't have *Red Dead Redemption 2* without retro games. They laid the foundation for everything you play today. Besides, *Tecmo Super Bowl* is much better than any yearly release of *Madden*."

"Oh, here we go," Charlie said, recalling countless online arguments between the two of them.

"In *Tecmo Super Bowl*," Dom continued, "you can actually *feel* the difference in the players' speed and passing accuracy. Each one is unique. Bo Jackson, Barry Sanders, Steve Young, Lawrence Taylor. They all have different abilities that you can feel on the field. With *Madden*, they all feel the same."

Johnny asked, "When was the last time you played *Madden*?"

"I don't know. 2004, I guess. *NFL 2K5* blew it away with much better graphics and animations."

"You're in no position to judge if you haven't played *Madden* since 2004. It's a lot better now."

Dom looked away and said, "I've seen videos."

"Yeah, but you haven't *played* it."

"I'm still pissed that *Madden* bought the exclusive NFL license just to stop every other football game from featuring pro teams and players."

"That may be," Johnny argued, "but the latest version looks amazing. Just like all the other games that came out this year. Sorry, man, but your retro games need to be left in the dust. Name me one game from back then that's better than any game nowadays. And don't say *Tecmo Super Bowl*."

"Easy," Dom said. "*Tetris*."

"*Tetris* is simple as shit. You really trying to tell me that it's better than *No Man's Sky*, with its eighty quadrillion planets?"

Dom sighed. "Making a game complex doesn't make it better. Simplicity is what makes them good. Apart from *Tecmo Super Bowl*, *Tetris* is the greatest game ever created. It's perfection in video game form. It's got logic, geometry, art, mathematics, tension, and critical thinking. Should I go on?"

"No," Johnny said.

Dom ignored him. "It works your brain, makes you feel smarter, lets you build things instead of shooting them. It made the puzzle genre popular, for fuck's sake. You could hand it to someone living in the Amazon rainforest, and they'd be able to play it within five minutes. Oh, and it had to be smuggled out of the Soviet Union, so it's got an amazing backstory, too."

Charlie said, "The man knows his video game history."

"I still say *Tetris* is boring," Johnny said.

Charlie laughed. "Give up, Dom. He'll never get it."

"Yeah, no shit," Dom said.

Charlie, impressed with Dom's classic video game rant, said, "I've heard you talk about games thousands of times. But what you just said was, like, *magical*."

"Get the fuck outta here," Dom replied.

A lightbulb turned on in Charlie's head. "You should invite this goofball onto your channel. It can be retro versus modern gaming. Hearing you two argue about this stuff is quite entertaining."

Dom turned to Johnny and said, "What do you say, goofball? You wanna be a guest on my channel and talk about games?"

"I'll consider it," Johnny said.

"I'm gonna use my winnings to buy some decent software so it looks more professional," Dom said, his excitement growing. "Maybe I'll do some streaming on Twitch. And there's that new app called TikTok. Looks like it might be huge."

Dom's childlike enthusiasm made Charlie smile.

"What about you, Charlie?" Dom asked. "Jagbag here tells me that you might want to start making games."

"I'm seriously thinking about it."

"Gaming's in your blood, brother. Go for it," Dom said. "Man, talking about this has got me pumped. I wish we could play another round of *Battle Theatre* right now."

CHAPTER 41

BONG DREAMS

C harlie's estranged uncle and his equally estranged cousins arrived late. He didn't want to talk to them, but he also didn't want to be rude, so he told Dom and Johnny that he would rejoin their conversation later. Johnny looked at Dom, then glanced toward the back door, signaling that they should go outside to smoke some weed. After grabbing the Fiery Phoenix and a gallon-sized bag of Johnny's premium cannabis from the trunk of his car, they set up a table right outside the back door and placed the bong on top of it. Within five minutes, they'd both blazed through two tightly packed bowls.

Dom hadn't felt this good in years. The *Battle Theatre* victory. The YouTube views. And now this mellow high. It all washed over him like a blanket of serenity. He finally felt like what he was doing mattered. He had created something that could make him some serious money. He leaned against the wall and tilted his head back. All the tension in his muscles melted away. At long last, he was content.

Johnny laughed. "You're baked like a Toll House cookie."

The high was kicking in fast. "I love cookies. Where are the cookies? I want cookies."

"You already had cookies."

"I did?"

"Yeah. You inhaled them," Johnny said, referring to the "Cookie" strain of weed that was in the two oversized bowls they'd just demolished.

"We gotta eat, man," Dom said. "I'm *so* hungry."

"Italian beef is waiting inside, baby."

Dom grabbed Johnny by the collar. "How do you do that? Like, I wanted cookies and you told me I already had cookies, so then I didn't know what I wanted. But then you said 'Italian beef,' and it was like hiding in my brain the whole time. I wanted it, but I never would've figured out I wanted it until you told me… I love you, man." He relaxed his grip. "Let's go smoke another bowl."

Johnny recalled the fake argument they had staged earlier to get Charlie out of his funk. "Didn't we already have, like, a different version of this conversation?"

"Yeah, maybe. But now it's beef time."

Francisco's Bar and Pizzeria was famous for its pizza, but its Italian beef was equally magnificent. The base of the sandwich was soft and chewy French bread, typically dipped in oregano-infused *au jus*, with a mountain of thinly sliced beef nestled inside. The whole thing could easily fall apart at any moment. Some preferred sweet peppers on their beef, even though there was nothing sweet about cooked green peppers. But most Chicagoans knew that giardiniera peppers—a mix of fermented carrots, celery, olives, sport peppers, and cauliflower—were essential for an authentic Italian beef. And it wouldn't be complete without drizzling some of the oil from the jar of peppers over the top.

Johnny and Dom walked back inside and watched the football fans getting drunk and stuffing their faces with food.

"I need some beef inside me. Now!" Dom yelled, attracting the attention of several barflies.

Johnny giggled at the thought that they might be thinking Dom was on the hunt for a very different kind of meat. Dom stumbled into the back room, sat on a chair, and tilted his head back again. Johnny grabbed two Italian beef sandwiches along with a basket of steaming golden fries, impressed with how fresh they looked. Then he made his way back to Dom, who stood up straight and gawked at the beef like an obsessive gamer anticipating the next *Grand Theft Auto* release.

"That's a beautiful thing," Dom said. He grabbed one of the sandwiches with both hands and gobbled it down in three minutes flat. It didn't matter that the beef, dripping in *au jus*, fell apart in his hands. His eating technique of taking a large bite, licking his fingers, grabbing a handful of fries, then taking another huge bite was entirely devoid of table manners. It was like he hadn't eaten for days. A sloppy, oily mess slid down his throat and probably clogged most of his arteries.

Johnny took a few modest bites of his sandwich and occasionally looked over at his caveman buddy eating like a starving man who'd just escaped from a dungeon in *Baldur's Gate*. "You take munchies to another level."

Dom, belly full, said, "Can you believe we won the fucking Midnight Multiplayer Match? I'm using my five grand to buy more weed and video games, as well as the software for my channel. What about you?"

"I've got something in the works," Johnny said. "I need a bit more to get it off the ground, but the five grand will help."

"You're gonna buy a ton of weed and sell it for triple the price, aren't you?"

"Not weed," Johnny said. "Bongs. I'm thinking of selling them as, like, works of art. I've been experimenting with new glass-blowing techniques to make them even more detailed than the Fiery Phoenix. I'm even learning how to improve my painting on glass. Five grand could go a long way to finding a financial backer."

"Just be careful with that, man," Dom said. "My cousin told me that Chong went to prison for selling bongs a few years back. You could get in trouble. Like, possession of drug paraphernalia or some shit."

"I'm well aware that Tommy Chong spent nine months inside for selling bongs. Such bullshit. An icon in the cannabis world sent to jail for selling bongs on the internet," Johnny said. "They raided his house with twenty agents like he was El Chapo. Thankfully, things have changed since then. They can be sold online as long as they aren't marketed for drug use. I plan to market mine as beautiful art pieces."

"I envy you, man. I wish I was young and bold enough to chase my dream. But fucking life, and video games, keep getting in the way. Maybe my YouTube channel will take off."

"If you want it to succeed, then it will," Johnny said. "I may play a lot of games, but I also love creating my bongs. Now, if I could just put a dent in my backlog of games…"

Like every serious gamer, Johnny's backlog seemed to grow larger every week, as PlayStation, Xbox, and Switch kept releasing new titles, not to mention all the weekly sales.

"There is another way to clear your backlog, you know."

Johnny asked, "How?"

"Gamble with Dimitri," Dom said.

MIDNIGHT MULTIPLAYER   257

"Dimitri and the mob don't fuck around."

Dom clenched his fists. "If I could get away with it, I'd love to punch that scumbag bookie right in the jaw for what he did to Charlie."

"Too much aggression, brah. You need to chill and smoke more cannabis."

Dom, still feeling the buzz, asked, "Why do you always call it cannabis? Why not call it weed like everyone else?"

"Brah, a weed is a useless, invasive species. Cannabis is medicinal. A beautiful, delicate flower that should be tended and loved," Johnny said, voicing his deep respect for the plant that had changed his life.

Charlie's father had told him his cousins' names earlier. As he approached them, he wondered if they knew his name. "Hello, Scott... Michael. Thanks for coming."

Scott was wearing a silver silk dress shirt with matching silver slacks and shoes that made him look like a Caucasian version of Kazuma Kiryu from the *Yakuza* game series. It was a shame that he dressed like a famous video game character, but he probably hadn't played a video game in twenty years.

Scott said, "Kinda weird having a party because you won a video game tournament. You still playing games at your age?"

"There wouldn't be a party if I didn't," Charlie said.

"I used to play games when I was little, but I don't have time for video games. Too much going on, you know."

Charlie hated it when people used the phrase: "I don't have time for video games." It really meant that they chose to make time for something else. Like binge-watching an entire season of a Netflix show in a single night.

Charlie wanted to test his theory.

"So, what TV shows are you watching?"

"*Black Mirror*," Scott said. "Great show. And *Homeland*, *Stranger Things*, *The 100*, *Ozark*, *The Last Kingdom*, *Brooklyn Nine-Nine*. Oh, and I'm catching up with *Breaking Bad*. Can't believe I missed that show. I'm trying to hurry up and finish it so I can watch *Better Call Saul*."

"I see why you don't have time for video games," Charlie said. "I wish we could talk more, Scott, but I just spotted my best friend. I really should say hello." He sped over to Johnny before his cousin could say another word.

There was a cardboard cake box on the table in front of Johnny.

"You baked a cake. How nice," Charlie said.

"The only thing that's baked is us. I set up the Fiery Phoenix out back, and now it's time to go tropical, baby." He opened the box to reveal his pineapple bong. "There's a bag of my most primo cannabis in here, too. Very high THC count. A few hits of this stuff and you're going intergalactic. Dom and I already cashed a couple of bowls. This place looks great, by the way. Did you do this?"

"My dad did."

"Very nice," Johnny said, before he spotted Dom waving his hands and signaling for them to come over. "Dom's getting antsy. Jesus, this guy likes to smoke more than I do. Why don't you come outside with us?"

"In a minute," Charlie said.

CHAPTER 42

THE PLAN

A group of people rushed to Francisco's front door to hold it open, almost as if a celebrity was arriving. Mary walked in with several different brands of beer in one hand and bottles of rum, vodka, and whiskey in the other. Joe rushed over to help her.

Then the door opened again. And a wheelchair rolled through.

Charlie recognized Tim immediately from the hundreds of times they'd FaceTimed over the past three years. But he'd never suspected his friend had a disability. He now understood why Tim was so afraid of putting himself out there, even though he had nothing to worry about. He was even more handsome in person, and as stylish as anyone with his sleek beige dress shirt, black tie, and dress pants.

They locked eyes, then both broke into huge smiles.

Johnny, being Johnny, said, "What the hell happened to him?" which led Dom to punch him in the arm.

Tim made his way across the bar and politely extended a hand.

Charlie shook it, then instantly leaned in and wrapped his arms around him. "You look amazing. Thanks for coming, pal."

The whole Chi-Town Crew chatted for a few minutes, until Charlie glanced at Johnny and Dom and said he wanted to talk with Tim alone. They managed to find a quiet corner of the party room.

Tim said, "I'm really nervous."

"It'll be fine. I promise."

"You've always been real with me online, so be real with me now."

Charlie looked at Tim's wheelchair and said, "You have a disability. So what?"

"Would you have tried to set me up if I'd told you about this earlier?" Tim asked.

"Absolutely," Charlie said. "I don't understand why you kept it from us. It's who you are. Why hide it?"

"I don't know," Tim said. "I guess I didn't want you guys to think I was weak."

"We could never think that. We love you, man. *I* love you. And Jasmine's friend is gonna love you too. You're smart. You dress nice. You even smell good. What cologne is that, by the way? Just be yourself. How could anyone not fall in love with you?"

Tim smiled and looked anxiously at the door just as Jasmine and her friend entered the room. "Oh my God, is that them?"

"Yup," Charlie said. "Relax. I'll introduce you." He waved a hand high in the air to get Jasmine's attention. "Just be cool, man. You got this."

Jasmine was wearing a dark-blue blouse and tapered gray slacks. Her friend was much more casual with a light-pink T-shirt, ripped blue jeans, and enough makeup to make Nicki Minaj jealous. Jasmine gave Charlie a light hug, then said, "This is my friend, Ayanna."

"Nice to meet you, Ayanna. This is my very good friend, Tim."

Tim held out his hand, but instead of a handshake, Ayanna waved at him. Tim quickly retracted his hand and waved back before tucking his chin into his chest.

"So, Ayanna, Tim was one of the key players on our team," Charlie said. "Without his expertise in geometry and mathematics, we never would have won."

Ayanna placed her left hand on her thigh and her right hand on her hip. "And what does that mean?"

Charlie tried to find the right small-talk response but came up empty. Instead, he blurted out, "It means he's very smart."

Ayanna rolled her eyes. "Well… I'm smart too."

"Well… then you two have a lot to discuss. We'll leave you to get acquainted. Jasmine and I need to talk about work. We'll be back soon."

"Okaaay," Ayanna said, holding the second syllable for far too long.

Charlie and Jasmine found a table in the far corner of the room.

"Do you want to eat first?" Charlie asked.

"No. We need to talk about work," Jasmine replied. Her tone was serious.

"What's on your mind?"

"What are we going to do tomorrow?"

"I'm just gonna tell him that the assignment was unreasonable, so I didn't do it," Charlie said. "Hopefully, he'll fire me on the spot."

"Why are you so eager to get fired?"

"So I can collect unemployment. But if not, I'll just quit. I have a plan."

Jasmine leaned sideways into her chair. "Oh yeah? What's that?"

Charlie beamed and said, "I'm going to develop video games."

"How'd you come up with that idea?"

"Let's just say I got a little inspiration from a close friend of mine."

"I'm glad you have a career plan," Jasmine said. "But we still need to figure out a strategy for tomorrow. I think he's going to fire me too, but part of me wants to expose his ass before he does."

"Expose him how?"

Jasmine bowed her head and rubbed the back of her neck. "I don't know if I should share this information with you." She grabbed one of the plastic knives and started gently stabbing the palm of her hand.

For a moment, Charlie thought she was testing it before turning it on him. "I know you're mad at me, but—"

Jasmine stopped herself, locked eyes with Charlie, and whispered, "He did something to me to try to get me alone in his room at the Atlanta conference."

Charlie clenched his fist, swiveled in his chair, and threw an uppercut into the open air, away from Jasmine. He knew DuPont was a sadistic bastard, but *this*? He scowled up at the ceiling, trying to calm his outrage. "Jasmine, I'm so sorry. Do you want to tell me what happened? You don't have to."

"It's okay. I can talk about it with you," Jasmine said. "He invited me to the hotel bar, and I had a glass of white wine. Then he pressured me to take a shot of tequila with him. After that, I started to feel really dizzy. He invited me up to his room, supposedly to get a report, but I told him I would wait in the hallway. While I was there, I felt like I was going to pass out."

Charlie ran his hand through his hair and said, "Jesus Christ."

"So, I ran away and locked myself in my room. Within seconds, I'd passed out. Like, I was totally gone. I'm pretty sure he drugged me with that tequila shot." Jasmine shook her head.

Charlie sat in total silence. Then he grabbed one of the plastic knives and started lightly stabbing his own hand. He tried to think, but his mind was blank. It was only when Johnny tapped him on the shoulder that he snapped back into full consciousness.

"Brah, the bong is waiting for you. Stop wasting time over here."

Charlie needed a clear head to think through this dilemma. "Not now, Johnny. We're dealing with some major work stuff."

Johnny might have been riding high, but he could tell that Charlie was serious. "All right, man. Later, then." He walked away mumbling to himself, "I mean, it's his party and he doesn't wanna party. I mean, it's not a fuckin' board meeting…"

Jasmine's eyes welled up with tears as she waited for Charlie to say something.

A few seconds later, he said, "If he did this to you, he may have done this to others. So, he's probably got a stash of pills. If we can find them in his office, we can get the bastard fired, not to mention arrested. I'm pretty sure it's a felony to have date-rape drugs in your possession."

"I've watched enough cop shows to know that DuPont will just say we planted them," Jasmine said.

"Not if I use my phone to record us finding them. Then we just put them right back where they were. We call the cops and get him arrested."

"Isn't his office locked?"

Charlie immediately thought of the die-hard Bears fan who was Head of Security at Unlimited Horizons. He had vented to Charlie multiple times about how DuPont had ignored his application for a junior financial analyst position. "I'll ask William to help us."

"The security guy? He's not going to risk his job to help us."

"He hates DuPont just as much as we do. That might be reason enough for him to help us."

Jasmine paused for a moment. "Let's say we get into his office and don't find anything. Then what?"

"Then we still report him to the cops. It'd be better if we had evidence, but if you report him, you could prevent him from doing the same thing to someone else. I'll be there to help you. One way or another, we'll expose him." Charlie extended his hand. "What do you say? Partners?"

Jasmine grasped his hand and said, "More like partners in crime. He's expecting a manila folder with your report in it. I have an idea what should go in that folder instead." She rubbed her hands together and added, "Let's just say it won't be a financial report."

"You're not gonna take a dump in it, are you?" Charlie said, grimacing.

Jasmine placed her hands on her hips and said, "That's disgusting. Why would you even think that?"

"I don't know. It just sounded like that's where you were going."

"Even though he probably deserves that, I have something else in mind. Something I bought a while ago for an occasion just like this one."

"As long as it's not a bomb or Anthrax," Charlie said.

"I don't want to kill the motherfucker," Jasmine shrieked. "I think you'll like what I have planned. That's all I'm going to say."

Charlie smiled and said, "It's gonna be one hell of a Monday."

CHAPTER 43

JOHNNY AND MARIE

A small bar station, complete with a bartender, was set up in the center of the party room. Marie, who could easily down four or five drinks at any social gathering, was first in line to order a Cosmopolitan. Dom was standing right behind her, having just ordered a beer.

Johnny approached him and said, "Why are you drinking that shit? Come out back so we can take a few more hits."

Marie turned toward her husband and said, "You don't need to smoke any more of that garbage."

Johnny motioned with an open palm toward the drink in Marie's hand. "What you're drinking is garbage. It causes seven different types of cancer."

"Bullshit," she said. "Everyone drinks. It's not that bad for you."

"You just think that because it's socially acceptable. Society has convinced you it's harmless."

"What about red wine? Everyone knows that's good for you."

It was time to go to school, with Johnny as the professor. "It contains the antioxidant resveratrol, which makes people think it's healthy. But you'd need to drink a hundred and fifty glasses in one sitting to get even a modest benefit from it. Cannabis, on the other hand, prevents seizures in epileptics, helps with post-traumatic stress disorder, reduces anxiety, and may even cure certain skin cancers." He pointed to her drink and added, "Alcohol destroys lives and livers. Drunk drivers kill thousands of people every year. Bad things happen when people drink too much. No man's ever beaten his wife after too many bong hits."

"I don't know," Marie said. "I just think that pot smokers are lazy."

Johnny rolled his eyes. "Some of them are, but a lot aren't. Plenty of people use it to help them sleep or deal with chronic pain. Others, like me, use it to spark their creativity. It helps people unwind and take a vacation from their worried minds. There are countless benefits to cannabis. There are zero benefits to drinking alcohol."

Dom, captivated by Johnny's speech, looked at Marie and said, "I'm going to take a few more hits from Johnny's bong… for research purposes only."

Marie took another sip of her Cosmo and waved her hand with a backhanded motion. "Go ahead and get high with your buddy, then."

Dom placed a hand on her shoulder and said, "Don't be like that. Come out back with us and check out the bong."

"Fine. I'll take a look at this goofy thing," Marie said, as she followed Dom and Johnny to the back door.

Even though the pineapple bong was right beside it, Johnny's Fiery Phoenix was still the main attraction on the table outside. Marie might have been against smoking weed, but she couldn't help but be impressed by Johnny's art glass masterpieces, with their multiple tubes swirling from the bowls to the mouthpieces like elegant decanters in a fine wine shop. Johnny had even molded a massive cannabis nugget into the shape of a Christmas tree, complete with tiny red ornaments and hundreds of trichomes resembling freshly fallen snow. Johnny the Budtender broke several pieces from the sticky cannabis tree and ground them into fine green shake to place in the Fiery Phoenix's bowl.

A minute later, four people exited the back door for a cigarette break. But they quickly put away their Marlboros for a chance to smoke something more interesting, lining up for a hit from one of the bongs. The woman at the front of the line opted for the Fiery Phoenix, filling its wings with white smoke. The swirling, intricate design mesmerized Marie and, like a tractor beam, enticed her to join the back of the line. She simply had to try it. It was too magnificent to ignore.

Dom raised his eyebrows. "Weren't you calling this stuff garbage a few minutes ago?"

"What can I say? I'm intrigued," Marie said as she stepped to the front of the line.

Johnny looked at her, then at Dom, and said, "Are you okay with her smoking?"

Marie said, "I don't need his permission to do anything. Just get it ready for me."

"I've met all kinds of cannabis smokers," Johnny said, "but never a demanding one."

"You don't have to live with her," Dom said.

Marie turned around and squinted at her husband with a "just you wait until we get home" look.

Without warning, Johnny ran inside and returned thirty seconds later with an ice bucket. He wanted Marie's hit to be extra smooth, so he gently placed a few cubes into the hourglass-shaped ice catcher to cool the smoke. Then he handed her the lighter and said, "Now remember to pull the stem out of the chamber as soon as you see the wings fill with smoke."

Marie used her shirt to wipe the mouthpiece and took a tentative hit, causing no more than a faint haze in the chamber that never even reached the wings. Then she blew out a weak plume of smoke.

Johnny said, "Try again."

Marie took another hit, but it had the same unimpressive outcome—no smoke in the wings. A brief fit of coughing followed.

"Honey, I think you've had enough," Dom said. "You don't want to overdo it."

Marie was high but didn't realize it because she was so focused on filling the Fiery Phoenix's wings with smoke. "No! I'm not done until the wings turn white!" she yelled.

Dom opened his eyes wide and stared at Johnny, who raised his eyebrows and shrugged in response. They both knew Marie was already halfway to Mars. She took another hit. Then another. The wings of the Fiery Phoenix finally turned whiter than the clouds of heaven. Marie pulled the stem out of the chamber, and the smoke rushed into her lungs. Her lips curled upward into a soft smile as she squinted at Dom and exhaled. For once, she wasn't squinting because she was annoyed with him. She was squinting because she was totally, unequivocally, baked out of her mind.

She started jumping up and down while shaking her head from side to side. "The wings! Did you see the wings? I did it!"

Dom leaned in to hug her and said, "I haven't been this proud of you since you gave birth to our children."

"I knew I could do it. I just knew it," she said, continuing to hop in Dom's arms.

"Gotta love the determination," Johnny said. "I guess the shape of the wings makes it hard for beginners to draw in smoke. This is why feedback from novices is important. I might have to make some slight modifications to the design."

Marie pointed her index finger an inch from Johnny's face and said, "Don't you dare change my beautiful Fiery Phoenix. I love her."

"I love her too," Johnny said.

Marie grabbed Dom by the arm and pulled him closer for another hug. "Why didn't you tell me weed makes you feel this good?"

"I don't know," he said. "You love to drink, but I didn't think you'd like to smoke weed."

"You know, I'm, like, seeing things, like, really clearly now. Like, why do I always worry about bullshit. Are the kids okay? Are they doing well in school? Does my sister love me? Do people like me? Who gives a shit? I mean, who really cares? This party is so amazing. Seeing you boys get together like this is so beautiful."

"Cannabis opens your senses, so you can appreciate the beauty that's all around you," Johnny said. "It takes away the worry and lets you see things as they really are."

"Absolutely," Marie said.

"So, what do you think of alcohol now?" Johnny asked.

"It sucks. Weed is *sooooo* much better."

Johnny crossed his arms and smiled. "Mission accomplished."

Even though she'd already eaten, Marie looked at Dom and said, "I can smell the food from here. I'm starving."

Dom placed a hand on her back and directed her toward the food trays. He looked over his shoulder at Johnny, who gave him two thumbs-up like Siskel and Ebert. Dom was glad his wife had finally gotten high, but he hoped she wouldn't embarrass him too much.

Charlie was finishing his meal with Jasmine when he glanced over at Tim and Ayanna, who were talking at a table at the far end of the restaurant. He smiled and said, "Isn't that nice? They're getting to know each other."

Instead of a quick glance, Jasmine focused on Ayanna's face. She wasn't smiling. Neither was Tim. Seconds later, Tim pushed a plate of food across the table, almost causing it to spill onto Ayanna's shirt. He grasped both push rims of his wheelchair and backed away before spinning around and wheeling himself straight out the front door.

Jasmine ran over to Ayanna and asked, "What the hell happened?"

Charlie arrived just in time to hear Ayanna say, "He asked me out on a date, and I told him it would never work because I'm not interested in a handicapped man."

"He's not *handicapped*," Charlie sighed. "He's got a disability. And he has feelings."

Jasmine shook her head. "Ayanna, why would you say something like that? You could have been more subtle."

Ayanna waved her hands in the air and said, "Subtle's not my style, baby."

Charlie grunted at Ayanna before running outside to search for Tim. He found him halfway down the block, already on his cell phone. Then he heard him say, "Mom. Come get me now. I want to go home."

"I'm so sorry," Charlie said.

"What did you think was going to happen?" Tim replied. "What did *I* think was going to happen? It's the same story every time. You'd think I'd be used to it by now." His eyes were glossy with tears. "What gets me is that we had a lot in common. I thought she was genuinely interested in me. For a few minutes,

I thought she could see the *real* me. But all she could see were these fucking legs that don't work."

"I don't know what to say, man. Please come back inside."

"There's nothing at that party that appeals to me."

Charlie paced around and said, "That's not true. Johnny's bong is in the back, waiting to be toked."

"You think you're being funny, but you're not."

Charlie stretched out his arms and pleaded, "Please, Tim. I'll get rid of Ayanna."

Tim wheeled himself ten feet away and said, "My mom was waiting for me at a restaurant nearby. She'll be here in a couple of minutes."

Charlie ran his fingers through his hair. "Don't leave like this, man. Fuck!"

"This is my fault. I should've told you I had a disability when you invited me. I don't know what I was thinking. Maybe for once. Just once, someone would accept me as I am."

"*I* accept you. And so do the rest of the crew. We love you, man."

A huge black SUV pulled up beside them. Vonda stepped out and opened the sliding door, revealing a wheelchair ramp.

"I gotta go, Charlie. This is my lot in life. The sooner I accept it, the better."

"Don't say that," Charlie said. "Please come back to the party."

Tim turned away from him, wheeled himself toward the ramp, and said, "Let's go, Mom."

Vonda looked at Charlie and said, "Thank you for trying."

Charlie rushed to the SUV and grabbed the wheelchair by the handles to help Tim up the ramp, but Vonda clutched his arm and said, "We got this, honey. We've been doing this for years." Charlie stepped back, let out a deep sigh, and waved.

But Tim never looked back.

———

Charlie stormed back to Francisco's. He had never wanted to yell at anyone more than he did right now. He arrived to find Jasmine standing outside her white Ford Explorer, which was parked directly in front of the restaurant. Ayanna was sitting in the passenger seat with the window rolled up. Charlie formed a fist and pulled his arm back. He was about to pound on the window when Jasmine grabbed his forearm.

"Charlie. Please don't. I already talked with her and told her what she did was wrong. She knows she made a mistake."

Charlie scowled as he said, "What the hell is up with her?"

"She was rude, yes. But why didn't you tell me that Tim was disabled?"

"Would she have come if I had?"

"I could have prepared her."

"Prepared her for what?" Charlie said, raising his arms in the air.

"You know what I mean."

He clasped his hands behind his head and said, "I didn't tell you because I didn't know. Okay?"

Jasmine tilted her head to the side. "You've known him for years. How could you not know that?"

"Tonight's the first time any of us have met him in real life."

"You online dudes are too weird."

"That may be, but we still have *feelings*," Charlie said, raising his voice on the final word so Ayanna could hear him through the window.

"I'm going now," Jasmine said. "I'm sorry about this. It won't affect our plan for tomorrow, will it?"

"It's not your fault that your friend is an *asshole*," Charlie said, again raising his voice at the end of the sentence.

"I'll call you in the morning," Jasmine said. Then she got in her car and drove away.

———

As soon as Charlie walked back inside Francisco's, he was greeted by Johnny, who said, "Brah, we're getting wasted out back. You should see Dom's wife. I got her so fucked up. It's hilarious. She's actually kind of cool when she's high."

Charlie thought about taking a few hits, but he knew it wouldn't ease the sorrow of seeing Tim leave like that. Besides, there was something else he needed to do. "Maybe later," he said. "First, I need to talk to my dad."

"C'mon, brah. This is our party. I've hardly seen you all night," Johnny said.

"I'm dealing with a lot of stuff. Don't worry. I'll be back there to try your bong soon."

"Don't let me down, man."

Joe was fidgeting with the food trays, trying to straighten them out. Charlie noticed that he didn't have a drink in his hand and looked uncomfortable, kind of like the one person at a party no one ever talks to. But his eyes lit up when he saw his son walking toward him.

"You're not drinking?" Charlie asked.

Joe raised his arms and gave Charlie a firm hug. "I wanted to stay sober for your party."

"You can have one drink."

"That's the problem. It's never just one," Joe said. "So, do you have a school in mind?"

"Polygon University. They specialize in video game development."

Joe started organizing the condiments and said, "Son, I'd like to help pay for your college."

"How? You're broke."

"I have a rainy-day fund I've set aside for an emergency. Since you might not have a job in the morning, I think that probably counts as one."

Charlie was skeptical. His father had always been the cheapest man he knew. His house looked like it was falling apart because he never spent a cent on it. "It'll be a substantial amount of money," Charlie said.

Joe smiled. "Don't worry about it. Just do me a favor."

"What's that?"

"Let me be the first person to play the first video game you design."

"But you don't play video games."

"Maybe you can teach me," Joe said, wiggling his thumbs at Charlie as if he were using an invisible controller.

For the first time in years, Charlie smiled at his father. Pleased that Joe was finally willing to invest in him—financially and emotionally. It was a bet neither of them could lose.

***

By nine o'clock, the party was winding down. But Charlie's cousin, Scott the TV binger, was winding up. He'd taken a few hits off Johnny's bong and was freaking out about getting busted. He found Charlie, grabbed his collar, and yelled, "I think someone called the cops on us. I'm really high. I can't go to jail. I gotta get out of here."

Charlie grabbed him by the forearm and said, "You need to see the cannabis professor."

They both stepped outside the back door.

Charlie said to Johnny, "My cousin is tweaking. Can you help him out?"

Johnny looked at Scott and said, "Take a seat and open your mouth."

Scott sat down and grabbed the armrests, but his eyes were darting back and forth like someone who'd just finished playing *Outlast* or *The Evil Within*. "What are you going to do to me?"

Charlie placed a hand on his shoulder. "Trust me. He knows what he's doing."

Johnny placed two dropperfuls of CBD oil under Scott's tongue. "Now, leave that under your tongue for a couple of minutes, then swallow. It will alleviate your paranoia."

Twenty minutes later, Scott's paranoia was gone. He took a deep breath and said, "How did you know that would help?"

Johnny replied, "You're not the first person to freak out. I always carry CBD for these types of situations."

Scott hugged him and said, "I owe you big time. Thanks, man."

Emma, who'd taken a few hits off the pineapple bong herself, smiled at Johnny's helping hand.

Charlie asked, "Do you need some CBD too?"

"I know exactly how much weed to smoke so I don't get like that," she replied. "Johnny's a dork, but that was cool how he helped our cousin. What's his name again?"

"Scott."

"Right. I gotta remember that."

Johnny snuck up behind Charlie and draped an arm around his shoulders. "Your sister was the captain of the boat that saved us." He placed his other hand on his chest and added, "And now she's the captain of my heart."

"Ewww," Emma cried.

Johnny laughed for a moment, then looked Charlie in the eye and frowned. "Where the hell have you been all night? I never got any feedback on my bong from the most important person at this party."

"I think you got plenty from everyone else," Charlie said.

The back door swung open, and Marie trotted over to Charlie to hug him. "Best party ever, dude." Dom followed right behind her.

Charlie, who hadn't witnessed Marie's *White Cloud Challenge*, asked, "What the hell did they do to you?"

Dom said, "I'm seeing a whole 'nother side of my wife I've never seen before... and I like it."

Marie reached into her purse and showed Charlie a cannabis bud the size of a golf ball. "Johnny's such a nice boy. He gave me this cute little bud to take home, but... shhh... don't tell anyone."

Dom, who felt sober since he hadn't smoked anything for almost two hours, said, "I think it's time to go home, babe."

Marie leaned on him and shouted, "Bye, everyone. We're gonna go home and have sex now. Johnny says that sex when you're high is amazing."

Dom turned to Johnny and said, "Wait! Why are you talking to my wife about sex?"

Johnny smiled at both of them. "She brought it up. You better step up your game, old man."

Dom flashed a nervous smile, excited to see what the rest of the night might bring for him. "I'll talk to you guys later. Thanks for turning Dr. Jekyll into Mrs. Hyde."

"Well, I guess the party's over," Charlie said. "Even though I'm probably getting fired, I still have to show up for work in the morning." *And give myself enough time to search DuPont's office before he arrives.*

Johnny groaned. "Let's keep the party going. Just show up late or, even better, don't show up at all."

"I'm really tired, Johnny. It's been a long weekend."

Johnny shook his head. "I can't believe you didn't get high with me... At your own party... Shameful."

"Next time."

"I'll hold you to that. Good luck dealing with that jagbag tomorrow."

Charlie hugged him, then went back inside to find his father and Emma clearing dozens of paper plates from the tables. "I'm gonna head out. Gotta go to work in the morning. Probably for the last time."

"What the fuck, Charlie?" Emma said. "You're leaving us to clean up after *your* party?"

"Let him be, Emma," Joe said. "He has a tough day ahead of him."

"Ugh. He never helps out..."

Charlie wrapped his arms tighter around his father than he ever had before. Emma watched in amazement as Joe gripped Charlie's shoulder with one hand and cupped the back of his head with the other. They finally released each other after seven seconds.

"You never hug me like that," Emma whined.

Joe went to hug her, but she brushed his arm away, saying, "Ugh. Save it." He clearly had another mountain to climb with his daughter.

"Dad loves me more than you," Charlie teased.

Charlie's first three words made Joe smile. All those years of pain, suffering, and regret were starting to fade away. There was a long way to go, but he felt like he'd finally established some sort of bond with his son.

Emma lunged at Charlie and tried to punch him in the arm, but he blocked the blow and then jogged toward the front door. "Later, Sis," he shouted over his shoulder. "Thanks for cleaning up. Bye, Dad. Thank you, too."

Joe waved goodbye, then tried to hug Emma again. She tried to resist, but Joe wasn't giving up. He pulled her into a tight bear hug and planted a kiss on her cheek.

Emma asked, "What the hell happened between you two?"

"We need to talk. Just me and you."

"About what?"

Joe released his hug, but kept his hands on her shoulders. "I'll tell you later. Just know that I love you. I love both of you so much. This has been one of the happiest days of my life."

CHAPTER 44

MANIC MONDAY

Jasmine's text arrived one hour before Charlie usually got out of bed: "On my way. Be there by 6:45." Three minutes later, she called him to confirm he'd received the message. Today was not the day to be late.

Jasmine said, "Did you get my text?"

"Yup. I'll be there soon."

"I wanted to apologize for Ayanna. I had a long conversation with her about her behavior."

"It's not your fault, but thanks for the apology. You nervous?"

"Hell yeah."

"Try not to worry. I'll be with you the whole time. I got you."

Charlie pulled into the empty parking lot at 6:50 a.m. and parked next to Jasmine's Ford Explorer.

She stepped out holding a large manila envelope that looked like a child's travel pillow and said, "You're five minutes late."

"What the hell's in that thing?" Charlie asked. "You sure it's not a bomb?"

"I told you I don't want to kill the son of a bitch. I stuffed it with blank sheets of paper, so it's the exact proportions of what the completed assignment should be. Along with a little somethin' somethin' for our favorite boss." Jasmine chuckled for a few seconds until the queasiness in her stomach returned. "What if he catches us searching his office?"

"I couldn't care less if he catches me," Charlie said. "He's gonna fire me anyway. The question is, do you care if he catches you?"

"What the hell kind of question is that?"

"I mean, are you ready for this?" Charlie asked. "No fear?"

Like a soldier preparing for a tough mission, Jasmine replied, "No fear."

They used their badges to enter through the main door. The security guard at the front desk was fully immersed with his Nintendo Switch, so he glanced at them for only a split second.

Jasmine whispered to Charlie, "Do you think he suspects something because we're here so early?"

"If there's one thing I know, it's that when you're playing a video game, you don't notice anything else. All he cares about is getting to the next level or beating a boss."

"The question is, will we be able to beat *our* boss?" Jasmine said.

"Love the analogy. This is the final boss. So, we need to make sure we have the right armor, weapons, and plenty of healing potions."

"But this isn't a game."

"We're either gonna win or lose, so I'd say it's pretty much like a game," Charlie said.

They entered the elevator and stood in silence as it carried them up to DuPont's floor.

Charlie called William as soon as the doors opened. He answered before the second ring. Charlie had phoned him the night before to let him know what he and Jasmine were planning. Part of that was to expect a call before 7:00 a.m.

"Hey, Billy. It's time. We'll be right in front of the asshole's door in about twenty seconds."

As Head of Security, William had several screens set up in his home office that enabled him to monitor every camera in the building. "I still don't know about this, Charlie. I could lose my job."

"DuPont's gonna keep stepping all over you," Charlie said. "He's never gonna let you become a junior financial analyst."

William squeezed the rubber hippo stress toy on his desk, causing its eyes to bulge out. "I know what you're doing, Charlie. You're trying to manipulate me. That's what *he* does."

Charlie didn't want to lie. "Bill, I'm sorry. Maybe I *am* trying to manipulate you. But he fucked with all three of us—me, Jasmine, and you. This is our chance to nail the bastard. But I understand if you don't want to go through with it. I'm sorry I bothered you." Charlie bowed his head and hung up the phone.

Jasmine said, "What the hell are you doing? Now we're screwed."

Charlie knew exactly what he was doing. He was taking the biggest gamble of his life. The four and a half grand he owed Dimitri paled in comparison to what he'd just wagered on William.

People don't remember all the casual greetings in the office, or the thousands of pleasant exchanges between coworkers. They remember the bad times. The knots in their stomachs when they have to discuss their performance with a deplorable boss. The injustices they face. Overlooked for a promotion just because a certain manager doesn't like them. Working long hours to show their dedication, only to be treated like they're invisible. Hidden away in a basement corner. Out of sight. Alone. Ruminating on what might have been.

Charlie felt the pain. And he hoped William felt it too.

He rested his chin on his interlaced fingers like a Buddhist monk, looked at Jasmine, and said, "Patience."

Jasmine replied, "I'm going to call that handsome motherfucker and give him a piece of my mind."

Charlie ignored her and grasped the handle of DuPont's door. He closed his eyes and pictured himself as a mage in *Final Fantasy*, about to conjure a spell. Thirty seconds passed. Still no call back from William. Charlie released the handle, dragged his feet toward a nearby cubicle, and sat down. Defeated.

Jasmine stood over him and said, "I'm calling him."

Charlie's shoulders drooped. "Don't bother. It's over."

Jasmine grabbed him by the collar and pulled him close to her. For a second, Charlie thought she was going to kiss him, but her grip transformed into two open palms that pushed him backward, almost making him lose his balance. "What was I thinking? Agreeing to come on your stupid mission. I could get in big trouble for this. I don't know why—"

Bzzzz. Click.

Charlie and Jasmine slowly turned their heads toward the sound at the same time. Charlie's eyes were laser-focused on the digital card reader next to DuPont's door. The panel read: "Door unlocked." He grabbed Jasmine by the shoulders, shook her, and said, "We're going in."

William called a few moments later and said, "I know you're manipulating me…" The next four seconds of silence made Charlie think the connection must have cut out, but then William added, "But I don't care. Burn that motherfucker down."

Charlie was so floored that he forgot to thank him. Instead, he referred to a famous character from *Resident Evil*: "Bill, you're better at unlocking than Jill Valentine."

"Okay," William said, clearly not understanding the reference.

Now that they were ready to go, a wave of panic washed over Charlie. "I don't know if I can do this. What if we get caught?"

"You won't get caught," William replied. "His secretary always shows up around eight o'clock, and DuPont arrives closer to eight-thirty. I'm watching all the cameras and badge swipes, so I'll let you know the moment the secretary walks into the lobby. That'll give you plenty of time to get out of there. But right now, you need to get started." He hung up the phone.

Charlie turned to Jasmine and said, "Let's go."

Jasmine looked at her phone. "It's seven o'clock. We have an hour."

Charlie opened DuPont's office door and immediately started searching the desk drawers for roofies, but found nothing. Jasmine placed the manila folder on top of DuPont's desk, then walked over to the large filing cabinet in the corner and opened the top drawer. She rummaged through the files to see if any drugs were hidden at the bottom. After ten minutes of searching, she called out, "Nothing here."

"Have you checked inside the folders?" Charlie asked. "Maybe they're in a Ziploc bag inside one of them."

"There are thousands of folders in this thing."

"Search as many as you can."

"What are *you* doing?" Jasmine said.

Games like *BioShock Infinite* and *Fallout 4* had taught Charlie to search every container in a room. "Checking the shelves. He's got fancy wooden boxes everywhere. Maybe he hid the roofies in one of them."

"Just hurry up. There are, like, fifty drawers here with a hundred files in each one. I need some help."

A few minutes later, Charlie walked over to the filing cabinet and opened the top drawer on the right. Jasmine was searching the third drawer down on the left, frantically leafing through each file.

It took them forty-five minutes to search through most of the drawers, but they found nothing.

Jasmine looked up at the clock and saw it was already 7:50 a.m. "We're not going to make it. What do we do?"

Charlie continued to rifle through the files. "Keep searching."

"My fingers are getting numb," Jasmine said. "I knew this was a bad idea. We have to leave before we get caught."

Charlie's hands were moving at lightning speed. "Just a bit longer. We still have a few more minutes."

At 7:58 a.m., his phone rang.

"His secretary just badged into the lobby," William said. "You have three, maybe four minutes, to get out of Dodge."

"Thanks, Bill," Charlie said. He hung up and turned to Jasmine. "The secretary's here. We've got four minutes, tops."

"There's nothing here," Jasmine said. "We need to get out. Let's just leave the folder on his desk."

Charlie scanned the office as if he were playing one of those hidden-object games that, for some reason, never go out of style. They had searched everywhere, except for the last ten drawers. He plopped into DuPont's luxurious leather chair and stared straight ahead at the bastard's pretentious portrait. It seemed to be mocking him from its elevated position on the far wall.

What am I missing? There's gotta be something here. I can't lose like this. Has the final boss defeated me?

Jasmine was already standing outside in the hallway, crying. "Come on, Charlie. It's over."

He couldn't move. He closed his eyes and saw a slideshow of vivid snapshots of his life: the final sniper shot to win *Battle Theatre*; the look of disappointment on Susan's face at brunch; his father hugging him; all the survival horror games he'd played, like *Silent*

Hill, *Resident Evil*, and *Alan Wake*; all the puzzles he had solved by pressing the right piano key, flicking the right switch, or…

Charlie opened his eyes. *Looking behind the right painting!*

He jumped out of the chair, rushed over to DuPont's portrait, then shouted out to Jasmine, "Record me."

She hurried back into the office and asked, "Do what?"

"Use your phone to record me."

Jasmine tapped on the video app and aimed the camera at Charlie. "Okay, go!"

Charlie unhooked DuPont's portrait from the wall and laid it face down on the desk. He grabbed an envelope cutter and sliced around the edge, not caring if the metal blade cut through to the canvas. He opened the tear to reveal a Ziploc gallon bag taped to the cardboard backing, filled with over a hundred dark green oval tablets. He pulled out his phone and took some snapshots of the roofies for good measure.

Jasmine locked her fingers behind her head and laughed in disbelief. "We got him. Holy shit. We got him."

Charlie heard the ping of the elevator at the end of the hallway. "Someone's coming. We gotta get this picture back up."

Jasmine helped him rehang the portrait. Then they dashed out of the office, closing the door behind them, and hid in a nearby cubicle.

Charlie checked his phone: 8:03 a.m. He called William and said, "Lock it."

"You get anything?"

"We sure did."

William said, "Thank God," as he locked the door.

Seconds later, Sarah Carson, DuPont's secretary, arrived at her cubicle. She dropped her bag and settled into her seat before glancing at the card reader on the wall outside his office. As usual, it read: "Door locked."

Charlie peeked over the top of the cubicle he was sharing with Jasmine, then quickly ducked back down. He turned to Jasmine and whispered, "Call the police."

Jasmine let out a sigh. "Can't you call them?"

"He drugged you and tried to get you into his room. You should be the one to make the call," Charlie said.

"Well, actually, he tried to fuck us both," Jasmine said.

"I'm glad you have a sense of humor about this. But we're not gonna be laughing if we end up in jail for breaking into his office."

"I don't want the cops to show up before he opens that envelope," Jasmine said. "I want to see the look on his fucking smug face."

"It's the Chicago police. We'll be lucky if they're here by lunchtime."

Jasmine called 911 and spoke to the operator for what felt like forever. Charlie started to fidget and asked, "How many questions are they asking you?"

Jasmine muted the call for a moment. "They say they won't come unless DuPont's here."

"Just tell them he's already here."

"Won't I get in trouble for lying?"

"If he's not here by the time they arrive, we'll just say he left the office to get breakfast," Charlie said. "He'll be here. Don't worry."

Jasmine unmuted the call and said, "He's here. Working in his office on the tenth floor."

CHAPTER 45

THE FINAL BOSS

D uPont entered his office at exactly 8:35 a.m. He placed his brown leather briefcase, monogrammed with the initials *E.D.*, on his desk. After unlocking the case's premium combination lock, he rummaged through the contents and pulled out a sleek, black-and-gold Montblanc pen.

Both Charlie and Jasmine peeked out from their cubicle. They were waiting for DuPont to open the oversized envelope on his desk, but he didn't seem to notice it.

Ten minutes went by while it just sat there. Unopened.

Jasmine turned her head to see the police talking to another secretary at the far end of the hallway. "Charlie, get him to open the envelope now. The police are here."

Charlie sprang up from the cubicle and dashed straight toward DuPont's office. As soon as DuPont saw him, he slammed his briefcase shut faster than a teenager closes their laptop when a parent barges into their room. *What else is he hiding in there?*

Charlie said, "Good morning. Just wanted to let you know that I completed the assignment." DuPont didn't react, so Charlie pointed to the envelope and added, "It's right there on your desk."

DuPont leaned back in his chair and placed his hands behind his head. "Good job, Charlie. How long did this take you?"

"I burned the midnight oil all weekend. Hardly had time to pee, sir," Charlie said, laughing.

"Well, thanks for your diligent work."

Charlie stood frozen in the doorway, his eyes fixed first on DuPont, then on the two police officers who were walking toward him, then back on DuPont again.

"I said thanks," DuPont repeated as he started typing on his laptop. "Now, kindly fuck off."

"I worked really hard on it. Are you sure you don't want to check to make sure it's been done correctly?" Charlie said.

DuPont stopped typing and looked Charlie square in the eye. "It's just another bullshit report. Completely meaningless. You want to see where reports like this go?" He grabbed the folder, stood up, and tossed it in the metal trash bin, generating a loud thunk.

Charlie placed both hands on the edge of DuPont's desk and said, "You mean it wasn't even important, but you still made me work on it all weekend. Why? To torture me?"

"Not to torture you, my boy. To see if you have the necessary resolve for a promotion," DuPont said. "And I'm pleased to say that you passed with flying colors, judging by how heavy that report was. I almost sprained my wrist when I tossed it in the trash. I just might promote you by the end of the week."

Charlie's face turned paler than the snow outside DuPont's plate-glass window. He turned to check on the police. They were now less than fifty feet away, talking to another secretary who pointed in Charlie's direction. He had twenty seconds to convince this sadistic, conniving bastard to retrieve the meaningless report and open it. His mind raced at a million miles an hour. He looked at Jasmine, who was still peering over the cubicle. Biting her cuticles.

Think, Charlie. Think.

The only option was the truth. He just hoped it would set him free. "The pages are blank," Charlie said.

DuPont looked up and smirked. "Bullshit. You don't have the balls."

Charlie crossed his arms and said, "There's only one way to find out."

DuPont raised his eyebrows and shot Charlie a searing look as he reached into the trash bin to pull out the report. Charlie peeked back at Jasmine. She was smiling. It was the kind of smile most people never see in their lifetime. And for that one brief moment, it made every decision he had made over the weekend seem worth it.

As soon as DuPont opened the overstuffed envelope, a spring-loaded explosion propelled hundreds of tiny, shiny, confetti-like dicks onto his suit and into his hair. And they stuck to his face, thanks to the film of sweat he was still sporting after his morning workout at the gym.

DuPont recoiled like the snake he was and yelled, "What the fuck?"

At that moment, a police officer walked into his office, grinned, and said, "Are you Edward DuPont?"

"That's what it says on the door. What the hell is this?" DuPont replied as he tried to brush the tiny dicks off his face.

"I'm Officer O'Brien of the Chicago Police Department. We have a report that you may be in possession of Rohypnol."

"Ro-what?"

"It's better known as the date-rape drug," O'Brien said.

DuPont was now brushing the dicks off his suit jacket. "And what is the source of this false accusation?"

Jasmine burst out of the cubicle faster than the tiny dicks had exploded out of the manila folder. She stormed into DuPont's office and stared him down like the DEA eyeballs a scummy drug lord right before a bust. "That would be me. And it isn't false. You drugged me, intending to get me alone in your hotel room at that conference a couple of months ago."

O'Brien said, "I see. So, I guess you were the one who made the call. Now, tell me, where are these drugs?"

Jasmine pointed to the portrait and said, "In that picture of him on the wall. Some days it's crooked, and others it's straight. I think he uses it to hide his drugs.

O'Brien said, "Well, we can't search it without consent, unless…"

Jasmine shrieked. "Unless what?"

"Unless someone with authority over this office gives us consent," O'Brien said.

Arthur Schreiber, the Chief Executive Officer of Unlimited Horizons, was standing in the hallway, watching all of this unfold. He glared at DuPont, then addressed O'Brien. "As CEO, I have authority over every office in this building. I give consent to search the portrait."

O'Brien put on a pair of latex gloves, took the portrait off the wall, and placed it face down on the desk. Then he removed the cut cardboard backing to reveal the bag of roofies. "Gomez, get in here," he shouted.

Another officer, also wearing gloves, entered the office. He transferred some of the roofies from the large Ziploc bag to a smaller one of his own, then said, "I'll be right back."

Two minutes later, he returned. "I checked the database. Dark green oval pill, scored on one side, with the number five-four-two on the other. We'll send it to the lab for confirmation, but it's most likely Rohypnol."

"Thanks, buddy," O'Brien replied.

The small crowd that had gathered outside DuPont's office let out a collective gasp as he pointed at Charlie and Jasmine and said, "These two must have broken into my office and planted those drugs. You saw that the back of the picture was cut. Arrest them both."

"How would we be able to buy that much Rohypnol on our salaries?" Charlie said. "And how would we break into your office? Your door is always locked."

"Not always. It was probably unlocked over the weekend," DuPont said.

Sarah, his underappreciated secretary, chimed in, "No, it wasn't. The card reader on the door showed it was locked when I arrived this morning."

"Whose side are you on, Sarah?" DuPont said. "They must have an accomplice." His mind raced through all the possibilities, until finally he blurted out, "The Head of Security. He can lock and unlock all the doors remotely. I knew that son of a bitch never liked me."

"Nobody likes you," Charlie said.

DuPont rolled his eyes. "I'll get to the bottom of this. We just need to review the security tapes, then you can arrest these two."

"Don't worry, we'll look at the tapes soon," O'Brien said. "But all I know right now is that there's a large quantity of potentially illegal drugs in your office, and that your suggestion that someone's trying to set you up seems a bit far-fetched."

DuPont slammed his fists on his desktop. "*Far-fetched?* I'm a respected executive and a pillar of this community. These two degenerates are trying to frame me solely because they don't like me."

"We have a woman here accusing you of drugging her with the intent to get her into your hotel room. And there's a large bag of pills in your office," O'Brien said. "If those pills turn out to be what we think they are, then that's a felony."

"Well then, arrest him," Charlie said.

"Will both of you numbskulls stop telling me who to arrest?" O'Brien said, glaring at Charlie and DuPont. "Where can we find this Head of Security guy so we can review the tapes?"

Charlie's throat started to tighten. They would end up in jail for sure if those tapes showed them walking into DuPont's office and rummaging around for an hour.

It wasn't supposed to be like this. I thought they'd just arrest him. Think, Charlie. Think.

"All right. Out of the office. All of you," O'Brien said.

Charlie's mind turned to games again. Specifically, puzzles to be solved. Forget what Edward DuPont might do. What would Edward Carnby from *Alone in the Dark*, the original survival horror game, do in this situation?

We already checked behind the painting. There are no pianos in his office. There were no switches to flip anywhere… But he closed his briefcase really fast when he first saw me.

"Wait," Charlie said. "Search his briefcase."

O'Brien looked at Charlie for what seemed like five minutes, but it was really no more than five seconds. He turned to DuPont, then to the initials on the briefcase. He cracked a smile, probably thinking that "E.D." stood for "erectile dysfunction," especially with the tiny dicks that were shimmering on the desk and all over DuPont's face. "Open the briefcase."

"Wait a minute, I know my rights. This is an illegal search and seizure. You need a warrant to search my briefcase," DuPont said.

O'Brien stared at DuPont's golden nameplate plaque on the desk: "Mr. Edward DuPont, Senior Vice President of Finance." He picked it up and rubbed his fingers over the raised lettering. "Senior VP of Finance. Impressive, Ed. Can I call you Ed?"

"I'd prefer Mr. DuPont."

"Well, you see, Ed... Normally, you'd be right. We wouldn't be able to search your briefcase. But the thing is, a shitload, pardon my language, boatload of what I reasonably believe to be illegal drugs were found in your office. So, I'm placing you under arrest on suspicion of possessing illegal narcotics," O'Brien said. He then turned to Officer Gomez and said, "Gomez. What have I established here?"

Gomez knew his senior partner was testing him. He paused for a few seconds before replying, "You've established a search incident to a lawful arrest to check his briefcase."

"And they say rookies don't know anything. Good job, Gomez," O'Brien said, smiling. "So, Eddie baby, open the fucking briefcase or, if you'd prefer, I can have your briefcase unlocked by another officer, who can be here in five minutes."

DuPont rotated the dial on his combination lock to 777. But today was not his lucky day.

O'Brien, still wearing his latex gloves, rummaged through the case and pulled out a small plastic bag containing ten roofies. He shook it and said, "Look what I found. The same little green pills that were in that portrait of yours."

"They must have planted them too," Dupont said. "My briefcase was here in the office over the weekend."

Fifteen minutes earlier, outside the building, O'Brien had met with a staging officer who arrived early enough to see DuPont step out of his yellow Porsche. It was time to call that officer on the radio. "Unit one-thirty-five, was the occupant of the yellow Porsche carrying a briefcase?" Two seconds of static echoed over the channel before the staging officer replied, "Affirmative, sir. A brown leather briefcase. Looked fancy."

"Copy that."

"This is ridiculous," DuPont said. "I—"

O'Brien interrupted him. "I'm adding a charge of suspicion of possessing illegal narcotics with intent to incapacitate a victim." He turned to Gomez and added, "Cuff this piece of shit. Sorry, piece of filth. The wife's been telling me to work on my language."

While Gomez was cuffing him, he glanced at the tiny dicks that were still stuck to DuPont's forehead. Trying to hold back his laughter, he said, "I always thought you corporate guys were dickheads, but I didn't expect you to advertise it."

Down in the lobby, William watched as O'Brien and Gomez guided DuPont toward the main door. He quickly stepped in front of them and said, "Excuse me. Could I have a word?"

O'Brien said, "Make it quick, pal."

William's smile was as wide as any Chicagoan's after the Bears won the Super Bowl in 1985. He said, "Last Friday, you said my chances of becoming a junior financial analyst were... What was it? Zero-point-three percent? That may be true, but your chances of avoiding jail are zero-point-zero... *statistically speaking*."

On the tenth floor, Schreiber looked out of his window to see DuPont escorted from the building. He turned to Charlie and Jasmine and said, "After you've given your statements to the police, come back to my office for further discussion. Jasmine, I don't know what to say, other than I'm sorry. Thank you for your bravery in coming forward and exposing that monster."

Jasmine let out a huge breath. "I'm just glad he won't be able to do the same thing to anyone else."

Later that morning, Charlie told Schreiber about the meaningless weekend assignment, while Jasmine gave him full details of DuPont's deplorable behavior in Atlanta. Schreiber took notes, shaking his head the whole time. Charlie then told him that he was quitting to pursue his dream of becoming a game developer. Jasmine looked over to Charlie and smiled.

He cleared out his desk by the time she made her way to his cubicle.

"I'm glad you're going to game development school," she said.

"Yeah. I've wasted enough time limiting myself at Unlimited Horizons," Charlie said.

"Dumb fucking name for a company."

"Yeah, dumb—" Charlie said.

Before he could finish, Jasmine embraced him tighter than a wrestler's bear hug. "Thank you, Charlie. For everything," she said. "I hope you make the best games in the world."

Charlie packed up his things, said goodbye to his coworkers, and left the building. For good. He would no longer work as a junior financial analyst and hide his true self. He was ready to be what he was always meant to be: a kick-ass game developer.

But there were a couple of things he needed to do first.

CHAPTER 46

NEGOTIATION TACTICS

T he problem with getting rid of a jagbag like DuPont is that another one always comes to the forefront sooner or later. A win doesn't erase the losses that accumulate over time. Win *Battle Theatre*; lose Susan and a game collection. Beat DuPont; still have to pay Dimitri, the jagbag extraordinaire, four and a half grand.

Charlie's curated game collection was a milestone of his youth. The precious artifacts he had acquired over the past two decades started to fade away in his mind. *I pay Dimitri, get my games back, but then what?* Dom and Johnny had sacrificed themselves during the tournament so that he could achieve glory. Emma could have easily left them all to die and faced SniperSnake47 alone for a chance to win five thousand dollars herself. But she didn't. She helped him and his friends win the money. *And what did I do? I bought her a fucking pair of jeans online.*

A few minutes after driving out of Unlimited Horizons' parking lot, Charlie received a text from Dimitri, requesting a meeting at a local pool hall called O'Malley's. It was the kind of place where people went to drown their dreams with spirits that never lifted them up. Dimitri took advantage of the hopeless by offering his services there to make himself some serious cash. It was the perfect place for him—dim, dreary, and grimy, just like his seedy existence. Charlie texted him back and agreed to the meeting. He had an email from the *Battle Theatre* developers with instructions on how to claim his prize money, but sharing that with Dimitri would be a last resort. He wanted to try something else first.

As soon as Charlie walked into the pool hall, a loud thwack echoed from the collision of the cue ball with the rack of balls on the far table. The click-clack of the balls continued as he walked over to Dimitri, who was playing nine-ball with a gargantuan beast of a man with a jaw that could chisel marble. Sitting on a stool watching them was a thin-framed man with noodles for arms. The two men were Mike and Steve—the lowlifes who had robbed Charlie last Saturday. Dimitri smashed the nine-ball into the pocket, causing a loud boom, to win the game just as Charlie arrived at the table.

Charlie took a glance at Dimitri's journal, which was sitting open on a nearby table next to three draft beers. Dozens of names, numbers, and sports teams were scribbled on the page.

Mike jerked his head at Dimitri and said, "You moved the cue ball closer when I wasn't looking."

Dimitri slammed his cue on the table and yelled, "You think I'm cheat?"

Mike stared him down for a few seconds before sitting down and taking a large swig of beer. "Whatever."

The testosterone in the room was thicker than a smoke grenade cloud in *Battle Theatre*.

Dimitri turned to Charlie and said, "Have seat, my little friend."

Charlie nodded at Mike and Steve, unaware that they were the ones who had robbed him. "Fellas."

Mike sat upright. His face was scowling. He looked like he was itching for a fight. Charlie swallowed hard, clenched his teeth, and tried not to stare back. He felt like a mouse caught in a trap.

Dimitri took a sip of his beer and asked, "How you feelin', buddy?"

"I know you want your money, but I have a proposition for your boss," Charlie said.

"And I know you want games back, so give me my forty-five hundred."

Charlie asked, "Don't you want to hear what I have to say?"

Mike's gaze pierced through Charlie like the optic beam from *X-Men*'s Cyclops. "Look, smart ass. You're lucky I don't chop off those precious little video game thumbs of yours like Dimitri and I talked about. Although that might be tough, seeing as you have more muscle definition in your thumbs than the rest of your scrawny body."

Charlie looked down at his thumbs. *Damn. He's right. My thumbs are pretty well defined.* He kept his head down, avoiding eye contact, and said, "I'll keep it simple. I have two requests."

Mike barked, "The balls on this guy. Now he's making requests."

Charlie's gut told him that Mike had something to do with the burglary. Instead of thinking of his well-being, the irrational part of his brain made him say, "You must be the guy who robbed me. You seem awfully aggressive."

Mike reached across the table, grabbed Charlie by his shirt, and pulled him close. He cocked his hand back, ready to throw a haymaker straight at Charlie's chin. "I'll show you aggressive…" The foul odor of his beer breath mixed with peanuts made Charlie recoil.

Dimitri pulled Mike off him and yelled, "Whoa. Whoa. Mike. Mike." He put his arm as far as he could reach around Mike's enormous back, led him to the front door, and said, "Wait outside."

"I'm not going to—" Mike said.

"If you want continue to work for us," Dimitri interrupted, "do me favor. Get the fuck outta here. Now!"

Like a scolded child, Mike dragged his feet out the door while Charlie straightened his shirt.

"Sorry about hot head. Mix coke with steroids. Never good idea," Dimitri said. "What are two requests?"

Charlie raised his index finger. "One, I need more time."

Dimitri rolled his eyes. He'd heard that excuse not only from Charlie, but from countless other gamblers. "I hope second request is better than first, or I call cokehead back in here."

Charlie held up his first two fingers in a peace sign, even though he knew that Dimitri was in anything but a peaceful mood. He pictured him chopping off both fingers as well as his thumbs if his plan didn't work. "Two, I need my games back."

Dimitri sprang up and said, "I get Mike."

Steve, up to now the silent partner of the criminal trio, placed an open hand on Dimitri's chest to block his path. "Let's hear him out."

Dimitri sat back down and took another swig of beer. "Go ahead."

"I can double your money," Charlie said. "My games are easily worth nine thousand dollars. Hell, maybe even ten. Plenty of people I've met online have made me offers over the past couple of years. If that doesn't work, I can easily sell them on eBay. I just need the games back... and enough time to sell them. It'll take a month, tops."

Dimitri shook his head. "You gamblers, all the same. Always trying to come up with bullshit scheme to avoid paying."

He had already taken a photo of Charlie's game collection and sent it to a pawn shop buddy of his, who offered him five thousand dollars for everything. But he wasn't aware that Steve was an avid gamer who'd secretly looked up all the prices of Charlie's games himself.

Steve cleared his throat. "I know games, Dimitri. He's not lying. They're worth at least eight grand, probably more. I say give him a chance."

Dimitri raised his phone to his ear. "I call boss. Hold on."

If the boss rejected the proposal, Charlie would have no choice but to show Dimitri the email from the *Battle Theatre* developers and hand over almost all of his winnings. But there was a reason why he didn't want to do that. That reason was Emma.

Dimitri got on the line with his boss and said, "I got guy here that owes the forty-five hundred. Yeah, guy with toys we got." He muted the phone, tilted his head toward Steve, and said, "He calls these games toys." He unmuted the call and spoke again to his boss. "Yeah. He say he pay double. But he need month." Dimitri's boss started yelling so loud that he had to move the phone away from his ear. It was twenty seconds before he was able to continue. "Is legit. Steve say we sell games for eight grand minimum. Maybe nine or ten. Expensive toys. Yes. Collector's items... No, I didn't. No. No. I'm not doing that. He good kid. I maybe break his thumbs... His kneecaps?" Dimitri paused to look Charlie up and down. "Is harsh, don't you think? No, I don't have hammer. The hardware store? Yes. Yes. I have crowbar in trunk. You won't change mind? You sure? Fine. I get Mike to do it."

Charlie's face turned pale as his insides twisted like an angry Amish man churning butter while dreaming of watching a porn video, but knowing he can't because of his faith. Charlie's throat tightened, and his breathing became shallow. He was seconds away from passing out. He reached into his pocket for his phone, ready to show Dimitri the email as proof that he was about to receive five thousand dollars. "Dimitri, please don't do this. I—"

Dimitri burst out laughing as if he were at a Yakov Smirnoff comedy show. Charlie wasn't sure if the laugh was from delight at the idea of causing him pain or just simple amusement.

"Relax. My boss say yes," Dimitri said. "He hung up phone as soon as I say 'collector's items.' Look on your face. Classic. That's what you get for dragging feet with debt."

Charlie closed his eyes and let out a loud sigh. "I guess I deserved that."

Dimitri stood up and said, "Steve, give games back to Charlie. If there's one thing boss never says no to, it's extra money."

Charlie rested his chin on his hand. Dazed.

"Don't sit there. Time is money. Go with Steve. Sell your toys," Dimitri said, before waving his hand to dismiss them. Charlie jumped up and was about to run out the door when Dimitri added, "Remember what Sosa say to Tony Montana before he got whacked."

"I wouldn't dream of fucking you. Thanks, Dimitri."

Charlie and Steve walked past Mike, who was still outside smoking a cigarette. He gave them a dirty look but went back inside the bar like a good henchman. Steve unlocked the trunk of his car, and then he and Charlie transferred the four overfilled boxes into Charlie's Accord. As they loaded the final box, Steve said, "I've been playing *Battle Theatre* all weekend. Great game."

"Hope you had fun," Charlie said.

Steve gazed at him, not like a criminal sizing up his victim, but like a teenage girl mesmerized by Taylor Swift. "The team that won the Midnight Multiplayer Match did some amazing shit. The way that Nighthawk34 and CyberLancer51 lined up that drone for the final shot blew my mind."

Charlie pressed his lips together and grinned. Steve had played dumb in the pool hall, acting like he had no idea who he was. But now it was like they were two lost souls who had found each other amid the chaos of a life of gambling.

Charlie sat on the hood of his car and asked, "How'd you know?"

"I recognized your voice from your *BattleTheatre* chat on YouTube. You have a distinctive whiny voice that's hard to miss."

Thank God Dom posted that video. "Whiny? Really?"

Steve sat next to him on the hood and said, "A bit. But who cares? You're, like, famous... At least in the gaming community."

"Why didn't you say anything back there?" Charlie asked, nodding toward the pool hall.

"How could I betray the winner of the *BattleTheatre* tournament? I wouldn't be able to live with myself. This is my way of saying 'Fuck you' to Mike and Dimitri. You must have a pretty good reason why you didn't just pay Dimitri the five grand."

"It's for RedBird21."

"The girl in the boat. Of course."

"She's my sister."

Steve reached into his pocket and handed Charlie his business card.

Since when do criminals have business cards?

"Here's my number in case you need help selling any of those games."

Charlie placed his right palm over his chest. "From the bottom of my heart, thank you."

"Go take care of your sister. Family is everything."

"So are friends. I'm lucky I found a new one today."

After driving back to his apartment, Charlie opened the trunk of his car and stared at the spines of all his games in the four bulging boxes. All those memories. Solving puzzles in *Little Nightmares* and *The Talos Principle*. Slaying dozens of dragons in *Skyrim* and *Dragon's Dogma*. Experiencing jump scares in *Dead Space* and *The Evil Within 2*. Going on challenging quests in *Divinity: Original Sin 2* and *Xenoblade Chronicles*. Managing his inventory in *Final Fantasy XV* and *Diablo 3*. Scoring touchdowns in *Tecmo Super Bowl* and *Madden*. Sniping enemies in *Sniper Elite* and, of course, *Battle Theatre*. He had lived a whole other life in the contents of those four boxes. But it was time to let them go. Sometimes you have to let go of what you love the most to let another love in.

He replied to the email from the *Battle Theatre* developers and gave them his bank account details. Thirty minutes later, they sent an email back confirming that his winnings had been transferred to his account.

There were still a few hours left in the day. More than enough time to go shopping for a super-powered PC.

CHAPTER 47

TIME AND MONEY WELL SPENT

The jeans Charlie ordered for Emma were lying in a package on his doorstep. They were slightly faded in the front, with a tapered fit around the thighs flaring to soft bell bottom. Gold rivets were stamped on the hip pockets, and embroidered sequins shaped like tiny silver stars ran down the seams. It was a nice gift for a kid sister, but not enough for a savior. It was an insult that everyone on the team was getting five grand, while Emma was receiving a gift worth less than a hundred fifty dollars. So, for the first time in his life, Charlie set aside his material desires and thought of someone else. Spending his prize money on a supercomputer for Emma would have been unthinkable yesterday. But not today.

He stopped asking himself, *Why am I like this?* and started telling himself, *I don't want to be like this anymore.* He drove to Best Buy and bought Emma a powerhouse computer with an Intel i9-9900K processor running at a turbo boost of 5 GHz, 32 GB of RAM, and an Nvidia GeForce RTX 2080. He paired it with a 32-inch 144 Hz monitor, featuring a 3440×1440 display panel and a 1-millisecond response time, complete with fancy RGB lighting and a built-in webcam.

He texted Emma to ask if she was at home. She replied with a suggestion that they should meet online instead, since she was in the middle of a *BattleTheatre* match. He told her he wanted to see her in person. It took three more texts before she finally agreed.

Charlie wrapped Emma's gifts in bright red, glossy paper. It was a crude wrapping job, but at least they were fully covered.

When he arrived at their mom's house, Mary answered the door, squinted suspiciously at the two boxes, and said, "What is happening right now?"

"Where's Emma?"

"Upstairs in her room. Playing her game."

Charlie set the boxes on the kitchen table and said, "These are for Emma. Sit tight."

He made his way up the stairs, then paused in Emma's doorway. The familiar terrain of *BattleTheatre* was on her TV screen. She was wearing her Turtle Beach headset. Charlie listened for a couple of minutes as she explained the controls to a newbie player. Not judging. Not being impatient. Just helping a fellow gamer. Charlie smiled, knowing that no one deserved a computer more than Emma. She was one of the next generation of gamers. Ready to take on the world and make her dreams come true. With a little help from Charlie, of course.

He crept up behind her and hugged her. It was only the second time he had ever done that. The first had been on the day of their parents' divorce. Emma removed her headset and turned to face him. Normally, she would have recoiled in terror, but this time she lifted her arm to embrace the back of his head.

Charlie asked, "How's the world's best *BattleTheatre* player?"

"Stop gaslighting, Mr. Champion," Emma said.

"It's not gaslighting if it's true."

Emma shook her head. "Yeah, whatever."

Charlie smiled and said, "You mad that I won?"

"You guys need the money more than I do, especially you with Dimitri."

Charlie sat on Emma's bed and rested his chin on his hand. "I thought I needed the money... until I didn't."

Emma squinted. "What are you getting at?"

"I can't explain why we never played together until this weekend," Charlie said. He paused. "Actually, I do know the reason. I wanted to be in control when everything was falling apart after the divorce. Then I just got used to the feeling of being alone. Part of it was because you were my little sister. I didn't think you took it as seriously as I did. But now I know that you do. I'm sorry that you can't get on an esports team because your computer is a piece of shit."

"I found a cheap graphics card on eBay," Emma said, "but I'm worried that my CPU will bottleneck the performance. I don't know. Should I buy it?"

Charlie walked into the hallway and said, "I have the answer to that question. Come downstairs."

Emma followed him down the stairs and saw Mary standing over a red box the size of a dishwasher on the kitchen table. On top of it was a smaller box with a card taped to it.

Emma's eyes darted back and forth between her mother and her brother. "What the hell is going on?"

"They're for you," Charlie said. "Open the small one first."

Emma ripped it open and screamed, "Wow! Thanks, Charlie. I've wanted these for so long. Should I open the card next?"

"Please do," Charlie said.

Emma pulled the card from the envelope and started to read:

To my Champion,

I used to think that all I needed was myself and my thoughts. I was alone even when I was with people. Instead of leaning on you, I ran away from you. And I ran away from Susan, who only wanted to spend more time with me. But this isn't about me. This is about you. My sister. Fellow gamer. Future conqueror of esports. A selfless, beautiful woman who did something her brother will never forget. The tournament wasn't for me to win. It was for you. It's always been for you. I just didn't know it at the time. You suffered with me all those years when Mom and Dad got divorced. Games got us through all those tough times, and they'll get us through all the hard times ahead. Go make your dream come true. Like mine did, when I was saved by you.

Love you forever,

Charlie

Emma wiped the tears from her eyes and looked up at Charlie. He smiled and nodded toward the large box. She tore a large section of the wrapping but paused as soon as she saw what was inside. It was the most expensive gift she had ever received. She ran across to Charlie and hugged him tight. Not wanting to let go. Afraid that she might wake up from this wonderful dream.

"What about your gambling debt?" she said.

"Dimitri is letting me sell my games to pay it off. A new friend of mine convinced him it was a good idea."

"Charlie. No! Those games mean everything to you."

"They're just small rectangular boxes collecting dust. But *this* box…" Charlie tapped the computer box with his palm. "This box is your future."

Emma jumped up and down, stomping her feet like she'd just won the Illinois lottery. She hugged Charlie again, then Mary, who said, "I've got nothing to do with this. This was all Charlie."

"I don't care," shrieked Emma. "I'm hugging everyone today. I'd hug Dad if he were here. He said he wanted to talk to me after the party… but you know what, I'm gonna call him first."

Emma was on her way to not only excel in esports but also to repair her fractured relationship with her father. Something told her that good ol' Joe would get it right this time.

It was ten o'clock at night by the time Charlie arrived back at his apartment. He couldn't stop thinking about how Ayanna had humiliated Tim at the party. He logged in on his PS4 Pro, hoping to see him playing *Battle Theatre* online, but no luck. He sent him three texts, but they went unanswered. He called him, but all five calls went straight to voicemail.

Charlie was lying in bed. Exhausted but unable to sleep. *He's usually online at this time and he always responds to my texts.* The chances of both his console and his phone being broken were almost zero. Something was wrong.

Charlie had sent Tim a physical copy of *Watch Dogs 2* last year, so he had his mailing address. He tapped the details into his phone, which told him it was an hour's drive, but that didn't stop him from bolting out the door. It was snowing. Hard. The salt trucks weren't out yet, so he'd have to drive slowly, which would add at least ten minutes to the journey. He gazed at all the Christmas lights on the way and thought about what he was going to say.

He arrived at Tim's house just before midnight and rang the doorbell, ready to apologize to Vonda for showing up so late. A minute passed. Charlie rang the doorbell again. Then he knocked on the door. If no one answered soon, he'd have to call the police. He imagined them breaking down the door and finding Tim dead on the floor. Or a goodbye note with no one in the house. Maybe Tim had convinced his mom to drive him to the Fox River, then, when she wasn't looking, wheeled himself in. Maybe he'd rolled off the overpass above the Kennedy Expressway.

Thirty seconds later, the porch light turned on. Charlie let out a sigh of relief.

Tim's mother opened the door. "Charlie. What on earth are you doing here? Come inside out of the cold."

Charlie wiped his feet on the welcome mat and stepped inside. His eyes were wide and frantic. "Hi, Ms. Maddox. Sorry for coming so late. Where's Tim?"

"He's sleeping."

Charlie was confused. "He always stays up past midnight. Is he okay?"

"He's been sleeping all day. I tried to wake him, but he grunted at me, saying he wants to be left alone," Vonda said. "Since you came all this way, why don't you try talking to him? I'm worried about him."

"I'm so sorry about the party," Charlie said. "I never should have set him up with that girl."

Vonda grabbed Charlie by his collar and pulled him close, just as Mike had earlier. She continued to hold onto him as a single tear rolled down her cheek. "You listen to me, young man.

Do not apologize for trying to help my son. He loves you, you know. You did what I couldn't do for years. You gave him hope."

Charlie bowed his head and said, "Only for it to be taken away from him."

Vonda released Charlie's shirt and crossed her arms. "Well, then, give it back to him."

Charlie shook his head. "How am I gonna do that?"

"Good friends lift each other up when they're down."

Charlie slumped forward. "Is that what I am? A good friend?"

"Honey, you his *only* friend," Vonda said with a smirk. "But you drove all this way in a snowstorm just to check up on him. I'd say that makes you a good friend, too."

"Thanks, Ms. Maddox," Charlie said.

"He's upstairs. It's the first door on the left after you make a right."

He headed up the stairs and knocked on Tim's door. He waited a few seconds, then slowly opened it and stepped inside. A wave of intense heat slapped him in the face. Tim was lying in bed with a thick, green *Halo* comforter featuring a large picture of Master Chief draped over him. An oscillating electric heater seemed to be the main cause of the oven-like conditions.

Charlie gently shook him and said, "Wake up, toasty Tim."

Tim opened his eyes. "Charlie? What the hell are you doing here?"

"You weren't online and didn't answer your phone, so I was worried about you."

"I'll be online tomorrow… and forever," Tim replied, sitting up. Video games were a way for Tim to run free in a virtual world without limitations. He didn't have to think about disabilities in a landscape filled with heroes, villains, and NPCs. Games gave him an intoxicating sense of power as well as a brief respite from the harsh truth that life was mostly filled with judgmental people who would never allow him to feel normal, let alone become their friend. "Let's face it, I belong in the online world, not the real one. I have no friends."

"Bullshit," Charlie said. "You have a whole crew of friends. Including me, your best friend. All you need in life is one best friend. You belong in the real world, with me, Dom, Johnny, and Emma. We should be doing things together, like eating pizza while watching the Bears game at Francisco's."

Tim buried his face in his pillow and said, "I thought Johnny was your best friend."

"Yeah, well, I have two, so shoot me."

"I don't think it works like that."

"Who made the fucking rules?" Charlie said. "I've said things to you that I've never said to Johnny. You and I are best friends online, so we should be best friends in the real world, too."

Tim tossed aside his pillow and stared at the ceiling. "The real world isn't friendly for people like me."

"Fuck everyone else. I got you. *We* got you. You just gotta give us a chance. And give girls a chance, too."

"That shit is definitely over," Tim said.

"Again with the bullshit. You're handsome, funny, and super intelligent," Charlie said. "And the way you piloted that drone behind SniperSnake47. That was greatness. Your calculations and planning won the match for us. If you can do something like that, you can easily win some lucky girl's heart with your love computations."

Tim turned his head toward Charlie and laughed. "*Love computations?* You couldn't come up with something better than that?"

Charlie raised his hands in the air. "I dunno. You're smart and you're looking for love, so, you know…" After five seconds of silence, he added, "Okay, yeah, that was pretty dorky. What can I say? I'm a nerd. Just like you. We're all nerds."

"I know," Tim said.

Charlie pulled out his phone and ran a quick search. Then he held the screen toward Tim. "See? There are plenty of dating websites for gamers and people with disabilities. But love'll never find you unless you look for it."

"Even if, by miraculous divine intervention, some girl wanted to go out with me, I wouldn't know what to do on our first date."

Charlie remembered Dom's advice. "She has to feel like the most important woman in the world when she's with you. Ask her about herself. Take an interest in what she has to say, then ask even more questions. Be confident, but humble."

Tim slid beneath his comforter like melted butter. "That sounds like a lot of work. What if she rejects me like Ayanna did?"

"It would be totally different," Charlie said. "She'd know about your disability beforehand. So, you'd just have to be yourself."

Tim swung his legs over the side of the bed and sat up. "I'll think about it."

"That's all I ask." Charlie paused and looked at the heater. "Jesus, it's hot in here. I don't give a shit how cold it is outside. Get dressed. You need some fresh air."

CHAPTER 48

THE POWER OF MUSIC

our months passed.

F The April sun warmed Charlie's skin like a plush blanket. He had learned to step outside and leave the cold days behind him. It was time to make room for things to grow. He spent his days strolling around the Polygon University campus between classes, while his nights were devoted to developing his first video game. After mastering Scratch MIT, he had moved on to Gamemaker and Godot before finally settling on Unity to create his 2D game, *Jubilant Jungle Jaunt*—a collect-a-thon platformer that was a cross between a modern-day *Pitfall* and *Metal Slug*. It featured gorgeous pixel art, lush green foliage, and stunning animation. Instead of collecting gold coins like in *Super Mario Bros*, the goal was to gather four-leaf clovers for points, and gold stars for special abilities like super speed and a jetpack.

Charlie's old programming notes had proved invaluable in helping him adjust the game's difficulty based on the player's performance. Every night, he would browse the Unity forums for ideas on how to troubleshoot bugs and glitches. He was the only one in his class ambitious enough to create a game after only a few months in school. It may not have been as polished as *Celeste*, the popular indie platformer at the time, but it was fun. And, more importantly, easier than *Cuphead*.

The day finally came to submit it. Charlie stayed after class and handed a USB drive to his teacher. "Professor Wilkes, I was hoping you could look at a game I've been working on for the past few months."

Startled, Professor Wilkes replied, "You mean to tell me you developed your own game?"

"Yes, sir," Charlie said. "The difficulty changes based on player performance. The worse you play, the easier the game becomes. The better you play, the harder it gets."

Professor Wilkes rubbed his chin. "What kind of game is it?"

"A platformer."

"I used to be pretty good at *Super Metroid*," Professor Wilkes said. "Let's see what we've got here."

Professor Wilkes loaded the game onto his laptop and pressed *Start*. Within a few minutes, the corners of his mouth started to lift, and his eyes filled with wonder. It was a look most gamers have when immersed in a fun video game. Almost like savoring a delicious dinner, reading a captivating book, or gazing at a majestic mountain landscape. Fifteen minutes later, he said, "Impressive. I felt the difficulty change you talked about. When I kept dying on that third section, my next run was easier. But it's missing one crucial element."

"What's that?"

"Music," Professor Wilkes said. "Are you okay if I send this to a composer who teaches here? You're not scheduled to take his class until next semester, but he sometimes helps exceptional students. He might be willing to write some chip-tune music for you if he likes your game."

Charlie's mouth dropped open. "I... I don't know what to say," he stammered. "That would be incredible. Thank you so much."

"I'd also like to meet with you after class so we can polish it up a bit. But this is already fine work, Charlie."

Professor Wilkes rummaged through his desk and emerged with the composer's business card, which he handed to Charlie. It read:

Carlos Cruz
Video Game Composer, Soundscapes
Professor, Polygon University

As soon as Charlie left the classroom, he pumped his fist in the air and skipped to his car. He didn't care if he looked foolish. Carlos's chip-tune music would elevate his game to a new level and prove that he belonged in the world of game development.

A few days later, Charlie was so starstruck when he received a call from the composer that he could barely speak.

Carlos laughed and said, "You're acting like I'm a celebrity or something."

"You *are* a celebrity to me," Charlie admitted. "I've listened to so much of your music over the years. Your work is amazing. You're incredibly talented."

"You have some talent yourself. Your game is quite fun. I'm guessing you've been tinkering around with game development for a while."

"About four months."

Carlos leaned back from his computer and placed his hands behind his head. "I know old man Wilkes hasn't taught you all this in four months."

"I used a few tricks Professor Wilkes taught me, but I'm mostly self-taught."

"Astonishing. Simply astonishing. How would you feel if I composed some chip-tune music for your game? Something upbeat and fun."

"That would be wonderful. Do you think you could compose something like *Streets of Rage* for the opening scene?" Charlie asked.

Carlos said, "You're familiar with the work of Yuzo Koshiro?"

"He's a master of video game music. I also like Harry Gregson-Williams's work on *Metal Gear Solid 2*, and what Richard Jacques did for *Headhunter*."

"Don't expect anything as grand as that, but I think you'll like what I come up with," Carlos said. "Call me next week. I'll let you know how things are going."

Over the next three weeks, Charlie worked closely with Carlos to integrate his music into the game. Between them, they came up with an innovative way to highlight Charlie's groundbreaking dynamic difficulty concept. In addition to corresponding to the action on the screen, the music's tempo increased when players performed well, and decreased if they played poorly. It was an idea that had never previously occurred to Carlos, who thanked Charlie for providing him with a new perspective on how to link his music to the gameplay. Soon, their mutual respect quickly developed into a strong friendship.

On his way home one evening, Charlie stopped at a local coffee shop and saw a small poster advertising a Battle of the Bands concert at the Ragin' Marlin. He scanned down the list of ten bands along with their single-sentence descriptions. The final entry read: "The She-Nannigans, featuring their new songs 'The Three A's' and 'The Bench at Dawn.'"

He knew that "The Bench at Dawn" had to be about his relationship with Susan. They had first met at a house party nearly two years ago. He was instantly drawn to her warm smile and infectious laugh. The questions they asked each other created an intense bond neither of them had ever felt before. They both fell in love that night. Charlie told Susan amusing stories about how relatable her life was to his. He also made sure she always had a drink in her hand, which made her feel special. After the party, they went to a local twenty-four-hour breakfast joint—a popular choice for local drunks. But Charlie wasn't drunk, and neither was Susan. They couldn't bear the thought of saying goodbye. Later, they found themselves on a park bench as the sun rose above the horizon. They gazed into each other's eyes. He kissed her for the first time. It was the best kiss he'd ever had. He ran his fingers through her blond hair and asked if she would be his girlfriend. She said yes.

Charlie still thought about Susan's laugh when he watched a funny movie, her perfume when he walked past a flower display, and her touch when he was holding his controller. But most of all, he thought about love. Something he'd never known. Until he met her. Like a rose's thorn, she never left his mind. After spending hours programming his game, he'd lie on his bed at the end of the night. Missing her. His loneliness was like a guest who never leaves.

Back in his apartment, Charlie sat at his desk and thought about the Battle of the Bands poster. He tried to focus on his game, but it was no use. He scrolled through photos on his phone until he found one of Susan staring at him across the dinner table at a fancy restaurant. It had been taken over a year ago. The warm glow of the lighting behind her, combined with her stunning smile, made her look elegant and angelic. He wanted to go to her gig, but figured that she probably never wanted to see him again. Nothing he could say would make her forgive him.

But maybe there was something he could do.

The next day, he called Carlos and offered to buy him an early dinner at Au Cheval, which was renowned for serving the best burger in Chicago, if not the world. Charlie drove thirty minutes to get there, but he would have driven two hours if necessary. They met out in front of the restaurant and signed up for a twenty-minute wait.

As they stood there, Charlie turned to Carlos and said, "I need a huge favor."

"Sure, kid. What's up?"

"Do you know anyone in the music industry who's looking for new talent?"

"Everyone in the music industry is always looking for new talent. Who do you have in mind?"

"My ex-girlfriend. Her band is called the She-Nannigans. They're performing tomorrow night at the Ragin' Marlin."

The chatter from the other people waiting in line grew deafening. A couple of Bears fans behind them kept talking about how the double-doink field goal tragedy from last January crushed their Super Bowl dreams.

Carlos rolled his eyes and said, "Let's get out of here for a second."

They squeezed past the crowd and stepped outside.

Carlos cupped his hands together. "I've done a lot of favors, but never one for an ex-girlfriend. She must be special."

"She is. She just doesn't know it yet," Charlie said. "I know this is asking a lot, but would you be willing to go to the gig and listen to her band?"

"Sure," Carlos said.

"Wow! I thought you'd need more convincing."

"My wife has been bugging me to take her out for a date night," Carlos said. "A concert sounds like fun. And if this ex-girlfriend's band is any good, I can get her in touch with the right people. Do you want me to call her if I like what I hear?"

"There won't be any need to do that. She'll call you. I just need one of your business cards."

Carlos said, "Sure. Let's head back inside."

As soon as they walked through the door, Carlos asked the host for a pen, pulled out his business card, and wrote something on the back before handing it to Charlie.

Fifteen minutes later, they sat down to eat. Charlie added a fried egg, while Carlos opted for hickory-smoked thick-cut bacon on top of their burgers. Charlie's moving account of his breakup with Susan made Carlos want to help him even more.

After the meal, Charlie called Dom on the drive home.

"*Paisan!*" Dom said. "How's the game coming along? Did you get a chance to tighten up the graphics in level three?"

Charlie asked, "How does one tighten up graphics exactly?"

"I guess we'll never know, since you chose to go to Polygon instead of Westwood College Online. Your graphics could have been tight," Dom said, referring to an obscure game design commercial from the nineties.

Charlie paused for a long time before saying, "The She-Nannigans are playing tomorrow at the Ragin' Marlin."

Dom tilted his head to the side and smiled. He knew where this was headed. "You're thinking about going, aren't you?"

Charlie turned north onto Halsted Street and said, "Do I just show up and say, 'I missed your last performance, so I figured I'd come to this one. Please forgive me.'"

"Do you want to get back with her?"

That was the question Charlie had been asking himself for the past five months. It seemed pointless, since he believed Susan was done with him forever. But he couldn't stop thinking of her. Especially at night.

All the studying, not to mention the effort he'd put into developing his own game, meant he no longer had the time or energy to play other games at night. But he was okay with that. He was part of something bigger now, able to tap into twelve-year-old Charlie's sense of wonder to create a digital world. Ambitious enough to achieve what he was meant to do. And brave enough to express himself through the one thing he had left to love.

He had trouble sleeping most nights. He would lie awake thinking about his game. And especially about Susan. He had pushed her away long before she'd broken up with him. All she wanted was to spend more time with him because she loved him. In the end, he got what he wanted: all the time in the world to play games. It reminded him of when he was a kid. Left alone by his father every weekend. Video games had filled the void then, but now she was the only one who could do so, by wrapping her arms around him, making him feel safe, bringing stability into his life, supporting him when he was anxious, feeding him chicken noodle soup when he was sick, having intelligent conversations with him, and giving him the love and affection he so desperately needed. He still loved her. Maybe there was a way for him to prove it.

He turned left onto Fullerton Avenue. "If I can't make it work with her, I can't make it work with anyone. If there's even a remote chance of winning her back, I'll take it."

"You'll need to talk to her about finding a way to include games in your relationship so she doesn't feel neglected," Dom said. "I had to negotiate with Marie about when I would play my games."

"How'd that go?"

"You ever notice that I never log in before ten at night?"

"Well, yeah, I mean, I figured you were busy with the kids and work stuff."

"I am, but I also spend a lot of time with Marie," Dom said. "I used to get home from work before she did, so naturally I'd play a game. She'd walk in and make dinner while I kept playing until it was time to eat. During dinner, I'd ask her about her day, but when she put on Netflix, I'd go back to playing in the basement."

"All of this sounds very familiar," Charlie said.

"Now, when we're together, she gets my full attention. I hit the *Pause* button a lot," Dom said.

Charlie stopped at a red light and lightly banged his head against the steering wheel. "I wish you had told me all this sooner. Maybe we never would have broken up."

"Nah," Dom said. "It took months of therapy before I was able to convince Marie that I could see her perspective. It sounds like Susan had already made up her mind to break up with you."

"Maybe I just deserve to be alone," Charlie said.

"No one deserves to be alone," Dom said. "Look. A relationship can be a pain in the ass sometimes, but no matter how bad life gets, it's nice having someone by your side to get you through the shit."

"I still don't know what I'm gonna do," Charlie said. "But thanks."

"Any time," Dom said. "Remember what I taught you, Luke."

Charlie laughed and hung up.

CHAPTER 49

LYRICS OF LOVE

Charlie spent half of Saturday morning playtesting *Jubilant Jungle Jaunt* and the other half brushing up on advanced Unity techniques. There was also time for what had become a new tradition: a weekly call from his father.

"Hi, Charlie. How's your game coming along?"

"Pretty good."

Charlie cut a sandwich in half and took a bite. It was Joe's turn to speak, but after ten seconds of silence, all he could manage was a long sigh.

"Is everything okay?" Charlie said.

Although Joe had quit heavy drinking back in December, he still allowed himself a couple of drinks every night. Recently, though, his daytime cravings had been increasing, so he'd decided to take the next brave step. He rubbed the top of his bald head and said, "I've stopped betting on basketball. And I've joined Alcoholics Anonymous. My first meeting was yesterday."

Before the *BattleTheatre* tournament, Charlie would have hung up on his father or said, "That's nice." But now he listened intently, deeply sympathizing with him. He tossed the controller he was using for playtesting aside and said, "I'm proud of you, Dad."

There was a long pause before Joe said, "That's supposed to be my line."

Charlie rubbed the back of his neck. "I used to want to hear you *say* it, but it's so much better when you *show* it. And you've been showing me a little bit every day."

Joe replied, "Well, I'm gonna say it anyway. I'm proud of you, son. I can't believe you've made a game already... Well, that's all really. I just wanted to call and hear your voice."

Joe was about to hang up when Charlie said, "Wait! Tell me more about your AA meeting."

And just like that, Charlie and his father had the longest conversation they ever had—over an hour. Charlie finally saw Joe not as an inattentive, drunk fool but as a man who was trying to turn his life around. First, by repairing his relationship with his son. Then, by breaking free from his twin addictions: gambling and alcoholism.

As soon as Charlie hung up, he opened the contacts on his phone, scrolled down to the name "Joe," and changed it to "Dad."

Nightfall arrived. Jessica was setting up the band's gear at the Ragin' Marlin, a psychedelic-themed venue decorated with multicolored lights, plastic bead curtains, polished wooden tables topped with stained-glass lamps, and a light-blue ceiling with hand-painted clouds. A few minutes later, Kat and Mimi showed up to lend a hand. Jessica had acted on her desire to date women back in January by asking out Mimi, but their relationship collapsed after a month due to her ongoing commitment issues.

When Susan arrived, she hugged all three of her bandmates before hooking up her guitar and amp. Then she placed the Dream Bin at the front of the stage. It was never meant to be a tip basket, but that didn't stop people from tossing in a dollar or two. This was the band's fifth gig since Susan's breakup with Charlie. They were maturing as a band, playing much better than they had in the past, and becoming more comfortable performing on stage. Tonight's show would be the first time Susan would try to sing in front of an audience since the disastrous gig at the Rusty Spoon five months ago. The band had tried to persuade her to sing back in February, but she wasn't ready. Like thrashers in a mosh pit, thoughts of Charlie kept banging around in her head. Her song "The Bench at Dawn" was about him, after all. She sometimes revisited the bench to write lyrics, hoping to recapture the feeling she'd shared with him that morning. Always at dawn, so she could watch the sunrise while the breeze blew through her hair.

The Ragin' Marlin could hold about three hundred people, with around sixty fitting in a large standing area directly in front of the stage. Stickers of alternative rock bands and profound quotes lined the walls. Twenty people were already hanging out in the standing area. The venue owner scheduled the She-Nannigans to perform first to boost the room's energy and get the women in the crowd dancing. An all-girl rock band would be perfect for that.

Thirty minutes later, the standing area was packed with fifty people, while another hundred were sitting at the lounge tables. Carlos and his wife arrived and found a table near the back.

The She-Nannigans had less than five minutes to get ready. As they tuned their instruments, Jessica said, "We'll start off with 'Radio Girls' to get warmed up. Then it's your time to shine, Susan, with 'The Three A's' and 'The Bench at Dawn.' We'll close out with 'Backhanded Compliment' and 'Unapologetic Crazy-Ass Bitches.' Everyone ready?"

Mimi and Kat nodded, while Susan rubbed the back of her neck and trudged to the rear of the stage.

Jessica followed her and asked, "What's going on with you?"

"Can I sing my songs last?"

"We've just decided on the set list. Why mess with it?"

Susan snapped back. "Because I feel like it, okay?"

Jessica placed her hands on her hips. "Something's going on. We're not starting until you spill the beans."

Susan ran both hands through her hair before interlacing them behind her head. She turned her back on the crowd. "It's stupid."

Murmurs from the audience grew louder, with one person yelling, "Let's go already!"

Jessica approached the microphone and announced, "We're experiencing some technical difficulties. They should be resolved in a few minutes." Then she hurried back to Susan. "If you haven't noticed, we have a crowd full of angry drunks waiting for us to start."

Susan's throat started to tighten. "I can't explain it. This feeling. It's like I can't sing unless I know Charlie's in the crowd. Like I need him there to show me everything's going to be okay."

Jessica grabbed Susan's head with both hands and turned it to the left, then slowly rotated it to the right, until she'd scanned the whole crowd. "Do you see him here?"

"No."

"Exactly. He's probably playing a video game with his friends," Jessica said. "Ugh. Men. Being gay is so much simpler."

Mimi scoffed and said, "No, it's not."

Susan couldn't stop scratching her forearm. "I'm scared I'm gonna mess up again."

Jessica placed her hands on Susan's shoulders and said, "Baby, I believe in you, and so do the girls."

Susan sighed. "I don't know if—"

Before she could finish her sentence, Jessica turned to Kat and Mimi and said, "Change of plan. We're gonna close with

'The Three A's' and 'The Bench at Dawn.'" Then she turned back to Susan. "That should give you some time to calm your nerves. You're gonna do great."

The band played the first three songs, then paused so Susan could say a few words to the crowd. Her mind raced, but her body remained perfectly still. She imagined Charlie's arms around her, saying, "Breathe in. Then out. You're okay. Clear your mind. Start over."

She exhaled slowly. Then took a breath and said, "This next song is called 'The Three A's.' Most people are lucky to get even one A from their partners."

The catchy guitar chords got everyone at the Ragin' Marlin swaying their hips before Susan started singing. This time, her voice was as smooth as glass:

> Attention, you never gave it to me.
> Admiration, is what I seek.
> Affection, do you know what it means?
> I wanted them all, but I came up empty.

The song ended with a modest round of applause before Susan approached the mic again. "This song is called 'The Bench at Dawn.' It's about a very special time and place for me."

Kat launched into a booming drumbeat, which was followed by a few simple chords on Jessica's rhythm guitar and a steady thump from Mimi's bass. Then Susan played a melodic twenty-second riff that made the crowd clap along. With every pluck of her guitar, an explosive and complex crescendo erupted. Her fingers glided across the strings as effortlessly as a champion surfer rides a wave. Her voice matched the chords, creating a passion-drenched symphony:

You say you won, I feel like I lost.
I loved you hard, it came at a cost.
I was your Queen, now I'm your pawn.
Will I see you again, on the bench at dawn?

The melodic beat paired with Susan's angelic voice was a huge success. The crowd cheered for almost a full minute. The performance couldn't have gone any better. Carlos scribbled notes like a man possessed. Then he sent a text to Charlie.

At the end of the night, a funky reggae outfit called Dead Dread Beat won first place in the Battle of the Bands competition due to their smooth sound and wild onstage antics. A synth band took second place. The She-Nannigans placed third, but Susan felt like she'd won the grand prize.

She was on her way to becoming the singer–songwriter she had always imagined herself to be.

CHAPTER 50

DAWN APPROACHES

There was a chameleon in the crowd during the She-Nannigans' performance at the Ragin' Marlin. A man who looked like a young and grumpy Mike Ditka, sporting a mustache with ten-day-old stubble, aviator sunglasses, a dark-blue Bears hat, and a gray windbreaker. He leaned against the back wall. He focused on Susan with a gaze more intense than when he'd tried to beat his high score in the bullet-hell shooter *Ikaruga*. He was mesmerized by her aura. She seemed different—her demeanor, her presence, the way she bobbed her head and moved her body to the bassline while playing guitar. She looked happy and free. The raw emotion in her voice made him feel like he was staring into her light-hazel eyes. Falling in love all over again.

With lines like "You think I'm tearing you down, but I only want you around" and "You love the game, I don't feel the same," both of her songs were clearly about him. But one lyric kept replaying in his head like a broken record: "Will I see you again, on the bench at dawn?" A tidal wave of guilt and anguish engulfed him as he kept listening. The pain in her voice was unmistakable, yet stunningly beautiful. She might have been an injured swan when they broke up, but now she was a majestic eagle, spreading her wings for the world to see. The breakup had given her what she needed to become an artist, just as it had made him realize he was meant to be a creator, too. The moment she stopped singing, he clapped louder than he ever had in his life.

His phone pinged. He looked down to see a text from Carlos: "It's a go."

Charlie's mission was clear: slip two items into the Dream Bin without her recognizing him. Susan had known him as a clean-shaven man who rarely wore a hat, so he hoped his disguise as Da Coach would be good enough. He'd completed over a hundred thousand missions in more than three thousand games during his lifetime, but this was his most important yet. And his well-defined thumbs couldn't help him this time. If Susan spotted him, it would lead to one of those awkward ex-lovers' conversations—all small talk, no substance. He wanted nothing more than to tell her how sorry he was, but now was not the time. Words were cheap. She deserved more.

He reached into his front pocket, grabbed Carlos's business card, and turned it over to see the handwritten message on the back. It was the most important message he would ever deliver. His movements were slow and calculated. Sticking to the shadows like Solid Snake, he made his way to the front of the stage and dropped the business card in the Dream Bin, along with a single short-stemmed rose. As he reentered the crowd, he glanced back at Susan. She casually tossed her lyric sheet into the Dream Bin, then unplugged her guitar from her amp. Charlie took a few more steps and looked back at her once more. His chest ached. He thought this might be the last time he'd ever see her. It was painful. But comforting that he gave her something without expecting anything in return.

Carlos's business card was a gift. Not an obligation to take him back.

CHAPTER 51

APEX LEGENDS

A week passed with no word from either Susan or Carlos. On Saturday night, Charlie logged in at twenty minutes to midnight to play *Apex Legends*, the hot new multiplayer shooter, with Emma, who was ranked twentieth and climbing fast up the leaderboard. She was already a top-ten ranked player in *Battle Theatre* and *Fortnite*, which meant she was making lots of connections with players who might get her a spot on an esports team. Although she primarily played the PC versions, she used her PS4 Pro for games with the Chi-Town Crew, of which she was now an official member.

Dom and Johnny joined the group chat.

Emma, who usually outplayed them, said, "You boys gonna beat me this time?"

"Let's hope so," Charlie said.

"Hard to believe you guys won the tournament since you all suck so bad," Emma scoffed.

"I'd play better if Johnny stopped fucking things up," Dom said. "He plays the game like Serious Sam, just shooting at everything like an idiot."

"You have a point there," Charlie said.

Johnny finally chimed in. "Boys, boys. No need for hostility."

"Have some respect," Charlie said. "Emma's here too."

Johnny took a hit from his bong and said, "Like I said, 'boys.'"

Emma snapped back, "I may be like a boy, but you play like a whiny little bitch."

Johnny exhaled a large plume of white smoke. "I'm the best player on this team."

Emma asked, "Do we have to play with him, Charlie?"

A few seconds later, Tim joined the group chat. "How's everyone feelin' tonight?"

"You sound like you're in a good mood," Charlie said.

Tim cleared his throat. "I got a date next week. With a die-hard gamer." He'd taken Charlie's advice and signed up to a dating site for singles with a passion for gaming. His date knew about his disability. And couldn't care less.

He found his unicorn.

"I'm so happy for you," Emma said, smiling.

Johnny said, "Hey, Tim. You want some tips on how to smash that?"

Tim groaned. "Do we have to play with him, Charlie?"

"Oh my God, Tim. I literally said the exact same thing just before you logged in," Emma said. "Hey, Dom. I saw your video on *GTA*. Congrats. Did all you fools see that his video got two million views?"

"And I hit three hundred thousand subscribers to-day," Dom added.

"Nice," Johnny said. "Congrats, old man."

Charlie said, "Dom, I meant to ask you. How are Jasmine and William?"

"Jasmine's doing well. She got DuPont's old job. And she gave a speech about preventing sexual harassment at one of the conferences," Dom said. "William's doing good, too. He's working for Jasmine now. Training to be a junior financial analyst."

Charlie smiled and shook his clenched fist like his crew had just defeated Extreme Behemoth in *Monster Hunter World*.

"When are we gonna get to play Triple-J?" Dom asked, referring to Charlie's *Jubilant Jungle Jaunt* game.

"I'm just waiting on Carlos for the music. Should be any day now."

Emma stretched out her legs and arms from her premium gaming chair, which she'd bought with the money she initially saved for a new graphics card. "I can't wait to play it."

"Speaking of music, what happened with Susan?" Dom said.

Charlie replied, "I saw her perform last week."

Johnny laughed and said, "And what exactly did she perform on *you*?" before simulating a fellatio motion on the mouthpiece of his bong.

Tim rolled his eyes. "This guy doesn't know when to stop."

"It wasn't anything like that," Charlie said. "She didn't even know I was there. She sang and played really well. I dropped Carlos's card in her Dream Bin. He has lots of contacts in the music industry who might be able to get her band an audition."

Emma bit her lip. "You think she'll call you?"

It was a long shot. A tiny opening in a door that had been closed for five months. Charlie wanted her, but did she want him? He'd turned away from her during their relationship, but now, without her, he wanted to run toward her. Would he reach her? Or slip on the icy roads of Chicago like he had done in the past? At least the card would bring her some joy after all the emotional scars he had caused.

Charlie said, "I did it for her, not me."

Right before their match was about to begin, a message popped up on Charlie's screen: "StevieB13 has accepted your invite." It was Steve, responding to Charlie's invite to join the game.

Johnny set down his bong and jumped up from his couch. "Who the hell is *this* guy?"

Charlie casually said, "He's one of the guys who robbed me."

Johnny sat back down and started rubbing his thighs. "Have you lost your mind?"

"Look. He could have told Dimitri about the *Battle Theatre* prize money and gotten me in trouble for trying to hide it. But he didn't. So, I forgave him. Please be nice to him."

"I'll be nice to him," Emma said. "Thanks, Steve!"

"So, we're playing with criminals now?" Johnny said. "He probably sucks at games."

"Johnny, you suck so bad that you die during game tutorials," Emma said.

Steve spoke up. "I've left that life behind me now. But I understand if you guys don't want to play with me."

"Please, give him a chance," Charlie said.

A message popped up on everyone's screen: "DonkeyBong57 left the chat."

Dom raised his hands in the air and said, "What? Did we piss him off?"

A few minutes later, another message appeared: "DonkeyBong57 entered the chat."

"Don't you think you're being a bit childish?" Charlie said.

Johnny replied, "I just got off the phone with Robert Stern."

Silence.

Johnny had posted pictures of his Fiery Phoenix and Dragonstone bongs on several online cannabis forums. Shortly after, they caught the attention of a millionaire investor. He added, "You know, the guy I've been chatting with about my bong designs?"

"Oh, yeah," Charlie said.

"He wants to meet me next Friday to talk about selling them as fine art," Johnny said. "He's a legitimate investor in the art world. What do I do? I don't know anything about business. I get nervous around executive types. I guess I could smoke some Indica, but I'm afraid I'll fall asleep during the meeting. I don't do well with Indica. I'm gonna mess up the meeting, I know it. What if it's a scam? What if I fuck it up? What if—?"

Emma interjected. "Take another hit, you idiot."

Charlie's lips formed into a huge smile. Johnny was on his way... just as Charlie was. All he needed was a little help from his friends.

"I've got nothing planned next Friday," Charlie said.

Dom shrugged and said, "Me neither."

"My schedule's clear," Tim added.

Emma pinched the bridge of her nose and shook her head before saying, "I guess I'm free too."

Johnny took a deep breath and, probably for the first time in his life, was at a loss for words. The supportive grace of friendship calmed him more than any Indica ever could. "I love you guys... and girl."

"Ewww. Gross," Emma said. "Let's just play the game."

The Chi-Town Crew—and Steve—played until two in the morning. Laughing. Cursing. Dying. And living. It was one of the best multiplayer gaming sessions they ever had. Steve shared stories of botched robberies and narrow escapes from the law. He might have been a criminal, but it was clear to everyone that he felt deep remorse and wanted to turn his life around. There was always room for another midnight multiplayer.

CHAPTER 52

THE BENCH AT DAWN

S unday afternoon. The She-Nannigans gathered to practice at Jessica's parents' house, which sat on top of a hill far from the neighbors, so they could play as loud as they wanted. On the way there, Susan rolled down her car windows to feel the cool May breeze flowing through her long blond hair. As soon as she pulled into the driveway, she heard her bandmates playing their latest song, "Love Surfing," in the open garage. Everyone stopped playing when Susan stepped out of her car. Almost as if they were in some weird cult ritual, they all smiled at her in a creepy, yet somehow tender way.

On the night of the concert at the Ragin' Marlin, Jessica had grabbed the Dream Bin off the stage and taken it straight to her parents' house, as she often did since it was their good-luck charm. She would have discovered Carlos's card two weeks ago if Susan hadn't tossed her lyric sheet on top of it. Or last week, if they hadn't skipped practice because Mimi had the flu. She finally found it earlier this morning because she wanted to type Susan's lyrics into her computer.

The smiles grew wider with each one of Susan's steps toward them.

Susan's fingers touched her parted lips. "Why is everyone looking at me like that?"

Kat and Mimi started fiddling with their instruments but kept smiling. Jessica grabbed Susan's arm and pulled her toward the Dream Bin, which was on the floor next to Kat's drum set. She pointed to it and said, "Look inside."

Susan glanced down and saw a dozen dried-up rose petals. Confused, she leaned over to grab the bin and noticed a small rectangular piece of paper beneath the petals. She brushed the petals aside to reveal Carlos's business card. Then she turned the card over and read his handwritten message: "Love your sound. You girls have potential. Call me." She flipped the card over again, then looked up from the bin. Her smile matched everyone else's. The words "video game" next to "composer" were dead giveaways. As were the rose petals.

"I can't believe this. It's just so… I don't know… *unlike* Charlie," Susan said. But then she thought back to how kind and thoughtful he'd been during their first magical year of dating.

Six months after the day they'd met, they took a camping trip to Starved Rock State Park. It was her first time sleeping in a tent. A few minutes past midnight, the blustering wind slapped the canvas tent in waves of terrifying volatility.

"Charlie. Wake up!"

Charlie turned toward her and asked, "What is it?"

"The wind. I'm scared it might blow me away."

Charlie rubbed his eyes and sat up. "Come here."

Susan eased herself backward into Charlie's arms. He held her tight against his chest and said, "You can't blow away now."

"You can't hold me like this all night. What if you fall asleep and let go of me?"

"Do you trust me?"

"Yes."

Charlie ran his fingers through her hair and said, "Then close your eyes. When you wake up, I'll still be holding you."

Six hours later, she woke up right where she had fallen asleep. Safe in Charlie's arms.

———

Susan howled at Jessica, "Why the hell did you wait two weeks to show me this?"

"You're the one who threw your lyric sheet on top of our bin."

Susan crossed her arms and paced around the garage. "What does this even mean?"

"I know that you and Mimi usually write the lyrics," Jessica said, "but I started writing a new song. It's called 'It Has to Be Love.' I got the inspiration from the *unlikeliest* of people. Guess who?"

Susan plopped down onto an oversized bean bag in the corner of the garage and tilted her head back to look up at the ceiling. "I thought you hated him."

"'Hate' is a strong word. I was never crazy about him, but what he did with that composer… Most guys would never do something like that. I know no one's ever gone out of their way for me. He did it for you… for us, as a band. To me, that seems like love."

"What do you know about love?"

"Not much," Jessica admitted. "But I know how to read between the lines of your lyrics."

Susan banged her head backward on the bean bag three times. "Oh? And what's between the lines?"

Jessica knelt in front of her, placed her hands on her shoulders, and said, "You're still in love with him."

Over the last few months, Susan had followed Charlie's journey from gamer to game developer through his social media posts. The captions gradually evolved from "How to Beat a Video Game Boss," through "Does Anyone Understand Unity?" to "Developing a Video Game—A Beginner's Guide." She could sense his joy in creating something. His bravery in chasing a dream. Just like she was doing. Almost as if their values were aligning, heading in the same direction. Making a game was no less important than composing a song. His last ten posts also contained meaningful quotes about regret and the importance of holding on to the people you love. It was clear he missed her. And she'd be lying to herself if she said she didn't miss him, too.

Susan's songs were like therapy to help her get over Charlie, but they were also a way to hold on to the faded feelings she still had for him. It was heart-wrenching for her to sing them, knowing that they might never be heard by the one person who needed to hear them the most. But now he had heard them. And done something she never dreamed he'd be capable of doing. He'd carved a path to her future.

"I need to shred for a while," Susan said.

"Shred?" Kat asked. "What is this, the nineties?"

Mimi shrugged. "It's a lot more fun than practicing scales, I guess."

Susan plugged her guitar into her Marshall amp and the band practiced Jessica's new song, plus a few others, for most of the afternoon. Afterwards, they all went to dinner at a nearby sandwich shop before going their separate ways.

Just as she was about to head home, Susan realized that she was within walking distance of the park bench where she and Charlie had first kissed. It was fifteen minutes until sundown.

Susan wandered into the park and spotted the bench in the distance. After sitting down, she reflected on the half-dozen times she'd visited the bench to work on her lyrics. She ran her fingers over their initials in the wood. Charlie had carved them with his car keys on their first date. She always knew exactly where to place her fingers to find them without looking. Her eyes filled with tears as she contemplated calling Charlie to suggest that maybe they should just be friends. She stood up, took three steps, then stopped as if she'd run into a brick wall. She turned around so she could look at their initials one last time. For a final goodbye. She glanced at them for a couple of seconds before turning her head away. But then she realized that something had been added just below their initials.

Probably some tweaker writing an obscenity. Should I read it? Nah. I should go home. Ugh. Fine. I'll give this park poet a quick look.

It took her about a millisecond to recognize the new words on the bench. They were selected lyrics from "The Bench at Dawn" and "The Three A's." For a moment, she wondered if a fan of the She-Nannigans might have written them. But then she saw the final line: "I love you, Susan."

Son of a bitch. He was here.

She looked up at the sky. Beaming. He had heard her lyrics. But most of all, he had understood them and taken the time to write some of them down on the bench where they'd fallen in love. He was showing her that he was ready to give her the three A's. He understood the pain she expressed in "The Bench at Dawn."

The sun would be setting soon.

Her hands trembled as she texted him: "Meet me at the bench at dusk."

Charlie was halfway through a bowl of pasta when his phone vibrated. He stared at the screen in disbelief before springing up from his chair, dropping his phone in the process. He looked out the window. The sun was no longer in the sky. *Dusk is... now!* He tossed what remained of the pasta into the trash, grabbed his phone off the kitchen floor, and ran to the bathroom to brush his teeth just in case he was lucky enough to get a kiss. He dashed outside. It was a miracle that he remembered to lock the front door, given the ten thousand volts of anticipation that were flowing through his veins.

He was out of breath by the time he arrived at the entrance to the park. There she was. Looking just as beautiful as she did when he first kissed her almost two years ago. The last sliver of sunlight was shimmering on the horizon. He walked toward the bench and sat beside her.

Susan asked, "How many times have you been back here?"

"I used to come once a month. But I've been back three times since I saw you at the Ragin' Marlin."

"Why didn't you tell me you were at the concert? Why go through all this?"

"I saw it in your eyes when you sang your song," Charlie said. "The pain I'd caused you. It didn't feel like the right time to talk to you. I was afraid you'd tell me to get lost."

Susan took a deep breath. "I've been thinking a lot. Trying to unpack everything. Maybe I should have taken the time to understand why games were so important to you, especially now that you're learning how to make them. I wanted this ideal version of you instead of seeing who you really are. Maybe there's a world where you can love games... and me. Maybe we should have talked it through. Or, like you said, maybe I needed to beat you over the head with how your gaming made me feel. You wanted to win your *BattleTheatre* competition, and I competed in the Battle of the Bands. Maybe those two things aren't so different."

"Games got me through a rough time with my dad. They made me feel safe, so I kept wanting to go back to them. Even when I was with you," Charlie said. "I thought they would make me feel less alone, but you're the only one who can do that... You should never feel alone when you're with me."

"I don't know anything anymore. I don't even know what the hell I'm doing here," Susan said. She glanced at the words "I love you, Susan" underneath her lyrics on the bench and said, "You didn't have to do that with the composer."

Charlie ran his fingers over their initials and said, "Yes, I did. It brought you back to me. For a chance to win you back."

Susan placed her hand on top of his and looked deep into his eyes. "Who knows? Maybe I'll let you win one day."

I hope you had fun reading my book and that it moved you in some way.
If you enjoyed your experience, please consider leaving a review.
It helps other readers discover my story and support my work as an author.
Scan the QR code or visit my website for a direct link to my Amazon review page:

paulchristou.com/leavereview

Thanks for Playing!!!

ACKNOWLEDGMENTS

You need fuel to get to the finish line.

My fuel was my family.

To my wife, Lorri. Without your support and guidance throughout my journey, this book wouldn't have happened. You were with me every step of the way, and I wouldn't have traded that for the world.

To my daughter, Maria, for reading the messy, disjointed 112,000-word first draft. You were my first editor, and your suggestions helped shape my story into something far better than I could have imagined. Without you, there would be no Emma.

My son, Deno, gave valuable feedback on story elements throughout my book, which helped refine it. You were able to show me what worked and what didn't.

If my family were the fuel, my best friend Harry Charalambous would be the engine. All you need in life is one true friend. And that friend is you. I don't think I've talked to anyone more about my story than you. Thank you for listening to me vent about every tiny detail in my book and for giving me some great ideas. Your words of inspiration are ones I will never forget. But most of all, thank you for believing in me.

Thank you to my editor, Dominic Wakeford. You taught me that the heart of the story is what truly matters, which helped me trim all the unnecessary parts of my book. Although I do miss the over 20,000 words that were cut, the result is a much tighter-paced story.

Thank you to my editor, Philip Parr, for helping with the final round of editing to get my book ready for publication. The lessons you taught me won't soon be forgotten.

I also want to thank my two beta readers, Trent Stafford and Raph Sangiovanni. I appreciate taking time out of your busy lives to read my book and for all your feedback.

Thanks to Nadia and the design team at Miblart.com for doing a great job with my book cover. They were able to take my vision and design a cover that visually showcases my story.

Finally, thank you to my narrator, Slade Hovick. Your voice helped bring my story to life, and I appreciate your patience and professionalism during the production of my audiobook.